14th

To Brian

With best-wishes for a

Happy Birthday.

FROM Mum & Dad.

By the Same Author

FAMILY AFLOAT
THREE GREEN BOTTLES

ONE GOOD TERN

Entering Yarmouth Harbour on Trial Trip.

Aubrey de Selincourt

ONE GOOD TERN

Illustrated by
GUY DE SELINCOURT

LONDON
GEORGE ROUTLEDGE & SONS, LTD.
BROADWAY HOUSE: 68–74 CARTER LANE, E.C.

First published . . 1943
Reprinted . . . 1943

THIS BOOK IS PRODUCED IN COMPLETE CONFORMITY WITH THE AUTHORIZED ECONOMY STANDARDS

Printed in Great Britain by Butler & Tanner Ltd., Frome and London

Dedicated to

IRENE, ANNE and LESLEY

WITHOUT WHOM NEITHER THIS NOR ANY OTHER
OF MY STORIES COULD HAVE BEEN WRITTEN

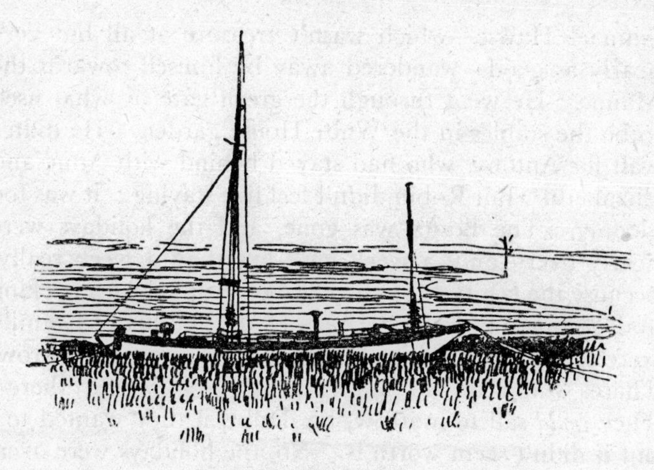

CHAPTER I

" It's a long time till Easter ! "

That is what the Bosun had said just before Mrs. Rutherford's car bore him away down the drive of the White House towards Burnham at the end of the summer holiday. The four children had stood in a melancholy group on the steps by the front door to wave good-bye.

Six months—it was a long time indeed ; six whole cold months before any of them could go for another sail, even in a dinghy. The interminable winter was between. Even Christmas was no comfort ; anyway, Christmas wasn't here yet—and the summer had gone. No wonder the children were gloomy.

You will understand, then, that the idea, when it came, was a particularly good one. And this is how it happened.

. . . .

Robin, his head still full of the best summer holiday he had ever spent, of the expedition to the Roach in *Puffin* and *Sheldrake* and the finding of the treasure of

Ishmael Hawse—which wasn't treasure at all but very nearly as good—wandered away by himself towards the Manor. He went through the green gate by what used to be the stables in the White House garden. He didn't wait for Antony, who had stayed behind with Anne and Elizabeth. But Robin didn't feel like staying ; it was too gloomy. The Bosun was gone, and the holidays were nearly over—only a week left—less than a week really, because the last two days would be occupied with packing and getting ready for term, and the Rutherford family were leaving the White House the day after to-morrow. There would be no more sailing. Or would there? They *could* sail to-morrow, no doubt, if they wanted to ; but it didn't seem worth it. No, the holidays were over. There would be no more sailing this year—not real sailing, anyhow. It was indeed a long time till Easter.

Robin shut the green gate carefully behind him, heaving it up on its hinge so that the catch fell into place. It was a burning, windless September afternoon ; the scorched grass in the fields smelt hot and sweet, and there was no movement of air in the innumerable bents dried white by the sun. To the left the river shone bright and smooth, curving away towards Redcliff and Bridgemarsh Island. Robin noticed an oyster-smack drifting home on the tide, her patched grey sails hanging limp. There were no other craft visible ; there wouldn't be, for there was no wind for sailing.

He trotted off across the flat fields towards the Manor a quarter of a mile away. Then he slowed to a walk, for it was too hot to run. There was no hurry, anyway ; there was nothing to do, and it was quite likely that Antony would stay to tea at the White House. He could have stayed himself if he had wished ; but he didn't. He didn't want any tea at all really. He wrinkled his nose and pushed the fringe of hair back off his forehead with a quick movement of his thin brown hand. How sickening it was that things always had to end! Elizabeth, now . . . she had enjoyed the treasure-hunt just as much as he had, but she didn't mind its being over—not in the same way as he did; Robin was sure of it. And as for Antony, he was older; and it's different when you're older. Anne was older too.

He entered the garden by his own private way, which was not through the gate, but through an inconspicuous gap in the hedge at the bottom of a dip in the ground towards the road. He wriggled through the gap, skirted the pond which lay just within it, and made his way indirectly towards the walled-in garden. The garden smelt of box and hot earth. Old Bramble was busy over something under the wall in the far corner. Robin went round by the fig-tree—there were plenty of ripe ones, some almost black. He chose two and pulled them off, with a precautionary glance towards Bramble, who continued to stoop over the earth. Not that he minded Bramble; and of course he could pick figs if he liked: but it was nicer not to be seen. Besides, he didn't feel that he wanted to talk to anyone just now, and when Bramble saw him or Antony picking figs, he usually made a jocular remark which was very difficult to answer. Robin had told Elizabeth about this, and Elizabeth had sympathized.

He ate his figs, spitting out the thick greenish bit by the stalk, and wiping his fingers on the seat of his shorts; then with another sideways glance at Bramble made his way out of the garden by the frames and tool-sheds and the rows of flower-pots until he came to the yard at the back of the house. In this yard was the shed which Robin and Antony used as a carpenter's shop; it was also full of interesting rubbish of various kinds, bits of old gear from the yacht *Ianthe*, two or three spars across the beams, a worn-out staysail in a heap under the window, and a number of sugar boxes half filled with rusty bolts, shackles, ends of rope, cigarette tins, and dust.

On the bench, amongst the tools, was the model yacht which Robin had made a year or more ago. It was lying on its side, dusty and neglected, with none of the sails up except the jib—and that was only half up, and hanging forlornly in a curve. Robin gave a twitch to the halyard—he wasn't really interested in the boat, at any rate not at the moment; he was feeling lost and vague. Nevertheless, it was remarkable how much the boat was improved in appearance when the jib halyard was tightened. He undid the halyard from its cleat, and made it fast again, properly. Then he put the boat in the vice, so that she stood upright. He rubbed the dust off her deck with his hand, and stood back to look at her. She wasn't really at all bad, he thought—and it had been fun making her. But it had been a very long time ago—before they had ever gone cruising by themselves, as they had this summer, with Anne and Elizabeth. And once you had gone cruising, real cruising, even though it was only in dinghies, you couldn't feel quite the same about *model* boats, however good they were. But she did look real, he thought, as he began to set the mainsail, leaving the peak not quite up—like *Ianthe's* when she was still on her moorings before getting under way. Antony was bored with model boats now; he was too old. Robin began to fiddle with the foresail; should he put it up, or leave it on deck, hanked to the stay? He decided to put it up. It was very dusty and stiff, and had some spots of mildew on it. It looked rather silly, Robin thought. However, he left it as it was, and wandered over towards the door. At the door he turned, and looked back at the boat again. Oh bother, he thought, she doesn't really look real at all; and what's the good of model boats, anyway? He had half thought of making another one during the winter, a bigger one; but now he knew he didn't want to. It might have been worth doing if Antony had been interested; but Antony was not interested, and never would be again—not in models. To make Antony interested, they would have to build not a model boat, but a real one; and that, of course, was impossible. Quite impossible. For one thing, they didn't know how; and it would be frightfully expensive.

Robin was still hot after his walk from the White House. He pushed his fringe back again, and left a broad smear of dust on his forehead. He was still staring at the boat on the bench.

But *was* it impossible?

Robin moistened his lips with the tip of his tongue. He no longer saw the boat on the bench, though he was still looking towards it.

"If only we could!" he thought. "If only we could!"

Then he heard steps crunching on the gravel. It was Antony.

"Hullo," said Antony, "what are you doing?"

Robin flushed. "N-nothing much," he said, stammering as he always did when he was excited or upset.

"Apparently not," said Antony cheerfully, and grinned. "Come on, let's go in to tea. I didn't stay after all."

Antony turned to go towards the house. Robin lingered within the door of the shed. Should he tell Antony about the boat? Would Antony laugh and say it was silly, or would he be pleased? It would be sickening if he laughed.

So Robin said nothing. He swallowed hard, and followed Antony towards the house.

But on the way he had another idea. He would not tell Antony; not yet. But he would write a letter to the Bosun. He would ask the Bosun whether it was possible, or just silly, to plan to build a boat, a real boat, that winter. The Bosun would know ; and the Bosun wouldn't laugh at him, even if it was silly and impossible. Then, if it was neither (and it might not be), he would tell Antony.

" Antony," he would say, " the Bosun and I have decided to build a boat. All of us, of course—Anne and Elizabeth too."

He would say it just like that, in a matter-of-fact way ; casually.

It would be marvellous.

By that time, they had reached the house. Then they washed their hands a bit, and went in to tea. All through tea (only their mother was with them) Robin was composing in his mind the letter he was going to write to the Bosun.

Antony ate a large tea. He had several crumpets and a great deal of bread and butter and apple-jelly. Robin had hardly anything. Once or twice he felt his mother's eye dwelling upon him ; but he didn't think she would ask him if anything was the matter ; she never did unless it was really necessary. She probably knew that it was beastly to have to say " Nothing " to a person when you knew perfectly well that they didn't believe you.

As soon as tea was finished Robin left the room and ran upstairs before Antony could ask him where he was going. On the top landing he paused and listened. He heard Antony come out of the drawing-room and go towards the garden door. Then he heard the door bang. Good ! He was alone. He trotted happily along the passage to his bedroom. The letter to the Bosun was all composed in his head ; he had only to write it down. He picked up Antony's pen which was lying on the dressing-table, and began to write :

DEAR BOSUN,

I've only just thought of it or I would have asked you before you went. Could we build a boat? A proper boat I mean, not a model boat. I would like to very much. What I mean is, would it be awfully expensive, and besides I don't really know about building boats, except model ones. We've got our money from the Reward, at least I have and so has Antony, and I don't expect Anne and Elizabeth have spent theirs yet as it was only about a week ago. The cruise was lovely, and so was getting the reward. Please answer quickly about the boat.

With best love

from

ROBIN.

He licked up the envelope, stuck it and addressed it. Then he took it downstairs. On the hall-table there was already a little pile of letters for the evening post. That was lucky. Robin tucked his under the others so that nobody would notice it. Then he wandered off into the garden, with no particular object. But he did not go back to the shed where the model boat was.

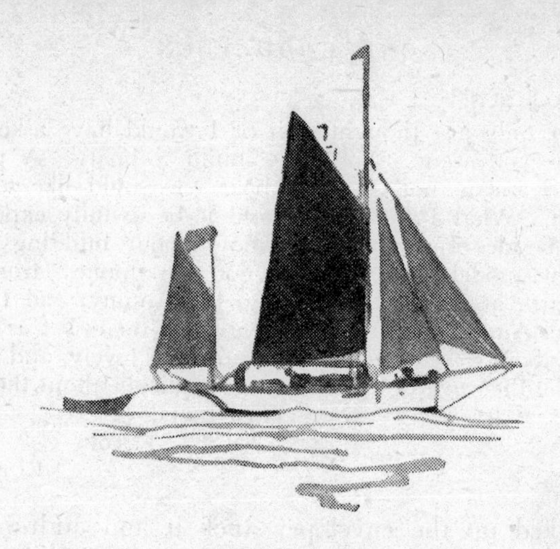

CHAPTER II

For those who have not read the previous history of Robin, Antony, Anne and Elizabeth, it is now time to give a short explanation about one or two things which were mentioned in the last chapter. For instance, what did Robin mean by the "reward"? And who was the Bosun, that Robin should have had such confidence in his judgment? The explanations will not take very long, for it is important to get on with the story as quickly as possible.

Anne and Elizabeth Rutherford (Anne was fourteen and Elizabeth was eleven) were already experienced mariners; that is to say, they had crossed the Channel the previous year in the yacht *Tessa* with their parents, and for part of the cruise, and that the most exciting part, the Bosun, who was a sort of cousin of Mrs. Rutherford, had been with them, and had been deeply implicated in their adventures. He was a very large man, and knew everything there was to know about sailing. Also, he specially liked Elizabeth. This summer, the Rutherfords had brought *Tessa* round to the River Crouch, and the Bosun, once again, had come too. Here they had made the acquaintance of Robin and Antony Chale, who lived at the Manor House at Creeksea, and were about the same age as Anne and Elizabeth. The circumstances of their first meeting were rather embarrassing to Elizabeth and Anne, who considered themselves, as I have said, to be experienced mariners : but they soon got over it, and before the holidays were half done they all four set off in the dinghies *Puffin* and *Sheldrake* on a cruise to the River Roach in search of treasure. This time the Bosun did not go with them ; nevertheless he was once again deeply implicated in the adventure. He was, indeed, the kind of person who always *is* involved in any adventure. They did not actually find the treasure, but they found something almost as good ; and the result of that find was the " reward " which I have mentioned.

I said just now that the Bosun specially liked Elizabeth ; but I am not sure that he didn't specially like Robin too. Certainly Robin liked *him*, and had a great respect both for his size, his strength and his knowledge, and for the faculty he had of accepting unusual situations without surprise. So it is easy to understand why Robin thought that the best thing to do about the sudden longing which had come upon him to build a boat was to write to the Bosun about it. If the Bosun approved, it would make a powerful influence in the Rutherford family, and Robin and Antony would then be able to approach their father with a certain amount of backing. Strictly, I suppose, Robin ought to have asked his father first ; but he was afraid he might be told that he had got a boat already, and what was the point of building a new one ? Of course he *hadn't* got a boat really ; for *Sheldrake* belonged to *Ianthe*, and wasn't his at all ; but that wouldn't make any difference to the argument. Besides, it was not only having a boat that was important; it was building one, and Robin was afraid that he might not succeed in making this clear. It was the kind of point very easily missed by anyone who did not particularly want to see it.

Robin's letter, then, was written and posted. Two days later he got a reply: his heart was in his mouth as he opened the envelope.

Dear Robin,

The idea is attractive, but it will want a bit of thinking out. (Thank goodness, thought Robin, he doesn't think it's just silly.) It's a long time since I've tried my hand at building (Gosh, thought Robin, he actually *has* built a boat. How marvellous!) and I'd greatly enjoy being in on another job of the kind. How much money, by the way, have you got between you? (Robin's heart sank a bit—he was sure it wouldn't be enough.) It *will*, of course, be expensive, but I dare say we can devise means. (Good old Bosun, thought Robin; of course we can, if *he* helps.) You will realize that I can't be very definite just at present (I do, thought Robin; but I wish he could all the same), as there are a good many things to consider, and a good many people to consult. *Where*, for instance, do you propose to build? And when—though I suppose the answer to that is "as soon as you jolly well can", i.e. in the Christmas holidays. (Obvious, thought Robin; of course it is.) Then there's the money (Bother, thought Robin. I wish there wasn't, though I know there is), and there's Uncle John Rutherford (He isn't an uncle, thought Robin; nobody's uncle), and your father (Bother, thought Robin again. But I'm sure the Bosun will make a difference); they've got to be consulted.

But you can count on me to weigh the matter properly, and to make all due enquiries. By the way, I shouldn't, if I were you, mention anything about it just yet to anybody except Antony and the girls. I'll write to you again as soon as I have anything to say. Meanwhile, let's hope for the best. Good-bye and good luck.

Yours ever,
Bosun.

Robin at once showed the letter to Antony, not without pride.

"I wrote to him," he said.

Antony's eyes widened. "I say!" he said; "that's pretty good. Did you think of it yourself?"

Robin nodded. "You see," he said, "I thought it would be nice to have something to do in the Christmas holidays."

Antony laughed. "It jolly well would," he said. "After all, we can't sail all the time, can we? Not in the winter."

"That's just it," said Robin.

The rest of the holidays (only three days) was spent in discussing the new plan with Anne and Elizabeth. Elizabeth wanted to tell Mr. Rutherford about it, because she was sure he would sympathize and make sensible suggestions; but Robin firmly upheld the Bosun, and would not let her. The fewer the things they could actually decide, the more it seemed necessary to discuss them; and what with reckoning up the amount of money they would have between them by the beginning of the Christmas holidays if nobody spent anything beyond absolute necessities during term, added to the Reward, and trying to determine whether it would be better to do the building at Creeksea or at the Rutherford's house in the Isle of Wight, and wondering how helpful and enthusiastic their fathers and mothers would be, not to mention visionary prophecies of what the completed vessel would be like, and the voyages she would make on either the Eastern or the Southern seas, the last days of the summer holidays passed much more pleasantly, and with fewer regrets, than they usually did; and when the time came for them to separate, there was no need to repeat the Bosun's words of sorrowful farewell, "It's a long time till Easter," for a whole epoch had been cut off from that age, and it was necessary only to say—privately, each to each—" It's a long time till Christmas." And it was not so very long either.

. . . .

About the term that followed nothing much needs to be said. Terms are not so interesting as holidays for most people; and they certainly were not for Robin. Antony minded less than Robin did when the holidays were over, and went back to his house in the Hillmorton Road at Rugby with hardly a qualm; but for Robin school was rather a nuisance—there were too many bells, and too many people watching you, and he did not like being separated from Antony, who always seemed to come back for the holidays a bit queer and strange, so that Robin felt uncomfortable about him until, after a week or so, the queerness and strangeness had worn off.

This term, however, was very important in one way; for during the course of it the general plans for the Christmas holidays were made. The making of the plans entailed a great deal of correspondence and conversation on the part of the Bosun, Mr. and Mrs. Rutherford, and Mr. and Mrs. Chale; for, even after the Bosun, with notable tact and skill, had persuaded both Mr. and Mrs. Chale that to build a boat of their own would be for all four children an excellent thing, both for their amusement and for their instruction, there was still the question to settle of where the building was to take place. It was finally decided that, as the Rutherfords did not intend to take the White House at Creeksea for the Christmas holidays, it would have to be done at their cottage in the Isle of Wight, and that Robin and Antony would stay in rooms in the village. The progress of these plans was communicated to the children at frequent intervals; and as they were all four at different schools, and each wrote to the other three to comment on each bit of news as it came, a great many letters must have been written. But before three-quarters of the term were done everything was settled, and Robin and Elizabeth (Antony and Anne were too old and had given up the practice) scratched off each succeeding day from their private calendar with greater zest than they had ever done before.

It was now definitely *not* a long time till Christmas.

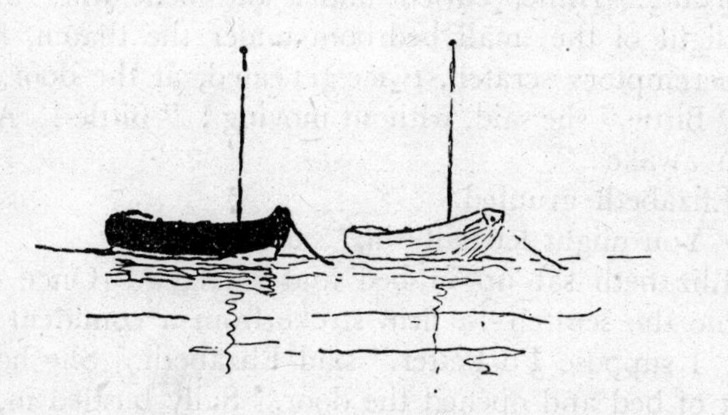

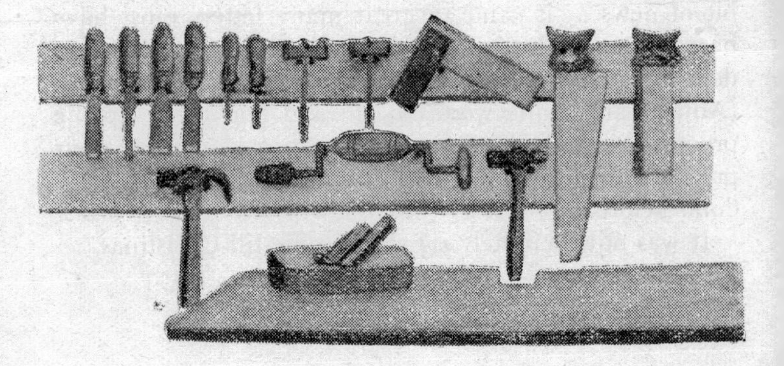

CHAPTER III

It was the last day of the year and eight o'clock in the morning. Anne, curled under the bedclothes in the twilight of the small bedroom under the thatch, heard a peremptory scratch, twice repeated, at the door.

" Bittle," she said, without moving ; " Bittle ! Aren't you awake ? "

Elizabeth grunted.

" You might let Sally in," said Anne.

Elizabeth sat up in bed and shivered. Once again came the scratch—a firm stroke from a confident paw.

" I suppose I'd better," said Elizabeth. She hopped out of bed and opened the door. Sally bustled in, very quick and close to the ground, scuttled over to Elizabeth's bed, looked up at it, then scuttled back to Anne's, jumped on to it and flopped down at the foot, her black and white nose pressed close to the blankets, and one bright brown eye watching the hump that was her mistress.

Elizabeth crossed to the open window and looked out. The postman was just coming through the gate ; she heard the faint plop of the letters as he dropped them through the slit on to the stone floor of the hall. It was a dull morning ; the road was moist and glistening ; there was a noise of wind in the bare boughs of the ash-tree. Elizabeth shivered again and drew back from the window ; then she began to wash without much enthusiasm in the small quantity of hot water which Emily had brought up a quarter of an hour before. The dining-room was under their bedroom, and she could hear the sticks crackling in the fire, a pleasant and encouraging sound. A door opened along the passage, and feet trod lightly down the stairs.

" Get up, Anne," said Elizabeth. " Mummy's gone down."

" Have you left any water ? "

" Yes, a bit. I don't expect the Bosun's up yet, do you ? "

" Bang on the wall."

Elizabeth banged.

" Bang louder," said Anne. " Wait a moment, *I* will." She got out of bed, ran across the room and slammed on the wall above Elizabeth's bed with a bedroom slipper.

" Oy ! " came a sleepy voice from the next room.

" Get up ! " called Elizabeth.

" Have you forgotten what day it is ? " called Anne.

" What's that ? " came the sleepy voice.

" What *day*—have you forgotten ? "

" I'm sleepy," said the voice.

" Go and wake him up properly," said Anne. " You're dressed, almost."

Elizabeth pulled her jersey over her head and chuckled. Then she went and opened the door of the Bosun's room. It was a little slip of a room almost filled by the bed, and the bed was quite filled by the Bosun.

"Go away," said the Bosun. "I thought this was holidays."

"Get up," said Elizabeth.

"Why?" said the Bosun.

"It's breakfast-time, and Robin and Antony are supposed to be coming to-day. They're almost sure to be."

There was a call from downstairs.

"Letters!" came Mummy's voice. Elizabeth slammed the Bosun's door and ran downstairs.

"Is it from *them*?" she asked eagerly.

Mrs. Rutherford nodded. "Two o'clock boat from Lymington," she said.

Elizabeth dashed upstairs again to take the news, first to Anne, then to the Bosun.

So Antony and Robin were really coming to-day! Until the letter arrived, it had been doubtful if it was to be to-day or to-morrow—it had depended upon various things which Mrs. Chale had carefully explained, but they had seemed to Elizabeth rather pointless and tiresome things, and she could never see why it should not have been to-day. And now it was. So that was all right.

The Bosun and Mr. Rutherford had already, several weeks ago, ordered from a shipyard at St. Helens the timber which would be needed for the building of the boat, and the family had decided to fetch it over to their own village of Yarwell in the car, as soon as Antony and Robin arrived. It would be a tremendous load; indeed, two tremendous loads at least—and very bad for the car. At any rate Mrs. Rutherford, who was especially fond of the car, said it would be; but Mr. Rutherford supported by the Bosun, rather wondered if the car could be more bent than it was already. Mr. Rutherford had also spent a good deal of time since Christmas (before Christmas there wasn't time for anything except shopping, hiding parcels, waiting for the postman, decorating the Christmas-tree, fetching threepenny bits for the puddings, and general expectancy) in fitting up the shed at the bottom of the garden as a workshop. This shed was called the Garage, because it happened to be the only place into which the car could be fitted—though a good many other things were, in point of fact, fitted into it too: the mowing-machine, for instance, and a derelict bedstead, a couple of chimney-pots (origin unknown) and a small table with a round hole in the top, which had probably been a washstand. The Garage had a sort of platform in place of a ceiling, about seven feet from the ground; and this made an upper story, or attic, under the slates, very useful for storing away the sort of property which everyone knows is useless but no one can bear to throw away. Into this attic Mr. Rutherford had removed the chimney-pots and the bedstead, and everything else which would get in the way when the transformation into a workshop was complete. ("Why," said Mrs. Rutherford, "didn't you do that years ago? It would have been much nicer for the car.") Along one side the Bosun had constructed a bench; he had also fitted up the stocks, a heavy piece of timber raised a couple of feet from the ground and running the length of the Garage. On this the boat was to be built. Anne and Elizabeth had driven pairs of nails into the wall above the bench, at suitable widths, to hold the hammers and chisels and screwdrivers.

"Nothing is more annoying," said Mr. Rutherford, "than to be unable to find a tool when you want it."

"As in sailing," added the Bosun, "a place for everything . . ."

"*Bosun!*" Elizabeth interrupted sharply; "you're *always* saying that."

The Bosun eyed her. " *And*," he remorselessly continued, " everything in its place."

" But it never is," said Elizabeth.

The Garage was just big enough, but only just, for the purpose ; for though there seemed to be plenty of room, to a casual eye, it was necessary, as the Bosun reminded them, to have enough space on each side of the boat, as her sides began to rise, to enable the builders to use their tools. But there certainly was not room for the car as well ; Mr. Rutherford thought that the car could very well stand outside the Garage, under the ilex tree, where there was a nice open space ; but Mrs. Rutherford was distressed at this suggestion, and a temporary shelter had to be found for it in a shed belonging to Mrs. Loveridge who lived in the square house on the other side of the lane, and sold milk.

The two-o'clock boat from Lymington reached Yarmouth at twenty to three. That meant early lunch, if they were to get there in time to meet the two boys. An early lunch meant rather a bustle. Emily was not very good at early lunch ; her method of achieving it, Mr. Rutherford said, was just to stop cooking sooner—a method which he commended rather for its simplicity than its success. So it usually happened that assistance was offered her. Elizabeth tended to get out of the way as much as possible when early lunch was wanted. It was not that she objected to helping ; but to have to contribute small, hot bits to a major work of somebody else's was, she felt, an unsatisfactory way of doing it. She preferred a larger plan of her own, even if it was less immediately useful : for instance, it was much better to put a new coat of creosote on the Hut, as far away from the kitchen as possible. To-day, however, she did find it necessary to go with Anne to Biggin's shop in the village to bring back onions and barley, without which

Emily's stew would have been distasteful, even if lunch was at the ordinary time.

At a quarter to two Mrs. Rutherford and the children were ready to start; that is to say they were very nearly ready, for when Elizabeth came out of the hall-door, in answer to urgent shoutings from Anne who was already in the car with Mrs. Rutherford, it appeared that she had not put on her overcoat.

"It's perfectly warm, Mummy," she said. Mrs. Rutherford, however, thought it was extremely cold; so Elizabeth had to go back into the hall and disinter her coat from underneath a thick bunch on a single peg. This was tiresome. But at last they were off, and rattling along the well-known lanes to Chale Green and Shorewell, on their way to Yarmouth. They arrived in good time; but even in winter Yarmouth is a pleasant place to wait in. The little harbour was almost empty; but the life-boat was there on her moorings, and a few small sailing boats lay at angles on the mud under the breakwater. Above the bridge yachts were laid up in the river, and from the quay you could see their masts. The wind was chilly, and stirred the dust in little whirls on the quay. Anne tucked her scarf closer round her neck and looked out over the Solent.

"There she is!" she called. The ferry steamer was in sight, coming out of Lymington River, by Jack-in-the-Basket. A quarter of an hour later (just time for Elizabeth to go to the shop on the corner for a necessary slab of chocolate) the steamer had arrived.

"I can see them," said Anne, and Mrs. Rutherford waved. Elizabeth hung back, and began carefully to unwrap her chocolate. Anne and Mrs. Rutherford walked forward to the gangway. A moment afterwards they were all five together, and Mrs. Rutherford was arranging the stowage of the boys' bags in the car,

Antony and Robin looked neat and unfamiliar in their travelling clothes, and a term at school had passed since Elizabeth and Anne had last seen them. So there was a certain difficult politeness and circumspection in their greetings.

" Come on," said Mrs. Rutherford ; " get in—I think Elizabeth has got the chocolate."

Elizabeth *had* got it, enough of it at any rate to be worth passing round, and to make them all feel more comfortable.

They packed themselves in, Anne, Elizabeth and Robin in the back, and Antony in front with Mrs. Rutherford. Mrs. Rutherford started the engine.

" One day," she said, " you'll be coming in here in the new boat."

" Rather ! " said Antony, and Robin nodded his head quickly.

The car started.

" It's a jolly good harbour," said Robin.

" The Solent's marvellous," said Anne. " There are hundreds of places. We know them all."

" Has the timber come ? " said Antony.

" We're fetching it to-morrow."

" Good."

Then their tongues were loosened, and the long term which had intervened began to melt away. But Elizabeth still thought that Robin looked all wrong in a hat.

CHAPTER IV

ANTONY and Robin had rooms with Mrs. Hackett along the lane. But they were to have all their meals, except breakfast, at the Rutherfords' cottage. It made rather a squash, because none of the rooms in the cottage were very big, and the dining-room table was not really meant for more than six at the most, especially when one of the six was the Bosun. But Robin and Elizabeth were both thin; so they didn't do so badly. It was not such a squash as in *Tessa's* cabin, as the Bosun said, when he expansively took his seat for tea just after the boys' arrival.

"But I do think," he added, looking at Mrs. Rutherford, "that you might have had a higher ceiling. I banged my head on that beastly beam."

"What, *again*?" said Mrs. Rutherford consolingly. "Poor Bob."

"The door's worse," said Robin.

"Much," said the Bosun. "I can only manage it on all fours."

After tea, which consisted of boiled eggs—as always on the first day of a holiday, or to celebrate a new arrival—and one of Mrs. Rutherford's thick golden curranty cakes (Mrs. Rutherford had to be tactful when she wanted to make a cake, to avoid hurting Emily's feelings) and new buns which they toasted themselves and ate with a lot of butter, and a honeycomb from the little house on the downs above the village, they all went along the narrow stone-flagged passage into the sitting-room.

Emily had just drawn the curtains and put the lighted lamp on the table. In the wide brick fireplace logs were burning. There was a faint smell of wood-smoke in the room. Tip and the Ancient Mariner (now bigger than his mother) were lying, furrily intermixed, in an armchair by the hearth. The lamplight was warm on the yellow walls.

Robin and Antony looked round appreciatively. It was a comforting room.

" Well," said Mr. Rutherford, filling his pipe, " I expect Antony and Robin would like to see the plans."

" Rather ! " said Antony.

" Are they here ? " said Robin.

" Good heavens, yes," said Anne. " We've had them for ages. Bittle and I know them by heart."

Mr. Rutherford reached up to the top shelf of the bookcase which filled the angle of the wall beyond the fire, and took down a neat blue roll.

" Come on," he said. Then he pushed the lamp a little to one side, and spread the drawings on the table. The four children pressed round.

" That's what she'll look like when she's finished," said Elizabeth, pointing to a small diagram in a corner of the print.

Mr. Rutherford laughed.

" Yes," he said, " but Antony and Robin will want to

see what sort of work they've got to do first. She won't look like that picture for a long time."

"If ever," said the Bosun from the hearthrug.

"What do you *mean*?" said Anne indignantly. The Bosun grinned.

"I was only warning you," he said benignantly. "There's many a chip, you know."

"*Chip?*"

"Between the cup and the ship. And the worst is," he added, "when the chips are all in the wrong places. I've built boats before. It's awful."

"Our boat will be *exactly* like the picture," said Elizabeth. "What shall we call her, Robin?"

Robin did not answer; he was too busy reading the *instructions to the builder*, written in white script in the bottom left-hand corner of the blue sheet.

"*Tern*," said the Bosun.

"Why *Tern*?" said Elizabeth. "It's quite a nice name though."

"One good tern deserves another," said the Bosun.

Mrs. Rutherford looked up from her chair where she was now sitting, underneath the cats.

"You stole that joke, Bob. I've read it."

"Naturally," said the Bosun mildly.

"*And* it's pointless. We haven't had one *Tern* yet."

"Sorry," said the Bosun. "But we can leave out about the 'other'. Just 'one good *Tern*'. That's all right, isn't it? After all, we don't *want* two, do we?"

The plans looked very complicated, and indeed they were. Antony, who was trying to read the *instructions* over Robin's shoulder, privately wondered if they would ever be able to do it at all. It was a good thing, he thought, that they had got the Bosun to help them. Robin was feeling quietly elated; he had finished the *instructions*, and his mind had leapt forward, and he was imagining to himself the pleasure of walking over to the building-shed after breakfast in the mornings, seeing the vessel taking shape—real shape ; large and powerful, not like the little model in the outhouse at Creeksea—doing the finishing jobs, painting and caulking, and driving home the few, last, culminating screws. He gave a little sigh, half of pleasure, half of impatience. This was going to be the best Christmas holiday they had ever had. Christmas itself was always good, and the rest of the time after it was all right too ; but not like this—they had never had anything like this before. It was nice, too, that the Bosun was there, and Elizabeth—and Anne. Not many people came to stay at the Manor—not that Robin minded being alone ; in fact, he rather enjoyed it, and would often go off for hours together without even Antony ; and there was always plenty to do, so long as nobody bothered you, or made suggestions. But it was nice all the same to have Elizabeth and Anne—especially Elizabeth. Yes, it was going to be a marvellous holiday.

Mr. Rutherford went to the fire, pressed it tidy with his foot, and put on another log. Then he turned Sally off his own particular chair, the one with the comfortably broken spring, and sat on it. Robin continued, alone, to pore over the plans. Elizabeth opened the corner cupboard to look for the Patience cards : then she looked again.

"Where are the cards, Mummy ?" she said.

"In the cupboard," said Mrs. Rutherford, in a practised manner.

"But they aren't," said Elizabeth. She got up on to the couch, to look better. "Oh yes, they are," she said. She spread them out on the table, opposite Robin, and began to stir them round, which was the easiest and most effective way of shuffling. Perhaps somebody would play

Racing Demon with her ; or Rum ? But perhaps they wouldn't. She gathered the cards up, looked across at the top of Robin's bent head, and began to hum. It was more likely they wouldn't, she thought. . . . She laid out the cards for a Patience.

" Well, Robin," said the Bosun, " have you mastered the plans yet ? "

" What ? " said Robin. " Oh, sorry," he went on ; " no—not really. It looks awfully difficult."

" It's a queer sort of design," said Mr. Rutherford ; " but quite good, I think. It's supposed to be an easy one for amateurs."

" How long will it take ? " asked Antony. " When do you think we shall get her finished ? "

" It's a long job," said the Bosun.

" There's only three weeks left," said Anne.

" Three weeks ? " said Mr. Rutherford. " That's hardly enough to begin in."

" But——" began Anne.

" Good Lord," said Antony, " I thought . . ."

" That we'd finish before the holidays were over ? " said Mr. Rutherford. " Impossible. But I did have an idea," he went on, " which would help us along a little. There are certain laborious jobs which only one man can work on at a time, and which have to be done right at the beginning—the slot for the centreboard, for instance, which has to be cut through the keel and the keel-plank. . . ."

" Which is the keel-plank ? " said Robin, running a finger over the drawings.

Mr. Rutherford went to the table. " Here," he said, pointing. " And I thought we might get Hackett (" The carpenter in the village where you're staying," put in Elizabeth, not looking up from her Patience) to do that for us, while we got on with something else."

There was a moment of silence.

" But," said Robin, " it wouldn't really be *our* boat then."

" There is that," said Mr. Rutherford. " But it's an easy job. We *could* do it. It's not like getting an expert to do for you what you can't do yourself."

" And then pretending you didn't," said the Bosun. " Personally, I think the suggestion is a good one. It'll save a week."

" *Then* could we finish by the end of the holidays ? " said Antony. Mr. Rutherford shook his head.

" No," he said.

Elizabeth stopped playing Patience. " Then Robin and Antony will have to come and stay with us next holidays too," she said.

" Exactly," Mr. Rutherford said.

" If they want to," said Mrs. Rutherford.

Elizabeth began humming her tune again. Then she turned up a great many cards very quickly. There was a pause.

" No doubt we could manage alone," said the Bosun.

" Without us ? " said Robin anxiously.

The Bosun grinned. " I only said we *could* . . ."

" Perhaps they'll want to be sailing," said Mr. Rutherford. " *Ianthe* will be fitted out at Easter."

Robin looked solemn. " I'd rather finish the building," he said.

" So would I," said Antony.

" And there's always *Tessa*," said the Bosun. " We could take a day off now and again, if we couldn't bear it."

Elizabeth continued her Patience at a more normal speed. It was going to be all right : Robin and Antony *were* coming again at Easter.

" I expect they could manage to come," said Mrs. Rutherford, " if Mrs. Chale didn't mind."

" She wouldn't a bit," said Antony.

" Then, with all of us working, we ought to have her ready for the summer," said Mr. Rutherford. " At any rate, if we let Hackett help."

" I suppose we shall have to," said Anne.

As a matter of fact it was a very good thing to get Hackett interested in their project, as they all agreed after a little more discussion ; for, as the Bosun pointed out, they would be able to borrow from him a number of things which they did not possess and which would be necessary for the building : a steaming box, for instance, and some large cramps. Whatever job you are working on it is useful to have a friendly carpenter at hand. Hackett was friendly, anyhow—he had advised Mr. Rutherford what apple-trees to plant in the garden years and years ago, when they first came to the village—and he would be friendlier still if he was taken into the confidence of the family over the building of *Tern*.

Mr. Rutherford put yet another log on the fire. Sparks flickered up the chimney. Sally blinked and edged away from the hearth. The wind sighed and swished in the trees outside. How foolish are the people who don't like winter in the country ! The room was the warmer and cosier for the wind in the tree-tops ; lamp-light and firelight more welcoming and alive.

Soon after supper Mr. Rutherford took Antony and Robin to their lodgings.

" Till after breakfast to-morrow," he said, as he left them at the door.

" Directly after," said Robin.

CHAPTER V

If all four children had gone with Mr. Rutherford to St. Helens to fetch the timber, there would have been no room left in the car, and they would have had to come back without it. Two was the most that could be managed ; and Mr. Rutherford wisely thought that the smaller they were the better. So Elizabeth and Robin went.

They left the car on the foreshore of the harbour, outside the railway station at Bembridge, and went across to Woodford's yard at St. Helens in the ferry. The tide was low, and the river only a narrow trickle between the steep sandy banks. To the right beyond the breakwater lay a chill and glistening expanse of crinkled sands, where many a time Elizabeth had bathed and basked in the hot sunshine of summer ; but now, as much as the wind which searched out the space between her scarf and her neck, the mere sight of them made her shiver.

Business at a shipyard is always leisurely, and this was

no exception Fortunately, however, no sensible person would ever wish to hurry in so delightful a place. In one of the sheds packed tight with boats of all sorts and sizes laid up for the winter, a workman was busy (fairly busy) with a tray of putty and a knife, going over a seam in the counter of a little yacht. He looked at Mr. Rutherford and the children as they walked by the entrance and gave them a friendly good morning ; but he was in no way curious about the object of their visit. Mr. Rutherford and Elizabeth made their way round to the back of the sheds where the office was. Robin lingered behind them, watching the man smoothing the putty into the seam ; then, hearing the sound of hammering from another shed a little farther along, he trotted away by himself to see what was going on. On the way he stopped to look up at the curving bilges and towering sides of a large ketch which had been hauled out of the water. There was a ladder propped against her and Robin wondered if he dared climb it and have a look at her deck, but decided he had better not.

Mr. Rutherford found the manager of the yard in the office. The manager said that the timber was ready, so far as he knew, but that he would just ask the foreman to make sure. He walked to the door of the office.

" Bill ! " he shouted to a figure in a blue jersey and dungarees which was just disappearing round the corner of the nearest shed. " Bill ! Have you seen Joe ? "

Bill thought that Joe might be down yonder on the slip, and said he would go and see. Mr. Rutherford and Elizabeth waited. The office was very small. The table was strewn with catalogues, and files of letters and accounts. There was a smell of paraffin from the oil-stove in the middle of the floor. On the walls were pinned photographs of boats offered for sale, and over the table was a beautiful half-model of a cutter yacht.

Bill returned, and said that Joe was not working on the slip, but that he was very likely over in the building sheds.

" I told Reg to give him a call," he said. " Is there anything the gentleman wanted ? "

" That timber," said the manager. Bill scratched his head and meditated.

" I doubt that'll be all that stuff in number ten," he said.

" That's it," said the manager.

Mr. Rutherford caught Elizabeth's eye and grinned. " I say," he whispered, and Elizabeth edged closer to him. " Pity Mummy isn't here—just the sort of shopping she enjoys ! " Elizabeth swallowed a giggle, and stole a glance at Bill who, finding his job was finished, ambled away to look for another one.

" I hope Reg is a good looker," said Mr. Rutherford softly. Then, " I say," he added aloud, " what's Robin up to ? "

" He went over there," said Elizabeth, pointing. Mr. Rutherford looked through the open doorway of the office.

" Ah," he said, " here he comes. And there's somebody with him. Perhaps it's Joe."

" Hullo," said Robin, hurrying to meet them ; " I've been watching them building. They're building an X-boat."

" Joe," said the manager (for it was indeed Joe), " the gentleman's come about the timber. Did you see Reg ? "

Joe shook his head. " Reg ? " he said slowly. " No, I ain't seen Reg, but I saw the young gentleman here. . ."

" I told him," put in Robin.

" All that stuff in number ten. That's what you want, I reckon," said Joe, and moved off through a narrow and draughty passage between two sheds towards the back of the yard.

" Come on," said Mr. Rutherford, and followed with Elizabeth and Robin.

It was a truly formidable pile. Mr. Rutherford, the two children and Joe stood and looked at it.

" Best thing we can do," said Joe, " is to take it over in a boat for you, and help you load up on the other side."

The four of them, helped by Bill and the elusive Reg (who had silently appeared beside them), carried the timber down to the water and put it in a large and grimy rowing-boat which belonged to the yard. It was not possible to get it all in at once, but Mr. Rutherford did not mind this, because it would be even less possible to get it all into the car ; so he decided to leave the topside planking behind and fetch it later on. There would be no need for it for a long time yet.

It was very difficult to get even what remained into the car. They lowered the hood, and stacked the shorter bits—the ribs and floors, the pieces out of which the stem-knee and transom were to be cut—into the back, and the long planks—the bottom planking, the keel-plank, and the keel—they stowed as securely as they could along the running-boards, with the ends projecting a considerable distance beyond the bonnet of the car. They were made fast by lashings to the bumpers in front and behind. When it was all stowed, Mr. Rutherford could not help wondering what Mrs. Rutherford would think of it, for the poor car *did* seem, as it were, to have rather less free-board than usual. But no doubt it would be all right, if he drove very slowly over the bumps.

It was now past midday, for their business at the yard had taken them over two hours—as business at a shipyard always does. So before starting for home Mr. Rutherford and the children went to a shop behind the railway station for a cup of coffee. It was a rather dingy shop, and they all hoped that the coffee would not taste like liquorice, but it did. Luckily it doesn't matter what sort of shop you buy slabs of chocolate at, so they bought an extra lot, to counteract the coffee. Then they started cautiously for home. As the back of the car was full, Elizabeth and Robin both had to squeeze into the front seat. When they entered Yarwell most of their friends seemed to be in the road to see them pass ; there was Mr. Brent the milkman, with his new van, Mr. Briskin the carpet-beater and mattress-maker, standing outside his casual-looking and untidy workshop, in his apron and spectacles, and Hackett, with a ladder on his shoulder and a bucket in the other hand, off to a job—all of them stopped, stood and stared, their eyes full of surprise and speculation, as the loaded car rattled by.

The Bosun and Antony were at the gate to meet them, for they had come the last hundred yards down Lacey's Lane with cheerful and premonitory hootings of the horn.

"Gosh," said Antony, as Elizabeth and Robin disentangled themselves and climbed out on to the road, "what a terrific lot!"

The Bosun began to untie the lashings and together, bit by bit, they transferred the timber through the gate under the ilex tree into the Garage, and stacked it neatly along the wall opposite the bench. By the time they had finished it was a good deal past lunch-time, and Mrs. Rutherford had had difficulty in preventing Emily from *cooking longer* in order to have it both hot and ready for them. Emily found it hard to calculate accurately, but then (as Mrs. Rutherford said, when she anxiously raised the lid of the potato dish), she was so nice—and it's much more important to be nice than to be clever.

CHAPTER VI

It would be a good thing at this point to explain what kind of boat *Tern* was going to be. Shipbuilding is an extremely difficult craft, and the perfection of it—even when the boat to be built is a small and humble one—is beyond the power of anybody but an expert. What makes the construction of a boat so much more difficult than the construction of any other wooden object, is the fact that in a boat there are no straight lines and no right-angles ; every piece of wood in the hull of a boat is curved ; and that, too, not in a regular curve, but a varying one. It is easy therefore to see that to get, for instance, the edges of two planks to fit exactly together under these circumstances is a ticklish task. And the worst of it is that they *must* fit. If you make a log-box, and there is a gap between the sides and the bottom, it may look silly, but the logs will not fall out ; but if you make a boat and there is a gap between the keel-plank and the garboards, it will not only look silly, but the water *will* come in. Nevertheless, though only an expert is able to build a boat with the beautiful exactness and finish that professional standards demand, any sensible person who has had some practice in the use of tools can, if he has a clear and adequate plan to work from, produce a vessel which will be strong and watertight, even if she is not beautiful. Her ability to sail once she is built—and to a great extent her beauty too—will depend, if the plans have been properly followed, not on the builder, but on the designer.

The Rutherford and Chale families were lucky. Robin and Antony had learnt years ago to use a chisel and a saw and a gouge, in the making of model boats at Creeksea, and they were able to work with accuracy and care. Mr. Rutherford had frequently been employed by Mrs. Rutherford to do Hackett out of a job, both in the house and in the garden at The Cottage (the extension of the summer-house, for instance, was all his work, and he was very proud of it) ; so he was used to the behaviour of wood, at any rate under normal circumstances ; and the Bosun, of course, had actually assisted at some point of his obscure and adventurous career in building a boat before. Anne and Elizabeth were novices ; but Elizabeth was a great hand with a paint-brush, and powerfully attracted by the thought of putty, and Anne (as Antony unkindly suggested) could at least embroider the burgee.

Tern, as shown on the plans, was to be a half-decked boat seventeen feet long and six feet broad, rigged with a mainsail and jib. She was to have a centreboard. The peculiarity of her design was the keel-plank, which has already been mentioned on several occasions : this was to be cut from a broad plank of elm, broadest amidships and tapering at the ends, and bolted flat on the upper side of the keel. Across the keel-plank at regular intervals pieces of oak, called the " floors ", were to be fastened, and to these floors were to be riveted the vessel's ribs. The ribs were not curved as the ribs of most boats are, but cut in angles, like this.

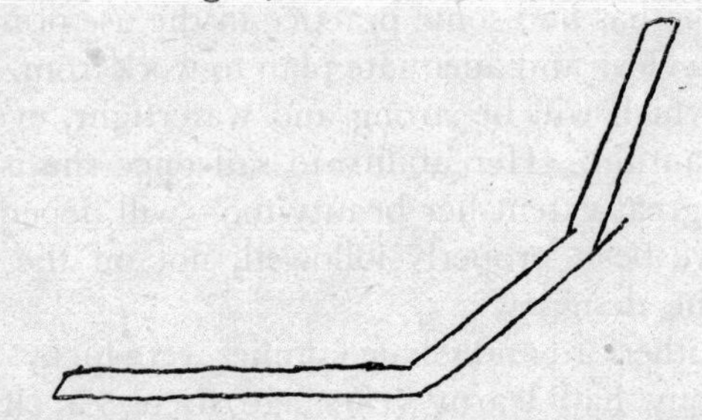

Each pair of ribs had to be of a different shape, as you will easily understand if you remember how boats bulge in the middle, and grow finer and narrower towards the bows. The exact shape of each pair of ribs was described in the plans (it had been worked out by the designer), and to save time and a very tiresome and laborious task Mr. Rutherford had told the manager of the yard at St. Helens to have them cut to shape on his steam saw. The same had been done with the floors. Both the ribs and the floors were of oak, and it was not worth while to spend days or even weeks cutting them out by hand from this exceedingly hard wood, when it could be done at the yard in as many minutes.

Immediately after lunch (which was all right except for the potatoes, which were mashed—and the Rutherfords never had mashed potatoes, unless there had been a miscalculation in the cooking) the four children, with Mr. Rutherford and the Bosun, hurried to the Garage.

" John," called Mrs. Rutherford, as he was going out of the door, " hadn't you better put the car away first, before you forget it ? "

" All right," said Mr. Rutherford ; " I won't forget." No ; of course he wouldn't forget, but when he got to the Garage and saw the beautiful new timber waiting for him, it seemed more sensible to make a beginning on the great task that lay before them. He would put the car away afterwards.

The best of having a lot of people working on a complicated job is that several different parts of it can be carried on simultaneously. Mr. Rutherford began to cut out the keel from two great slabs of elm, four inches thick; the Bosun, after marking the shape of the keel-plank with a pencil (everybody helped in this, checking the measurements from the plan) handed it over to Antony who took it out into the open space under the holm oak (the plank was sixteen feet long), put it on trestles and started to rough it out with a saw. Then the Bosun began to fit together the frames; and as this involved the use of copper rivets, Robin was set to the task (watched by Elizabeth) of cutting a large number of short pieces, each carefully measured, from copper rods a quarter of an inch thick. He put a rod in the vice on the bench and cut off the bits with a hack saw. The sawing made an unpleasing noise, but Elizabeth bore it because it was interesting, and neither Robin nor she had known before that one could cut metal with a saw. Anne meanwhile was under the holm oak with Antony, and took a turn now and again, when Antony was tired, in the sawing of the keel-plank. Sixteen feet is a long way to go with a saw, and it had to be done twice—once on each side. In fact it was such a long way that after a time both Antony and Anne felt a bit sick of it, and came into the Garage to see what the others were doing.

Robin had cut enough pieces of copper rod for the time being; the Bosun was now going to show him how riveting was done, and Antony thought that he might as well prolong his rest, and stay and watch too.

The Bosun took one of the floors and carefully fitted

on to it the corresponding rib, telling Robin to hold it firmly in position. Then he drilled three holes through both floor and rib, and through each of the holes (which had to be exactly the right size) he drove one of Robin's pieces of copper rod. The pieces of copper projected about a quarter of an inch on each side. Then he put a rove, which is a disc of copper about the size of a sixpence with a hole in the middle, over one of the projecting ends, and with a hammer (a special one with a convex instead of a flat face) began to tap gently at the end of the rod with little, outward, smoothing taps. Copper is very soft, and the end of the rod, under these taps, gradually splayed out over the edges of the rove, until they finally held it down firmly. Then the frame was turned over, and the same thing was done on the other side. Robin had a try at fixing the second rivet, and so did Antony, but it was not as easy as it looked ; for they found that if they just hammered straight, as if they were driving a nail, nothing much happened ; and it obviously needed practice to acquire the right kind of smoothing movement : outwards and inwards, and always away from the centre. But it was interesting, and Robin, who liked practising things, quickly decided that he would become a good riveter.

But there was not much chance to practise that afternoon, for by the time they had fixed the second rivet (which had to be finished off by the Bosun), it was getting dark, and they had to stop work. So they put the tools away, and Elizabeth hung the hammers and saws on the nails above the bench.

"We haven't done much," said Antony. "At least, it doesn't *look* much."

Mr. Rutherford laughed.

"Give us a chance," he said.

The children went down the path between the apple-trees towards the house. Just as they reached the edge of the lawn, Elizabeth stopped.

"Hsh!" she said. "Listen. Somebody's at the door. Talking to Mummy."

They listened. Anne looked at Elizabeth, and her jaw dropped.

"Gosh," she said, "it isn't *Arthur*, is it?"

"Who's Arthur?" said Antony.

"I believe it is," said Anne.

"Help," said Elizabeth, and giggled.

"You needn't laugh," said Anne.

"But who *is* Arthur?" said Antony.

"A ghastly boy," said Elizabeth. "He's perfectly frightful. He . . ."

"Shut up," said Anne. "He's coming."

Shepherded by Mrs. Rutherford, who was doing her best to look both welcoming and cheerful, a tall thin boy of about sixteen came across the lawn towards them. He wore a cloth cap set at a jaunty angle. He had a pale face, and not much chin. He wore spectacles.

"Here's Arthur," said Mrs. Rutherford encouragingly. There was no need to say it; but it would have been worse if she had said nothing. There was a short pause. Then Anne said "hullo", and shook hands. Arthur's clasp was limp.

Antony hung back. Elizabeth stole a look at Robin; Robin was solemn, his eyes on the newcomer. Elizabeth's fingers crept to the sleeve of his jacket and gave it a little twitch; but Robin took no notice. Then they all shook hands, one after the other—with Arthur. Nobody could think of anything to say, and for a moment or two there was an uncomfortable pause. Then Mrs. Rutherford thought of something.

"They've all been very busy," she said. "They're building a boat."

Robin wished she hadn't said it. He felt he didn't want Arthur to know ; at any rate not yet. It would not have mattered if Arthur had been different. But Elizabeth was right : he *was* rather ghastly. Besides, they had only just begun ; *Tern* was not a boat at all yet. Robin, of course, already saw her, in his mind's eye, complete and beautiful ; and for that very reason she was at the moment a secret : a secret between themselves. He looked quickly at Antony, and wondered if he felt the same, but thought that he probably didn't. It was the kind of thing he always wanted to explain to Antony, but never could—not properly.

Arthur smiled politely. " That's pretty good," he said. " What is it ? A model, I suppose."

" No," said Anne. " A real one."

Arthur whistled.

" By Jove," he said. " But you're not pulling my leg, are you ? "

" No," said Anne.

" They began this afternoon," said Mrs. Rutherford.

" Can I have a look ? " said Arthur.

Robin's heart sank. He was afraid Arthur would say that.

" It's getting rather d-dark," he muttered—stammering a little, as he always did when he was excited or worried. But nobody heard him.

Arthur had already started forward towards the Garage ; Elizabeth, Antony and Anne followed reluctantly. Robin lingered.

" Aren't you going too, Robin ? " said Mrs. Rutherford.

Robin shook his head.

" I don't th-think so," he said.

" Don't be long," Mrs. Rutherford called to the others. " Tea's almost ready ; and there's the right sort of fire for toast."

Then she took Robin's arm, and led him off across the lawn towards the house. " I *think* it's the right sort of fire," she said, " but if it isn't, we'll arrange it—to be ready for them when they come in."

" Will he stay to tea ? " said Robin. Mrs. Rutherford laughed.

" I don't know," she said. " But we'll have to ask him."

" I hope he w-won't," said Robin.

Emily had lighted the lamp in the sitting-room, but had not yet drawn the curtains. Through the french windows the room looked warm and happy.

" We *ought* to go round to the front door," said Mrs. Rutherford, " and wipe our boots. But we won't."

The evening was still and frosty. The Bosun's voice could be heard from the Garage, then Mr. Rutherford's ; they were saying how-do-you-do to Arthur. Suddenly it seemed much darker. Mrs. Rutherford paused with her hand on the knob of the french window.

" Look," she said, and pointed up through the branches of the ash-tree, " there's a star."

Robin nodded solemnly. Then they went in. Tea was on the table. Mrs. Rutherford drew the curtains, and then cut some thick slices of bread for Robin to toast. Robin himself had gone straight to the fire, and was kneeling in front of it with the tongs in his hand, making some delicate arrangements of the logs so that it would be better for toasting. Some sparks flew up the chimney, and left a company of little glittering ants in the soot at the back of the fireplace. Sally, who was in a chair close by, stirred uneasily.

As each piece of toast was finished Robin propped it up against the brick fender to keep warm. Most of the time he was thinking about *Tern*, and sometimes about Arthur. He went on hoping that he would not stay to tea. He would have liked to ask Mrs. Rutherford to tell him more about who he was ; but it wasn't a very good opportunity, as the others would be coming in at any minute. The piece of bread on his fork curled suddenly, dangled on one prong, then fell off into the fire. Robin snatched it. Then he looked back over his shoulder, and caught Mrs. Rutherford's eye. Both chuckled.

"It's not burnt much," said Robin.

"Blow the ashes off," said Mrs. Rutherford. Robin blew, and went on toasting.

Voices were heard. The others were coming in. They passed the french window, and their feet crunched on the gravel path which led to the front door. Then the latch of the gate clicked.

"Robin," said Mrs. Rutherford, "he's not staying to tea."

"Why?" said Robin. "How do you know?"

"Didn't you hear the gate?"

Robin nodded.

"Good," he said.

The engine of a motor-bicycle started with a splutter and cough, roared for an instant, hiccupped, roared again, then faded in diminishing thunder along the lane. Mr. Rutherford and the Bosun and the three children came into the sitting-room. They were all talking and laughing, and hungry for tea. Emily brought in the teapot. They took their places round the table—except Mr. Rutherford, who sat in an easy chair by the fire and balanced his cup on the arm of it. This was a habit of his ; Mrs. Rutherford rather wished he wouldn't do it ; sometimes she told him he was sure to upset his tea, and sometimes that he was unfriendly ; but Mr. Rutherford said he was not unfriendly at all, and that there was no danger whatever of upsetting his tea, unless one of the children bumped into his chair.

Tea began. There was honey and toast and cake, and apple-jelly, bright and clear and amber-coloured in a glass jar. Tea in winter is the best meal of the day. In summer it is pleasant enough, but it always interrupts something important that you are doing ; in winter it comes just at the right time, at the lighting of the lamps, when the work of the day is over and the long warm comfortable evening is before you. Moreover in summer you cannot have toast. Honey is good, and apple-jelly is good, and home-made cake and yellow butter and new bread are all good too ; but it is toast that makes tea the best of all meals—not toast brought in by Emily, warm and slithery in a covered dish, but made as you want it by the sitting-room fire—made quickly and evenly by a bright hot patch, tasting very slightly of wood smoke, and eaten at once with knobs of cold butter freshly applied for each bite.

Everybody talked a lot as tea went on, except Robin ; Robin was still wishing that Arthur hadn't come. The others were discussing Arthur, and Robin listened. The only other silent one was Mr. Rutherford ; he had happened to notice a particular book in a shelf within reach of where he sat, and he had quietly abstracted it and was turning over the pages as he sipped his tea. But he didn't feel at all unfriendly ; he could hear them all talking perfectly well, though he did not always know what they actually said—except once when Mrs. Rutherford said very clearly " don't you think so, John ? " and he inconsiderately said " yes ", which was the wrong answer. In the pause which followed he caught Mrs. Rutherford's eye, and both laughed ; so that was all right, and Mr. Rutherford continued unrepentantly to turn the pages. Presently, however, just as he had begun his third cup of tea, he shut his book with a snap and said " Good heavens ! "

" What's the matter ? " said Mrs. Rutherford.

" I've forgotten to put the car away."

" Now if only . . ." began Mrs. Rutherford, but Mr. Rutherford interrupted her.

" You were right," he said ; " absolutely right. I just forgot. You see, I meant . . . " He got to his feet.

" Look out," said Mrs. Rutherford. " Your cup." The spoon tinkled in the saucer and fell on the floor.

" It's only the spoon," he said.

" Did you turn the lights on ? " said Mrs. Rutherford.

" No . . . but it'll be all right. I expect it's Frank's night off."

" Who's Frank ? " said Antony.

" Our Policeman," said Anne.

" I meant to put it away before tea," said Mr. Rutherford.

" Yes, dear," said Mrs. Rutherford.

" You see . . . " began Mr. Rutherford, on his way to the door ; but then stopped. He knew that Mrs. Rutherford did see perfectly well : that was the trouble. As he passed her chair, he very gently pulled a small curl at the back of her neck, and hurried out of the room.

At about half-past nine Antony and Robin went back to their lodging to bed. It was a pity that there wasn't room for them in the cottage. If it had been summer they could have slept in the Hut at the end of the garden near the Garage. Various members of the Rutherford family always did sleep in the Hut during the summer holidays, not only to make extra room but because they liked it. It was not really a hut at all. It had once, very long ago, been a chicken-house, and Mr. Rutherford had removed two of its sides and cleaned it up and beautified it with white and blue paint and creosote, and the chicken-run outside it had gradually turned, under his and Mrs. Rutherford's hands, into a small and lovely garden about nine yards square, shut in on one side by a neat hedge of privet, and on two others by a trellis of climbing roses. On the roof of the Hut a fig-tree from the garden next door had generously spread its branches, as if especially to give Elizabeth delight ; and when you awoke on an August morning at sunrise you were welcomed to the day by a smell of sweet-peas and the sight of hollyhocks within a few feet of your bed ; and perhaps the wrens who had built under the beams of the Garage would already be busy about nothing in the apple-tree, whose growing branches reached in across the privet.

But now it was winter ; there were no hollyhocks or sweet-peas in the garden, and the climbing roses were nothing but interlacing stems of bare thorn. The camp-beds in the Hut had been put away. The Bosun, of course, had suggested that Robin and Antony might sling hammocks somewhere, and when Mrs. Rutherford had asked where, had replied blandly but vaguely, " Oh, anywhere." Robin secretly liked the idea, and so did Elizabeth, who preferred to feel that he and Antony were staying with them really properly. But it did not seem practicable ; so they were obliged to find a room in the village. The room Mrs. Rutherford had taken was along the lane which led up towards the downs. It belonged to Mrs. Hackett, the wife of Mr. Hackett the carpenter. This was convenient. Mrs. Hackett was a comfortable person ; she was by nature friendly to boys, having had quite a shoal of them herself in the distant past, and as soon as you saw her you could tell that she had enjoyed it ; with Hackett himself Robin and Antony now knew that they were going to stand in a very special sort of relationship. He was to help them build *Tern*, and it was important to make friends with him. Moreover, a carpenter's shop is a delightful place under any circumstances—inferior, thought Robin, only to a shipyard ; and Hackett's shop, for the time at any rate, *was* a shipyard, for it was on Hackett's bench that *Tern's* keel was to be shaped.

Mr. Rutherford took Antony and Robin to the door. There was no need to take them all the way to Mrs. Hackett's to-night ; they could find it easily enough by themselves. It was a cold night, with a feel of frost. It was black dark, and the stars were large and liquid. Antony switched on his torch, and flashed its beam on the green gate. Robin hunched his shoulders and put his hands in his pockets. He heard Bittle's laugh—diminished by the shut window. Mr. Rutherford said "Goodnight" and shut the front door.

"Antony," said Robin, "let's go round this way. Come on." And instead of opening the green gate he began to walk along the gravel path which led past the sitting-room windows to the lawn.

"Why? Where are you going?" said Antony.

"Round here. Round by the Garage—by the Building Shed."

"What for?"

"Just to have a look at *Tern*."

Antony thought there wasn't much point in it—there was very little of *Tern* to look at, anyway ; and it was pitch dark, and they had only their torch. But he followed Robin round the corner of the house, and across the lawn and along the path under the rose-arch, until they came to the Garage.

The doors stood open. There was a fresh sharp smell of wood. Robin took the torch from Antony and flashed it round on to the bench and into the corners. He didn't say anything ; but his thoughts were busy. With wonderful rapidity *Tern* grew before his mind's eye. He would become an expert riveter. Stopping seams with putty and red lead would be lovely. What would his father think when he first saw *Tern* under sail—with Robin at the helm? Would it be possible, if they worked really tremendously hard, to get her finished these holidays? No, of course not. The Bosun had said they couldn't. But they might.

Antony stamped his feet and began to whistle.

"Come on," he said. "It's jolly cold. Let's go." He moved towards the gate under the ilex tree.

"Bring the torch, Robin," he said.

Robin followed. They went through the gate together, and along the lane. A dog barked, high and shrill.

"That's Sally," said Antony. "She must have heard us open the gate."

"Antony," said Robin. "What did Arthur *say* when he went to look at *Tern*?"

Antony laughed. "Something about a metacentric shelf," he said.

"What's that?" said Robin.

"*I* don't know," said Antony. "He said he'd lend us a book about it—to help us."

"Did he say anything else?"

"Not much—I don't think. Except that he'd give us ten minutes an hour handicap in his snipe, when we get her to Poole."

"What's a snipe?"

"A sort of racing boat he's got."

Robin thought for a minute in silence. They reached Mrs. Hackett's door. Then with his hand on the door handle he said solemnly: "I think he's pretty l-loathsome, really; don't you?"

Antony laughed again.

"He might be worse," he said. "He's got a motor-bike. He said he'd take me on the carrier."

They said goodnight to Mrs. Hackett and went upstairs to bed. The bedroom smelt of clean linen, faintly sweet. The candle glinted on the polished brass rails of the beds. They undressed quickly. Robin was in bed first. The sheets were icy cold, and he curled his knees up under his chin, and pulled the bedclothes over his head. Then he came up to breathe, and began cautiously to extend his toes into the chilly wastes. Shivers crept up his spine, then suddenly stopped. He lay limp and warm. They didn't talk much—which was unusual. Robin was thinking—or rather his mind was thinking for him, and he rather wished it wouldn't. Would Arthur come every day? It would be sickening if he did. Elizabeth didn't like him, thank goodness; nor did Anne. Antony? No, of course, Antony didn't like him either. He couldn't possibly . . . but he did wish he hadn't said anything about his motor-bike.

The church clock struck: probably half-past ten. Robin said goodnight to Antony—just to see if he was asleep. He was.

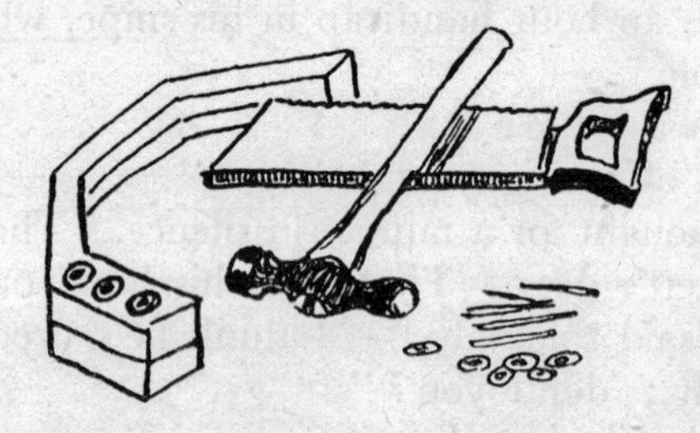

CHAPTER VII

Hackett was a satisfactory person. Robin soon made friends with him. Robin was quite good at making friends with people, on the whole, in spite of the fact that he was shy—almost as shy as Elizabeth; but whereas Elizabeth never knew what to *say* to strangers, and hoped they would not make remarks to her which were difficult or embarrassing to answer, Robin was content to say nothing at all, at any rate for a time. One of the best ways of getting to know people is to be with them—if they will let you—while they are at work. Robin knew this. Obviously, you can't do it with everybody; but you could with Hackett: he was the right sort of person.

During the days which followed Robin spent quite a lot of time, after breakfast in the mornings, before he joined the others at the cottage, in Hackett's workshop. At first he hardly spoke. But he liked to watch the beautiful precision of Hackett's tools as he worked. There was something comfortable and pleasant in the leisured certainty of his movements, in his large and kindly presence, and in the gentle voice in which he would drop inconsequent sayings, not so much to Robin as to the workshop itself and all it contained. Robin quickly felt at home, and knew that Hackett liked him to be there. Sometimes Hackett would tell stories, long and rambling, and full of confusing people whom Robin had never heard of; they were not very interesting stories, but Robin quite liked them, nevertheless, because they were companionable. Hackett of course knew nothing whatever about boats, and though Robin did not actually try to teach him, he did do his best to persuade him not to call the keel "that there fin". But he was not very successful.

It was lucky that Robin made friends with Hackett; for when it was first suggested by Mr. Rutherford that Hackett should help with certain parts of the building of *Tern*, it was Robin who was most doubtful about the propriety of asking him. Would it still be *their* boat, if Hackett helped? But Robin's doubts soon disappeared. Mr. Rutherford had explained that they could do it all themselves, if they were willing to afford the time; and that made it better; but now it was better still, and Robin was almost willing, tacitly, to accept Hackett as one of the company—*Tern* would be their boat *and* Hackett's. He explained this to Antony, but Antony did not seem to think it was so important as Robin did. He had not felt the difficulty, and he did not properly appreciate the solution.

"Obviously," he said, "we want to get *Tern* finished as soon as we can. It would be hopeless if she wasn't done by the end of next holidays." But for Robin that was not quite the point. It was difficult sometimes to get Antony to see things. Elizabeth understood better what Robin meant.

"He's not a boat-builder," she said. "He's an ordinary carpenter, and couldn't do anything without *us*." Then she added with a chuckle: "Has he told you about his mother who's a hundred? He told me once, when he came to mend the plaster in the kitchen. All about her birthday party. It was awful."

Robin shook his head. "But he's nice, though," he answered.

"Yes," said Elizabeth. Elizabeth was good at seeing things.

Tern was getting on nicely. After a fortnight's work (more than half the holidays gone—for they had not begun until after Christmas !) she was already beginning to Robin's prophetic eye to look a little bit like a boat. The keel (made and slotted by Hackett) and the keel-plank had been set up on the stocks, and the floors and ribs fixed in their places. To an eye that was not prophetic she looked more like the skeleton of a whale than a boat: but it was easy to imagine the ribs clothed with planks, smooth and sweetly curving—and a great deal more besides. Robin had improved as a riveter; Antony had done a lot of laborious sawing to accurate measurements, and Elizabeth's thoughts were turning ever more strongly towards putty and paint: especially towards putty. The Bosun pleased her with the information that two sorts of putty would be required: one called "luting", very squashy and damp, to seal certain joints, the other a delightful compound of white and red lead, linseed oil, and size. Present days were good—but there were even better days coming.

It would be pleasant to describe in minute and exact detail every process in the building of *Tern*, all the difficulties that each of the builders encountered (except Hackett, who didn't encounter any), and how they were surmounted—at least it would be pleasant for some people. Certainly it would be pleasant for me ; and I think Robin, if he were telling this story, would undoubtedly insist upon doing so. To know how things were done was always important to Robin : useful things at any rate—like building a boat. True, he was less interested in some other things : gardening, for instance. The garden at the Manor House at Creeksea, where Robin and Antony lived, was a beautiful one : moreover, Bramble the gardener was a friend of Robin's up to a point (the point was usually reached just before the figs were ripe in the summer holidays, Robin being ahead of Bramble's time by a week or so) ; and Mrs. Chale herself used to spend many quiet and happy hours in it with a basket and a pair of scissors. Robin loved the garden—especially he loved the walled garden, and the smell of the box-borders on a hot day. But that is not the same thing as being interested in gardening. On the few occasions when Mrs. Chale suggested that he should come round with another basket and another pair of scissors and cut off a few deads himself, he felt almost miserable. But boats were another matter. Where boats were concerned Robin would have thought no detail uninteresting or unimportant. But perhaps it is just as well that it is not Robin who is telling this story ; for there must be a lot of people who do not much want to be told about chine-strakes and doublings, and do not fully sympathize with the exquisite pleasure of getting two curved edges to fit precisely together along a length of seventeen feet. The really important thing in this story is, of course, what the children did with *Tern after* she was built. If Antony, now, had done the telling, he would probably have gone straight to that—after just mentioning casually that they had built the boat themselves. Possibly even Elizabeth would have done the same ; but I am not sure—Elizabeth might have tried to tell a certain amount about the building ; she enjoyed it enormously, but not in the same way that Robin did. And Elizabeth would have been cheerfully inaccurate about the words. She would also, no doubt, have put in quite a lot about what they did in between their actual hours of work. I know this, because I have talked to them about it—to all of them ; so in telling the story myself, and knowing as I do what each of them found most important in it, I feel that the best thing is not to favour any one of them too exclusively, but to borrow a bit from each as I think fit.

One bit I must borrow at once from Robin, and describe how he and Hackett made the transom. This is worth describing, because not even the Bosun really knew the proper way of doing it. A transom is a square stern. *Tern's* transom was more than three feet wide, and about three feet deep, and was made of elm an inch thick. It had to look, when it was finished, like a single solid piece, but the difficulty was that no plank could be got which was wide enough. Two planks had therefore to be joined together, edge to edge, strongly and exactly. The whole party had a conference about how this should be done, but no satisfactory solution was proposed. Elizabeth suggested glue.

" I'll melt some," she said. But nobody approved. Antony thought that they might screw strips of wood at right-angles to the join.

" Like a hencoop ? " said the Bosun.

" Why like a hencoop ? " said Antony indignantly.

The Bosun threw a covert glance at Elizabeth.

" Transom is as transom does," he whispered. Elizabeth giggled, and looked at Robin who remained solemn.

" I still think glue," she said.

" It wouldn't stick," said Robin. " N-not for long," he added politely.

"There must be a way," said Mr. Rutherford.

"Exactly," said the Bosun and began to fill his pipe. "Now when I was in Bechuanaland . . ."

"Bosun!" said Elizabeth; "you never were."

The Bosun raised his eyebrows and began luxuriously to light his pipe.

"Doesn't it tell you on the plans?" said Anne.

"That's an idea," said the Bosun, and blew out his match.

"It doesn't," said Robin.

There was a short pause. Mr. Rutherford was holding the two pieces of elm, edges together, one above the other, balanced on the bench. He was looking at them attentively, his head cocked. Elizabeth nudged Robin.

"Look at Daddy," she said.

Mr. Rutherford dropped the boards and knocked a chisel off on to the floor.

"The best chisel," said the Bosun calmly. Mr. Rutherford picked up the chisel.

"We don't seem to be getting anywhere," he said.

"Nowhere," said the Bosun. "Only glue and hencoops. It's absurd."

"Surely it *would* stick," said Elizabeth.

"Don't be an ass, Bittle," said Anne.

There was another pause. Then Robin broke it.

"Let *me* do it," he said. "M-me and Hackett, I mean."

So that was how it was arranged.

Hackett's method was this: he told Robin to put one half of the transom into a vice, and bore eight holes at regular intervals in the upper edge of it. Each hole was to be three-quarters of an inch deep. Then with a narrow chisel he himself cut little slots, extending also about three-quarters of an inch from the left-hand edge of each of the holes which Robin had bored. This he did very carefully and deliberately.

"We'll soon get your boards fixed for you," he said.

"It's the transom," said Robin.

"That's it," said Hackett with soothing assent, and tapped his chisel firmly with the mallet. Steps crunched in the lane outside the workshop. A man's voice called a greeting: "'Morning, Jim!"

"'Morning, George!" sang Hackett, without looking up from his bench. The steps moved on. Somebody was whistling. Out of the corner of his eye Robin saw Mrs. Hackett go round to the back of the house with a pail. Hackett went on tapping. Once he glanced up at Robin over his spectacles.

"I didn't ought to be doing this for you this morning," he said. "There's Mr. Biggin waiting for them new hinges on his cupboard."

Robin felt that he didn't much mind about Mr. Biggin.

"But there," said Hackett, giving a final tap, "we can't do more than our best, can we?"

Robin nodded his head quickly and solemnly. The next thing Hackett did was to put the other half of the transom in the vice, and drive into the corresponding edge of it eight screws—one for each of the holes which Robin had made. He drove them half in only; not upright, but all with an equal slant in the same direction. Their protruding heads were exactly opposite the holes. Then he took the other half and fitted it to the first, the screws dropping neatly into the holes. Robin was intently watching.

"B-but," he said, "it isn't right—it's sideways. Look, it sticks out. We didn't—I mean *I* didn't—make the holes in the right place."

Hackett pushed back his spectacles and gave a slow smile.

" We ain't finished yet," he said. Then he picked up his mallet again, and on the edge of the upper half which protruded sideways over the lower half he dealt several sharp and deliberate blows, forcing it along until it was exactly in position.

" There now ! " he said. " There's your board—just right. Now there'll be trouble for me if I don't get on with them hinges."

" Why did we put the screws in crooked ? " said Robin.

Hackett wiped his hands on his apron. " Why," he said, " being set on a slant like that, they pulls the edges together like. It stands to reason, don't it ? "

Robin was not quite sure that it did, and privately resolved to practise a joint of that kind himself one day when he was at home. But the result was eminently satisfactory. The two halves of the transom were as one : firm and neat and beautiful.

He put it under his arm and, heavy as it was, ran back along the lane to the cottage, and in through the gate under the ilex tree.

" My transom," he said, as he dumped it down, out of breath and panting ; " mine and Hackett's."

The Bosun, when Robin arrived, was planing off the edges of the keel-plank to get them flush with the frames, an awkward and distressing job because it was, so to speak, upside-down, and you had to stand on your head to do it. Moreover, if you took off too much in any one place, the whole boat (so the Bosun said) would be ruined, because the plank which was to fit to it would not lie close and the water would get in. He straightened himself out and came to inspect the transom. Elizabeth, who had been stirring some ancient paint in the bottom of a tin for no particular purpose, and talking to the Bosun as he worked, came too. Anne was not there ; nor was Mr. Rutherford—he had gone to the village, to remedy a certain deficiency in the larder which Emily had discovered rather too late for the remedy to be of much use ; but he had gone all the same.

Elizabeth removed a shaving which was clinging to one of her pigtails, then looked at her fingers : there was not much paint on them.

" You've been an awful long time," she said.

" No I haven't," said Robin, then added : " Where's Antony ? "

Elizabeth sniffed. Then she looked hard at Robin.

" Arthur came," she said.

" Well done, Robin," said the Bosun ; " you've finished one good job. What about another ? Have a go at the keel-plank. My back aches."

Robin took the plane from the Bosun and squatted down on his haunches by the stocks. He ran his finger along the edge of the keel-plank, then jabbed at it with the plane. The plane slithered unsatisfactorily over the surface. He jabbed again. Then he dropped his arms.

" It's blunt," he said. Elizabeth stood by his side and looked down on the top of his head.

" Bosun'll sharpen it," she said. Then she began to hum.

" D-did he come on his motor-bike ? " said Robin.

" Of course," said Elizabeth defensively. " He always does."

" I know," said Robin.

" Daddy said he could go," said Elizabeth quickly. " Antony, I mean . . . on the back of it. He only told Arthur not to go too fast."

There was a short silence. The Bosun was turning over some planks which lay along the bench, looking for something.

" Where did you put the ruler, Elizabeth ? " he asked.

Robin attacked the keel-plank with sudden energy.

Crisp shavings curled from the plane. After a minute he stopped. His arms ached.

"Why don't you go on?" said Elizabeth.

"I am going on," said Robin. Then he gave another jab, and the plane slithered.

"It *is* blunt," he muttered. He pushed the fringe of hair back from his eyes, got up, and threw the plane down on the bench. The Bosun had found the ruler, and was leaning over the skeleton of *Tern*, his pipe in his mouth, measuring things.

"Pity that piece of oak for the stem hasn't come," he said. "It'll hold us up."

Elizabeth began to hum again. Robin fingered a bit of waste wood on a pile in the corner of the shed.

"When did they go?" he asked, his voice a little husky.

"Ages ago," said Elizabeth in as off-handed a way as possible.

Robin did not want to do any more work that morning. He felt suddenly listless. Making the transom with Hackett had been fun. But now everything felt different. He hoped it was nearly lunch-time—but obviously it wasn't. Perhaps it was half-past eleven: they had cocoa and biscuits at half-past eleven. But probably it wasn't even that. He hoped Elizabeth wouldn't begin asking him what was the matter; but he didn't think she would. And what *was* the matter, anyway? He hardly knew himself. Oh yes, he did though—Arthur was loathsome: he simply couldn't bear Arthur. He had known that the first time he had seen him, when he had come into the garden with his silly long nose and condescending manner, and asked to see *Tern*. He couldn't possibly know anything about sailing—though he was always bragging about what he had done in his snipe. Indeed, he bragged about most things. And his father had a sort of motor-boat with sails : Arthur called it " our fifty-fifty ". Horrible ! It had Diesel engines, or something. And whenever he looked at *Tern* (which he quite often did) he made some disparaging remark about her design.

" A bit heavy in the stern, isn't she, Antony, old man ? " What did *he* know about it ? Of course, the Bosun himself had said when he first saw the plans that the stern might drag a little—but that only made it worse. It wasn't Arthur's *business* to know anything.

And then there was the motor-bike. Not that Robin disapproved of motor-bikes. When he was quite young he often used to ride his own bicycle at Creeksea, sitting on the carrier and reaching forward to the handlebars, and pretend he was on a motor-bike himself. But that was ages ago. Still—motor-bikes were all right. Indeed, he wouldn't mind riding on the carrier of one—if Antony would take him. But of course Antony was not old enough to have a licence ; besides, he couldn't drive. There was nothing really wrong with motor-bikes. He'd have one someday himself, probably. But Arthur's motor-bike he hated—almost as much as he felt at that moment he hated Arthur. He had known for days now that Antony would go with him ; it had been obvious. Yet Antony jeered at Arthur as much as any of them. He couldn't possibly *like* Arthur, could he ? No. Nobody could like Arthur. But Antony was queer sometimes. . . .

Elizabeth had gone back to her tin of paint and was looking at it pensively with a bit of stick. The Bosun was still measuring, and making marks with a pencil. Elizabeth knew Robin was gloomy about something ; altogether, she thought, it wasn't much of a morning : first Robin spending hours and hours alone with Hackett, and, now that he was back, being gloomy ; Daddy being busy indoors half the morning and then going fussing off to the village ; Anne lazing about in the sitting-room ; and Antony being away with horrible Arthur. Only the Bosun was going quietly on with *Tern*—but she didn't feel very interested in what he was doing. It looked dull —and there wasn't the least chance of any putty being wanted for weeks. If it was Emily's day out, she might help Mummy with the cooking ; but it wasn't even that.

It was a good thing, therefore, when Mrs. Rutherford opened the french window of the sitting-room and called in a cheerful voice that coffee was ready. Yes, she said *coffee* ; for she and Mr. Rutherford and the Bosun had coffee, though the children preferred cocoa. The Bosun stopped measuring and marking, and straightened himself up with a pleased and anticipatory smile. He put his ruler on the bench. Then he put one large hand on Elizabeth's shoulder, gently removed the tin of paint with the other, and urged her towards the door of the shed.

" Come on," he said.

Together they walked down the path between the apple-trees, and Robin followed behind.

They were half-way through their coffee when a motor-bicycle roared up the road, and with a splutter and pop stopped outside the gate. Robin heard voices, raised and excited—Antony's and Arthur's. A minute later Antony flung open the sitting-room door and marched in. His face was flushed, his hair wild, his eyes still streaming from the wind.

" Gosh," he said. " That was marvellous." He took a cup. " Is this mine ? " he said. " Is there sugar in it ? " And without waiting for an answer he began to drink.

Robin had looked up at him quickly as he came in

then he looked down again, and bent his head over his cocoa. He did not say anything. He wanted very badly to tell Antony about the transom ; but somehow he thought he had better not—not just yet.

CHAPTER VIII

The Christmas holidays are much too short. Mr. Rutherford was a schoolmaster, and there are certain misguided people who think that schoolmasters' holidays are much too long. Envy has a strange effect upon the judgment. Even the Bosun sometimes spoke as if Mr. Rutherford's life was mostly fun; but Anne, who was present on one of the occasions when he did so, indignantly replied that it was most unsuitable for the Bosun to talk in that manner, for *he* never seemed to do any work at all—or hardly.

The Bosun was not perturbed by this reproof. He was having breakfast at the time, a nice lingering breakfast, after the others had finished. A massive slice of toast, well loaded with butter and marmalade, was on the way to his mouth; he stopped it, and beamed benevolently.

"Ah!" he said; "but when I do . . .!"

He poured himself another cup of tea. The pot being nearly empty, the tea trickled out rather thin and strong. The Bosun sipped.

"It doesn't look very nice," said Anne; "is it, Bosun?"

"Repulsive," said the Bosun cheerfully.

"Would you like some more water?"

"Yes, please," said the Bosun.

Anne picked up the kettle from the hearth.

"I'm afraid there isn't any," she said.

The Bosun sighed.

"I once thought of being a schoolmaster myself," he said.

"*You,*" said Anne. "Why?"

"Really . . ." replied the Bosun in a dignified manner. "Why not?"

He continued to eat toast and marmalade. Anne watched him. Suddenly she chuckled.

"How would you like to teach Arthur?" she said.

The Bosun swallowed.

"Very much," he said.

"You *would*?"

"It would be so easy."

"Why easy?"

"He knows everything already," said the Bosun.

Anne snorted. "He *thinks* he does," she said. Then she added inconsequently: "Where's Robin?"

The Bosun looked carefully under the table.

"No," he said; "he's not there."

Anne ignored him. "I expect he's gone up to the Garage with Antony," she said. "I know they've come."

Anne was probably right. Robin nearly always did go up to the Building Shed immediately he came from Mrs. Hackett's. Often Antony went with him. Anne and Elizabeth went later, for they had jobs to do in the house—beds to make and so on. Tiresome but necessary. They also helped Emily clear the breakfast-table, making a horrific pile of dirty porridge plates and cups and knives and spoons by the scullery sink. But they didn't wash up—thank goodness, they didn't wash up. Even on *Tessa* washing up was bad ; though you did get used to it. But Elizabeth thought she would never get used to it at home. Emily washed up. Sometimes Elizabeth would linger a minute or two in the scullery, in order to watch her wade in and begin. Emily would cock an eye at the straggling heaps as she turned on the tap.

"Lor', Miss Elizabeth," she would say ; "there's quite a bit this morning, isn't there though ?"

Then she would fill the bowl with crocks, sprinkle soap-flakes with a liberal hand, and stir the mixture merrily round with a mop until everything clinked. Mrs. Rutherford had tried to cure Emily of this habit ; but alas it was inveterate. Mrs. Rutherford would sigh, and say : "Still, she's so *nice*. That's the great thing really—Emily's *nice*." Elizabeth agreed.

Robin liked going to the Building Shed by himself in the early morning, when he didn't stay with Hackett. He liked going with Antony too ; for it was a good time for talking, almost as good as the half-hour in bed before going to sleep. Moreover, he always liked having Antony to himself. The holidays were nearly over, and very soon they would be going back to their different schools. But he liked going alone too—just for a short time before the others came. It was a good opportunity for thinking. Robin was an energetic person ; he had always spent a lot of time doing things and practising things ; if he hadn't practised so much with his air-gun, for instance, last summer, he would never have found the bottle which contained the map of Ishmael Hawse ; and ever since he learnt to sail he had spent hours and hours on the river at Creeksea practising difficult manœuvres in the dinghy. But he was also quite good at doing nothing in particular. The desire to do nothing in particular would at times irresistibly descend upon him, and then he would just moon. Antony often found this annoying. Antony did not practise things as often as Robin did; but he always liked to have something definite to do: patball, for instance (their own special kind of fives, invented by Uncle Lance), when they were at home—or going out on Arthur's motor-bicycle. But Robin liked mooning.

A good place to moon—or to think, which can often be much the same thing—was the Building Shed after breakfast, on the days when Antony didn't come. Robin was there this morning. It was a cold dark morning with a westerly gale blowing, which roared like the sea in the trees at the bottom of the garden and made the branches of the ilex flow continually. It would be horrible working outside; but inside the Building Shed it seemed by contrast quite warm and pleasant.

For the last few days *Tern* had not seemed to get on very quickly. There had been a number of fiddling and delicate jobs to do which made no difference to her appearance or apparent growth. And the lack of the timber for her stem was annoying. Robin wondered whether he should work a bit on the groove into which fitted the bottom of the transom—*his* transom, and Hackett's. He took off one or two shavings with a chisel. But he didn't feel like work, so he stopped. For a minute or two he just looked: looked and stared—not thinking of anything special, but thinking all the same. It was nice in the Building Shed; it looked nice, and it smelt nice—still more, it *felt* nice. He liked the workmanlike muddle of chips and shavings, the wooden box full of copper nails, the neat cardboard packets of brass screws, the sawn or half-sawn planks stacked along the wall, the odd bits of copper rod lying about the floor, and the shining tools. And *Tern* herself was lovely.

He lifted a long plank from the stack by the wall and heaved it laboriously up until it pressed against *Tern's* ribs. He wished Antony was there to hold the other end—then they could bend it round into position, just to see what it looked like. But it was quite easy to imagine—it looked lovely. *Tern* was going to be the finest boat ever built.

He dropped the plank, and his eyes wandered to her stern—where his transom would soon be. Was it true that the stern was too wide? The Bosun had thought it might be: so did Arthur. Would Arthur be here next holidays too? Perhaps he would be sailing in his fifty-fifty cruiser. He hoped to goodness he would be. Why was Arthur horrible? He was utterly different from Elizabeth and Anne. And from Antony—though Antony seemed quite to like him, worse luck. Though perhaps he only liked the motor-bike rides.

Even if *Tern's* transom *was* too wide, she was still the best boat ever built. He didn't mind if she was a bit slow—she'd be jolly sea-worthy, anyway. If they'd had her last year when they went treasure-hunting in the Roach river, he and Antony could have slept on board instead of in a tent; there would have been heaps of room. Next year they *would* sleep on board—he and Antony; for he supposed there would hardly be room for Anne and Elizabeth too.

But she wasn't nearly finished. It took an awfully long time to build a boat—even when there were six people working—and Hackett. And the beastly timber for the stem hadn't arrived. He had asked the Bosun why they couldn't cut a bit from a thick branch of the ilex—that was oak of sorts; but the Bosun had said it wouldn't do because it would be green timber and not seasoned. So they'd have to wait.

He heard his name called in a voice which was at once merry and imperious; then steps on the path between the apple-trees. A moment afterwards Antony, hands in pockets, was at the door of the shed.

"Hullo," he said, "what are you doing?" He came over to where Robin was standing.

"We could sleep on her," said Robin.

"Gosh, yes," said Antony. "Easily."

He took a plane from the bench and began to work briskly at the bevel on the keel-plank. Robin stood by him and looked down on the back of his head as he drove the plane. He wished he was as strong as Antony —Antony was lucky to be so strong; and his hair didn't flop in a fringe over his forehead as his own did. Antony's hair was nice.

"The bike's got a puncture," Antony said, still planing.

"Arthur's?"

"Yes—of course."

"Did he come?"

"He was here just now," said Antony. "Just after I got down. He asked me to go there to tea."

Robin swallowed.

"Are you going?" he said.

Antony laughed.

"No," he said. "I told him we were too busy—building."

Robin was relieved.

"He said he'd teach me billiards," said Antony. "It would be quite fun really."

Robin's heart sank again.

"And he asked me if you'd go on his bike some time —when the puncture's mended. Do you want to?"

"Not m-much," said Robin.

Antony began to whistle. He was still working vigorously with the plane, stopping every now and again to test the bevel with the edge of it. He glanced up at Robin with a half smile.

"Why on earth not?" he said, and then added in a lower voice, almost to himself: "He's an awful ass, really."

Robin was glad when he said that. He felt he didn't mind—much—if Antony *did* go out with Arthur, so long as he thought he was an ass. Robin was happy again.

"I say," he said, "I've been making a cleat." He rummaged amongst some odds and ends of wood on the bench. "It's this. I made it out of a bit of holly I found in the garden. It was the right sort of shape. The grain's right—look. And I'm sure it's seasoned. Do you think it will do?"

Antony took it from him. "Jolly good," he said. "It's a bit big though. It'll do for the main halyard perhaps. And the transom's marvellous."

"Hackett did most of that," said Robin.

"I know," said Antony.

Not a great deal of progress was made that morning. Anne and Elizabeth and the Bosun came along to the shed later and did various small jobs. Mr. Rutherford didn't come at all; he was digging the vegetable garden. The Bosun was inclined to deprecate this, as insufficiently nautical.

"I understood," he said, "that *good* gardeners do their digging in October."

"But in October," replied Mr. Rutherford, "good choolmasters teach."

The Bosun sighed, and then looked sideways at Anne.

" How right I was," he said meditatively, " not to be a schoolmaster."

But the real thing that was checking the proper progress of the building was the absence of the timber for the stem. To make and set up the stem was now the next essential thing to be done. With that finished—and the transom also in position—they could begin to think about putting on the planking. It was very annoying of the yard at Bembridge not to have sent the timber. Moreover, it was not the kind of thing that an ordinary carpenter would be likely to have in stock. Certainly Hackett hadn't. You can't pick up a nice piece of seasoned English oak, six inches thick, just anywhere.

Everybody was glad when it was lunch-time. It was roast mutton, and it was Elizabeth's turn for the knuckle. Then there was a steamed pudding with a great many raisins and sultanas in it, to be eaten with a large helping of sugar. Steamed pudding was Emily's *chef-d'œuvre.* It was doubtful if she could make anything else, and Mrs. Rutherford was inclined to be cowardly about letting her try, preferring to make other sorts of puddings herself. But the steamed puddings were a triumph, and Emily knew it. She was always happiest on steamed pudding days. " And a nice steamed pudding to follow," she would say, when Mrs. Rutherford went into the kitchen after breakfast to discuss the menu. It disappointed her when Mrs. Rutherford was compelled to say, " Well—perhaps not to-day."

Seven people in the little dining-room made a tight fit ; but who cared ?—as the Bosun said, lifting his elbows and digging Elizabeth in the ribs with one and Robin with the other—they had often been tighter in *Tessa's* cabin.

It was still blowing hard ; the trees at the bottom

of the garden in the dell, and in front of the Vicarage opposite, still writhed and roared as if they were alive. But the cottage was snug and warm, and cheerful with firelight. They all ate a lot, and went into the sitting-room afterwards feeling comfortable and somnolent.

"I'll just get a few more logs," said Mr. Rutherford. The Bosun lit his pipe. Soon the fire in the broad hearth was nobly piled.

"Be an angel and pass me that cushion," said Mrs. Rutherford. Antony passed it. There was a happy silence.

Then Mrs. Rutherford asked if anybody was intending to do more work that afternoon. The Bosun stretched his legs.

"They can if they like," he said. No one else answered. Anne gave a little comfortable yawn; she was sitting on the stool with her back against the brick fireplace. Robin was squatting cross-legged, leaning against Mrs. Rutherford's chair. Elizabeth was wondering if she should look for the Patience cards, and making a slight disturbance in the neighbourhood of the corner cupboard. Then she saw an exercise book sticking out of the bookshelf, and thought she had better draw instead. But there remained the question of a pencil.

"Mummy," she said, "do you know where the pencil is?"

"No," said the Bosun.

"*Mummy*," said Elizabeth.

"On the mantelpiece," said Mrs. Rutherford firmly and precisely. "On the right-hand side. In Daddy's High Jump Cup."

After about a quarter of an hour Robin began to get restless. He got up and went to the window. The leaves of the magnolia tree were tapping on the pane: a gentle irregular tapping. A car went by, with a soft hiss, on the road at the other side of the hedge. Robin remembered with pleasure that Antony was not going to tea with Arthur. Should he ask Antony to come to the Building Shed? He looked over his shoulder at Antony, and thought not—he was curled in a big chair, reading.

Presently he slipped out of the room by himself. Directly he opened the door the wind struck at him with violence, and made him catch his breath. He trotted up the garden towards the Building Shed. Almost as soon as he got there Elizabeth followed.

"Hullo," she said.

"Hullo," said Robin.

"Are you going on working?"

"Not specially—I don't think," said Robin.

For a minute or two they idled about the shed, doing nothing in particular. The wind seemed to be getting stronger; on the smooth patch outside the shed it made little whirls and eddies of last year's ilex leaves.

"I say," said Elizabeth, "do you know Rocken End?"

"No," said Robin. "Why?"

"It would be terrifically rough to-day, with this wind."

"Where is it?"

"Near the lighthouse. Let's go."

Robin readily agreed.

"I'll just tell Mummy," said Elizabeth. She ran back to the house, Robin following.

"Mummy," she said, opening the sitting-room door, "we're going for a walk; Robin and me."

"All right, darling. You'll want your coat."

"Oh——" said Elizabeth; "shall I?"

Getting coats is a nuisance.

Soon they were on their way—two small figures on the road to the village, heads bent, pushing against the wind. They didn't talk much; it wasn't worth it—the wind made such a noise in their ears.

A quarter of an hour's walking brought them to the top of the old road which leads down between low stone walls overgrown with brambles, across rough, sloping fields, to the lighthouse. The sea was full before them, torn white by the wind. Beyond the trim white lighthouse stood a solitary farmstead, on the very verge of the land. It looked desolate and grey. Elizabeth and Robin hurried on down the lane over the loose stones. It was difficult for them to keep their eyes open against the force of the wind. The lane ended at the gate of the farmyard.

"Through here," panted Elizabeth and pushed open the gate. A sheepdog with a matted coat was lying outside his kennel; he barked and shook his chain. The yard was thick in mud. The farmhouse itself seemed to lower, and to crouch against the gale. Chickens pecked about some bins, and scattered in a fluster when Robin and Elizabeth went by. Nobody else seemed to be about. The wind clutched them and roared.

"Where's Rocken End?" shouted Robin.

Elizabeth turned her head to hear him, one pigtail blown and flattened across her face. They passed the gate at the farther end of the farmyard.

"Nearly there," she shouted back, and staggered sideways into Robin.

"Gosh," she gasped. "I can hardly stand up. Come on; it's only just over there."

A few hundred yards over rolling ground, and the path suddenly dipped. At once the air was filled with

That's Rocken End.

fine blown spume, like driving rain. The pressure of the wind was like a solid weight.

"That's it . . . that's Rocken End," said Elizabeth, her voice high and thin against the noise.

"Gosh," said Robin.

The sea in front of them was a cauldron on the boil. A dent in the coastline made a small bay; it was strewn with great grey boulders, shapeless and jagged. Around and against them the white sea surged and smashed. It had a living but purposeless savagery. The wind tore at their eyelids so that they could hardly see.

Farther offshore—in the Race—the confusion of water was worse. It was horrible. The waves were not like any waves that Robin had seen before; they did not march in procession as ordinary waves do, however tremendous. They had run mad. They fought together, and met, and clashed, and reared up into towers and pinnacles which collapsed upon themselves with a continuous and horrifying roar. It was the Milky Way of the sea.

Robin was fascinated. "Gosh," he said again. "Oh, gosh." But the words were inaudible, snatched from his mouth by the wind.

Elizabeth took hold of his arm and pulled him forward. A big rock on the curve of the bay gave them a little shelter. The sea swirled almost to their feet; but it was easier to breathe here. They stood close together, pressed against the rock. They could still see half the bay from where they stood.

Elizabeth shivered.

"We'd better go back soon," she said.

Robin was shading his eyes with a thin brown hand and staring out on the water.

"Suppose there was a boat there?" he said. "Out there . . . in that sea."

"Come on, Robin," said Elizabeth. She pulled at his sleeve. They left the shelter of the rock—back again into the furious wind. Elizabeth's hair was dark with spray.

Above the tide-mark, on the path, Robin stopped and turned to look again at the sea. "Oh, gosh," he thought, "suppose there was a boat out there . . . ?" Elizabeth put her arm through his and pulled. "Come on," she shouted, "we must go."

Robin resisted her pressure.

"Look," he said; "what's that?" He had made a shield of his two hands over his eyes and was staring at the sea not far from its edge. He jerked his arm free and hurried as fast as the wind and the rough stones would let him back to the water's edge. Elizabeth stayed where she was, wondering. She saw Robin stop, and peer again under his hands. Then with a quick look to left and right he half jumped half scrambled on to a flat-topped boulder round the base of which thin tongues of water foamed. He crawled across it on all fours, then disappeared over the farther edge.

Elizabeth had a moment of panic. What was he doing? Surely he wasn't going farther out . . . it was all right *there* . . . but farther out—he would be dashed to pieces. If only she could *see* him . . .

"Robin!" she shouted—but what was the good of shouting? You could hardly hear even when you were by a person's side. And now he was miles away—against the wind. Elizabeth knew he couldn't hear. But she shouted again: "Robin! Rob-*in*!"

Then she felt desperate. She ran to the edge of the sea, slipped on a stone, floundered into a pool, and scrambled as well as she could on to the rock from which Robin had disappeared. Her hands and knees were cut and scratched, but she didn't notice. She crawled across it to the edge. Then she saw Robin. He was on a farther rock, a little to the left; he was lying face downwards, his feet towards her, one arm reaching—or was it dangling?—down towards the water. For one frightful moment Elizabeth thought he was dead. She tried to shout again, but couldn't. Then Robin moved—he heaved himself still nearer the edge of his rock. Then he turned his head and saw Elizabeth.

"Come and help," he shouted. Elizabeth heard—the wind brought his words. Everything was all right. Her throat was dry; she swallowed, and gave a little inward laugh. It was silly to have been frightened.

But was it *quite* all right? Robin's rock—and her own—were practically on the shore: they were not really *in* the sea at all. But the sea reached them all the same—it came in sudden white rushes, and swirled and sucked and foamed around them. The water wasn't deep—at least it didn't look deep. It couldn't be deep, because when the sea sucked back between the waves, the stones at their base were bare. The spray, from both far and near, whipped by the wind, drove over them like a cloud continually.

"Come and help," shouted Robin again. "Come and hang on to me. I can't reach."

Elizabeth picked her way, with handhold and foothold, on the slippery stones across the intervening space. The wind stung her. Robin hauled her up by her hands on to his rock. She was panting.

"What is it?" she gasped, still hanging on to Robin's hand—to keep her balance.

"Salvage," shouted Robin. "Look—it's there. It's coming nearer."

Elizabeth looked.

" Where ? " she said.

" Over there. Quite close. It's gone again. No—*there*. Look ! "

Elizabeth saw a dark object spewed up by the churning water, about ten yards beyond their rock to seaward. It turned, and writhed, and bumped against the stones, disappeared in a welter of foam, reappeared . . . and was swept nearer.

Elizabeth's teeth chattered. She was wet. The wind blew through her, icy. She suddenly longed to be indoors.

" Oh, come *on*, Robin. Come *back*," she panted. " It's only a bit of wood."

But Robin wouldn't listen. " It's salvage," he shouted. " I want to get it. We'll reach it soon."

He forced Elizabeth down on to the rock beside him. They lay on their stomachs side by side. It was better lying down.

" It's coming," said Robin. " It's much nearer." A fierce wave from seaward, broken and scattered into eddies and swirls by the inshore rocks, had lifted it ; it reared and twisted—and leapt nearer by a yard. Elizabeth was caught by the fascination of watching it. She found herself wanting it—whatever it was—as much as Robin did. It leapt again ; then stuck between two stones. A wave came, and the eddies swept over it ; then another—and still it did not move. But it was very near.

" It'll come," said Robin. But it didn't. It was stuck tight.

Robin measured with his eye the space between. It wasn't much : only eight or nine yards—eight or nine yards of hissing foamy water, dotted with small rocks. If it had not been for the gale it would have been dry land. Even as it was, every few moments the white water was sucked away, and left the rocks black and bare. But then it surged back again—fiercely.

"I'm going to g-get it," said Robin.

"I'll come too," said Elizabeth.

"No—don't. You'll get w-wet," said Robin.

"I *am* wet—sopping," said Elizabeth.

"I shan't be a s-second. Wait for me," said Robin.

He slithered down off the rock, waited a moment for the water to recede, gauged the distance to the nearest boulder, and plunged for it. He arrived safely on all fours. He clung on while the next wave came and drenched him with spray. Elizabeth watched. He picked his way from boulder to boulder cautiously. They were slippery with weed, and spiky with limpet shells. He noticed that with each boulder gained, the water when the waves came was a bit deeper around it. He struggled to the next. His foot slipped, and his leg was plunged into water up to the knee. But the salvage was very near : only a couple of yards away—almost within reach, still jammed between the stones. Almost—but not quite : between him and it there were no more boulders. Could he dash for it between two waves? Between waves the bottom was still dry—but when the waves came, the water surged in much deeper than before. Was it worth making a dash?

While he was hesitating, his eyes fixed on the salvage, Elizabeth saw, far out beyond the rocks, a tremendous wave approaching. It was like none of the others ; it was much bigger and swifter and more terrible. It was sweeping shoreward athwart the cove. It was lithe and supple like the muscles under the skin of a monster. It was high and steep and dark. Its advancing face was smooth, like a wall. It reared perpendicular. It glistened darkly, like marble. Its rushing crest hollowed and toppled, and broke with a slow crackling roar, speeding on towards the rocks.

Elizabeth yelled to Robin to look out, but she could not make her voice heard against the wind. She yelled again.

Then Robin saw it himself—oh, golly, what a wave! He turned and began with all the speed he could to scramble back towards Elizabeth. He slipped on a patch of weed, scraped his shin on the rough stone, half saved himself with a clutch of his hands, and hurried on, hopping, scrambling, climbing from boulder to boulder. The wave broke on the outer rocks: it broke with a spreading, gathering roar. Into the cove, round rocks and boulders, it rushed and twisted, in channels and tongues of foaming water. Robin glanced back. Then he made a dash for the next stone. Elizabeth watched, her heart in her mouth. He was almost within reach of her. She stretched out her hand to catch him. He slipped again, his foot in a hollow, and came down on all fours. The white water swirled about his knees and elbows.

"Oh, Robin," yelled Elizabeth. "Oh, Robin. Look *out*!"

He got to his feet and staggered, dripping and frightened, to the base of Elizabeth's rock. Elizabeth, on her stomach, caught his hand and heaved.

At that moment a piece of timber was carried past his legs, missing him by an inch, and bumped against the rock.

Robin pulled his hand from Elizabeth's and grabbed at it.

"The s-salvage," he stuttered. "The s-salvage . . . catch it . . . catch hold of it . . ."

He got it, and heaved up one end towards Elizabeth. Elizabeth took hold, and lifted it on to her rock. Then

Robin climbed up. The white water from the wave receded.

Together they conveyed the salvage, sometimes carrying, sometimes dragging it, to the grass above the cove. There they threw it down and looked at it. It was a curved piece of wood, about three feet long, very thick, and extremely heavy for its size. It was almost black from long immersion in the sea. It did not look very interesting. Now that her excitement and fright were over, Elizabeth suddenly felt rather cross and miserable. She was wet, and the wind was icy cold—and she had bruised her shin. For one unpleasant moment she thought she was going to cry.

Robin was squatting down, his back to the wind, by the side of the salvage, fingering it. He looked up, and saw Elizabeth's face.

"I s-say," he stammered (*he* was cold too), "you're frightfully w-wet."

"Of course I am," said Elizabeth. "Soaking."

She turned away.

"Oh, come *on*, Robin," she said. "Let's go home."

Robin was still fingering the salvage.

"Elizabeth," he said.

"What?"

"We must t-take it with us."

Elizabeth had never before thought Robin was silly, and she had never before been angry with him. But at that moment she thought he was perfectly idiotic, and she felt very angry indeed. It was silly enough to have made all that fuss about a piece of wood in the first place; but it was much sillier to want to lug it all the way home. Besides, it was late; it would be getting dark soon; she was horribly cold. And what was the good of the beastly salvage, anyway?

"I'll go by myself if you don't come," she said.

Robin looked at her solemnly. Elizabeth didn't usually speak like that—not in that voice. He saw she was shivering.

" I'll come with you," he said. " I'll come back for the s-salvage afterwards. I'll get Antony."

Elizabeth relented a little, though she was still longing to be home.

" But what do you want it for ? " she said.

Robin's words, as he answered, came in a rush. " I th-thought of it," he said, " when it hit the rock . . . you remember . . . at first I just wanted it because it was salvage . . . but when it hit the rock, I knew it would do . . . that it's just what we need for *Tern* . . . for the stem . . . I'm sure it'll do . . . we can start on it to-morrow . . . it'll be marvellous . . . it's oak . . . I'm certain it's oak . . ."

Robin paused. He was not looking at Elizabeth. He was looking at the timber, and rubbing it speculatively with his forefinger.

" But we'll go home," he went on. " It's awfully c-cold, isn't it ? I can get Antony. It'll be all right here—the timber, I mean—for a bit." Then he added wistfully : " At least, I *think* it will."

Elizabeth hesitated. She looked at Robin's anxious face. He was blue with cold, and his wet fringe was stuck to his forehead. Then she realized that she had stopped feeling angry.

" Come on," she said. " Let's take it."

So they did take it. It was a most unpleasing thing to carry, but they managed it. They took it in turns, for about two hundred yards each ; sometimes each took an end and they carried it between them. But though it was less heavy like that it was more awkward.

When they reached home it was half-past four, and almost dark. Robin dumped the timber in the porch, and they went in—to get warm and dry again, and to tell their story.

Tea had already begun. That was good. Nothing is more delightful than to find tea actually on the table when you come home.

CHAPTER IX

In fact tea was nearly finished by the time Elizabeth and Robin came into the dining-room. They both had to have a bath first, and to change all their clothes. But that made tea more delightful still. All the family was round the table. There was an atmosphere of crumbs and cosiness, and the Bosun had already lighted his pipe. There was a perfect fire for toast. Robin made piece after piece for himself and Elizabeth. The wet and the cold and the wind had slipped away into a memory.

As they ate they told their story.

"But where is it?" said Antony, when they were nearing the end. Robin answered that they had left it in the porch.

"I'll get it in," he said; "I'll take it into the other room. I want the Bosun to see it."

Mrs. Rutherford looked a little anxious. "Is it *very* large and wet?" she said.

Elizabeth reassured her. "It won't make a mess,

Mummy," she said ; " not really. It'll soon dry by the fire."

Robin fetched the timber, and they all left the tea-table and went into the sitting-room. Mr. Rutherford turned up the lamp.

" Come on," said Robin. " Here it is—here's our salvage."

They all crowded round to inspect it. Mr. Rutherford poked it with a penknife, and pronounced it to be oak. The Bosun examined the run of the grain—holding it up-ended in the hearth, where the water which trickled from it made a pool—and confirmed Mr. Rutherford's statement.

" Undoubtedly," he said. Robin was pleased ; he nodded his head quickly, and glanced at Elizabeth.

" It's a funny colour," said Antony. " Sort of blackish."

" That's because it's old," said the Bosun. He laid it down across the fender, one end protruding over the mat.

" Must you put it where it drips on to the rug ? " said Mrs. Rutherford. Mr. Rutherford picked it up and propped it against the bricks of the fireplace.

" It's hardly dripped at all," said Elizabeth. " I'll mop it up."

" Elizabeth ! *Not* with your handkerchief ! "

Elizabeth chuckled.

" I think it's Robin's," she said. She cautiously unwrapped a corner of it. " It *is* Robin's," she said.

There was a good deal of speculation about what the piece of salvaged timber had originally been. It was about five by four inches thick ; one end was cut smooth, the other jagged and broken. It was slightly curved. It was obviously very old, but—as Mr. Rutherford said—none the less serviceable on that account. It was perfectly sound and very hard.

" Oak," said Mr. Rutherford, " keeps sound for centuries—especially in sea-water." He told them the story of how an ancient Norse galley had been dug up from the mud on the river-bank near Botley, her oaken frames still sound. The Bosun said he had seen, in a museum, a pointed oaken pile, one of a row driven by the ancient Britons into the bank of the Thames above London to keep the Romans from crossing.

" It was a bit moth-eaten," he said. " But it had been out of water for years, mouldering in a glass case."

Elizabeth watched the Bosun while he told them this. He was not laughing. So Elizabeth knew that it was true. The Bosun didn't make jokes about things which were important.

Exactly *how* old the piece of timber was, nobody liked to say. It might have been in the sea ten years, or a hundred—or even more.

" Obviously it's a bit of a ship," said Antony.

Nobody denied it.

" What bit, do you think ? " said Mrs. Rutherford, who felt more drawn towards it now that it was no longer making a pool on the mat. But it was difficult to say. Mr. Rutherford thought it might be a piece of one of the ribs of a fishing-smack—of a good big fishing-smack, like a Brixham trawler, built in the days when they still used timbers of grown oak. It couldn't have been actually the stem of a vessel, because it wasn't quite the right shape. Robin wondered for a happy moment if it might possibly have been part of the poop-rail of a Spanish galleon—for it *could* have been in the sea (Mr. Rutherford had said so) for more than a hundred years. But whatever it was, there was no doubt at all that it would make a magnificent stem for *Tern*.

" Fit to break ice with," the Bosun said.

" Why ice ? " said Elizabeth.

"He means Captain Slocum," said Antony. "That's what Captain Slocum's friends said when he was building *his* boat."

"*Spray?*" said Robin.

"It'll be a job to work," said Mr. Rutherford. "It's as hard as iron."

Robin thought for a moment. "Let *us* do it," he said. "Hackett and me."

Everyone thought this was a good idea, except Antony.

"You're always with Hackett," he said.

"I'm *not*," said Robin.

"Practically every day," said Antony.

Robin was privately rather pleased that Antony had said this, though of course he didn't show it. But if Antony minded his spending so much time with Hackett (though it wasn't really very much) why did he keep going off with Arthur on his beastly motor-bike? He gave a quick glance at Antony under his eyebrows, and suddenly the knowledge that the holidays were almost finished swept over him like a little cold wave of emptiness and desolation. He edged himself nearer Mrs. Rutherford's chair, and leant his back against it, his shoulder touching her knees.

Elizabeth squeezed past the Bosun and began a speculative tour of the room. It was time, she felt, to do something else. She cast a backward look at the mantelpiece, paused at the bookshelf in case there was an exercise book sticking out somewhere, then hopped on to the sofa and opened the corner cupboard. It seemed to have mostly bits of stuff and old medicine bottles in it—and one squashed tube of seccotine. She shut it softly, and began to hum a tune. Mr. Rutherford reached for his book, but before he could open it Mrs. Rutherford forestalled him.

"Let's *all* have a game," she said. Mr. Rutherford put his book down again.

"What shall it be?" said Mrs. Rutherford.

"Rounders," said the Bosun. Anne looked at him with a rather chilly eye. The Bosun relit his pipe, and blew neat puffs towards the ceiling.

"Your turn, Anne," he said.

"*I* don't mind," said Anne.

Elizabeth called Sally. Sally, pleased and responsive, trotted across the room and jumped up on the sofa beside Elizabeth.

"Down, Sally. Naughty dog," said Elizabeth, no less pleased. Then she trailed a bit of string over the floor. Sally seized the other end.

"Don't riot with the dog," said Mr. Rutherford.

Mrs. Rutherford waited patiently. It was a curious thing how games always began like this in the Rutherford family—nobody ever seemed to want to do anything; but when they did begin, everyone enjoyed it. Mrs. Rutherford knew it would turn out all right in the end. The only question was to decide on which game.

The statutory games in the family were Rhymes and Picture Consequences. Charades were appreciated, but usually confined to the occasions when they were on a visit to Grandpapa. Charades need a biggish room; in a cottage they are inconvenient, because it is impossible for the audience (if there is any) to get off the stage. Sometimes, I regret to say, they played Old Maid. But Old Maid with the Rutherfords was not quite the same as Old Maid elsewhere—it was a game of skill. The cards, too, were particularly pleasing; they had been bought for sixpence-halfpenny (old stock) from Mr. Biggin the grocer. Elizabeth's favourite was Mr. Crackshott Fullbagge, with close competition from Miss Euphemia Dulcet Screech. It was a game of skill, because the Old Maid herself was bent; the skill was to conceal the bend. This was best done with the thumb; the Bosun was excellent at it—he had a large thumb. She—the Old Maid—had, of course, to be the right way up before your thumb could be properly brought into action. All through the game everybody knew exactly who had got her, and the thing to do when she reached the person on your right was not to give him time to get her arranged and to apply his thumb, but to make a swift grab. Elizabeth was a very swift grabber.

Rhymes was a good game too—provided that you liked that sort of thing. All the Rutherfords liked it; so did Antony and Robin. The Bosun hoped it would be Rhymes this evening, because he knew if it was that there would be a lot about Arthur in it. Elizabeth was good on Arthur.

In Rhymes you begin by writing a line of poetry. This is easy, provided you get the tum-ti-tum right—the rest comes by instinct. Then you pass what you have written to your neighbour, who writes two more lines. He then folds down the first two, and passes the poem on, so that the next person can read the last line only. You go on like this until you reach the bottom of the paper. Then you read the poems aloud. The method of composition renders them inconsequent but agreeable.

Antony was particularly fond of Rhymes. Only the other evening he had given everybody great pleasure by relating an Awful Incident which had occurred the previous Christmas at the Manor House, when he and Robin and Mr. and Mrs. Chale (their father and mother) and Uncle Lance and Aunt Dora had been playing the game. Just when they had got to the reading aloud, a visitor was ushered in. He was an unnecessary and pointless visitor—they had only seen the man once before in their lives. Moreover, he was a dim sort of man: rather shy, and extremely polite. He became aware that some game was in progress, and was politely loth to interrupt it. He hoped—nay insisted—that they would continue . . . It was most awkward. Mrs. Chale deprecated; Antony giggled; Mr. Chale looked down his nose. But there was no getting out of it. One poem at least had to be read. Antony read it. It was a most unsuitable poem: unsuitable, that is, for a strange dim visitor. The first line was received in breathless silence. Then, after a short pause (Robin's handwriting was a little irregular), Antony began to giggle again. The visitor was not at all sure what at. Then Mrs. Chale started. Then Uncle Lance (as the poem proceeded) sort of burst. Mr. Chale, though silent, was seen to wipe a tear from his eye. Probably (so Antony thought afterwards) the visitor supposed they were laughing at him: but of course they weren't—not at all. But it was bad luck on the visitor.

Elizabeth was trying to stop Sally rioting. Her method was to keep saying, "Be *quiet*, Sally," and to go on pulling the piece of string. Sally's four feet were braced for the tug. She growled delightedly through her mouthful of string. Elizabeth let go, and she skidded round the carpet with great rapidity, the string trailing.

"Oh, *Sally*, be quiet," said Elizabeth, and started in pursuit.

The Bosun smoked his pipe, more pained than surprised.

"Why not Rum?" said Mrs. Rutherford.

"What's that?" said the Bosun, brightening. "Yes please."

Elizabeth, checked by the barrier of his legs, came to

a stop. She tossed back a pigtail which had lost its ribbon.

"It's cards," she said.

The Bosun sighed. "Oh," he said, "I thought—but I'm sure it's a rotten game. No rum, thank you."

Mrs. Rutherford had got up, and was quietly collecting pencils from the High Jump Cup.

"Let's have Rhymes," said Elizabeth.

"Oh *no*, Bittle," said Anne. "We had them yesterday."

"It wasn't yesterday; it was the day before," said Antony.

"Oh well—it's the same thing."

"Not quite," said the Bosun. Anne glared at him. Elizabeth looked at Robin who was still sitting on the floor.

"I've thought of a bit of one," she murmured.

"What?" said Robin.

"Like a candle, bent and smooth," said Elizabeth, "Arthur is a spotty youth."

"Why 'bent'?" said Antony.

"A warm candle," said Elizabeth. "There's one in the scullery."

Mrs. Rutherford, having exhausted the High Jump Cup, had opened the corner cupboard.

"There aren't any pencils there, Mummy," said Elizabeth casually, "I looked just now."

Mrs. Rutherford moved a small roll of blue casement cloth from the right-hand bottom corner, and produced three. The Bosun and Mr. Rutherford each had one in his pocket. These, with the contents of the High Jump Cup, made enough to go round.

They didn't play Rhymes. They played Picture Consequences. The great thing about Picture Consequences is to be able to draw quite well, but not too well : not so well, I mean, as Uncle Lance. If everyone who was playing drew as well as Uncle Lance, the game would be solemn and rather dull, because they would know exactly what every picture was meant to be. As a matter of fact, if one or two of the players can hardly draw at all, it doesn't matter, provided that some can. Robin, for instance, was hopeless at drawing.

You begin by thinking of a Subject. This you write on the extreme top edge of your piece of paper, and pass it to your neighbour ; he then draws a picture to represent it, folds back the original title, and passes his picture on. The next person writes underneath what he thinks the picture is meant to be, folds it back, and hands his neighbour the new title. This goes on as long as possible—in fact, until the paper is finished. The last picture is usually a bit different from the first.

The subject Mr. Rutherford thought of was *Robin salvaging.* He was sitting next to Antony ; so it was Antony who had to draw the picture. Antony was a pretty poor draughtsman (though a bit better than Robin), and the picture he drew was this :

When it was finished (and when the others had all finished theirs) he passed it to the Bosun, who interpreted it as *A beetle about to have a bathe.* Elizabeth was next to the Bosun. This was Elizabeth's picture :

Anne called this picture a *Floppy quadruped drying a bowsprit and singing* ; whereupon Mrs. Rutherford drew this :

For this, Mr. Rutherford's title was *Musical spectre* ; and the Bosun, to whom it had come round again, drew the last picture like this :

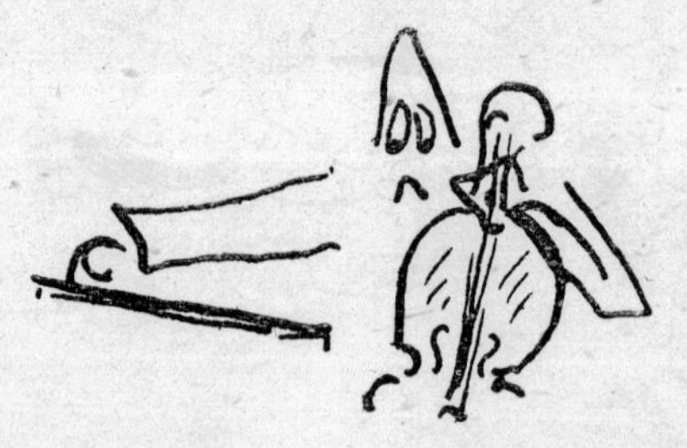

Elizabeth liked Picture Consequences. But she still rather wished it had been Rhymes. In Rhymes you could get in more about Arthur. Just for fun (though it isn't really part of the game) she wrote her first Subject in rhyme. She wrote:

> He rides his bike with clattering sound
> And wears his cap the wrong way round—

and hoped that her neighbour would interpret it satisfactorily. But he didn't—very, because he was Robin, and found a man on a motor-bicycle extremely difficult to draw. I have not actually got Robin's picture; but I think that Mrs. Rutherford, who came next, gave it the title of *Thin coalheaver, with a shovel on his head, learning to ride a fairy cycle.* But I am not sure.

When the game was finished Mrs. Rutherford collected the pencils and put them back in the High Jump Cup on the mantelpiece. It was getting on for supper-time, and Emily was beginning to rattle about in the kitchen. Plates seemed to be on the move, and, from the sound of it, she was poking the fire to some purpose. After supper the Bosun pulled back the curtains from the french window in the sitting-room, to look at the night. The gale had spent itself. The clouds had broken and there were patches of stars. The wind rustled and sighed in the ash-tree; but the roaring was gone—instead of it, like another roaring, but much fainter and farther away, could be heard the sound of the surf on the beach. The Bosun shut the window, and drew the curtains again.

It was the last hour of the evening—perhaps the most delightful of all—before bedtime. Mr. Rutherford called it the antepenultimate and drowsy hour; Elizabeth never asked him why, but she liked the sound of the words. In winter, in the country, this hour is best: better than in other seasons or in other places. In summer it is good, when the light lingers, and the blackbird whistles from the top of the pear-tree, or the water in the harbour is pearly grey and smooth, and your vessel sleeps at her anchorage ; but in winter it is better still—if you are in the country, in a small warm house, with the people you would choose, and the fire flutters and whispers in the wide hearth, and the firelight and the lamplight are warm on the walls and the curtained windows.

To-night, in this hour, they had reading aloud. To Elizabeth, ever since she had been old enough to enjoy it, Mr. Rutherford had always read aloud when she was in bed : every night for years and years—and to Anne before that. But this had now stopped. Instead, there was reading aloud to the whole family : not every night, but just sometimes, when they felt that they wanted it. This was a good thing to do—but for mothers and fathers every change is a little sorrowful.

The book was *Moby Dick* : not the whole of it, but large bits chosen by Mr. Rutherford. The parts which Elizabeth would have called " thick " he skipped. They had not yet got to the final chase of the White Whale ; but they had reached the description of the typhoon, when the corpusants burned in blue fire on the three masts of the *Pequod*. As Robin listened, his thoughts kept going back to Rocken End, and the race. Suppose, he thought again, there had been a boat out there —in that sea ? He had not known before that the sea could be like that. He had read about storms often enough, and thought he knew what they were like ; but he didn't know. Now he had seen the sea at Rocken End, and he did know.

It was later than usual when Antony and Robin went off to Mrs. Hackett's for bed. It was ten o'clock—a reprehensible hour ; but obviously it was not possible to stop reading in the middle of the typhoon. Mrs.

Hackett was in bed herself when they came in. Like most women who live in the country and work hard, she preferred to go early. She had already told Antony and Robin that should they be late any night they were not to mind if she had gone up—and Mr. Hackett too ; but would they please remember to draw the bolt, and blow out the lamp at the bottom of the stairs. This they did, and took their candle up the narrow staircase to their room.

They were both very sleepy, especially Robin. He had had a tiring day. But it had been successful, and he was happy. The only thing that spoilt his happiness (for he wasn't bothering much about Arthur to-night) was the knowledge that there were only four more days of the holidays left—four more days at the cottage, then one day at home to pack in, then school. Antony would have two days at home : his term began later. Lucky Antony.

To-morrow he would make a beginning on *Tern's* stem —he and Hackett. It would be a splendid stem : fit to cut ice, yes—fit to cut ice . . .

He was pretty sure that it *was* the poop-rail of a galleon . . . of a Spanish galleon.

. . . .

The remaining days of the holidays passed all too quickly. Robin and Hackett cut out and shaped the stem. The timber had an oblong section, like this ; and it had to be sawn to look like this  . That meant a long slanting cut, to exact measurements, which, especially in that hard wood, was very difficult to do. So Hackett did the sawing, and Robin trimmed it up afterwards with a plane. The others, meanwhile, finished fixing the transom in position. There was just time to bolt the new stem to its knee, and to fix that in position too. This was the last job they were able to do. They were busy to the last, all working their hardest. Arthur did not come again—thank goodness; but even if he had come, Antony would have refused to go out with him on his motor-bike. Time was precious. Everybody was glad that they were able to finish the transom and the stem; for with her frames and her two ends complete, *Tern* looked already a boat. You could see her shape—and imagination could easily supply her planking, and all the lovely details that were still needed. Hackett came to see her too. Robin brought him. He beamed upon them with benevolence, and pronounced *Tern* a grand job.

The day came for Antony and Robin to go. They arrived at the cottage after breakfast in their clean clothes and horrible hats—Elizabeth thought they were horrible—Antony carrying a shiny suitcase. They both went up to the Building Shed for a good-bye look at *Tern*. The Bosun was in the shed.

"W-will you do any more to her when we're gone?" said Robin.

The Bosun shook his head.

"I don't expect so," he answered. "We're going ourselves the day after to-morrow."

"I hope you w-won't," said Robin. He saw a hammer on the floor, half hidden in a heap of shavings. He picked it up and laid it carefully on the bench. It was the riveting hammer.

"It's not so long till Easter—now," said the Bosun.

"It's ages," said Antony.

Mrs. Rutherford drove them in the car to Yarmouth. Anne and Elizabeth went too, to see them off. They bought chocolate at the shop on the corner near the church, and walked to the end of the pier, Antony carrying the suitcase. They watched the steamer coming across from Jack-in-the-Basket. The steamer arrived.

Antony and Robin said good-bye to Mrs. Rutherford and Anne. They walked to the gangway. Elizabeth suddenly began to undo her chocolate.

" They're just going, Elizabeth. Come and say good-bye." Elizabeth came towards them reluctantly.

" Good-bye, Antony, good-bye, Robin," she said as casually as possible. Her face was pinker than usual.

It was horrible to see them go—but it was even worse to say good-bye.

They went aboard. The paddles began to churn ; the ropes were cast off ; the steamer moved away. From the top deck Antony and Robin waved.

Mrs. Rutherford and her two daughters drove silently home.

CHAPTER X

About the eleven weeks which followed, the less said the better. Perhaps if Mr. Rutherford had been telling this story—but no ; I don't think Mr. Rutherford would have said much about them either.

The last day at the cottage was spent as last days usually are. The Bosun left in the morning. I suppose he went back to work—but you never could tell with the Bosun. Anyway—he went. Mr. and Mrs. Rutherford were busy packing and clearing up. The cottage had to be put to bed until the spring.

Anne and Elizabeth felt aimless and disconsolate. Elizabeth hated packing. Not that she did much of it herself ; but she hated other people doing it too. Packing produced a peculiar and disagreeable feeling : the comfortable stream of time ceased to flow, and was broken up into shallow eddies and spurts which kept leaving her, so to speak, high and dry. Even before a holiday packing was unpleasant ; after a holiday it was intolerable. There was nothing to do ; and even if you found something, you were sure to be interrupted, and asked to go to the village to buy a bit of box-cord. Mummy and Daddy, too, were uncompanionable when they were packing.

The only relief was the bonfire. Mr. Rutherford always made a bonfire on the last day of the holidays. Mrs. Rutherford had turned out the larder and the cupboard in the bedroom, and produced a surprising heap of squashed cardboard boxes, old pattern books, newspapers, unrecognizable fragments of garments long since dead, and a number of other objects more or less combustible. These, with a still surviving pile of last autumn's hedge clippings, made a tolerable fire. But it didn't burn to the end—the hedge clippings were too wet.

The morrow came—and another good-bye—this time to the cottage itself. The car was loaded as no car but the Rutherford's was ever loaded before. Mr. and Mrs. Rutherford sat in front ; Anne and Elizabeth and Emily and Sally squeezed in behind. Just as they were all settled, and the ultimate flotsam of parcels and miscellanies had found its level, Sally decided that she would prefer Mrs. Rutherford's lap to Anne's. She scrabbled vigorously over the back of the seat.

The car started. They turned their heads for a parting look at the grey stone walls, the green gate, the thatch, and the sycamore in the corner by the stream. Then they were gone.

Two days later there was another packing, and yet another good-bye ; Anne went back to school. So did Elizabeth, but not to boarding-school ; not yet, thank goodness.

So now they were all at work—and most of them scattered. This chapter is a dismal one ; it shall therefore be very short. The next will be more cheerful ; for the year was steadily revolving—moving towards the time (not so very distant, as even Robin admitted after the first few sorrowful weeks were gone) when the young sun should have run half his course in the sign of the Ram, and the sweet showers of April pierced to the root the drought of March—and holidays were come again.

CHAPTER XI

When the Rutherford family returned to the cottage, the daffodils were out in the dell and on the banks under the trees at the bottom of the garden ; the japonica was gay with blossom on the stone wall outside the dining-room window ; on some of the hedges in the lanes there was already a faint flush of green. Wallflowers were in bloom. Old Puttock had been busy about the garden-beds ; the lawn had been mown, and was fresh and pleasant to the eye. Outside the Hut, on a bright day when the wind was north of west, you could sit and sun yourself, almost as if it were summer.

It was always Elizabeth's habit as soon as they arrived to look quickly into every room, before going out into the garden—just to say hullo, as it were. Anne usually went straight round into the garden. Then they both came back to help Mr. and Mrs. Rutherford get the things in from the car. Elizabeth was still not good at this ; but she had improved—the parcels she chose were a size larger than a year ago, and she managed to deposit them more nearly where they were meant to go.

The first thing Elizabeth noticed about the cottage was that it smelt nice : a sort of dim cool smell, sweet and faintly musty. The rooms were unnaturally neat : they looked as if they were still half asleep—but expectant. There was a fire in the sitting-room ; it was still cold enough for a fire, morning and evening. And even if it hadn't been, Emily (who had come down the previous day) would have lighted one ; for a fire helps a house to wake up quickly, and to give its people a proper welcome.

Antony and Robin were not to come for a week. They were to have a week at home—at the Manor House at Creeksea—before joining them. It would have been bad luck for Mrs. Chale if they had spent the whole holidays away ; moreover, *Ianthe* was being fitted out in Burnham, and both boys wanted to lend a hand. In any case, everybody wants to be at home for part of the holidays. No one quite knew when the Bosun would arrive. He would probably send a post card : or he might just arrive, without a post card. It was hard to tell with the Bosun. But Mrs. Rutherford had his room ready for him.

It was fun to see *Tern* again. The whole family went up to the Building Shed as soon as they had finished tea —the customary first day's tea of boiled eggs and one of Emily's spectacular currant cakes. *Tern* seemed to have got through her eleven weeks of desertion quite satisfactorily. She was a bit cobwebby and dusty, and in need of air and open doors, otherwise she had not suffered. Elizabeth was surprised to find how big she looked.

" Isn't she huge ? " she said to Anne. " Much bigger than I thought." Probably Elizabeth had been thinking of *Puffin* and *Sheldrake*, in which they had cruised the previous summer : *Puffin* and *Sheldrake* were just ordinary dinghies. *Tern* was a boat. Indeed, she was almost a ship—or would be, when they had finished her. And they were going to finish her these holidays.

" I believe we *could* sleep on board," said Elizabeth. " All of us—all four of us. Couldn't we, Daddy ? "

" I wish they were here now," said Anne ; " Antony and Robin, I mean."

" Daddy," said Elizabeth, " are you *sure* we can finish her these holidays ? "

Mr. Rutherford thought they could, provided that they all worked hard and didn't waste any time.

" Anyway," he said, " we've jolly well got to."

" I know," said Elizabeth. " But . . ." She stopped, frowning a little, and fiddling with the ribbon on one of her pigtails.

" What ? " said Anne.

" We promised," said Elizabeth. " We promised Robin—not to go on with her when he wasn't here. At least, we sort of promised."

" Robin won't mind," said Anne. " Nor will Antony," she added.

" Antony won't," said Elizabeth. " But Robin will. I'm sure Robin will."

" It doesn't matter," said Anne. " Besides—we've *got* to go on. Otherwise we shan't finish her. It's a whole week before they come. A week's ages."

But Elizabeth was not convinced. She was sure Robin would mind ; and she was equally sure that it did matter. Mrs. Rutherford agreed with her. Mr. Rutherford reminded her that it was not exactly a promise they had made to Robin : it was only that the Bosun had said he didn't expect they would do any more after the boys went.

"And we didn't say anything about not going on before they came," said Anne. "About *these* holidays, I mean."

Elizabeth saw the justice of this; nevertheless she felt as certain as before that Robin would be disappointed. Even though it was not an actual promise, it was as good as a promise.

"But surely," Anne persisted, "Robin *wants* us to finish her?"

Of course Robin wanted them to finish her—as much as any of them. But Elizabeth knew that that was not the point. Her face flushed, and she drew down the corners of her mouth. She looked at Mrs. Rutherford.

"He *would* be disappointed, wouldn't he, Mummy?" she said.

Mrs. Rutherford nodded. There was a silence for a minute. Then Mrs. Rutherford had an idea.

"We could write and ask him," she said. "We could get his permission."

"Or send a telegram," said Elizabeth.

That seemed the best thing to do. Robin would be sure to say yes—he would be sure to give them permission; obviously, he would rather be there while the work was being done; but he *did* want *Tern* finished—and provided they told him that they were working—or that they wanted to work—it would (Elizabeth thought) be all right. It would be quite different from just doing it when they had practically promised not to. Elizabeth was glad that Mummy understood what she meant; probably Daddy did too, really—though he didn't say anything.

They went out of the shed—except Mr. Rutherford, who seemed to want to spend a little more time examining *Tern*.

"Let's cut some daffodils," said Mrs. Rutherford. "I want a *lot* in the sitting-room."

Outside the Building Shed, in the corner of the vegetable bed under the ilex tree there was a big heap of straw. It came from a bit of the roof of the cottage which had had a patch put on it while the family was away. Elizabeth thought as she stopped to look at it what a lovely bonfire it would make. They might light it to-morrow—or perhaps they ought to wait until Robin came. Yes; that would be better. Robin liked bonfires too. She hoped Daddy would not want to dig it into the garden for manure: that would be waste.

"Come on," said Mrs. Rutherford. They went down the path between the apple-trees towards the lawn.

Elizabeth called back to Mr. Rutherford. "Daddy," she said, "you're not doing anything, are you?"

Mr. Rutherford laughed. "No," he called back, "I'm only looking."

They picked their daffodils, a large bunch. Elizabeth always liked picking. She skipped from clump to clump, choosing the best, and as she picked she composed in her head the telegram to Robin. *Do you mind if we go on building . . . ?* No; that didn't sound like a telegram at all; and it would come much too long. Telegrams were difficult. She saw a specially lovely daffodil, and ran to it.

"Mummy," she said, squatting on her haunches before the clump, "*you* make it up."

"Make up what?" said Mrs. Rutherford.

"Robin's telegram," said Elizabeth.

"We'll just take in the daffodils," said Mrs. Rutherford, "and then we'll do it. I say!" she added, "you *have* got a lot!"

Elizabeth certainly had. Daffodils, of course, are easy;

but it was just the same with primroses or blackberries: Elizabeth always picked the most.

The telegram was made up, and there was just time to send it before the post office closed.

"Come with me, Anne," said Elizabeth.

"Just a moment," said Mrs. Rutherford; "as you *are* going to the village, there are just one or two things we want from the shop. . . ."

Anne and Elizabeth exchanged glances. That was the worst of going to the village. However, it was impossible to mind much on the first evening.

When they had walked a few yards along the road, Sally squeezed through the hedge and followed them—guiltily but hopefully. Sally was bad at motor-cars, so she was not supposed to go on the road without a lead. If you put on her collar and lead, she thought she was going for a walk—and got more excited than was really decent; so to do it merely for going to the village—which was not a walk at all—was hardly fair. Besides, it was rather a nuisance; for one seldom knew exactly where her collar and lead were. Sally, therefore, was not supposed to go to the village for shopping. She knew this perfectly well. You could see she did by her peculiar manner of walking after she had squeezed through the hedge—guilty but hopeful.

"Sally," said Elizabeth, "go back. Naughty dog."

Sally hunched her shoulders, cowered into the road, and looked at Elizabeth with appealing eyes. Then she came on a little farther.

"Go back!" said Elizabeth. Sally stopped again. Elizabeth looked at Anne and chuckled. They walked on. A moment later Sally was at their side, trotting briskly. She must have heard the chuckle.

The post office was dark and smelt of dust. Anne wrote out their telegram. It went like this: *Cannot wait, must continue building, otherwise cannot finish, do you mind? Rutherford.*

Then they went on to Mr. Biggin's shop. Mr. Biggin in his apron, behind the counter, was like a small and benevolent mole. Elizabeth felt as she saw him that he must have been there—behind his counter—ever since last holidays. She could not imagine him anywhere else. They bought what was required of them, and a bar of chocolate besides—the special kind which Mr. Biggin never forgot to get into stock before the holidays, because he knew that it was Elizabeth's favourite.

On their way back to the cottage, just as they had reached the corner by the post office, a motor-bicycle, driven at considerable speed, was coming down the hill from the direction of Newport.

" Sally—where's Sally? " cried Anne, as she saw it. Sally was twenty yards behind, peering with interest through somebody's garden gate, on the farther side of the road.

" Sally ! " called Elizabeth sharply.

Sally turned her head, then came pattering with an air of cheerful insouciance across the road. The motor-bicycle came speeding on.

" *Sally !* " shouted Anne shrilly.

Sally, feeling that something might be amiss, stopped —half-way over.

The motor-bicycle was upon them. The brakes were jammed on. It swerved, it spluttered ; then swerved again, missed Sally by inches, and brought up with a jerk against the stone wall on the wrong side of the road.

Anne's heart was in her mouth ; so was Elizabeth's. But Sally was safe. They hurried back to her, frightened and angry. As they reached her a voice addressed them.

" Hullo," it said. " That beastly dog nearly had me off."

It was Arthur.

Elizabeth was already by Sally's side, scolding her with outraged affection. Anne joined in.

"Good Lord," said Arthur, backing his bicycle from the wall, "is it *your* dog? I didn't recognize her. She nearly had me off. There might have been the dickens of a smash. You ought to keep her on a lead, you know."

Anne and Elizabeth were speechless with indignation. Anne picked Sally up. Arthur restarted his machine—and then remembered he had not seen the Rutherford family for three months.

"Just arrived, I suppose," he said sociably. "Well, how's life?"

"Come on, Bittle," muttered Anne. Then she shot a single glance at Arthur. "You might have *killed* her," she said.

They went home, Elizabeth carrying the parcels from Mr. Biggin, Anne with Sally still firmly tucked under her arm.

"Beast," said Elizabeth, when they were safely in the garden. She said it with quiet conviction. She stooped and kissed Sally on the nose. "*Naughty* dog," she said.

Sally wasn't naughty at all, really: she was simply rather foolish and vague. Anne and Elizabeth knew perfectly well that they ought to have put her on a lead. So did Arthur. That was partly why they felt they hated him so much at that moment.

"Nearly had *him* off!" said Anne. "Gosh! What about poor Sally?"

During the next few days Mr. Rutherford spent a good deal of time in the Building Shed. Anne and Elizabeth helped him occasionally, but they found on the whole that building was less attractive when Antony and Robin were not there. Not that either of them ever did do very much actual building—but the fact that they did not was more apparent, to Elizabeth at any rate, when they were alone with Daddy. It would be different when the time for paint arrived—for paint and putty. Meanwhile, there did not seem to be very much that she could do, except hold things for Daddy, which was dull. But she and Anne were, of course, extremely anxious that the building should progress ; it would be dreadful if *Tern* were not finished by the end of the holidays ; everybody would be bitterly disappointed, especially Robin. And they *would* begin working again when the boys came. But just for the present it was better, they felt, to let Daddy get on with things by himself, and not to interrupt him. So apart from frequent visits and inspections they spent most of their time messing about in the garden, or going for little expeditions with Mummy in the car, or taking her to the beach at Castle Cove and trying to persuade her to paddle. The sun was hot, as it often is in a fine April, and once or twice they succeeded.

" It's not a bit cold, is it, Mummy ? " said Elizabeth, as a small wave creamed over Mrs. Rutherford's toes. But Mrs. Rutherford thought it was—rather.

Sometimes they met Arthur on his motor-bike. He would grin at them as he whizzed past.

" Did you see his cap ? " said Anne. Elizabeth giggled.

" Yes," she said. " It *was* the wrong way round."

Once Arthur called at the cottage—to see how the old tub was getting on, as he put it. Anne and Elizabeth were in the garden, brushing Sally. When Arthur came back from the Building Shed, he was smoking a cigarette. He stopped by the girls, and flicked the ash off with a gesture of conscious elegance.

" I left your father an article I cut out from the *Sailing Monthly*," he observed. " It's got some tips in it."

Really—Arthur was intolerable.

Antony and Robin came on the Friday. Mrs. Rutherford, with Elizabeth and Anne, went as usual in the car to meet them at Yarmouth. Their hats were not quite so bad this time : Elizabeth must have been getting used to them. Robin's first question, after they had all said hullo to one another, was obviously about the progress of *Tern*. Elizabeth's reply was a little vague : Daddy had been very busy with the chine something, she thought. But he was getting on—she knew he was getting on.

"You're sure you didn't mind us not waiting ?" she said. "I mean, *Daddy's* not waiting," she added, and looked at Anne. Anne laughed.

"We'll work terrifically hard now you've come," she said.

Robin didn't mind at all that Mr. Rutherford had been at work ; indeed, he was glad. It was different, he said, from when he had asked the Bosun not to go on ; then it had been the end of the holidays, and he couldn't bear to think of going dismally back to school—of not being there while *Tern* was growing. But now it was the beginning.

"Is the Bosun here yet ?" asked Antony.

It was disappointing to learn that he was not.

They got into the car and set off for home. Mrs. Rutherford drove fast and joyfully.

"I say, Antony," said Anne, swaying towards him as Mrs. Rutherford rounded a bend, "Arthur smokes."

"Good Lord," said Antony, clutching his hat as Mrs. Rutherford accelerated down the straight. He looked sideways at Robin. Antony never smoked : that is, practically never. But he looked at Robin, because he had once made him buy a packet of five cigarettes from a small grimy shop in Burnham, and they had smoked one each in the stable-loft when they got home.

"And he nearly killed Sally with his motor-bike," said Anne.

"Beast," said Elizabeth over her shoulder—she was sitting in front with Mrs. Rutherford. Robin said nothing. He had taken his hat off, and his fringe was blown sideways by the wind of the car's speed. He said nothing—but he hoped that Arthur would be going for a cruise in his father's fifty-fifty.

When they drew up at the cottage, the four children hurried off at once to the Building Shed.

"Anne," said Elizabeth, as they were crossing the lawn, "Daddy's talking to someone—someone's there."

A laugh rang out: a large and hearty laugh—six feet three of it at least. Elizabeth broke into a run.

"Bosun!" she called. "Anne, quick, it's the Bosun. He's come."

It was indeed the Bosun. A moment afterwards all four children were round him, on the gravel patch under the ilex tree. Elizabeth hugged him. They all talked at once, asking questions and not waiting for the answers. When had he come? How had he got there? Why didn't he send a telegram? But none of the answers mattered. The only thing that mattered was that he had come.

Elizabeth let go, and ran back to the house to tell Mrs. Rutherford. They came back together.

"Bob!" said Mrs. Rutherford. She put her hands on his arms and stood on tiptoe. "Bend down," she said. "I can't reach." The Bosun bent. Then he stepped back and looked at Mrs. Rutherford apologetically.

"I wrote a post card," he said. "Really I did."

"We never got one," said Anne.

The Bosun put his hand in his coat-pocket. "I'll give it to you now," he said. "By the way, Janet," he went on, "if I've caused you any inconvenience . . ."

" Don't be silly, of course you haven't."

" I mean, if you'd like me to make up the bed in my room . . . or anything . . ."

" It won't take long," said Mrs. Rutherford.

" Let *me* do it," said the Bosun gallantly.

" Thank you, Bob," said Mrs. Rutherford.

The Bosun's eyebrows lifted.

" *What* did your mother say, Elizabeth ? " he murmured.

Elizabeth began to giggle.

" She said, ' Thank you, Bob.' "

There was a brief pause.

" Dear me," said the Bosun. He turned to Anne. " Anne," he whispered, " are you a good bedmaker ? "

" Rotten," said Anne. " Bittle's much better."

Mrs. Rutherford was laughing. Mr. Rutherford knocked his pipe out on the heel of his shoe. " As a matter of fact," he said, " Emily did it while you were all out. I saw her go upstairs with the sheets."

" So did I," said the Bosun.

Robin had slipped into the Building Shed, and was devouring *Tern* with his eyes. It was marvellous to see her again. Antony soon followed.

" She looks fine," said Antony. And indeed she did ; for Mr. Rutherford, with the Bosun's help, had succeeded in getting on two broad planks—the chine strakes—one on each side, and fixing them stem and stern. *Tern* had definitely ceased to look like the skeleton of a whale. She was a boat—now and for ever.

" And now there's a big job for you, Robin," said Mr. Rutherford, who had followed them into the shed. " Those planks want three screws to each frame. You'll find the oak and the elm pretty tough to bore. And you'll have to go straight."

Robin wanted to begin at once, but tea was ready,

Besides, it is unsuitable to start boat-building in one's best clothes.

"Come on," said Mrs. Rutherford. "Let's have tea first."

Even Robin was not really loth to have tea. The Bosun, however, was positively eager. So they all went in.

"Gosh," said Robin, as he came on to the lawn behind Elizabeth; "what a lot of daffodils!"

Elizabeth looked at him with the special, small, suppressed smile which meant that she was pleased. It was nice, she thought, that Robin had come back again. He didn't look very different—at least, he wouldn't after tea, when he had put on his old clothes.

CHAPTER XII

WITH the return of the boys and the Bosun there was once again fervent activity in the Building Shed. The work was planned to give everybody, so far as was possible, something to do ; only thus could there be any hope of having *Tern* ready for sea before the holidays ended. Mr. Rutherford and the Bosun shaped and fitted the planking ; Antony and Robin helped to bevel the edges, and drove and countersunk innumerable screws to fasten the planks to the frames ; Anne and Elizabeth —a job in which less exactitude was needed—made the floor-boards and began to rough out some of the deal planks for the foredeck ; Hackett made the centreboard case. For certain joints, notably that between the garboards and the keel-plank, luting was required, and Elizabeth spent some delightful hours compounding it on a board with a putty-knife and a bottle of linseed oil.

The whole village got to know about the building of *Tern*. To be sure, the whole village got to know about most things—that is the way of villages ; but the buildng of *Tern* was an event of more than common interest. Islanders though they were, the villagers, apart from the wo fishermen, knew little of ships and the sea; they knew more of "turmuts" and "taties", so that the building of a boat in a cottage garden gave them a fruitful subject of comment and speculation. For the most part they regarded it as an act of harmless lunacy: more harmless, perhaps (and less lunatic), than sleeping in the Hut on a wet night in September. The Rutherford family, they knew, did strange things—but they were used to regard them with amused tolerance. Tom Mould, who was eighty, would stop his barrow when the gate under the ilex tree was open, nod his old head, grin, and call out to Mr. Rutherford.

"Don't worrk too 'aard, young Master," he would say, then shuffle on laboriously down the lane. Frank Tibbets, when he brought the milk in the morning, would make jocular enquiries of Emily at the back door. The children on their way home from school would hang about in wondering knots outside the gate, and nudge one another and stare.

And all the time *Tern* was growing. She was growing fast—the only trouble was (and it was a real trouble) that April was growing too. It was already past the middle of the month; more than half of the holidays were gone; and though the work sped, and not one of them was idle, there yet remained a very great deal to do. Would they succeed in getting her finished in time? It would be bitterly disappointing if they did not. However delightful and interesting the task of building a boat may be, not one of them wanted to have to continue it in the summer. In the summer they must sail. For the summer all their plans were already made: *Tern* would be at Poole; Mr. and Mrs. Chale would join them in *Ianthe*; with *Tessa* and *Ianthe* as headquarters of the two families, what cruises and what adventures might not the children have in *Tern*? But if *Tern* were not finished in time, everything would be spoiled. They had all assumed, at Christmas, that she *would* be finished in time; they pretended to assume it still—nevertheless, doubt was beginning to gnaw them. There was a terrible lot still to be done.

The dreadful possibility that they might fail was first suggested to the children by Arthur. Unhappily, Arthur's father had decided against an Easter cruise in his fifty-fifty, and Arthur in consequence paid frequent visits to the Building Shed. He came, partly to try to persuade Antony to go for rides on his motor-bike (which Antony refused, as he was too busy), and partly to exhibit his new cigarette-case. Perhaps he was also interested in *Tern*. One day about the middle of the holidays, while the family was at work, he was leaning against the doorpost of the Building Shed, and giving an account to anyone who would listen of a race he had sailed in his snipe the previous summer—a race which he would undoubtedly have won, had it not been for the folly and ignorance of his companion. The story fell rather flat, so Arthur, after a short pause, changed the subject.

"When's the launch to be?" he said. "When's the great day?"

Antony, who was trimming up the mast (a nice clean larch pole which they had bought from Hackett for half a crown), replied without looking up that they expected to be ready during the last three or four days of the holidays. Arthur whistled.

"You'll have to get a move on, won't you?" he said. "I'd have given you another six weeks myself."

Antony said nothing, but continued to drive his plane. Indeed, none of the children paid much attention to Arthur's remark at the time. But when he had gone,

Robin suddenly realized that he was feeling uncomfortable.

"B-bosun," he said, "we *shall* finish her in time, shan't we?"

Robin did not really doubt it, any more than the other children did. He merely wanted confirmation. It was very distressing, therefore, when the Bosun did not immediately answer his question. Mr. Rutherford did not say anything either—but Anne thought she saw him and the Bosun exchange a significant and disconcerting glance.

"Sh-shall we?" repeated Robin more urgently. The unpleasant truth then came out. Neither the Bosun nor Mr. Rutherford would definitely say that they would not be ready by the end of the holidays. If everything went well, there was still a chance . . . a small chance. But on the other hand . . .

"Oh, *Daddy*," said Anne. "Why didn't you tell us before?"

Mr. Rutherford temporized. . . . There was nothing to tell. . . . After all, you could never be *certain*. They still *might* get done . . .

"You don't believe it, Daddy," said Anne. There was cruel disappointment in her voice. Robin was silent.

The truth was that Mr. Rutherford did *not* really believe it. Nor did the Bosun. For a number of days past their doubt had been growing, and it was now almost a certainty. They knew they would have to tell the children some time: now it was done. However, there was still a chance. Mr. Rutherford would not admit that there was not a chance.

The first effect of this realization on the children was not to spur them to further effort. On the contrary, they were less inclined to work than they had been before. The least affected of the four was Elizabeth;

she could not help feeling Robin's disappointment, and sharing in it ; but red-lead putty is in itself so agreeable a thing that it was not possible for her to be as disappointed as she ought to have been. It was not only the upsetting of their plans for the summer ; it was also the actual launching and trial of *Tern*, which they had been expecting to take place so soon. They had had no sailing these holidays : it had all been sacrificed to *Tern*. Had she been finished in time, and the trial trip achieved before school began again, all would have been well. It would have been no sacrifice at all. On the contrary, it would have been all gain. It was what they had counted on. But now it was not to be. It was no good Daddy pretending that there was still a chance of getting her finished. There wasn't. Obviously there wasn't —if there were, he and the Bosun would have said straight out that Arthur was an idiot. But they had not said so. They might as well admit it—there was no chance at all.

Antony felt like giving up work altogether. So did Anne. Robin for an hour or two tried to persuade himself that if they worked really frightfully hard they might yet succeed, and drove screws with desperate energy. But his arms began to ache, and he was forced to stop. Yesterday it had seemed that every screw he drove was a step towards the end ; but now he felt that even if he went on all day, however much his arms ached, it would not really make much difference. Indeed, he wanted to go on ; but somehow he couldn't, and the sight of Antony loitering about outside the shed, listless and bored, made it more difficult still. If only Arthur hadn't said that they would want another six weeks . . . It was all Arthur's fault. Arthur was a beast. He'd be certain to ask Antony to go on his motor-bike again . . . and Antony would go.

Mr. Rutherford and the Bosun continued quietly and

methodically to work. So did Elizabeth—mixing red-lead putty. But for the others the day was a dismal one.

Lunch was a more silent meal than usual. Mrs. Rutherford knew at once that something was amiss, but she did not ask what it was. She knew even better that it is horrible to be asked what's the matter when one is feeling gloomy. If she had needed further proof that something had gone wrong, she had it when both Robin and Elizabeth refused a second helping of steamed pudding.

It was only at the end of the meal that their trouble was mentioned. Mr. Rutherford began tentatively to recall certain incidents which had occurred during their cruise to France in *Tessa* two years ago.

"It was fun, wasn't it, Janet?" he said.

"Lovely," said Mrs. Rutherford. "The best cruise we've ever had."

Then Mr. Rutherford began to wonder—only as a possibility, of course—whether it might not be a good thing to go foreign again this year—*Tessa* and *Ianthe* in company.

Mrs. Rutherford looked surprised.

"But I thought . . ." she began. Then, seeing the expression on Robin's face, she stopped.

After that it all came out; the bitter fact that it was impossible to finish *Tern* in time.

Elizabeth tilted her chair, and began to hum—a quiet tuneless hum—as she usually did when the family atmosphere was electric or oppressive.

"*Arthur* said we'd want six weeks," she said.

Anne looked at her scornfully.

"You are an ass, Bittle," she snapped. "It's nothing whatever to do with Arthur at all."

"But he did say it," said Elizabeth.

Robin too felt that it was somehow Arthur's fault,

though it would have been difficult to say why. But what did it matter whose fault it was? It was true: that was what mattered.

Yes—it *was* true. Before the day was over, even the Bosun and Mr. Rutherford gave up the pretence that there was any hope. It was better, they felt, to have it clear.

Under these unhappy circumstances, it was a good thing that Mr. Rutherford was able to propose an expedition to Southampton to order *Tern's* sails. The thought of it was a welcome diversion. They would go to-morrow. They would go to Barton's—to Barton's sail-loft near the ferry at Woolston. They would all go: all except Mr. Rutherford and the Bosun. Mrs. Rutherford would drive them in the car to Cowes.

Antony thought that it might be a bit difficult to order sails—unless, of course, Mrs. Rutherford knew how to do it. Wouldn't it be better, therefore, if Mr. Rutherford or the Bosun came too? But the Bosun said that Mrs. Rutherford knew perfectly well how to do it, and had done it (helped by Mr. Rutherford) years before any of them were born. In any case, it was not difficult at all: one merely had to take the measurements, and tell the sailmaker what they were.

"And to tell him to be quick," added Mr. Rutherford.

When he said that, Robin felt a small new pang. What was the use of being quick—now? But the pang was only momentary. And it *would* be fun going to the sailmaker.

In the afternoon they lit the bonfire which Elizabeth had saved up for Robin. They had been too busy to do it before. The weather had been dry, and the straw was in good condition. It was a very superior bonfire. It singed the lower branches of the ilex. The flames roared. Dove grey, solid and swirling the smoke poured over the next-door garden in a most unneighbourly manner. It smoked out the Bosun who was engaged on a delicate job in the Building Shed. The wind blew, and fanned, and fed it. With scorched faces, choking lungs and streaming eyes, the children stoked it. Once the wind snatched a bit of it and whirled it like a fiery butterfly into a heap of shavings on the gravel patch. The shavings took fire. They crackled. The wind fluttered them, and burning flakes eddied nearer to the shed. Antony leapt, and beat them out, and trampled them. It was glorious.

By tea-time the flames had subsided. The bonfire was a small black mound sullenly smouldering in a wide circle of ashes. Mrs. Rutherford suggested potatoes—why not? They had not roasted potatoes in bonfire ash for years. It was a good suggestion. Anne went into the larder and chose seven big ones, shapely and all of a size. Then they found a place—hot, but not too hot—and poked them in. In an hour and a half they would be cooked.

Tea was a more cheerful meal than lunch had been. The bonfire had done them good—and there was the prospect of to-morrow's visit to the sailmaker. After tea they spread the plans of *Tern* on the sitting-room table, and took the measurements for a mainsail and jib. Robin wrote them carefully down on a sheet of note-paper. They were almost happy again.

Suddenly, at about half-past six, Elizabeth remembered something. She was lying on her back on the sofa, with her knees cocked up, drawing horses. She threw down her exercise book and pencil, and scrambled to her feet.

"Robin!" she said. "Anne! We've forgotten the potatoes."

She ran out into the garden through the french win-

dow, and Robin followed. They scrabbled in the ashe
with a stick, and turned up three small blackened husks
Elizabeth giggled.

"It's not worth looking for the rest," she said.

CHAPTER XIII

Next morning Mrs. Rutherford and the four children made an early start to catch the 10.30 boat from Cowes. They arrived in plenty of time, for Mrs. Rutherford (as was to be expected) had not loitered on the wide road from Newport. They put the car into a garage, bought their tickets, and went on to the pontoon. It was another fine morning with a pleasant westerly breeze. The water of the harbour was deep green and almost unruffled under the shelter of the town, but out in the Solent there were quick little waves, flecked with white. On the pontoon two men, one in a blue jersey and the other with a canvas apron tied round his waist, were loading crates on a van. Two or three dinghies were tied up at the landing-hard ; in one of them a small ragged boy was sitting, rocking it to and fro. The green water slopped lazily against the stone. A noise of hammering came from the boatyard just up the river : yachts were fitting out—and a small company of them were already on their moorings along the edge of the Shrape.

"There she is," said Elizabeth—the ferry-steame was coming. Robin watched her come alongside th pontoon. Steamers are not very interesting, compare with sailing-boats, but they are interesting all the same Robin liked to see the man throw his line: to see hin balance it for a moment, a part in each hand, the swing his arm with a casual, easy gesture; and then t see the man on the pontoon catch it across his back and haul it in—rapidly at first, then slowly when th weight of the hawser came.

The steamer was less familiar to Antony and Robi than to Elizabeth and Anne; it was natural, therefor that the boys should spend at least a part of the crossin in exploring her. Robin soon found that the pleasante places on board were the two extreme ends: eithe right up in the bows (where you could watch the bow wave—how fast a steamer goes!) or on the gratin astern, when you could sit amongst the coiled hawser It was necessary, however, to spend a certain amount c time in the dining-saloon; here they were served by weary but courteous steward with a pot of coffee (som what peculiar in flavour), and a packet of pink biscui for Elizabeth.

Anne, who had sailed much in the Solent, enjoye telling Antony and Robin the names of the buoys they passed them: West Bramble, North Thorn, Cast Point, Black Jack, Hook, Hamble Point, Dean's Elbow- delightful names. Anne remembered most of them, ar Mrs. Rutherford could prompt her when she forgc Elizabeth was bad at buoys; Baldhead was the on one she could constantly remember, and even of th she was never sure of the exact position. But she kne it was a very small one.

As they passed the docks, the liners were worth lookir at: first a ship of the Union Castle, tied up to t wharf. She was blue-grey and huge; little, diminished men moved remotely on her decks and alley-ways; then other ships, bigger still, tucked away in odd corners, their towering sides and sloping funnels visible over intervening roofs. Robin wondered however they got there. He stared and stared—sitting on his hawser in the stern—until his attention was taken by a little fishing-smack from the Itchen, her grubby brown mainsail triced up at the tack, her staysail ill-setting, her bowsprit bare, and a solitary fisherman in a blue jersey sitting aft, one arm over the tiller, smoking his pipe at his ease. Robin watched her as she went by, lazily ambling; he watched her till she was out of sight—the great ships forgotten.

After the bustle of landing they made their way along the wide dreary street, past the entrances to the docks and the offices of the steamship companies, to the chain ferry. The ferry was coming in as they turned the corner. It disgorged its cargo: first a car or two, then a couple of vans, then the passengers—an indistinct and hurrying stream.

The sailmaker's premises were on the left hand, just before the road dips to the waterside. Mrs. Rutherford stopped and looked dubiously at the entrance. Why is it, she thought, that sailmakers always seem to make a special point of having the outside of their premises as gloomy and as dirty and as mean as they possibly can? The most fashionable and expensive sailmakers in the world—who receive without lifting an eyebrow an order for a couple of new racing mainsails at three thousand pounds apiece—have a shop which, to judge by the front door and the dingy office inside it, would be rejected with scorn by a bankrupt seller of fried fish in a slum. Barton's was no exception. The paint was peeling off the door, the small window covered with dust and cobwebs.

"It can't be it," said Elizabeth, and wrinkled her nose. But it was. Mrs. Rutherford plucked up her courage.

"Come on," she said. "Antony, it's for you to do the business."

"Me?" said Antony. "Why me?"

Mrs. Rutherford laughed.

"What would the Bosun say," she said, "if you let *me* do it?"

"Go on, Antony," said Elizabeth.

They went in, Antony feeling awkward and embarrassed. It was a small dark room. Behind a dirty glass screen in one corner there was a desk with some papers on it. There was no other furniture. In another corner a steep, narrow stairway led up through the ceiling and disappeared. There was a man with spectacles behind the glass screen. As the party entered he looked up without interest or surprise. The room felt uncomfortably full. Elizabeth hung back by the door.

Antony swallowed—this didn't look like a sailmaker's at all.

"We want to order some sails," he said.

The man led him to the stairway.

"Will you step up, sir?" he said mildly.

Antony felt a little better. It still didn't look like a sailmaker's; but it was nice to be called "sir".

The man clumped slowly up the stairs. Antony, and all the others, followed him in silence.

At the top of the stairs all the children felt a sudden flush of surprise and delight. They found themselves in a huge, light, airy room; the ceiling was open to the rafters; there was a smell of tarred twine, pungent and delicious. Between two rafters a great sail, brand new and snowy white, was stretched. Spread on the clean floor were others, with men working at them, sewing on bolt ropes with needle and palm, or putting in cringles. At one end of the loft a man was working the treadle of a sewing machine ; the machine purred, the white canvas heaped and billowed beside it. Rolls of canvas and drums of rope were stacked round the walls.

Robin was happy. He felt he could stay here for hours. Mrs. Rutherford laughed and whispered to Anne.

“ Anne,” she said, “ aren’t you glad you and I haven’t got to do such *enormous* sewing ? ”

Meanwhile Antony ordered the sails. It was easy now, and he no longer felt awkward or embarrassed. He pulled from his pocket the sheet of paper with the measurements on it in Robin’s writing, and explained what they wanted.

Elizabeth, who had strayed over to watch the man with the sewing machine, came back and nudged Antony.

“ Don’t forget to tell him to be quick,” she whispered. Antony hesitated : he didn’t much like telling him to be quick.

“ How . . . how long will it take ? ” he said.

The man put his pencil behind his ear and looked mildly and benignly at Antony.

“ I dare say we could have them done in a week or two,” he said. “ It’s only a small job.”

Ordering sails is different from ordering—say—sausages. In anything to do with boats there is impropriety in hurrying. One just goes quietly on. The man scratched his ear, and spoke again to Antony, as if he were humouring him.

“ We’ll do what we can for you,” he said.

They all enjoyed their visit to the sailmaker, especially, perhaps, Robin—Robin privately decided it would be a good thing to learn sailmaking. Then, when *Tern* wanted a new jib, they could make it themselves. But it looked difficult and would want a lot of practice. He wondered if his friend Wilkinson at Creeksea (the oysterman who owned *Britannia* and a brown dog and had taught him knots) would be able to give him some lessons.

There was an hour or two to wait before the next steamer back to Cowes, so they had lunch in a restaurant and saw a bit of a film. There wasn't time to see it all, but it was the kind of film which one could, so to speak, begin or end almost anywhere. It was a western, in which men in check shirts on horseback chased other men in check shirts (also on horseback) through a great many similar ravines. Sometimes they fired their revolvers backwards, sometimes forwards. There was also a girl, who seemed very fond of one of the men—he too had a check shirt. There wasn't time to see if she married him; but she is practically certain to have done so. This kind of film is great fun if you eat plenty of ices and chocolate while it is going on.

They had tea on the steamer, and by the time they got home it was nearly supper-time. The Bosun and Mr. Rutherford were just knocking off work in the Building Shed when they arrived. Sally met them at the green gate—she had knocked off work long ago.

Robin and Antony went up the garden to the Building Shed. Elizabeth, after a quick look into the kitchen to see what Emily was doing for supper, followed (Emily was doing rice squash—what Mrs. Rutherford tried to remember to call risotto when she told Emily to make it). The Bosun and Mr. Rutherford were putting away tools.

"We ordered the sails," said Antony.

"And we went to the pictures," said Elizabeth.

CHAPTER XIV

THE first thing to do was to borrow a kettle. Their own kettle was not big enough. To steam satisfactorily one needs a very big one. Mrs. Rutherford knew that Mrs. Babbitt had the biggest kettle in the village—an iron one. Mrs. Babbitt lived in the cottage opposite, at the corner of the lane, and used occasionally to help Emily, in times of stress, with certain aspects of the housework. She would often bring Mrs. Rutherford useful presents of vegetables from her garden. Mrs. Babbitt was fond of flowers, but there weren't any in her garden: only vegetables. This was the fault of her husband, Joseph.

"Flowers?" she would say to Mrs. Rutherford. "Not him—Joe's all for vegetables and that. There's no sentiment in Joe."

So Mrs. Rutherford, in exchange for the vegetables, would take now and then a bunch of flowers to Mrs. Babbitt. Thus it was that Mrs. Rutherford was familiar with Mrs. Babbitt's kitchen; and being familiar with her kitchen, she knew about her kettle. Mrs. Babbitt's kettle was just the thing.

Antony carried the primus to the Building Shed. It was *Tessa's* primus, which the Rutherfords always kept on shore when *Tessa* was not in commission. Elizabeth brought Mrs. Babbitt's kettle. The children were good at primuses, for they had had plenty of practice in *Tessa* and *Ianthe*, and also during their cruise last year in the dinghies *Puffin* and *Sheldrake*. That is to say, Anne and the two boys were good at primuses; Elizabeth was not so good: she always had difficulty in pumping at the right moment. It is important, when lighting a primus, to pump at the right moment; for if you pump too soon you get a most alarmingflare; and you get a vile smell (and no flame at all) if you pump too late.

Robin pricked the primus and poured in the meths. Antony had the matches. Elizabeth watched. Anne was still indoors, doing her after-breakfast jobs—the older you get, the more there is to do after breakfast, especially if you are a girl. Mr. Rutherford and the Bosun said they would come along soon—when the kettle was beginning to get hot.

Antony lighted the stove, and when it was going properly Elizabeth put the kettle on it. Being so large a kettle, it took some time to boil.

"I'll go and hurry up the Bosun," said Antony, "and see what Anne's doing."

"It won't be boiling for ages," said Elizabeth. She had stopped watching the kettle and was standing by the bench, within reach of the putty-knife.

Robin was looking at *Tern* intently and abstractedly. Elizabeth's eye wandered from the putty-knife and dwelt affectionately on a pot of paint. Mr. Rutherford had said she would probably be able to begin painting the topsides to-day.

"Robin," she said, "shall we mix the paint while we're waiting?"

Robin did not answer. "He's gone vague", Elizabeth thought to herself. Robin did go vague sometimes, when he was not actually busy, or practising something. He would just stare and seem not to see what he was staring at. When he did this, Antony would get irritated; but Elizabeth didn't mind—and she never asked him what he was thinking about. He was sure to say "nothing", anyway. Moreover, it is quite possible to think about nothing—and it is not the same as not thinking about anything. In the former case you think, in the latter you don't: that is the difference. What about, does not matter; and very often you cannot possibly explain, even if you try.

Elizabeth began her tune; she hummed with quiet contentment. Then she picked up the putty knife and poked at some remains of putty on the board. It had gone hard. Perhaps she might moisten it with a little more linseed oil . . .

"I say," said Robin, "she'll be very *nearly* finished, won't she, when the stem capping's on?"

Elizabeth didn't answer—it was not really a question. She tilted the bottle of linseed soil.

"Bother," she murmured. "I've put too much."

She stirred vigorously with the putty-knife.

"Robin."

"What?"

"Does *your* father make things? Like building *Tern*, I mean?"

Robin squatted down by the primus and gave one slow extra stroke with the pump.

"He's f-frightfully good at carpentry," he said. "He can do everything."

"But does he make things—like us?"

"He *has* made lots of things," said Robin.

"But does he now?"

"No," said Robin, "why?"

"I just wondered," said Elizabeth, she began to hum again, still stirring the putty. She thought it was a pity that Robin's father didn't make things, or build boats; but she didn't say so. She had hardly seen Robin's father last year, when they were all at Creeksea.

The kettle began to sing. Robin gave one more gentle pump to the stove. Then he stood up and peered over *Tern's* rail—just to see how big she was inside. Elizabeth was close to him. She privately measured herself against him, shoulder to shoulder. They were just about the same height—but then Robin was on tiptoe, peering into *Tern*.

Robin looked round at her. Elizabeth looked quickly away.

"It was awful," said Robin, "when your father said we shouldn't finish in time."

"I know," said Elizabeth.

"All the same," said Robin. "I don't think . . . I mean, even if we don't, I shan't mind really frightfully much."

There was a silence for a moment. The kettle sang more briskly. Then Robin went on.

"Building is fun," he said. Elizabeth nodded.

"We *could* build next holidays as well," said Robin.

"You could come here again," said Elizabeth. Robin looked solemnly, and nodded too.

"I know," he said. "That's what I mean. But still . . ." He hesitated.

"What?" said Elizabeth.

"Creeksea . . ." said Robin; we couldn't be at Creeksea . . ."

"Of course not," said Elizabeth.

"Is Arthur *always* here . . . in the village?" said Robin.

"Yes," said Elizabeth. "In the holidays. Like us."

Robin was prevented from saying any more about Arthur by two events: the return of Antony with Mr. Rutherford and the Bosun, and the boiling of the kettle.

"Good," said the Bosun as he came into the Building Shed. "Everything's ready."

Mr. Rutherford removed the square end of the steaming box—the end opposite the small round hole—and told Antony to put the stem capping in. Then into the hole itself he pushed the spout of the kettle, and replaced the farther end. The box was now sealed up, and steam was getting into it. Mr. Rutherford propped it carefully on bits of wood, at the right height to prevent it from upsetting the kettle. The kettle bubbled, the steam hissed, and little wisps of it escaped through the joints of the box.

"Now we can leave it for a bit," Mr. Rutherford said. "All we need is to keep the stove going with a pump or two occasionally, and to see the kettle doesn't boil dry."

While the steaming went on, they occupied themselves with other jobs about the boat. Elizabeth painted the top sides—the first coat of pale pinkish-grey paint, not a very interesting colour. But Elizabeth didn't mind. Antony helped, beginning on the opposite side. Robin watched the primus and the kettle. The morning passed quickly and pleasantly. Everyone was surprised when Mrs. Rutherford told them that coffee was ready.

"We can have our coffee, and then the stem capping will be just about cooked," said the Bosun.

They drank their coffee and cocoa and hurried back to the shed, Mrs. Rutherford with them. Robin turned out the primus. The Bosun pulled the spout of the kettle from the hole. Antony opened the further end of the box. The Building Shed was full of steam. Mr. Rutherford tipped out the stem capping on to the floor.

It was important to bend the capping to shape as quickly as possible, while it was still soft from the effect of the steam. If they waited too long, it would harden again. Mr. Rutherford and the Bosun got the lower end of it into position and chocked it up firmly with a chunk of thick wood, so that it would not shift when pressure was applied at the opposite end. Then the Bosun (being the strongest) took hold of the upper end (the projecting one) and with gradual pressure began to force it upward, thus making the whole plank fit to the curve of *Tern's* bows. Mr. Rutherford watched the chock to see that it did not slip. When the upper part of the capping was a foot or so from *Tern's* stemhead, the Bosun's strength gave out.

"Quick, Antony," he said, "get the cramp on."

Antony jumped to obey. With Robin's help the iron cramp (Hackett's again) was soon adjusted, and the screw tightened to take the strain.

"Right," said Antony.

The Bosun let go. "All right underneath, John?" he said.

"Fine," said Mr. Rutherford.

The Bosun stepped back with a satisfied sigh. Mr. Rutherford got up.

"Screw him up, Antony," he said.

Antony took a few turns on the screw. The capping bent farther inward. Then Mr. Rutherford told Antony to stop—one must not go too fast with the last bit, or the plank might break.

Little by little they tightened the cramp—just a few

turns every ten minutes or so—until the capping was pulled flush with the stem. It was then ready for the bolts and screws which should finally fix it. Meanwhile Elizabeth and Antony went steadily on with the painting.

The remaining days of the holidays passed all too quickly. The children had become used to the knowledge that it would not be possible to finish *Tern* in time ; indeed, it was now obvious to all of them. The first horrible disappointment, which had made them feel that it was hardly worth while to go on working at all, had been alleviated by the fresh interest of ordering the sails and the making of the stem-capping ; but now, as the holidays drew towards an end, the feeling of failure returned. To a casual eye *Tern* looked so very nearly finished ; there she stood on the stocks, her hull complete, and bright in its new paint. Mast and spars were ready, and stored in the loft above the shed—you could see their projecting ends. The deck-beams were on. But *Tern* was not finished—there still remained innumerable jobs to be done inside her before she could be ready for sea.

Nor was it only that they had failed in the task of getting the building done ; almost worse than that was the fact that they would have no sailing these holidays. They had so long looked forward to spending their last few days in trying *Tern* at sea. They always sailed at Easter ; and this Easter they were to have had not only the pleasure of sailing, but the added delight of sailing in their new vessel—the vessel built by their own hands. But it was not to be. They would have no sailing at all. And even next holidays—the summer—goodness knows how long they would have to waste before they could do what they had planned to do.

Arthur, moreover, became a more frequent visitor.

He liked, he said, to have a squint at the old tub now and then. He congratulated them condescendingly on *Tern's* construction. He shook his head knowingly as his eye lingered on the transom.

"You've made quite a job of her," he would say. "But she's a homely old packet, isn't she?"

Then he would tell more stories about the excessive speed and weatherliness of his snipe, and praise with faint damns his own prowess in the handling of her.

"We'll have some races," he said; "next hols. Handicap races. I don't suppose you'd want to start level, would you?"

The Bosun would wink—but Robin writhed.

"*If* you ever finish her," Arthur added.

Arthur took Antony for more rides on his motor-bike—for Antony was no longer busy. That made it seem worse—for Robin. But the worst thing of all happened two days before the holidays ended—Arthur came to tea. I say it *happened*, because it wasn't really Mrs. Rutherford's fault. It wasn't really anybody's fault, except Arthur's own. But it was a great pity.

Arthur had dropped in (those were his words) to say good-bye; he was leaving the village next day, to go back for his last term at school. But the sickening thing was that he dropped in just as the family was sitting down to tea. In fact he and Emily (with the tea-pot) dropped in practically at the same moment.

Mrs. Rutherford was naturally hospitable; so what could she do? It was obvious what the children *wanted* her to do; you could tell from their faces. But it was too difficult.

When a person comes to say good-bye, the one impossible thing to do is to say it, except after saying a number of other things first. Everybody knows that. What other things does not in the ordinary way matter a bit;

but when tea is on the table and the family is sitting expectantly round it, the field of choice is necessarily narrowed.

"Won't you stay and have some tea?" said Mrs. Rutherford. She really couldn't say anything else. Of course, there was just the chance that Arthur might refuse: he might have a pressing engagement elsewhere—or he might have other friends to say good-bye to.

But he hadn't. He stayed to tea.

Even without Arthur there was rather a squash round the table; with him, the squash was worse—much worse. He squeezed in between Elizabeth and Robin.

During tea Arthur was on the whole less tiresome than he usually was. He didn't talk much, and never mentioned his snipe once. This was surprising. He refused a second helping of cake. In fact, he made a very poor tea, and seemed depressed. This was all to the good; for Arthur was one of those people who are nicer when they are not too cheerful.

When they went into the other room after tea, Mrs. Rutherford proposed a game. Not Rhymes—certainly not Rhymes; but perhaps some good safe game with cards. Arthur, however, was afraid he must be going.

"Oh not yet, surely?" said Mrs. Rutherford, hospitably but rashly.

But all was well. Arthur *was* going. Robin was so much relieved (he had expected to be saddled with Arthur all the evening) that for a brief moment he felt almost fond of him.

Arthur went, and it was over. Tea had been grim, but not so grim as they expected. Mrs. Rutherford was quite worried: was Arthur ill? It was a beautiful cake . . . and such self-effacement was unprecedented.

"The poor boy can't have been feeling well," she said. But none of the children believed it. It was only school, they said—the end of the holidays. It was the end of their holidays too ; and they had enough sympathy, even for Arthur, to be sorry for him.

But Mrs. Rutherford was right. The next day she learned that poor Arthur was in bed with a temperature. He felt very ill, and had a singular discomfort in his neck—just under his ears. His mother, in great distress, called at the cottage to report to Mrs. Rutherford.

It was *so* unfortunate . . . with a houseful of children too . . . just as term was about to begin . . . the doctor could not yet be sure ; but he suspected mumps . . .

The doctor was right—just as Mrs. Rutherford had been. It *was* mumps.

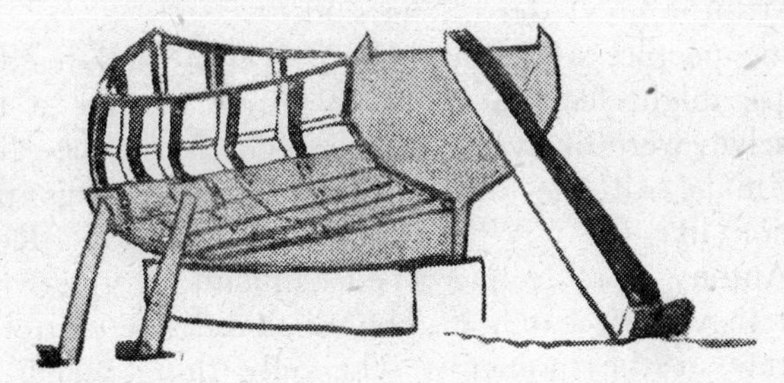

CHAPTER XV

It was coffee-time. The whole household was quite disgracefully cheerful, for they had just got the news. The full significance of it had taken some minutes to become apparent. Now they understood.

Mrs. Rutherford sipped happily. " You see," she said, " they've been in contact."

" Close contact," said the Bosun.

" Especially me and Robin," said Elizabeth. " He sat between us."

" And b-bumped our elbows," said Robin.

" He must have had it coming for days," said Antony. " And I went on his motor-bike."

" He breathed down my neck after tea," said Anne.

" Antony," said Mrs. Rutherford, and a shade of anxiety crossed her face, " I suppose you haven't *had* it, have you—you or Robin ? "

" Had what ? "

" Mumps."

" No," said Antony.

"Of course they haven't," said the Bosun. "What an idea."

Mrs. Rutherford looked relieved.

"Thank goodness," she said. The Bosun grinned.

"Arthur's good deed," he said.

Some people, when they have recently had tea with mumps, might feel uncomfortable and wonder if they themselves were likely to catch it. Circumstances, however, make all the difference to one's feelings in a situation like this. What Anne and Elizabeth, Robin and Antony were feeling is not difficult to guess. No doubt they *might* catch it; but that did not matter, at any rate at the moment. The only thing which did matter was that it was obviously impossible for them to go back to school for ages—for at least a fortnight—or three weeks. Anyway, for ages. The holidays were not over after all. That in itself was good; but even better was the knowledge of what they would now be able to do: they would be able to finish the building of *Tern*. They would finish her—and the summer holidays would not be robbed of precious time.

It was no wonder that the whole household was cheerful.

They couldn't even be sorry for Arthur. "*Poor* Arthur," Mrs. Rutherford said; but she said it with a sort of twinkle in her eye, and in the wrong voice for genuine sympathy. Besides, was there any need to be sorry for Arthur? Mumps hurts rather; but it hurts much more at school than it does at home; and Arthur wouldn't be going back to school either. Arthur was lucky: not nearly so lucky as themselves—but still lucky . . .

And Arthur was nicely out of the way. That was another good thing. He wouldn't come bothering, until they had finished.

The only person who had taken no part in the general rejoicing during the past few minutes was Mr. Rutherford. Up till now he had sipped his coffee in silence. To say that he was not glad would be unfair to Mr. Rutherford and not true; but there was an unhappy fact which, though it had not yet occurred to the others, had at once occurred to *him*. His rejoicing therefore was tempered with regret.

He finished his coffee, put down his cup, and waited for a pause in the babble of happy excitement.

"But what about poor father?" he said.

The only person who knew what he meant was Mrs. Rutherford. She went and sat on the arm of his chair. There was a short silence.

"You see," said Mr. Rutherford. "I've *had* mumps. And even if I hadn't . . ."

"Oh *Daddy* . . ." said Anne.

"But you don't mean . . ." said Elizabeth.

"Good Lord, but surely . . ." began Antony. Robin stared, and said nothing.

But that was the truth. Poor Mr. Rutherford *had* had mumps. He must return sorrowfully to school on the day appointed. He must go to-morrow. He must teach Greek to hundreds of tiresome boys who didn't want to learn Greek a bit, and who were too stupid, or too inconsiderate, to get mumps themselves.

"And I shall go with him," said Mrs. Rutherford.

There was another silence, while the significance of this grew gradually clear. Then Mrs. Rutherford spoke again.

"We shall take Emily with us," she said.

The Bosun filled his pipe.

"Anne," he said anxiously, "have you been practising your cooking lately?"

"N-no," said Anne. "Not much. Hardly at all, in fact."

"And your housework?" said the Bosun. "Scrubbing the floors, sweeping, dusting, washing the clothes, ironing . . ."

Anne looked a little blank. Mrs. Rutherford laughed.

"Don't be silly, Bob," she said. "I'll get Mrs. Babbitt. After all, it's not for long . . ."

"But it *is*, Mummy," put in Elizabeth. "It's ages . . . at least . . . but how long *is* it?"

"About three weeks, I think," said Mrs. Rutherford.

Elizabeth looked relieved. Even though Mummy and Daddy had to go, it would be awful if it wasn't very long after all.

"You'll have a lovely time," said Mrs. Rutherford.

"Lucky children," said Mr. Rutherford.

It was arranged, then, that Mrs. Babbitt should come in every day and help with the housework and cook the lunch. Everything else they would do themselves, each taking a share.

"Like cruising," said Mr. Rutherford.

"Exactly," said the Bosun; "I'll navigate."

It was going to be fun. They would, as Mrs. Rutherford had said, have a lovely time. It was sad that Mummy and Daddy had to go back to work: sad for the children, and perfectly frightful for Daddy. But all the same . . . they would have a lovely time. . . .

"John," said the Bosun, "I've said it before and I say it again. It's a good thing I decided not to be a schoolmaster."

Elizabeth went and sat on the other arm of Mr. Rutherford's chair.

"Daddy," she said, "couldn't you *forget* that you've had mumps?"

Anne was leaning her elbows on the back of his chair, and looking down on the top of his head.

"*Poor* Daddy," she said.

Yes, it was sickening. But though they grieved for him, and for his coming absence and Mummy's, yet cheerfulness could not but break in. They were going to have a lovely time. And *Tern* was to be finished.

" I'll tell you one thing," said Mr. Rutherford.

" What ? " said Anne.

" We'll come down for the trial trip. Mummy and me. I'll get a week-end off."

" Urgent private affairs," said the Bosun. Mr. Rutherford nodded.

" That's it," he said. " Frightfully urgent. You must see that *Tern's* ready on a Sunday."

That made it better. Poor Daddy would have something to sustain him while he was teaching Greek during those three weeks of exile, something to look forward to. They would all be together again for the trial trip. Everything was right . . . very nearly right, anyway . . . as right as it could be in a world in which it is difficult entirely to avoid mischance. *Tern* was to be finished ; Arthur was temporarily eliminated ; Mummy and Daddy were coming back for the trial trip—and it would be quite fun, really, having to cook breakfast and supper themselves : almost (as the Bosun had said) like cruising.

There was no doubt that they were going to have a lovely time.

" Incidentally," said the Bosun, " I hope, Anne, that you won't give me scrambled eggs for supper *every* night."

One other thing was clear : with Mr. Rutherford away, they would have to work tremendously hard to get the building done. But none of the children minded that. To work hard was just what they wanted, now. Achievement was in sight : indeed it was certain—or practically certain ; and that is the sharpest spur to effort. The dullest jobs they would now do with zest. Moreover, they would get Hackett ; if necessary, they would get him to join them in the Building Shed, and work by their side. Hackett (Robin said) would love to come—if he wasn't too busy. Hackett was a quick and expert craftsman ; nobody would object to his coming now ; he had done so much already that he might truly be considered as one of their company. With Hackett, there could be no doubt at all of their finishing the work.

" And even if there were," said the Bosun tentatively, " one of you—Anne, for instance—might, on the last day, become conscious of a pain . . . just a small pain . . . under the ears . . ."

That was a very improper suggestion, and nobody (I am glad to say) would have thought of it except the Bosun. It was unlikely, however, that there would be any need to put it into practice.

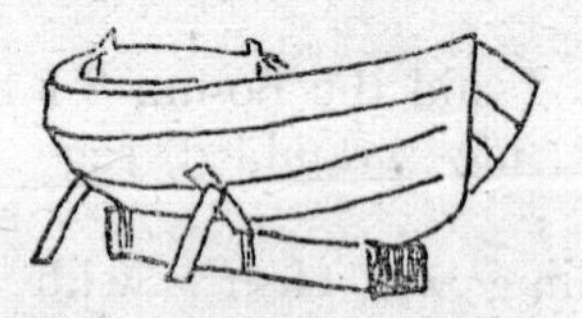

CHAPTER XVI

As it is not Robin who is telling this story, you will have to skip the details of the next three weeks. Robin would have insisted upon telling everything. For Robin, every screw and every nail they drove was interesting and important. Indeed, he was right; but what is interesting and important in the actual doing is often a bit monotonous in the telling. I will merely record that during those weeks the four children, and the Bosun, and Hackett (who had, he said, two or three jobs on hand, but would like to oblige Mr. Rutherford—and Master Robin) were exceedingly industrious and happy; that Anne, taking the necessary hours from her work in the Building Shed, scrambled eggs with much verve and some success, varying the dish on certain days with exciting compounds of rice, bacon, cheese and potatoes; that Elizabeth helped her with advice and encouragement; that they all—even the Bosun—made their own beds after breakfast and reduced their bedrooms to the outward semblance of order and decency; and that Mrs. Babbit scrubbed and dusted the rest of the house with cheerful competence, and uncomplainingly washed up each morning the piles of plates and dishes which had horribly accumulated on the scullery table.

In the Building Shed, the centreboard case was fitted, the thwarts and floorboards finished and put in, the deck planking screwed on and covered with canvas; cleats and fairleads were fixed, rigging prepared, the fittings of mast and spars completed. Innumerable jobs—all interesting, and all delightful. Best of all, for Elizabeth at any rate, was the orgy of painting which came at the end: the bottom to be covered first with black varnish (inside and out), then—on the outside—with anti-fouling composition of a beautiful rich red, and the top sides to be given their final coats of white: the last coat being enamel, exquisitely smooth and shining.

The days galloped by; but the work kept pace, and within the time allotted *Tern* was done.

While the paint was drying, and the last touches being put to the internal fittings, a telegram was dispatched to Mr. and Mrs. Rutherford. They were to come on Saturday. On the previous day *Tern* left the Building Shed. Three men came with the lorry which was to carry her to the sea; these with the help of all the family and Hackett, coaxed her from the stocks on to rollers, slid her out to the gravel patch under the ilex, steered her through the green gate, and lifted her (she weighed a ton) on to the waiting lorry. A ton is a lot, but there was no lack of lifters; for, in addition to the three lorrymen, a crowd soon gathered in the lane to see so unusual a sight. In the gardens opposite the diggers stopped digging, and left their spades; housewives, bucket or broom in hand, emerged into porches, loiterers stayed their steps and stared, the baker's boy with his basket on his arm ceased to whistle and stared too. Then all, as if at a signal, onverged upon the spot outside the green gate where he lorry was standing.

" Coo ! " said the baker's boy.

" My goodness alive ! " said old Mrs. Mould.

" 'Ere, catch a holt," said a loiterer. And Joe Babbitt pat and said nothing.

But not even twenty pairs of hands can lift a ton of *Tern* and dump it neatly into a lorry, and the Bosun and he lorrymen had not a little difficulty in restraining the ash attempt. Little by little, on her rollers, *Tern* was manœuvred into the lane until she stood directly behind the lorry ; two rollers were laid on its floor, and then with a well-timed heave *Tern's* bows were raised to a sufficient height ; the lorry backed a yard until its tail was under the uplifted keel ; gently the bows were lowered—they rested, propped on the lorry's floor. Then all hands moved aft, seized *Tern* by the gunwale, hove again at the Bosun's word, and, when she was raised to an even keel, shoved her forward on the rollers until she lay snugly ensconced in her proper place.

Then the gear was piled in : the mast and spars, the rudder and tiller, the sails, the ropes, the floorboards and the rigging, and a precious wooden box containing an assortment of shackles, bolts and screw-eyes, a ball of twine, half a tin of grease, a bailer, a couple of paint brushes and some tools.

The lorry was well loaded, but there was still just room for Elizabeth and Robin. Under Tern's quarters they each found a nest, narrow, nobbly and comfortless ; and there they curled themselves—squashed but content.

The lorrymen and the driver resumed their seats on the box, the engine was started, the gear engaged, and the lorry began to move off down the lane. The baker's boy attempted to raise a cheer ; Mrs. Mould shook her old head and chuckled ; the loiterers continued to stare, and one by one the diggers turned and went back to their spades. The lorry disappeared round the corner of the lane.

The Bosun was to follow with Antony and Anne in the bus—there was no car in the family now that Mr. and Mrs. Rutherford had gone. The next bus for Newport, where they would change for Wootton, left in half an hour. When the lorry was gone, Antony strolled back into the Building Shed ; a moment or two later the Bosun and Anne followed him. The shed looked strangely large and bare and unfamiliar. Antony, his hands in his pockets, kicked at a little heap of sawdust beside the bench.

" Gosh," he said, " we never thought we'd do it. But we have."

" Arthur's good deed," said Anne, and looked at the Bosun.

The Bosun was lighting his pipe. When he had blown out the match he looked down at Anne and grinned.

" Nice chap, Arthur," he said.

Anne snorted. Antony stirred the heap of sawdust with his toe.

" He's not so bad, really," he said casually. " Though he does swank a bit."

" A bit ! " said Anne.

But none of them were much interested in Arthur at the moment. There were too many other things to think about.

" Come on," said Anne. " We mustn't miss the bus."

" I say," she added, " what shall we do about lunch ? "

" You're cook," said the Bosun, " what have you got ? "

" Well . . .," said Anne, " I don't think there's anything, really. I mean . . . not what we could take."

" Then I suppose we do nothing," said the Bosun practically.

"We could buy things in Newport," said Antony.

"So we could," said the Bosun.

They went into the house. It was cool and clean and empty, and smelt faintly of floor polish. The morning sun lay in a broad bar on the carpet of the living-room. They got their coats from the pegs in the narrow hall.

"Good Lord," said Anne. "Here's Bittle's. She's forgotten it."

"And Robin's," said Antony. "We'd better take them."

Then they walked up the village to the crossroads, where the buses stopped.

Meanwhile Elizabeth and Robin were bumping along over the familiar road (familiar to Elizabeth) towards Wootton. They couldn't talk much, because they were one on each side of *Tern*, tucked away under her quarters; they could not see each other, and it was difficult to hear even if they shouted, because of the noise of the engine, and of the bumps. But their thoughts were busy. Elizabeth was enjoying the ride in so unusual a motor-car; she liked expeditions of any kind, and this was a very special expedition; she liked watching the greening hedgerows stream past her from behind; she liked the mixture of smells in her nostrils—the musty smell of the lorry and the sharp smell of *Tern's* sails and gear; she liked being with Robin; and she liked not being at school. Robin's thoughts were all with *Tern*: *Tern* perfect and complete at last, *Tern* on her way to the sea, this very day to be afloat. He craned his neck to look up at her smooth bottom—how big and strong she seemed, as he crouched in his corner under her quarter! She would be the finest vessel that ever sailed, and they had built her! Perhaps she would be fast too . . . snipes were fast . . . but even if she wasn't so very fast, she was sturdy and strong. "Stiff as a church": that's what she would prove—as the Essex oystermen said ; she would be as stiff as a church.

The lorry bumped and grumbled through Newport, where everyone in the street stopped and stared as it passed, took the road towards Ryde, and turned left at the narrow lane which leads down to Fishbourne. Carefully it sidled past the little circular green and crept on down to the shore of the creek, where the lane ended. There it stopped.

Robin and Elizabeth hopped out. The lorrymen climbed from their box. Robin asked the driver to wait while he ran to the shipyard to get help for unloading *Tern*. The Bosun had told him to do this, and Elizabeth knew where the yard was, because she had often come to Wootton before in *Tessa*. So Robin and Elizabeth set off together along the shore of the creek, past the landing-place where the car ferry from Portsmouth comes in, and over the flat tongue of marsh and shingle at the bend. A few vessels were laid up in little inlets in the marsh, looking desolate and rather forlorn ; others in their new spring paint were lying at moorings in the river. Farther down, by the wooden dolphins which mark the channel past Wootton rocks, a dinghy was sailing, her varnished hull and scarlet sail bright against the grey water. Robin looked at her over his shoulder as he stumbled along across the shingle, and thought to himself with quiet rapture that soon—very soon—*Tern* would be there too.

The shipyard was just round the bend. Elizabeth was not very good at dealing with strange men, and Robin too preferred, as a general rule, to have the support of Antony except when the business to be done was of the simplest. Doing business in a shipyard is not simple except for those who are used to it ; the trouble is that one never knows whom to ask—and if you don't ask, nobody takes any notice of you at all ; nobody even looks at you—they just go on scraping, or whatever it is they happen to be doing. Some shipyards of, course, have a conspicuous office, and though an office makes things less difficult and uncertain, it makes them in a way even more embarrassing.

Robin, however, was too excited to be embarrassed. He addressed the first person they saw—a young man in brown dungarees who was varnishing a spar outside the sheds.

" We've brought the b-boat," Robin said, " and we want some help to get her off the l-lorry." He was rather out of breath, and the urgency of the occasion made him stammer more than usual.

The young man balanced his brush across his pot of varnish and strolled into the sheds to see what could be done. The children waited impatiently. The clean, bitter smell of wet varnish was in the air. A boat was rowing beyond the point ; its rowlocks clanked. Five minutes later the young man returned, bringing with him another man in a grey sweater and flannel trousers tucked into sea boots.

" For Mr. Rutherford, isn't it ? " he said.

" Y-yes," said Robin. He hadn't known they were expected.

The second man turned to the first. " Better see if you can find Bill," he said.

The first man nodded and once again strolled away towards the sheds. One does not hurry in a shipyard. Robin wished that one did.

" Where did you leave her ? " asked the man in the sea boots.

Robin pointed back down the river.

" Over th-there," he said. " She's on the lorry."

The man in sea boots considered.

"It'd been better to drive up to the yard," he said.

"I'll tell them," said Robin. "I'll ask them to bring her round."

"I daresay we can manage without," said the man. One is seldom precise in a shipyard.

The young man in dungarees was a long time looking for Bill. Robin grew more impatient. When you are cruising and happen to have a morning to spare (because the tide will not serve until the afternoon) few things are more agreeable than loitering in a shipyard. Then you can happily spend a couple of hours in buying, say, a few fathoms of new rope for sheets. The very leisureliness of the procedure is an added source of pleasure. There is so much to look at and to feel, that clocks (upon which the tide does not depend) are unimportant, and every moment is its own self and delightful. But to-day it was different. Robin was impatient to get on; it was not the present moment but the next, which called and urged him. *Tern* was waiting.

After about a quarter of an hour the man in seaboots also strolled away towards the sheds. Elizabeth glanced at Robin with a small smile, and quickly looked grave again. Robin fumed.

"What are they d-doing?" he muttered. "I do wish they'd buck up."

"Let's go and see," said Elizabeth. "Let's go back to the lorry."

Another man, this time in a blue sweater and serge trousers appeared at the entrance to one of the sheds. Robin hoped it was Bill. The man was carrying a pair of oars under one arm and a coil of rope was slung over his other shoulder. Apart from the oars and the rope, he looked as if he might be Bill. He came on down towards the water, dumped the rope and the oars into a dinghy which was lying on the mud, considered them for a moment, and trudged back again. He took no notice of the children.

Evidently he was not Bill.

"Come on," said Elizabeth. "Let's go." Elizabeth knew that Robin was fretting with impatience. She didn't mind waiting herself; she was quite content to be where she was, so long as Robin was there too—though she was getting a bit hungry, and wished they had asked the lorrymen to stop in Newport so that they could have bought some chocolate. But the Bosun would be coming soon, and Anne and Antony—with lunch.

"Oh, all right," said Robin.

But before they could move there was the sound of an engine and heavy wheels somewhere behind the sheds: then of men's voices. Robin and Elizabeth looked at each other.

"They've come," said Robin.

They had. The lorry had driven round with *Tern*. At this very moment they were hauling out *Tern's* gear and piling it on the ground. Robin and Elizabeth ran. When they got to the lane behind the sheds, there the lorry was, and there was *Tern*, with six men looking at her with a speculative stare. The man in brown dungarees was there, and the man in the grey sweater—and a third, who must have been Bill. And the three lorrymen.

The man in the grey sweater nodded to the children with an air of having arranged it all nicely.

Then they proceeded to unload *Tern* herself.

"She's a lump of a boat," said the man in the grey sweater. "Go easy, Bill."

The rollers were laid on the ground behind the lorry; *Tern* was slid out, and the after end of her keel lowered on to them. Then four of the men laid hold of her bows.

F

A moment later she was safely on the ground. Robin sighed with relief and satisfaction.

" Shall we put her in the water straight away ? " said the man in a grey sweater—who seemed to be the boss. Robin would have dearly liked to say yes ; but obviously they must wait for the others. A launch is a serious thing. It wouldn't be fair on the others if it were done before they came. So Robin said No : they would wait. He thought, however, that it would be a good plan to get the mast stepped : then he and Elizabeth could employ themselves in bending on the mainsail and setting up the rigging while they were waiting.

Tern, therefore, was taken round (on her rollers) to the front of the sheds—it was a pity to leave her beside the road ; she didn't belong there ; she belonged to the water—and two of the men (the job was much too heavy for the children) got the mast into her.

Robin gazed. With the stepping of the mast *Tern* had come wonderfully to life. She lay on her bilge, tilted a little, and other boats were about her, and the smell of mud and of seaweed, and seagulls, and the river. She was in her proper place at last. The two men also were considering her with critical eyes.

" We b-built her ourselves," said Robin.

The man in the grey sweater nodded, not unkindly.

" Yes," he said, " I can see you did that." Then he added : " She's like a Yorkshire coble, something, isn't she ? "

Perhaps she was ; but Robin neither knew nor cared. At any rate she was beautiful.

Then the men went away, the lorrymen back to their lorry, the others to the sheds. Elizabeth and Robin were left alone with *Tern*.

" I wish they *had* launched her," said Elizabeth. But she was ready to agree when Robin said they could not possibly have done so without Antony and Anne and the Bosun.

" And Mummy and Daddy ought to be here too," she said.

" I know," said Robin.

But Mummy and Daddy were coming to-morrow ; and that was the next best thing.

" I wonder when the others *will* come ? " said Elizabeth " They ought to be here soon."

Robin did not answer. His impatience was gone. Apart from wanting Antony to see *Tern* there—with her mast stepped and her gear aboard—he would not now have minded waiting hours for the launch. Time had come right again. There was no hurry now, no possibility of accident or disappointment. *Tern* was lovely : he could not take his eyes off her. And there was plenty of work to do : lovely, leisurely jobs with tarred marlin, bending the mainsail to the hoops on the mast.

" Aren't you hungry ? " said Elizabeth.

" Not specially," said Robin.

" They're bringing lunch."

" I know," said Robin. " We can have it on board."

" Like cruising," said Elizabeth.

Robin nodded happily. " Come on," he said. " I'm going to start getting the mainsail ready."

Both children climbed on board. Robin had often been on board before—in the Building Shed, when *Tern* was on the stocks ; he had been on board sometimes to work, sometimes just to imagine and pretend. Now he was on board to work, and there was no need to pretend at all. It was a good feeling. He looked up at the short stout mast ; a seagull wheeled and flashed overhead. The wind blew cool through his hair. The dinghy with the scarlet sail was sliding gently in round the point, almost becalmed by the trees on the farther bank.

For nearly an hour they worked contentedly : that is to say Robin worked ; Elizabeth was just as contented, but she worked less. First Robin set up the shrouds, port and starboard, pulling them tight with a piece of brand new, stiff codline ; then the forestay. After that, which took only a few minutes, he began work on the more laborious task of bending on the mainsail. He laced the head of the sail to the gaff, lashing it firmly at throat and peak ; then to the boom he made it fast at tack and clew.

" I'm fitting out," he said to himself. " I'm fitting out *Tern*."

Building had been good, but fitting out was better. Robin was happy, and cared not how time went by. The hour was his own.

" Pass the marlin, Elizabeth," he said. Elizabeth passed it. She was happy too—though she was getting hungrier and wished the others would hurry up and come.

Robin had lashed three mast-hoops to the eyelet holes in the mainsail when Elizabeth saw them.

" They're there ! " she cried. " Robin, they've come."

Robin dropped the sail. He hopped on to the foredeck, one arm round the mast and waved.

" Hullo ! " he shouted. " Hullo ! We're fitting out."

They were crunching across the shingle, away to the left, the three of them in a row with the Bosun in the middle. They were laden with coats and paper bags. They couldn't wave back, but they shouted instead.

" *Tern* ahoy ! " roared the Bosun.

" Ahoy . . . ahoy . . ." called Antony and Anne together.

" Marvellous," said Anne as she followed a moment later.

Antony and Anne put their paper bags and mackintoshes down on the seat aft. The Bosun came up and did the same with his. His mackintosh clinked, because the pockets were full of bottles.

"I'm bending on the mainsail," said Robin. "I've done the shrouds and the forestay."

Elizabeth cast an expert eye on the paper bags.

"Come and help, Antony," said Robin.

Antony stepped over the rail and came aboard. Elizabeth looked inside a bag: it was sausage rolls.

"Lunch first," said the Bosun. "We'll have lunch first, and get to work afterwards."

It was the best thing to do. They had it on board, as Robin had suggested: that is to say, the four children did. The Bosun would not actually come on board, because he said it wasn't too good for the boat to have large weights in her when she was not afloat.

"And don't put your feet on her planking," he said. "Tread on the floorboards, or on the ribs."

But he was very nearly on board: he propped himself, half sitting, half leaning, on the side-deck. It was quite comfortable like that, and near enough to be convenient for the food.

While they ate their lunch ("Elizabeth," said the Bosun, "don't make crumbs in the clean new bilge"), the tide was coming up. Robin watched it. The water was already much nearer *Tern* than it had been when he had begun to fit out. She was not more than a dozen yards or so from the edge.

When they had eaten all they could, the Bosun reached for his mackintosh and extracted the bottles. Elizabeth eyed them.

"I'll have *that* one," she said. "Unless," she added, ". . . unless anyone else wants it."

There was silence.

"Do *you* want it, Anne?" she said challengingly.

Fortunately Anne didn't—much.

"Why are there six?" said Antony.

"Six?" said Anne.

"Yes: six bottles. It's one too many—we're only five."

"You've forgotten the ship," said the Bosun. "We want one for the ship."

"What . . ." began Elizabeth, but Robin interrupted her.

"I know," he said. "To ch-christen her. We want it to christen her with."

The Bosun nodded. "Just before the launch," he said. Robin was privately thankful that he hadn't let the men from the shipyard put *Tern* in the water immediately she was off the lorry. He had never intended to let them: that he knew; but all the same, he had not remembered the christening.

The Bosun dusted the crumbs off his trousers and took his pipe from his pocket.

"We'll launch her now," he said. "We can finish the fitting out when she's afloat."

Antony and Robin fetched a couple more rollers from where they had been left just outside the sheds. They laid them down, six feet apart, in front of *Tern's* bows. Elizabeth and Anne climbed out.

"We'll work her round so that she goes in alongside the jetty," said the Bosun. "Now heave."

They hove. If you have rollers and hard ground it is surprising how easily a heavy boat will move. *Tern* slid forward.

"Easy now," said the Bosun. Robin let go his hold, picked up the roller which *Tern* had left behind (there were still two under her keel) and laid it down again in front. In this way, a yard or two at a time, *Tern* approached the water. Just before she reached it, all four children took their shoes off.

Then they hove again.

"Ow!" said Elizabeth. "It's frightfully cold."

Robin was in the water on the other side, but he said nothing.

"Easy again," said the Bosun.

Tern now lay close to the jetty, her bows just in the water. The Bosun told Antony to take one end of the jib halyard off the cleat, and then to tie it round the christening bottle. Then he made him measure the length, to see that it reached to the outside of *Tern's* bows.

"Right," said the Bosun when Antony had done. "Now we'll get her nearly afloat, so that the moment the christening is over one heave will float her properly."

They shoved again; then stopped to roll up their shorts—*Tern* drew nearly two feet of water even without her centreboard. The water was icy, the bottom knobbly with stones, some of them sharp. But nobody noticed or cared.

When *Tern* was almost afloat, the Bosun took a rope which was made fast to her bows and climbed on to the jetty.

"Now," he said, "one more heave will do it. Elizabeth, you're to perform the ceremony. You know what to say?"

"Yes," said Elizabeth. "Like Mummy—when she christened *Sheldrake* last year."

Elizabeth took the bottle (strictly, it should have been champagne, but it wasn't) and waded as far from *Tern* as the rope attached to it would allow.

"Ready?" said the Bosun. Elizabeth nodded. The Bosun took the strain on his rope; Antony, Anne and Robin grasped the gunwale and prepared to heave. Then Elizabeth raised the hand with the bottle in it and said, speaking slowly and clearly: "I name . . . this . . . vessel . . . *Tern*."

As she said " *Tern* " Elizabeth let the bottle go—with a little extra push. The bottle swung in, and hit *Tern's* bows with a smack, and burst into fragments.

" Heave ! " called the Bosun. They hove. *Tern's* keel crunched for another moment on the gravelly bottom. Then she slid away from the children's hands. The Bosun hauled her in to the jetty. She was afloat.

" Hooray ! " said Antony. " Jolly good ! "

Robin still said nothing ; his eyes were fixed on *Tern* ; he stared and stared—with the water lapping up round the bottom of his shorts. Elizabeth, Antony and Anne splashed ashore.

" Come on, Robin," said Antony. " I'm going aboard."

For another minute Robin did not move. Then he glanced down at his shorts, waded ashore, and hopped up on the jetty.

The Bosun had made *Tern* fast alongside.

" She'll want a lot of ballast," he said. " Three or four hundredweight, I expect."

An obscure small shadow passed from Robin's mind when the Bosun said this. *Tern* wanted ballast—lots of it. *That* was why she looked so queer. Robin had not really admitted to himself, when first she took the water, that something had seemed wrong. But it had—*Tern* did not look as he had so often dreamed that she would look. She looked queer—and a bit ungainly. But now it was all right. He had never thought of ballast—of course she wanted ballast. She would look right then ; she would be as beautiful as he had always known. She would be like *Spray*—like Captain Slocum's *Spray*. What was it that Mr. Rutherford had said ? *Like a swan :* that was it. *She sat on the water like a swan.* That is what *Tern* would do—when she had got her ballast.

All the men from the yard were on the foreshore,

watching the launch. None of the children had seen them come: they had been too busy. The man in the grey sweater came along the jetty, and stood looking down into *Tern*. The Bosun was by him, relighting his pipe.

"She'll want four hundredweight," he said.

The man in the grey sweater nodded. "We've plenty of scrap we can let you have," he said.

"Good," said the Bosun. "And now there'll be plenty of work for all hands," he added.

Robin had wanted at first to finish bending on the mainsail; but now it was clearly more important to get the ballast on board. For the next hour and a half all hands were busy. They brought from the yard a great quantity of old iron—some of it lumps, some of it bars, some of it just bits—all of it of different shapes and sizes, and all of it covered with red rust; and as each piece was brought, it was carefully stowed in *Tern's* bilge, under the floorboards. There was one immense pig, shaped like a tin-loaf, which only the Bosun could carry. He brought it, and with extreme caution lowered it in, and stowed it aft, under the after seat.

"Why is there all this *water* in her?" said Anne after they had been stowing ballast for an hour. Actually, all the children had been a little uncomfortable about it—for it was quite obvious that water was coming in; but none of them had liked to mention it before. After all, it would be pretty awful if *Tern* leaked. . . . The trouble was, she evidently did leak. Fortunately, however, this trouble too (like Robin's other one) was short lived. For when Anne, speaking the thought of the three others, asked why it was that *Tern* was gradually filling up with water, the Bosun was in no way perturbed. He merely laughed.

"Don't worry," he said. "She'll soon take up.

A boat always leaks when she's put into the water. You ought to know that from *Tessa's* dinghy. She'll probably fill right up to-night; then we'll bail her out to-morrow and she'll be as tight as a drum."

They finished stowing the ballast; it made a wonderful difference to *Tern's* appearance, and Robin was satisfied; then Robin and Antony went on with the mainsail. They still had to work with their shoes off, because of the water which was slopping about in *Tern's* bottom. Robin and Antony still hoped that it might be possible, when they had finished, to take her out into the creek for a sail: just a short one. But the Bosun said No: she must be allowed to take up first—she must be allowed to leak as much as she liked, so that the planks could swell properly. They would have to wait for the trial trip until to-morrow.

"And then Mummy and Daddy can come too," said Elizabeth. Robin nodded. The Bosun was right (of course he was); but so was Elizabeth. It was only fair that Mr. and Mrs. Rutherford should be with them for the trial trip.

It was half-past six before they left her: in no job does time go so quickly as in that of fitting out a boat. Tea-time had slipped by unnoticed; and it was only when the children were putting on their shoes again that they realized they were hungry. It was a good thing, therefore, that the Bosun had hidden two of the paper bags in a neighbouring dinghy, to provide for this very emergency. They ate what was inside with the contentment of a job well done. Then they made ready to go home.

Again and again, as they crunched over the shingle, they stopped to look back. Yes—there she was—there was *Tern*, afloat at last, tied up to the jetty. To-morrow they would sail.

"Come on, Robin," said Antony. But Robin kept lingering for one more look.

"Yes," he thought to himself, "she's all right now. She's like *Spray*—sitting on the water like a swan."

CHAPTER XVII

On the next morning, at eleven o'clock, the whole family was assembled at the yard. Anne had telephoned to Mrs. Rutherford the previous night after they had got home (Anne liked telephoning ; Elizabeth loathed it—all her *sang-froid* deserted her as soon as she picked up the receiver, and she was so much afraid of not hearing what the other person said that in point of fact she never did hear), and had told her to come direct to Wootton as early as possible. Mr. and Mrs. Rutherford had accordingly started at the crack of dawn—Mr. Rutherford having obtained leave of absence on extremely urgent private affairs—driven to Southampton, where they left the car in a garage, and caught the first steamer to Cowes. From Cowes to Wootton is only a short ride in a bus.

Anne and Elizabeth met the bus at the end of the lane, where it joins the main road to Ryde, and helped to carry the luggage back to the yard. There was a good deal of luggage, because Mrs. Rutherford had taken the precaution of bringing a lot of extra sweaters and other woolly objects for the children to wear, in case it was cold. It was, after all, still early in May, and sailing in May can be very chilly indeed. She had taken the further precaution—a much better one, Elizabeth thought—of buying a lot of extra provisions in Cowes, in case they were hungry. You can't have too many provisions—in May or at any other time.

When they arrived at the yard, Antony, Robin and the Bosun were already on board, bailing the water out and putting the finishing touches to *Tern's* gear.

"To think," said Mr. Rutherford when the greetings were over, and he stood on the jetty looking down into the little ship, "to think that at this very moment I ought to be teaching Greek to a lot of scrubby boys who don't know one end of a boat from another."

"And to think that I," said Mrs. Rutherford, "should be *pitying* him for it."

"Do you like her?" said Anne.

"Rather!" said Mr. Rutherford. "She looks first rate."

"We worked jolly hard."

"I can see you did. Well done!"

It was a happy moment for all of them. They were lucky indeed—it was a fine morning, the wind was northerly. *Tern* was afloat and ready, and they were all together again. It was an ill mump (as the Bosun remarked) which blew out nobody's neck to good purpose.

To get out every drop of water, Robin finished the bailing with a sponge. When *Tern* was dry, the Bosun examined the seams, especially the garboards, and the joints of the centreboard case. He looked up at Mr. Rutherford with a satisfied nod.

"She's taken up beautifully," he said. "She's not leaking a drop."

Then they put back the floorboards and stowed the

luggage and the food under the deck in the forepeak. The deck extended for about a third of *Tern's* length ; except for a narrow side-deck, six inches wide, the rest of her was open ; but the space under the foredeck made a sort of fo'c'sle, big enough for two children to sit upright in (one on each side of the mast), or to lie at full length under cover. It was very useful for stowing things in. If there was nothing much to stow, it was also useful as a cabin provided that you were not too big. It wasn't much good for the Bosun ; he could insert only about half of himself into it at a time. It also contained the anchor and warp.

When everything was tidily stowed (it is important to start tidy when you are sailing ; if you don't, the frazzle gets steadily worse), Mr. Rutherford hauled *Tern* to the outward end of the jetty and made her fast with a slip-line round one of the posts. Then he joined the others who were already on board. *Tern* was lying head to wind. Robin made fast the tack of the jib to the stemhead, fixed the cliphooks to the stay, and bent on the halyard. Antony set the mainsail. The Bosun was at the tiller. Mrs. Rutherford, Anne and Elizabeth were for the moment occupied in saving their heads from the boom, which flicked to and fro above them, inconveniently near.

" All ready ? " said Mr. Rutherford.

" All ready," said the Bosun.

Mr. Rutherford canted *Tern's* head from the jetty. The mainsail filled on the starboard tack. The slipline was let go, and they were off.

Once clear of the jetty, Mrs. Rutherford lowered the centreboard. The Bosun put *Tern* on the other tack, so that she headed down the river towards the bend.

" Look," said Antony, " there's the man—grey sweater —on the jetty. He's come to see us off." He waved, and Robin waved. The man raised his arm in reply.

"Let's have the jib, Robin," said the Bosun. Robin hauled on the halyard. The little red sail ran quickly up the stay with a light rattle of cliphooks. Elizabeth made fast the sheet to the cleat. *Tern* bowed to a puff which came, darkening the surface of the creek, from a gap in the trees; the water rustled under her forefoot. They were off indeed.

The puff died, and they were almost becalmed; but the ebb soon took them round the point and within sight of the line of moored fishing boats. Here the northerly wind blew straight in, unchecked by the baffling trees on the shore, and *Tern* was sailing again. In short tacks with the tide under them they beat out past the wooden dolphins which mark the channel, and in half an hour from the time when they left the jetty *Tern* was in the Solent. Here they could lay their course for Cowes—and the west.

The boys were alive to *Tern's* every movement, watching how she behaved, speculating on what she would do, proud of her qualities already revealed.

"Isn't she stiff?" said Robin.

"There's a lovely lot of room," said Elizabeth.

"She's like a fishing boat, but better," said Antony.

"She'd be grand in a strong wind," said Robin.

"I wish there was more now," said Anne.

The Bosun was still at the tiller. He grinned contentedly, an eye cocked at the masthead.

"Good to be at sea again?" he asked.

There was no need for an answer. It is always good to be at sea again. It had been (in the Bosun's words) "a long time till Easter"; indeed, it had been longer than ever this year. But they were at sea now—and they were at sea in *Tern*, the vessel they had built with their own hands. And *Tern* was good: there was no doubt about that. She was all they had hoped, all they had dreamed.

With the wind just forward of the beam—sailing full and by—*Tern* was reaching down the Solent towards the west. The sun was on the water, there was haze on the distant shore beyond Beaulieu, the sails were asleep, and under *Tern's* forefoot the bow wave chuckled.

"Who would be a schoolmaster?" murmured the Bosun.

"John's not one, either," said Mrs. Rutherford. "Not to-day."

Robin was lying flat on his stomach on the foredeck, looking down at the bow wave. "My stem", he thought to himself. "Elizabeth's and mine." How long ago it seemed, that day at Rocken End! He remembered for a moment that terrible sea, and with the memory there passed through him the little quick thrill of fear which always—mysteriously—made a part of his delight in sailing, and which he had never confessed to anyone, not even to Elizabeth.

"Who wants to take her?" said the Bosun.

"Me," said Mrs. Rutherford.

She changed places with the Bosun; and after that they all took their turn at the helm—to try her. Robin was last; lying on the foredeck, watching the bow wave, rapt and content, he didn't seem to want to move. It was only when Antony called him that he really noticed the changes of helmsman.

"Come on, Robin," Antony said. "Come and take her."

"M-me?" said Robin. Then he got up and skipped quickly aft to the tiller, and sat there solemn and without speaking, taking his trick.

While Robin was steering Elizabeth rummaged amongst the bundles in the forepeak and found lunch. Lunch was good, because not only had Mrs. Rutherford taken precautions in Cowes, but the Bosun had also taken precautions in Newport. So there was even more than usual to eat. Elizabeth did her best not to make crumbs in the bilge, but not to make crumbs with sausage rolls is difficult. She found it much easier with the bananas.

The Solent grew gay with craft as *Tern* approached Cowes. It was still early in the season, but it was Saturday, and a company of small yachts, and a few big ones too, were out for their week-end airing. A liner was anchored in the roads. Away to their right an old tramp steamer with a black smoke trail was ploughing her way up the Thorn channel to Southampton Water. A small smack with her trawl out lay just ahead, in Osborne Bay ; they passed close to her, and the single fisherman aboard signalled a greeting and looked hard at *Tern*. A few minutes later, on the last of the ebb, they were off the town.

"Well," said Mr. Rutherford, "what about it? The boat seems all right, so . . ."

"Daddy!" interrupted Anne. "*All right*. I should think she is!"

Mr. Rutherford laughed. "I didn't mean she wasn't," he said. "But this is a trial trip. We've not made any plans really."

"Let's go on," said Antony. Everybody supported him. Indeed, it would have been absurd to do anything else. They decided, therefore, to make for Yarmouth, where they would leave *Tern* for the night, and then see if to-morrow was a suitable day for continuing the voyage to Poole.

The trial trip had now turned into a cruise. The difference (Robin said) between a sail and a cruise is that in a sail you come back on the same day to where you started from, but in a cruise you end up somewhere else. Cruising is better than sailing.

The general opinion was that there were enough provisions on board for one more meal. It would not exactly be tea, because there would be no tea to drink. It was impossible to boil a kettle in *Tern*, except on a calm day in harbour, even if there was a stove on board ; and at present there wasn't a stove—and the northerly wind was blowing pretty fresh. But it would be a meal ; and there were still (owing to the double precautions) several bottles of peculiar fizzy drinks. The ebb was now finished ; the flood would soon be making against them, but once they were round Egypt Point, with a good breeze on the quarter they ought to be at Yarmouth in four hours or so.

Antony relieved Robin at the tiller. It was not as warm as it had been, and Robin thought he might as well put on an extra sweater.

"They're up in the bows," said Mrs. Rutherford, "under the deck."

"In the fo'c'sle," said Elizabeth.

Fo'c'sle was the right name. Robin privately decided that it should always be called the fo'c'sle. You must have a fo'c'sle when you're cruising : they were cruising now—and they would be cruising much more in the summer holidays, when they explored Poole harbour. Robin did not know Poole harbour yet ; but he had seen a chart of it. It was full of Islands.

He crawled into the fo'c'sle and put on his sweater. Anne and Elizabeth wanted theirs too, so he passed them out. Then he stayed in the fo'c'sle a bit.

Robin had always liked to tuck himself away in odd corners of boats. The work of a ship he loved—the work of getting under way, of bringing up, sounding, or trimming the sails, or steering : all those things, of course were lovely ; but he also liked, when the vessel was sailing, to hide himself away in this part of her or that, and do nothing at all. Often in *Ianthe*, on a day when the sun was shining and there was a perfect sailing breeze, he would creep below into the sail-room aft, and curl up amongst the sailbags like a dormouse in its nest, and lie shere for an hour or more. Mrs. Chale would ask him tometimes how he could bear to miss everything that was going on outside, and Robin would find it difficult to answer. All he knew was that he didn't *feel* that he was missing anything at all : on the contrary, there was something there, in his nest amongst the sailbags, when *Ianthe* was under way, that he could not have found anywhere else.

One side of the fo'c'sle was pretty well filled up with luggage ; but there was room for Robin on the other. He found that if he crawled right in as far as he could go, so that his head was almost touching the stem, he could just stretch his legs out straight and still be all under cover. It was better if he curled up a little. The anchor warp was awkward ; but he managed to push it more or less out of the way up against *Tern's* side.

He lay still. It was warm and snug and separate. The others, out in the well, looked a long way off. The deck beams were close above his head. He listened to the gurgle and talking of the water as *Tern* slid over the gentle seas. He could hear the creak of the shrouds as she rolled.

Elizabeth, who had been sitting next to Antony as he held the tiller, clambered over the centre thwart, and came forward. She squatted down by Robin's toes.

"Hullo," she said.

Robin propped himself up on his elbow, and looked at her with round solemn eyes.

"It's nice in the fo'c'sle," he said.

He drew up his legs to make more room. Elizabeth squeezed a little farther in.

" *Tern*'s marvellous," she said.

Robin could just see Antony's head past Elizabeth's shoulder. He was looking at something with evident interest, and talking to Mr. Rutherford, and pointing. Presently he called out.

" Robin," he shouted. " Come and see."

Elizabeth and Robin scrambled into the well.

" What is it ? " said Elizabeth. But Robin had already seen. Fine on the weather bow a great racing yacht was coming towards them. She was quite near, and would pass them very close indeed. Robin watched her. She had a bone in her mouth. She looked immensely tall as she came swiftly nearer, her sails a sloping spire, flushed faintly golden against the sun. Her crew lay along her decks. She swept by, and as she passed, *Tern's* boom swung in with a jerk and she was left an instant helplessly rolling and becalmed.

" I say," said Robin, when she was gone, " we've come a jolly long way, haven't we ? "

" Look," said the Bosun. " Newtown River's just in there." He pointed away under the lee.

" That's where we started from in *Tessa*," said Anne, " two years ago—when we went to France."

" We'd never seen you then," said Elizabeth. It seemed queer, somehow, that there was a time when they hadn't known Antony and Robin.

" You're lucky," said Antony. " You must have had a marvellous time. I wish *we* could have come."

Tern sailed on. With the fine steady breeze on her quarter she made perhaps about two knots over the tide. Yarmouth pier, with the cluster of masts beyond it, had been clear in sight for a couple of hours, but only very slowly did it seem to get any nearer. But getting nearer it was. They were passing the Solent Banks now, and away over to the right they could see the ferry steamer coming out of Lymington river, by Jack-in-the-Basket.

They were hungry again, and had their meal. It was almost exactly the same as lunch, but none the worse for that. All food is delicious when one is sailing.

At last they were off the pier. Mr. Rutherford was steering.

"Who remembers the way into the harbour?" he said.

"I do—I think," said Anne.

"I've seen it on the chart," said Antony.

"Leading marks in line," said Anne.

Mr. Rutherford nodded.

"You take her in," he said.

Anne took the tiller. Entering port is always fun; and in *Tern* it was much easier than in *Tessa*, because *Tern* drew so little water, and it didn't matter if you failed to keep the leading marks quite exactly in line. Besides, if you *did* run aground, you could pull the centreboard up and get off again. You could—but, of course, it was better and more dignified to keep afloat.

Anne got *Tern* in without mishap. The harbour-master was at the end of the quay, as he always is when a vessel is entering. *Tern* was too small to need to be directed to a berth, but no doubt the harbour-master was interested, and wondered who she was. They sailed round the breakwater: there on their left was the life-boat, gay in blue and red paint, at her habitual station; and along the edge of the mud a line of yachts were moored, sometimes two deep, between the buoys. *Tern* slipped quickly past them, bore away round the bend, and brought to by the wooden steps at the bridge.

The first voyage was over, and *Tern* was in port again: a different port—because she was cruising. Her sails were stowed, and she lay quietly. The warm red bricks of the little town and the old stone quay welcomed her in. Mrs. Rutherford was happy—Yarmouth was her favourite harbour. Indeed, they were all happy, and any harbour would have been good ; but Yarmouth was especially good. Of all the Solent harbours it is the most delightful, and (what makes it better still) it stands at the very gateway to the Channel seas beyond. In the inland waters amongst the quiet marshes of Newtown, or opposite the green gateway of Brooklands Farm at Bursledon, adventures should end, but at Yarmouth they should begin.

CHAPTER XVIII

THERE is not much to tell about the further voyage to Poole. The whole party spent the night at an hotel in Yarmouth, because it would have taken too much time (without the car) to go back to the cottage, and they wanted, if the weather was suitable, to make an early start on the following morning. Robin wanted to sleep in *Tern* : it seemed waste to go ashore, and even though there were no blankets on board, there were plenty of sweaters and things which, he thought, would be quite enough to keep him warm. He could sleep in the fo'c'sle. The Bosun, however, succeeded in dissuading him ; and this was a good thing, for the nights in early May are chilly, and it would have been a stiff, weary and frozen Robin who faced the long voyage to Poole on the morrow. But to sleep in an inn (a Yarmouth inn, within a stone's throw of the harbour) was a good second best.

"We can get up early," said Elizabeth, "and come and see *Tern* before breakfast."

Robin nodded.

"All the same," he said, "I would l-like to sleep on board."

Every sailor knows that it is silly to make a passage against the tide unless it is absolutely unavoidable to do so. In the present case it would have been more than silly; for the tide in the narrow entrance to the Solent by Hurst Castle runs so swiftly that it would hardly have been possible for a small boat like *Tern* to make headway against it. It was therefore important to get under way at the top of high water, just as the tide was beginning to set towards the west: thus they would have it with them throughout their passage.

The tide was due to turn at half-past nine. By half-past eight the ship's company, after an early breakfast, was assembled on board. It was a grey morning. The wind had gone round into the north-east, and was much stronger than it had been yesterday. Indeed, when Mr. Rutherford first woke up and heard the sound of it amongst the chimney-pots, he was afraid that their voyage might have to be postponed. *Tern* was not *Tessa*, and outside the shelter of the Solent one cannot take risks with an open boat. But a glance out of the window of his bedroom was enough to reassure him.

"It's all right, Janet," he said; "it's north-east. The very wind we want. We shall have smooth water all the way."

The clock on the church tower pointed to just after nine when they cast off their ropes. A few minutes later *Tern* was in the Solent. The Bosun was at the helm; he kept her headed for Hurst Light. Elizabeth, crouched on the floor by the centreboard case, was watching the sea—it was not at all like what it had been yesterday. Always, indeed, even in the calmest weather, the sea west of Yarmouth suffers a change; it assumes an urgency and power which it had not before. To-day it was tur bulent. The last drains of the flood tide were still coming in, and the brisk north-easter blew against it. Swift, steep waves hurried *Tern* along on their crests, and sucked her down into the hollows between. To the left, the Shingles bank was white with a line of foam.

Gay with her thoughts Elizabeth hummed a tune. Robin, his arms round his knees, was sitting just outside the fo'c'sle, on the floorboards, with his back against *Tern's* side. Had anyone spoken to him, he would not have heard. From where he sat, low in the boat, the waves seemed to tower above the stern for one threatening moment before she lifted, and they passed underneath. Sometimes his heart was in his mouth, and his little imp of fear chuckled inside him. But he did battle with it and was happy.

Antony was at the Bosun's side, serene and merry.

"Gosh," he said, "isn't it fine!"

Mrs. Rutherford could not but wonder what the sea would be like when they were outside—really in the open. She looked at Mr. Rutherford.

"Smooth water all the way, John?" she said.

Mr. Rutherford laughed.

"Almost," he said. "Once we're round Hurst Point, it will be calm as a millpond. You'll see."

Mr. Rutherford was right. *Tern* passed close—within a few yards—of the shingly bank at Hurst, and quite suddenly all the waves were gone. It was like sailing into another sea. The Narrows were behind, and *Tern* was under the weather shore. In smooth water, with the tide now turned in her favour, she was sailing steadily and swiftly for Hengistbury Head, six miles away.

The rest of the voyage was uneventful. It was easy and delightful sailing. The wind blew strong and fair, and three and a half hours after she had passed Hurst Point, *Tern* was at the entrance to Poole Harbour.

They went in through the passage which the fishermen use, at the north end of the bar ; thence they worked their way past the chain ferry and Sandbanks to the creek, populous with small craft, which runs to the eastward opposite the South Deep and Brownsea. Here at a wooden jetty they disembarked.

And now the time had come for the party to break up. Not even mumps could postpone it again. The Bosun remained at Sandbanks till the following day ; then he put *Tern* in charge of the yard until the holidays should come again. He had to wait till to-morrow, because to-day was Sunday. Mrs. Rutherford and the four children, by a complex collaboration of bus, train and steamer, found their way back to the cottage in the Isle of Wight, where they collected their luggage before going their several ways to school. Mr. Rutherford returned disconsolately to school by himself, his leave expired, to be left, until Janet could join him, to the care of Emily, Sally, and the steamed puddings.

Just before they said good-bye, a look half anxious half hopeful came into the Bosun's eye. He put one large finger behind each of Elizabeth's ears.

" Elizabeth," he whispered, " *do* you feel a bulge . . . even a *little* bulge . . . ? "

But alas ! Elizabeth didn't. None of them did. The days of quarantine were over, not to be prolonged.

Good-byes were said. Lucky Bosun, thought Robin envying him his one more day with *Tern*. Soon he would be in the train ; and travelling in a train is a dreary thing after sailing in a boat.

As they walked up the foreshore, they stopped for a last look at *Tern*. Yes, she was a good boat ; she was staunch and strong—better than they had dared to hope They walked on, except Robin who lingered last.

" Come on, Robin," said Antony.

Robin ran to catch them up. "I say," he said, "that boat out there, what is she? Is she a snipe?"

Mrs. Rutherford looked where Robin pointed.

"Yes," he said; "I believe she is."

"L-like Arthur's," said Robin.

They watched her for a moment. Then, "Gosh," said Antony, "she looks jolly fast. Do you think *Tern* could beat her?"

Mr. Rutherford hesitated. "They're built for racing, you know," he said, "but in anything of a breeze, give me *Tern*. She's more of a boat."

"I'm sure we *could* beat her," said Elizabeth.

Antony and Robin said nothing. They both hoped that *Tern* could beat her, especially Antony; but Robin was thinking of what Mr. Rutherford had said last: *She's more of a boat.* It was a satisfying phrase—and it was true. Next holidays they would make Arthur, too, see that it was true.

CHAPTER XIX

ANNE was standing on *Tessa's* deck, one arm round the shrouds, looking out over the water towards the entrance to the harbour. The smell of cooking was coming up through the fo'c'sle hatch. Suddenly she stamped with her foot on the deck and called out excitedly.

" Mummy, Daddy, Bittle ! " she exclaimed. " There she is. She's coming ! I can see her ! "

Elizabeth tumbled up the companion ladder, and looked to where Anne was pointing.

" There's someone on the cross trees," she said. " It's Robin—it must be."

Mr. and Mrs. Rutherford followed. All looked at the white ketch which was coming in.

" It's *Ianthe* all right," said Mr. Rutherford.

" There's somebody up aloft," said Mrs. Rutherford. " Look." She pointed with the spoon she had been cooking with.

" Robin," said Elizabeth. " It would be Robin."

The white ketch came about, and not many minutes

afterwards she was lying at anchor only a hundred yards away.

. . . .

It was the second week in August. Since the Bosun was left with *Tern* after her first voyage, a great deal (I suppose) had happened, but nothing (I am sure) which was interesting enough to record. For everybody, except the Bosun, had been at school. I don't know where the Bosun had been.

During the course of the term Mrs. Rutherford had had a long and complicated correspondence with Mrs. Chale about their plans for the summer holidays. Obviously it was necessary that the four children should spend at any rate a part of the holidays together; for it is no good building a boat if you don't get an opportunity of sailing in her. On the other hand, nobody wants to be away from home for the greater part of three holidays in succession, and Antony and Robin had already spent most of the Christmas and almost all of the Easter holidays (not to mention the joyful days of quarantine) in the Isle of Wight. Nor was it possible to get *Tern* to Creeksea, where the Chales lived: the voyage would have been much too long and much too hazardous. Fortunately, however, Mr. and Mrs. Chale would have felt that the summer holidays were wasted without a cruise in *Ianthe*, just as Mr. and Mrs. Rutherford, and the Bosun, would have felt that they were wasted without one in *Tessa*. It was agreed, therefore, that *Ianthe* and *Tessa* should both make their headquarters for the last three weeks of August in Poole harbour. Antony and Robin would enjoy the trip in *Ianthe* from the East Coast, and once at Poole the two families, the two yachts and *Tern* would all be together. There would be nothing to prevent either *Tessa* or *Ianthe* from cruising farther along the coast from time to time if they wished to do so; for the four children after their experiences in the Roach river the previous summer, when they had recovered the treasure of Ishmael Hawse, were already hardened mariners, and with *Tern* herself, and a couple of tents in case of inclement weather, would be quite able to look after themselves.

Tessa had left Newtown river four days ago. The family was all eager to be off, and had remained at the cottage only until the gooseberries were finished and the earliest apples ripe. The other apples (and the figs) would be ready when they returned for the last three weeks of the holidays.

Tessa now lay in the South Deep, under Brownsea Island. *Ianthe* was moored to one of the harbour buoys just below her, within comfortable hailing distance *Tern* was lying to her own anchor abreast of *Tessa*, bu farther inshore, on the edge of the channel—you coul get to her in the dinghy with half a dozen strokes of th oars.

. . . .

When *Ianthe* arrived, Anne and Elizabeth at onc went off to her in the dinghy. This time there was n trouble about hats, and after a brief moment of mutu inspection, the children forgot the intervening montl and felt that they had never been separated at all. was just possible, however, that Antony was not qui the same as he had been; Elizabeth wondered for moment, but Anne (when Elizabeth mentioned it afte wards) indignantly denied that there was any differenc It may have been merely because he was wearing a ve clean pair of new white canvas shoes.

The Rutherford family was invited to supper on boa *Ianthe*. The Bosun was a little anxious about th because of his trousers. He was afraid they wouldn't tone in with *Ianthe's* cabin as well as they did with *Tessa's*.

"What are Mr. Chale's like?" he asked.

"White," said Elizabeth.

"Help," said the Bosun.

Mrs. Rutherford rummaged in a locker and took out another pair, which she gingerly tendered to him.

"I think these are a little better," she said, shaking them dubiously out.

"What about our own stew?" said Mr. Rutherford, looking at the pot which Mrs. Rutherford had been stirring.

"It will do for lunch to-morrow," said Mrs. Rutherford.

It was an agreeable supper party, though somewhat demure. *Ianthe's* cabin was not like *Tessa's*; it had a virginal look, different from the workaday homeliness to which Anne and Elizabeth were accustomed. And it felt odd to have the dishes brought in by the fo'c'sle hand and set with a sort of manly deference (unlike Emily's) on the cabin table, instead of arguing amongst themselves about whose turn it was to do it next. Evidently it wouldn't do to have an accident with one's chop in *Ianthe*. Not that it did very well in *Tessa* either; but one got over it sooner.

Anne and Elizabeth had seen Mrs. Chale quite often last year at Creeksea; she had usually been occupied in the garden, carrying a basket and cutting off deads with a pair of scissors. They had never imagined her in a boat; but she made it clear during the course of the meal that she was almost happier on *Ianthe* than in her garden, and that she knew nearly as much about sailing as Mrs. Rutherford did.

Mr. Chale they had met very seldom; he was usually in London—"Worse luck," as Robin said. He was older than Mr. Rutherford, and Elizabeth began by being very shy of him and not knowing what to say. But he had kind eyes and a soft slow voice, and when the fruit came at the end of supper, he carefully selected the ripest fig and put it on Elizabeth's plate—" just to show " (as he said) " that there's no ill feeling." After that Elizabeth felt better.

The next day Antony and Robin rowed over to *Tessa* after breakfast. They were to take *Tern*, with Anne and Elizabeth, to Sandbanks to fetch provisions. *Tern* had already proved useful for this purpose during the past few days since *Tessa's* arrival. The South Deep is a delightful anchorage, but its one disadvantage is that it is a very long way from the grocer. In order to provision your ship you have to row a couple of miles in the dinghy, and as the way lies across the main channel of the harbour, you have to contend with a strong tide and also, if there happens to be a breeze, with a disconcertingly choppy sea. This is exhausting. *Tern*, however, made the expedition both easier and more amusing ; for instead of rowing, you could sail.

The four children went aboard and were soon under way (with the shopping list) for Sandbanks. It was the first time they had been in *Tern* by themselves. As they passed *Ianthe*, Alf (the deck-hand who had brought in the chops the previous evening) was polishing the brass rods on the skylights. He grinned broadly.

" Now you're off, Mr. Antony," he said.

With the westerly breeze behind them it did not take long to reach the creek—the same creek where they had left *Tern* after her maiden voyage. Antony steered her through the crowd of small craft which lay moored there, and made for the jetty. Robin stood by the halyards. At a word from Antony he lowered away. The mainsail was stowed, and Tern slid up alongside the jetty. They hardly bumped at all.

"Not bad," said Antony, pleased with their seamanship in a boat which was still strange. It would have been a pity to bungle it, for there were a lot of people watching.

They went ashore with the shopping list and a sailbag. They did not go immediately to the streets, because it is almost impossible to pass a shipyard without lingering. Moreover there was plenty of time. As they stood on the foreshore in front of the yard, there was a broad sweep of gravelly sand on their left, now dry, but covered at high water. A dinghy or two and a couple of small sailing boats were lying on it. Children in bathing dresses, or with shorts tucked high up their thighs, were running about the sand, or paddling or bathing in the creek. A brown retriever, his coat matted with wet, was barking spasmodically at the water's edge. Behind them the yard hands were moving leisurely about the sheds.

One of the sailing boats lying on the sand was painted a vivid orange. Elizabeth was staring at her. It was not only her unusual colour which attracted her attention, but a certain hubbub of which she seemed to be the centre. A tall youth stood close by her side; he had evidently been bailing her out, because he still held the bailer in his hand; but he was not bailing now—he was haranguing half a dozen boys, mostly small and all of ather ragged appearance, who were standing in a emicircle around him.

Elizabeth nudged Anne. "Look," she said. Anne ooked. The tall youth was still haranguing, and gesticu- ating with his bailer. They couldn't hear what he aid because he was too far off. He was obviously nnoyed. One of the small boys kicked at a puddle nd splashed the water at him. Then he turned and an off with a derisive laugh, his companions following.

The tall boy shouted something after them. Then he threw his bailer into the boat and began to walk towards the yard. He was coming straight to where the children were standing. As he got nearer, Robin's heart sank. The gait was familiar.

"Come on," he muttered. "L-let's go."

"Good Lord," said Antony. "It's Arthur."

It was too late to go now, for Arthur had recognized them. He quickened his pace.

"Hullo," he called, "how's life?"

"Those infernal kids," he went on after he had said how do you do to Antony and Anne, and nodded to Elizabeth and Robin; "I told them I'd report them to the police."

"Why? What have they been doing?" said Antony.

"Mucking about with the *Whynot*. They're always doing it. But I put the wind up them this time," he ended with a satisfied air.

Anne thought privately that the infernal kids had not been so very frightened, despite Arthur's belief that they had. But she said nothing.

"Where are you staying?" said Arthur.

Antony pointed over to the South Deep. "On *Ianthe* and *Tessa*," he said. "We've just come across in *Tern*."

"*Tern*?" said Arthur. "What, the old tub? Where is she? Let's have a look at her."

He strolled down to the end of the jetty with Antony and Anne. Elizabeth and Robin hung back behind them. Arthur surveyed *Tern* with a professional eye.

"Well, well," he said. "You've made quite a decent job of her, haven't you? Is she tight? I expect she leaks round the centreboard case, doesn't she?"

"No," said Antony; "she doesn't leak at all."

(This was true in fact, if not strictly true in intention

for *Tern had* leaked round the centreboard case after the first cruise. The defect had been remedied by the yard during term-time.)

Robin saw that Arthur's pale eye was dwelling on the transom, and inwardly writhed.

"Not a bad job at all," said Arthur. "How does she sail? A bit slow to windward, I should say, with that heavy stern."

One of the sickening things about Arthur was that he was so often right. Right in a way, that is. In another way, of course, he was utterly wrong. *Tern was* a little slow to windward—though none of her crew would have dreamed of admitting it just then. But who cared, anyway? *Tern* was never meant to be a racing machine. And with the wind a point free she wasn't slow at all—in fact she was jolly fast. And she was as stiff as a church.

"I must be getting along," said Arthur. "We're taking *Zephyr* out this afternoon—our fifty-fifty, you know. But I'll be seeing you. How long are you staying?"

"About three weeks," said Anne.

"That's fine," said Arthur; "we must have some races. I'm pretty well fixed up at week-ends with the class races. But we'll find a day. I'll give you a quarter of an hour handicap on the course."

"We'll sail level," said Antony.

Arthur grinned. "Oh come," he said; "that'd hardly be fair, would it?" He put his hands in his pockets and strolled off up the foreshore. Presently he stopped.

"Have a look at the *Whynot*," he said. "You'll like her. Oh, and by the way, if you leave your boat ashore, look out for those blasted kids. They'll pinch anything they can. I warn you."

Then he disappeared round the back of the sheds.

After waiting long enough to give Arthur a good start, the four children took their sailbag and went to the street where the shops were. To come suddenly from boats to pavements, trams and buses always gives an odd feeling ; but it is quite a pleasant one, provided you know that in a few minutes you are going back to boats. For one thing, it is not only groceries that you can buy : you can also buy chocolate and ices. In fact, this was the first thing they did. They went into a café and ate their ices sitting round a glass-topped table. They hesitated a moment before going in, because it occurred to them that Arthur might have gone in too. It is always tiresome to meet somebody you have just said good-bye to ; but it is more tiresome still when it is Arthur. Elizabeth, however, after a cautious and comprehensive look through the window, pronounced that the coast was clear.

" He's an awful ass," said Antony, as he scraped up the last liquescent spoonful of his ice. He was still smarting under Arthur's offer of a handicap. " I bet we can beat him if only we have a good breeze."

Robin still had half his ice left. He took a very small shaving of it off the edge. " W-why do you know him so well ? " he asked.

" Why not ? " said Antony casually. " I suppose they can't help it."

Elizabeth began to giggle. She caught Anne's eye. Anne, who was also irritated by their late encounter with Arthur, looked at her with an elder-sisterly manner and asked her what the matter was. Elizabeth still giggled, and glanced at Robin.

" *Why-not*," she murmured. " That's the name of his boat. It's such a silly name."

" We've known him for ages," said Anne.

"He comes here for the *yachting*," she added with a grimace. Antony snorted.

As a matter of fact, they all knew that Arthur would be in Poole this summer—and had, as they remembered, already challenged them to a race (with a handicap) long ago, before *Tern* was finished. But it was annoying to find him all the same.

"Mummy knows his mother," said Anne, as if to excuse their acquaintance with him.

"Mummy loathes her," said Elizabeth.

"She doesn't loathe her," said Anne. "She . . ." Then she stopped, caught Elizabeth's eye again, and began to laugh. The exact nature of the relationship between the two families was difficult to explain. Mummy did know Arthur's mother; she had known her for years and years. But she didn't like her much. Actual contact was restricted to about one reluctant tea-party a year—apart from unavoidable meetings in the road. But still . . . she did know her. Apparently the acquaintanceship was one of those social obligations which seem so unnecessary, but somehow aren't. And that being the case, it was impossible for Anne and Elizabeth altogether to escape Arthur. And now it was equally impossible for Antony and Robin to escape him either. It was a pity, but so it was.

Robin minded most. Antony didn't mind so much—which was partly why Robin *did*. Antony knew Arthur was an ass; but it might be quite fun, he thought, having a few races with the *Whynot*, especially if they could get some windy days. *Tern* was obviously better in a breeze. And there was always the motor bicycle . . .

Anne and Elizabeth, however ghastly (that was Elizabeth's word) they knew Arthur to be, were nevertheless pretty well used to him. It would, indeed, have been nicer if he were not there—but he *was* there, and it didn't really matter. But Elizabeth was sorry for Robin ; for she knew Robin couldn't bear him.

They did their shopping and started back to the creek, taking turns with the sailbag. Luckily there were not many tins in it this time ; tins are not only heavy, but the edges are painful to the back when the sailbag bumps as you walk. When they were half-way there Anne remembered that they had forgotten the cheese.

" Come on, Antony," she said. " We'll go back and get it."

Elizabeth and Robin went on to the yard by themselves. Robin's eyes searched eagerly for *Tern* as soon as he got to the front of the sheds. There she was, at the end of the jetty—the best boat within sight.

" We'll go on board and eat our chocolate," said Elizabeth.

Standing on the jetty, looking down into *Tern*, was a little boy. He had on short trousers and braces and a whitish-grey singlet with a large round hole at the back. He looked at Elizabeth and Robin as they passed him with a wary and measuring glance.

Elizabeth and Robin went on board, settled themselves comfortably outside the fo'c'sle and unwrapped their chocolate. The little boy was still watching them. Elizabeth looked up—he was staring straight at her. Elizabeth gave a small smile, her mouth full of chocolate.

" Hullo," she said.

The little boy didn't answer. Elizabeth stood up.

" Have a bit," she said, and held out a square of chocolate. The little boy looked at it for a moment, took it with a quick movement, then turned and scampered off to join his accomplices farther along the beach.

Elizabeth chuckled to herself. She was used to small ragged boys (and girls), and this one, she thought, was a rather nice one. He was perky like a sparrow, and had a brown face which looked as if it could laugh a lot if it tried. He reminded her of the one she always left apples for outside the gate, on the stone wall, at the cottage. She could still see him, farther along on the foreshore, with others . . . probably they were the same who had recently got into trouble with Arthur.

Ten minutes later Antony and Anne arrived with the sailbag. They stowed it in the fo'c'sle, hoisted the mainsail and got under way.

It was not so easy to get out of the creek as it had been to get into it : for this time the wind was against them. The creek, moreover, was both narrow and crowded, and as they worked their way down it in short tacks they needed all their judgment and skill to avoid a collision. As they were going about on one of the in-shore tacks, Elizabeth saw the little boy again, on the beach. Two others were with him. They were on the edge of the water, scooping for something with empty tins. Elizabeth waved her hand. The little boy stopped scooping, and stared. He didn't wave back.

"Who was that? Who were you waving to?" said Anne.

"Oh, just a boy," said Elizabeth casually. "I gave him some chocolate while we were waiting. They're Arthur's boys, I think."

"Arthur's?"

"The ones he said he'd tell the police about."

"Oh—those," said Anne.

Pilotage was too tricky to let them think about the boys any more for the moment. They were fully occupied —Antony was once again at the tiller, and Robin and Anne were tending the jib sheets. Elizabeth, it is true, was not particularly busy. So she continued to think that the little boy, even if he did mess about with other people's boats, was nice—and that it was disgusting of Arthur to say he would report him to the police.

CHAPTER XX

It had taken them only ten minutes to sail to the yard. It took an hour to sail back. For one thing, they were beating to windward ; for another the tide was ebbing : this meant that though it was with them down the creek, it was sideways in the main channel, and against them up the South Deep. But it does not matter how long things take in boats—or if you think it does matter, you had better not sail at all.

As it was lunch-time Antony and Robin went straight back to *Ianthe*. They sailed *Tern* alongside. Robin was a little anxious about the propriety of doing this ; for they were not yet fully accustomed to *Tern*, and it is difficult to bring a boat any larger than a dinghy neatly alongside a yacht at anchor. There is more danger of bumping, and—*Tern* being heavy—less chance of fending off if you do bump. Moreover, *Ianthe* was not at all the sort of boat that one can bump with impunity. Not, indeed, that one can bump any boat with a happy conscience : to bump *Tessa* was highly reprehensible ;

but to bump *Ianthe* would be much worse. Alf would be deeply pained, and Mr. Chale would undoubtedly look down his nose, both of which things would be more disconcerting than the Bosun's cheerful abuse or Mr. Rutherford's well-drilled resignation. Alf, however, was ready for them ; he had been watching their approach for half an hour ; and with the help of some anxious and skilful work with the boathook, he enabled Antony to accomplish the manœuvre without disaster.

Anne and Elizabeth were then left to sail *Tern* the remaining hundred yards to her anchorage opposite *Tessa* by themselves. Anne had had plenty of practice last year in a dinghy, but a dinghy is not quite the same thing as Tern. She felt rather hot and flustered, and gave a great many orders to Elizabeth—some of which, with her usual insouciance, Elizabeth carried out. But in a voyage of a hundred yards on a fine day one cannot really come to grief, and they succeeded between them in getting *Tern* anchored more or less in the right place after a couple of tacks. The Bosun came off in the dinghy from *Tessa* and fetched them.

It wasn't quite lunch-time after all, because the potatoes were not done. There was, therefore, time for a bathe.

" Why not swim to *Ianthe* ? " said the Bosun.

" It's an awful long way," said Anne.

" Nonsense," said the Bosun. " You needn't swim at all—the tide will take you."

" What about getting back ? "

" Robin'll bring you back in the dinghy."

It was a good idea. Anne and Elizabeth got into their bathing-dresses. Anne climbed up on to the mizzen boom, and hailed.

" *Ianthe* ahoy ! " she shouted. The wind was behind her, so Robin soon heard.

"I'm going to swim to you," shouted Anne. "Will . . . you . . . row me back . . . in . . . the dinghy?"

Robin waved assent, and ran aft to get the dinghy ready. It was a new sort of bathe. Anne was a good swimmer. She dived in, and struck out towards *Ianthe*. It was surprising what a long way off *Tessa* looked after a few strokes. She stopped swimming and lay on her back, paddling gently with her hands. Still *Tessa* receded. How strong the tide was! Bittle could have done it easily. It was a pity she hadn't come too—but she preferred (as usual) to lower herself into the water by the steps, with Daddy waiting in the dinghy to fish her out.

In another minute Anne was there. *Ianthe*'s bows loomed above her. Anne swept past her smooth white sides—and there was Robin, waiting in the dinghy, under her stern. Anne caught hold of the dinghy's gunwale, but she couldn't get in. Robin tried to explain how she should do it—over the stern with a quick kick and a heave. But Anne couldn't; so Robin had to tow her, rowing mightily, to *Ianthe*'s gangway steps, which Alf put over the side. As they rowed back to *Tessa*, Anne could see Bittle standing on deck with a towel round her shoulders, drying.

Lunch is improved by a bathe. Anne and Elizabeth were both hungry. When they had got to the oranges and bananas, Mr. Rutherford asked them what they were going to do that afternoon.

"We haven't arranged," said Anne. "But I expect we shall sail."

"I shall sleep," said Mr. Rutherford.

"Oh, *Daddy*!" said Elizabeth.

"You might circumnavigate Brownsea," suggested the Bosun, "on the evening tide." He took down the chart, cleared a space amongst the orange and banana skins, and spread it out on the table. Elizabeth gave it a swift but casual glance.

"We saw Arthur," she said. "He was bailing his snipe. She's called *Whynot*."

"That was nice for you," said the Bosun.

"Robin loathes him more than ever," said Elizabeth.

"Who's going to clear the table?" said Mr. Rutherford. The Bosun looked across at him.

"I thought I'd done so already," he said, "for the chart." Anne and Mrs. Rutherford began to collect plates.

"But I'm *not* going to wash up," said Mrs. Rutherford.

"Certainly not," said the Bosun. "We shouldn't dream of letting you. Should we, Anne?"

"It's your turn, Bittle," said Anne. "I'll dry, if you like."

"Is there any hot water, Mummy?" said Elizabeth.

"Plenty," said Mrs. Rutherford.

"Oh," said Elizabeth.

After waiting just not long enough to make it necessary for anybody to tell her to hurry, Elizabeth began to wash up.

"Daddy," she said, as she handed a wet plate to Anne; "he told us the beach-boys spoilt his boat."

"Who did?"

"Arthur. When we met him. He said they'd pinch things out of *Tern*, if we left her ashore."

"He was having a row with them just before we met him," said Anne. Elizabeth giggled.

"He said he'd set the police on them," she said. "But I don't believe they would steal things out of *Tern*. Do you, Daddy?"

Mr. Rutherford was doubtful. He said he had once

lost a couple of blankets from *Tessa*, when he had left her for a week in Brownsea Roads.

" That wasn't boys," said the Bosun. " That was men. Large, evil men."

" I didn't see them all," said Elizabeth. " But one of them was nice."

" She gave him some chocolate," said Anne.

The Bosun chuckled. " Sensible girl," he said.

Mrs. Rutherford smiled to herself. She thought of Anne, years and years ago at the Cottage, and of the large hospitality with which she invited the village into the garden when the apples were ripening. There was plenty of room in the garden—but it might be inconvenient if Elizabeth did the same, and invited all the beach-boys on board *Tessa*. However, she didn't think it was likely.

" If I were a beach-boy," said the Bosun, " I'd probably spoil Arthur as well as his boat."

Elizabeth pondered this for a minute, with pleasure, as she slowly rubbed the traces of ham-fat from another plate with the mop. When she next spoke, it was anxiously.

" I hope he *won't* tell the police," she said. " He'd be a beast if he did. What would they do—the police, I mean ? "

" Nothing much," said the Bosun. " Don't worry. I knew a man once who told the police about boys robbing his garden."

" And what did they do ? "

" They said they'd have a look round."

" And did they ? "

" Yes," said the Bosun, " *all* round. If they'd looked straight they might have seen something."

Soon after the washing up was done there was a knock on *Tessa's* side and Antony's voice hailed them. Elizabeth and Anne hurried on deck.

"Come on," said Antony. "Let's go out." He had rowed over in *Ianthe's* dinghy with Robin.

Elizabeth and Anne got into the dinghy and they pulled across to *Tern.*

"We ought to have brought the Bosun," said Antony.

"Why?" said Anne.

"To take the dinghy back."

"I'll shout," said Robin.

Robin shouted. The Bosun appeared on deck, smoking his pipe.

"We forgot to bring you to take the dinghy back," Robin called.

"Bring her back yourself," said the Bosun. "Tow her alongside."

This would have been a rather difficult manœuvre, so they decided instead that Robin should row the dinghy back to *Tessa* and that they should then bring *Tern* alongside, unencumbered, and re-embark Robin. The Bosun would take *Ianthe's* dinghy back to *Ianthe*—towing their own. It was all rather complicated. It would have been less complicated if Robin had rowed back to *Ianthe*, and had re-embarked from there; but they still hesitated to sail *Tern* alongside *Ianthe* unless it was really necessary—because of Alf and his anxious (though helpful) boathook.

There was a puff of wind as Antony luffed to come alongside *Tessa*, and *Tern* had more way on her than was strictly desirable. This made it all the luckier that it was *Tessa* and not *Ianthe.* However, they didn't actually bump. Antony shouted to Robin to jump as *Tern* came up into the wind, and Robin jumped. The Bosun grinned as Robin landed in a heap on the floorboards aft and Antony hurriedly disentangled the main sheet from his arms and legs.

"Pretty poor," the Bosun said benevolently.

Antony put the helm up, the mainsail filled again, and they were off. Robin scrambled on to the foredeck and set the jib. There was still a pleasant breeze from a little south of west. The harbour was full of craft, large and small, as it always is in summer. Dinghies and one-designs flitted this way and that, happy and aimless as butterflies; motor cruisers and launches were passing in or out of the harbour along the main channel; a paddle steamer was off the Haven, on her way to Bournemouth; far away, beyond Old Harry and Durleston Head, they could see little pyramids of sail, white or grey according as they were in sunlight or shadow, of yachts out at sea. A big black ketch (Robin thought she was a converted Brixham trawler) was reaching down through Brownsea roads on the last of the ebb-tide. She had her boat lashed on deck, so she must have been starting on a passage to the westward, perhaps, or to some distant port on the Cornish coast, or to the Scillies.

Robin had taken the tiller from Antony. They were in the main channel now, sailing close-hauled towards the entrance of the harbour. The wind came a little stronger, and *Tern* heeled to it, and the bow wave began to hiss and whisper. The big black ketch passed them to leeward, and was soon far ahead. For a moment Robin's thoughts were with her, a little enviously; where would she be to-night and to-morrow? But they came quickly home again to *Tern*. It was lovely sailing in *Tern*—much better than in the dinghies they had sailed in last year. *Tern* was a *boat*. His eyes travelled affectionately round her, and he saw her again on the stocks, in the Building Shed at the Cottage, and remembered the slow labour of building. Yes, she was roughly built, no doubt. But she was sturdy and strong . . . fit to go anywhere. . . . Arthur called her the old tub . . . but Arthur was an ass and didn't really know anything about boats at all, though he thought he did. Was *Whynot* really so much faster than *Tern*? They'd have a race soon . . . it would be marvellous if *Tern* won. But even if *Whynot* *was* faster, *Tern* was the better boat. Of course, Arthur would never admit it . . . Robin wished he could somehow make him admit it. But he knew he couldn't. Anyway, it didn't really matter.

"Look," said Antony, "there's a big motor-cruiser coming in." She was approaching them fast—a large vessel of some forty tons.

"Can you read her name, Bittle?" said Anne.

Elizabeth looked. "It begins with Z," she said.

"Good Lord," said Antony. "It's *Zephyr*. I can read it."

"She'll pass frightfully close," said Anne.

Robin put the helm up a little. A moment later *Zephyr* was almost on them.

"Look," said Elizabeth. "Arthur's steering."

Willowy and conspicuous, Arthur was standing at *Zephyr's* wheel. He was wearing white flannel trousers, a blue serge jacket, and a yachting cap. He had recognized *Tern*, and was passing her as close as he could. He took a hand from the wheel and raised it in a lordly greeting. Antony and Anne waved back—one always greets an acquaintance at sea, even when it's Arthur: at least, almost always. Robin didn't, but that may have been because he was too busy steering. Elizabeth didn't either, because she could think of nothing but how funny Arthur looked in his yachting cap.

Zephyr swept by—brilliant with white paint, glass windows and polished brass. Just before she was out of earshot Arthur turned his head and shouted.

"I'd give a pull on your peak halyard if I was you. It's slack. She'll sail better if you do."

Then she was gone, and *Tern* was left rolling in her wash.

Elizabeth chuckled to herself. Arthur was more like a candle than ever in those trousers. She tried to catch Anne's eye, but Anne wouldn't look. Robin glanced up at the throat of the mainsail, and then looked at Antony. Antony sniffed, and settled himself with rather conscious deliberation, his back against the middle thwart. They had got under way in a bit of a hurry . . . of course, he knew perfectly well that the peak halyard wanted setting up a little. He had been meaning to do it for ages. It was Robin jumping on board like that when he had gone alongside *Tessa*—much too fast—which had made him forget. . . .

Robin knew too ; he was just going to tell Antony to give the halyard an extra pull when they saw *Zephyr* coming. It was sickening. He felt he could bear Arthur even less than usual. Anyway, the mainsail was practically all right—and *Tern* was sailing jolly well.

They went on for a minute or two without speaking, past the line of black buoys under their lee. Elizabeth was humming to herself. Presently she stopped humming.

"Shall *I* do it?" she said.

"What?" said Antony.

"Pull up the peak."

"No," said Antony irritably, without turning round. "It's perfectly all right as it is."

Robin silently assented—of course, it was all right. Elizabeth began to hum again, dabbling a hand over the lee side in the water until it spurted up her arm.

When, a quarter of an hour later, they put *Tern* about near the Bar Buoy and stood in towards Studland, Antony without saying anything went forward and (as casually as possible) gave a small quick extra pull on the peak halyard.

That done, Arthur was temporarily forgotten. They sailed *Tern* close in-shore at Shell Bay. The white curve of the beach was dotted with picnickers.

"Let's anchor," suggested Anne.

"We might have a bathe," said Antony.

Antony and Robin—as they often used to do at Creeksea—had their bathing things already on under their clothes. You never knew when they might come in useful.

The water in-shore was smooth and clear under the lee of the land. Robin brought Tern to within about thirty yards of the beach. Anne sounded with an oar. It was quite shallow—not more than four feet deep. They lowered the sails and dropped the anchor overboard. *Tern* lay to it, softly lifting to the smooth and gentle swell.

Anne and Elizabeth had not brought their bathing-dresses; but Robin and Antony both bathed. Antony swam ashore with the brisk strong strokes which Robin always secretly admired and envied. He ran up the beach and waved to them, then splashed back into the sea, and swam vigorously out far beyond where *Tern* was lying. Robin paddled quietly round *Tern*, keeping just far enough away to see her properly. She looked lovely, her mainsail lying loose in the well, her jib, still clipped to the stay, bunched on the foredeck all ready for hoisting again. The water close under her side was deep olive green and smooth. He could see the anchor when he swam over it, and the warp growing slackly from it along the bottom. It was much better bathing like this—from *Tern*—than bathing from the beach, like the picnickers. The picnickers would go on foot, or by bus, or by car, back to their houses; how much better it was to go back by *Tern* to *Ianthe* and *Tessa*!

"Is it warm?" called Elizabeth.

" Lovely," shouted Robin.

By the time the boys were on board again (it was hot; there was no need to dry; they put on their clothes over their wet bathing dresses) the tide had turned and was beginning to flow again. Like sensible sailors, they had arranged to have a fair tide both ways. They got under way, and ran back towards the Bar Buoy. It would have been nice, Elizabeth thought, if they had remembered to bring things to eat with them; Robin thought so too, especially as he had had a bathe. But unfortunately they hadn't brought anything.

" We ought to keep a special tin," said Antony.

" Yes," said Anne; " for iron rations."

" Why iron?" said Elizabeth.

" They're what you keep," said Robin. " You keep them for emergencies."

Elizabeth chuckled. " Like Bosun," she said, " and his rum—when we went to France. Iron rum."

But it was a good idea: they would certainly get a large biscuit tin next time they were ashore. It could be stowed conveniently under the after seat, next to the bailer and the box of nails and spare shackles, and they would keep in it always slightly more than they were likely to want at any one time.

Elizabeth took the helm. Elizabeth didn't often steer —and never at critical moments, like getting under way or coming alongside or mooring. But she liked steering sometimes, so long as Anne didn't fuss her and tell her she was doing it wrong. If Anne did fuss it always made it much worse and quite impossible to remember what was the right thing to do. Elizabeth really preferred steering when Antony was on board; for Anne was less likely to fuss with Antony there. Antony himself never fussed her at all.

Tern was running before the wind, slowly and easily.

Robin was on the stern seat at Elizabeth's side. Elizabeth screwed her head round and looked back at the receding beach.

"Anne," she said, "look, there's somebody riding." Elizabeth continued to look behind her until she felt a gentle pressure on the tiller—Robin had quietly put his hand on it.

"I was afraid she might gybe," he said.

"It's a girl," said Anne. "She's going right into the water. Like those people at Bembridge—you remember, Bittle."

"Yes," said Elizabeth. "On the sand, where we bathe." She abandoned the tiller to Robin, and continued to watch the girl on the horse—small dark figures against the bright sand.

Anne and Elizabeth both loved horses, and had learnt to ride almost as soon as they could walk. Elizabeth (as has been often remarked) spent a lot of her spare time drawing horses; and she drew them because she loved them.

"Do you want to steer again?" said Robin.

Elizabeth shook her head. "Not specially," she said.

Along the long lane of buoys *Tern* sailed back into the harbour. As before, Antony and Robin went straight to *Ianthe*; Alf was down below getting tea for Mr. and Mrs, Chale, so he was unable to stand by with his boathook. This, however, was perhaps an advantage, his anxiety about *Ianthe's* paint being apt to make the helmsmen nervous. But they were all getting more used to *Tern*, and with every boat use brings confidence. Robin brought her alongside without a scratch.

On *Tessa* also, tea was almost ready. Mrs. Rutherford had waited until she saw *Tern* coming in by the Haven, and then had put the kettle on.

"Hallo, Daddy," said Elizabeth when she came into the cabin. "Did you go to sleep?"

"Yes," said Mr. Rutherford.

"While I," said the Bosun, "did all the work."

"What work?" said Elizabeth.

"*What* work?" said the Bosun, raising an eyebrow. "Buying potatoes, of course."

"But we did the shopping this morning," said Anne.

"You forgot the potatoes," said the Bosun.

"I didn't know we'd run out," said Mrs. Rutherford.

"Poor Bosun," said Elizabeth.

The Bosun sighed. "And what's more," he said, "as you'd gone off with the luggage-van, I had to row all the way in the dinghy."

"Luggage-van!" said Elizabeth. "*Tern's not* a luggage-van."

"We had a marvellous sail," she added. "And we saw Arthur."

"He had white ducks and a yachting-cap," said Anne.

"Quite the gentleman," said the Bosun, and cast an affectionate glance at his trousers. "As a matter of fact," he went on, "I saw Arthur too."

"*You* did?" said Anne. "But he was on *Zephyr*."

"He must have gone straight ashore," said the Bosun; "directly they got back to their moorings. *Zephyr* was home two hours before you."

"Where did you see him?" said Elizabeth.

"On the beach by the yard. He'd gone to look at his Yellow Peril."

"The *Whynot*," murmured Elizabeth.

"But he *wasn't* looking at her," said the Bosun.

"What was he doing?" said Anne.

"Fighting," said the Bosun calmly.

"*Fighting?* Why? Who with? What do you mean?"

Mr. Rutherford brought in the teapot. The Bosun took his pipe from his mouth and put it carefully down on the top of the locker by his elbow. Anne and Elizabeth kept their eyes on him with pleased expectancy.

"A battle," said the Bosun. "Definitely a battle. I missed the beginning of it, worse luck." He looked at Elizabeth out of the corner of his eye, then held out his hand towards Mrs. Rutherford. "Tea please, Janet," he said. "You don't know how thirsty I am."

"But *tell* us, Bosun," said Anne impatiently. "Who was he fighting *with*? He wasn't *really* fighting, was he?"

"Certainly," said the Bosun, as he received his teacup. "At least, he had been. I think he'd been defeated. His trousers were no longer white. Poor Arthur, I think it's a shame."

Elizabeth's eyes were sparkling. She chuckled.

"Was it the beach-boys?" she said.

The Bosun sipped his tea, and nodded slowly.

"It was," he said. "All of them—a savage horde."

Elizabeth pondered the idea for a moment, and found it not unpleasant.

"Did they kick the water at him?" she said.

"Undoubtedly," said the Bosun.

"He jolly well deserves it," said Anne.

"Bosun," said Elizabeth.

"What?"

"Was *my* beach-boy there?"

"How should he know?" said Anne. "He's never seen him."

"What's he like?" said the Bosun.

Elizabeth thought—her slice of bread and honey suspended.

"Like Robin," she said, "but redder and dirtier—*and* fatter."

The Bosun considered.

"It might have been him," he said, "who had the trophy. But I couldn't be sure."

"What trophy?" said Anne.

"The yachting-cap," said the Bosun.

CHAPTER XXI

After tea, as nobody seemed to want to do anything particular, Elizabeth paid a call on *Ianthe*. It would be a good thing, she thought, to tell Robin and Antony about Arthur's battle. Anne didn't want to come, so Elizabeth took the dinghy and went by herself. When she got to *Ianthe*, she found that Antony had gone ashore with Mr. and Mrs. Chale, and that only Robin and Alf were on board. Robin was in the fo'c'sle with Alf, watching him smoke his pipe and listening to stories of the days when he had worked on a Brixham trawler. He came on deck when Elizabeth knocked on *Ianthe's* side (their usual signal when they called on each other).

Elizabeth told him what the Bosun had said, and Robin listened with solemn satisfaction.

"I hope it *was* our beach-boy who got his cap," she ended.

Robin nodded. He liked talking to Elizabeth about Arthur, because Elizabeth understood what he felt about him. Antony and Anne were different. Of course,

Anne didn't *like* Arthur. No sensible person could. But at the same time (Robin felt) she didn't really mind him. She thought he was an ass ; but it was all right, so far as she was concerned, so long as she didn't have to see him too often. Antony—well, that was just the trouble. Antony didn't really like him either—but he went out with him on his motor-bike : at least, he had done so last holidays. And whenever Arthur was there, Antony was different. Robin could not have explained *how* he was different ; he just felt that he was. And Arthur was beastly about *Tern*. He thought that because she wasn't all smooth and polished (so to speak) like the *Whynot*, that she was therefore not so good. Robin knew she was much better. *Tern* was lovely. He would rather have her than a hundred *Whynots*—even though she *was* a bit slow to windward.

" But it doesn't matter," said Elizabeth, " even if he *does* think *Whynot* is better than *Tern*." But although she said this, she understood what Robin meant, and she knew that it did matter.

" *We* all like *Tern* best," she added.

Robin nodded again. Of course they all liked *Tern* best. But at the same time a little arrow of doubt shot through him. *Did* they ? Of course, Antony had never *sailed* in *Whynot* ; they had only seen her lying on the beach. But Robin remembered how Antony had been annoyed when Robin had tried last year to explain to him why he liked *Tessa* even better than *Ianthe*. *Ianthe* was beautiful—nobody thought her more beautiful than Robin did—but at the same time there was something about *Tessa* which Robin felt, though he could hardly say why, that *Ianthe* could never have. *Tessa* was old. She had never actually been a fishing smack—but she almost might have been. The Falmouth men who built her (forty years ago) had no thoughts of the sunny Solent and smooth water and clouds of white canvas: they thought rather of the grey seas off the Dodman, and of what happened in a blow. But Antony didn't understand properly what Robin meant. Suppose he felt the same about *Tern* . . . and the *Whynot.* Arthur, of course, could never possibly understand—really understand—why *Tern* was beautiful. But Robin was desperately anxious that Antony should. Perhaps Antony did . . . but Robin could not be absolutely sure. And the fact that he couldn't be sure made him miserable. If only they could *prove* that she was better—better in every way—than the *Whynot*: if only they could make Arthur see that she was "more of a boat." Racing wouldn't be any good. Robin was pretty certain that *Tern* would lose . . . worse luck. Not that *he* minded if she did . . . not really; but Antony would mind—and then it would be harder than ever to make him understand what Robin felt.

It was nice (Elizabeth thought) being on *Ianthe* with Robin—and with Alf. She could smell Alf's tobacco smoke as it came up through the fo'c'sle hatch. Robin took her into the sail-room, and showed her his favourite place where he used to curl himself up amongst the sail-bags when they were under way. And he took her into the fo'c'sle—to see Alf. Alf had a sunburnt face and twinkling blue eyes, enormous hands, and *Ianthe* embroidered in white cotton across the front of his jersey. He told them more stories of his trawling days in the West Country—pleased to have another listener.

"The smacks are all right," he said. "The men may give out, or the gear may go; but the smacks will never let you down."

When Elizabeth got back to *Tessa* she found Anne cooking supper. Anne said she ought to have got back sooner in order to help. Elizabeth was glad she hadn't.

Supper was scrambled eggs. It usually was when Anne cooked it—mixed with chopped bully beef. Elizabeth and Mrs. Rutherford washed up.

When Mrs. Rutherford came to say good night to them, Elizabeth, already sleepy, suddenly remembered the girl on the horse she had seen when they were leaving Shell Bay. She told Mrs. Rutherford about her.

"They were on the beach, Mummy," she said. "Right in the water."

Anne thought of Twinkle, the brown pony with a star on his forehead, which she and Bittle used to ride at home. She had a sudden longing to see him again.

"Mummy," she said, "I wish we had Twinkle *here*." Mrs. Rutherford smiled.

"Twinkle *and Tern*?" she said. "It would be rather difficult, wouldn't it?"

"I suppose it would," said Anne.

"But I'll tell you what," said Mrs. Rutherford, "we might have an expedition one day: we might go to the New Forest for a picnic. Then you and Elizabeth could ride. I know some stables there." Her eyes seemed to be remembering. "I've ridden myself in the New Forest."

Anne thought a moment. Then, "Antony rides," she said.

"Robin can't," said Elizabeth.

"Antony loves it," said Anne. "He might come too."

Elizabeth chuckled to herself. "I bet Arthur can't ride," she said.

"Except a motor-bike," said Anne.

. . . .

The next morning, soon after they had cleared away breakfast, there was an unusual noise forward, in the

forepeak. Actually it wasn't in the forepeak, becau
Anne went to look : it was outside. Elizabeth hurrie
up the companion ladder on to the deck, and just as h
head appeared above the hatch, Robin's head al
appeared over the bulwarks in the bows. They stare
at each other, and both laughed.

"Hallo," said Robin. "I sw-swam over."

It was Robin's morning bathe, and as the tide w
flowing he thought he would do as Anne had done—on
the other way round—and swim to *Tessa*. He ha
climbed on board by way of the bobstay and the bowspr
shrouds. It was a nice way of paying a call.

Robin perched himself on the edge of the skylight, an
sat for a minute without speaking, hugging his w
shoulders.

"But isn't Antony bathing?" asked Elizabeth. "Wh
didn't he come too?"

"I d-don't know," said Robin. "I mean—I didn
wait for him." He stopped a moment; then he went o
speaking rather quickly.

"It's about Antony," he said, "I c-came to tell yo
He . . ." But before he could get any further Ann
came on deck. She had heard the voices, and had com
to say good morning.

"Hallo," she said. "Did you swim? Where
Antony? Haven't you had breakfast yet? We ha
ours long ago."

Robin did not seem inclined to go on about Anton
while Anne was there. He continued to sit on th
skylight hugging his shoulders. Elizabeth thought h
seemed gloomy. Presently she suggested that she shoul
row him back to *Ianthe* in the dinghy (a necessary pa
of that kind of bathe). Robin at once assented.

When they were in the dinghy, Robin went on wit
what he had to say.

" He's g-going out with Arthur," he said. Elizabeth
ɔked at him as he sat there in the stern—thin, brown,
:t and solemn, his fringe stuck by the seawater to his
·ehead. Suddenly she felt angry with Antony.

" On his beastly motor-bike ? " she said.

" No," said Robin. " Worse than that . . . He's
ing in *Whynot*. He's going to race. He met him
sterday afternoon, and arranged it."

Elizabeth said nothing. She dug the oars deeper into
e water and gave a vicious stroke. The dinghy
ɔbbled. It was sickening of Antony. He'd no business
do it. . . . Why, they'd hardly sailed at all in *Tern*
t. They hardly knew what she was like. If he *must*
out with horrible Arthur, he might at least have
aited a bit longer.

" I think he's a beast," she said at last.

" Who ?—Arthur ? "

" No, Antony," said Elizabeth.

" *Arthur's* a beast," said Robin.

The rest of the way (it wasn't far) they rowed in silence.
'hen they were alongside *Ianthe* they could smell bacon
ying. Nobody was on deck. Robin scrambled on
ɔard and stood a moment looking down at Elizabeth.

" Robin," Elizabeth said, " let's take *Tern* out by
ırselves."

" With Anne too ? "

" No. By ourselves."

Robin nodded his head quickly and ran off to the
ɔmpanion. He disappeared below to put on his clothes
ıd have breakfast.

Elizabeth returned to *Tessa*. Mr. Rutherford and the
osun were putting the blankets out to air ; they were
anging them over the booms to get sweet in the morning
ınshine. Anne and Mrs. Rutherford were still tidying
p down below. Elizabeth hoped that Anne would not

want to come with them in *Tern.* It would be safer, s
thought, not to ask her, in case she said yes, but simp
to announce the fact that she was going with Robin.

" Robin and I are going in *Tern,*" she said, firmly a
defiantly.

" What's Antony going to do ? " said Mrs. Rutherfo
Elizabeth told her.

" Good Lord," said Anne. She was busy with a dus
pan and brush on the cabin floor, and didn't seem
surprised as Elizabeth had expected she would be. B
then (Elizabeth reflected) Anne wouldn't be so ve
surprised—she didn't really feel in matters of this ki
as Robin and herself did. Probably it was because s
was getting so old. Fortunately, however, she didn
say that she wanted to come with them in *Tern.*

When they were all on deck after lunch, the Bosu
pointed down the channel towards the entrance to t
South Deep.

" Look," he said : " there she comes."

" Who ? " said Anne.

" The Yellow Peril."

It was the *Whynot.* Nobody could mistake her brillia
orange hull. Arthur was coming to fetch Antony o
Ianthe. He was beating up the South Deep against t
westerly breeze. One more tack, and he would b
alongside *Ianthe.* Elizabeth could see Antony on dec
and Alf—anxiously waiting with his boathook.

" I hope he bumps," murmured Elizabeth. But h
didn't. He brought *Whynot* alongside in a neat a
professional manner, and Antony jumped on board. I
a moment *Whynot* was off again. As she squared awa
to run back, Elizabeth saw Antony wave good-by
Somebody on *Ianthe's* deck (probably Mr. Chale) wave
back.

Half an hour later Elizabeth saw Robin's signal ; sh

was expecting it, and was on the look-out. Robin signalled in semaphore: they had all learnt semaphore the previous year; it had come in useful then, and might, indeed, come in useful at any time. Elizabeth answered his signal, and saw Robin get into the dinghy with Alf. Alf rowed to *Tessa*, and then put them both aboard *Tern*. He lingered a minute, his hand on *Tern's* rail as Robin got the mainsail up.

"Are you going after Mister Antony?" he said.

"No," said Robin. "He's racing."

Alf glanced up at the fluttering red mainsail, his eyes humorous but not unappreciative.

"That's it, Master Robin," he said. "Some's built for speed, some's built for comfort. That's where it is, eh, Master Robin?"

Then he pushed off and rowed back to *Ianthe*. Soon *Tern* was under way, running down the South Deep.

"Where shall we go?" said Robin.

"I don't mind," said Elizabeth. "Anywhere."

Then she remembered the suggestion which Antony had made the previous day.

"Let's go ashore and get the tin for the iron rations," she said. "*And* some iron rations."

They turned out their pockets and found that they had three shillings and fivepence between them.

"That's heaps," said Elizabeth.

They went ashore at the usual place and left *Tern* tied up to the jetty. As it was Saturday afternoon the yard was shut; but there were a great many people on the beach of the creek. Elizabeth's eyes wandered over to where *Whynot* was used to lie.

"Robin," she murmured, "don't you wish we'd seen him with his trousers all muddy—after the battle?"

They bought their biscuit tin and as many iron rations to go inside it as their money allowed. When they got back to the jetty Robin put his hand on Elizabeth's arm and stopped.

"Look," he said; "there's someone in *Tern*."

Tern, from where they were standing, was half hidden by the jetty; they could see only her bows and part of her foredeck; but above the intervening jetty, they could see a boy's head—and it was pretty obvious that the rest of him was in *Tern's* well. He was looking up at another boy who was standing on the jetty, evidently talking to him.

"B-bother," said Robin. "They're b-beach-boys."

Elizabeth, however, was not at all perturbed.

"Of course they are," she said. "Come on. I think one of them's ours. The one in *Tern*." She started off again towards the top end of the jetty. Robin followed, carrying the iron rations. He was glad Elizabeth was with him, rather than Antony: Elizabeth had had more practice with beach-boys than he had, for they (or their inland equivalent) never came by invitation or otherwise into the Manor garden at Creeksea to share the apples. Bramble would never have allowed it.

Hearing their steps the boy on the jetty looked quickly over his shoulder; he whispered something to his companion in *Tern*, jumped off the jetty into the shallow water and scuttled off along the beach to the right. The boy in *Tern* stayed where he was.

"He *is* ours," said Elizabeth.

The boy looked up at them as they reached the end of the jetty with an expression half anxious, half impudent.

"Hallo," said Elizabeth.

The boy got to his feet and scrambled up on to the jetty.

"I was just keepin' an eye on 'er for you," he said.

"Thank you," said Elizabeth gravely. Robin, the ration tin under his arm, cast a hurried glance over *Tern*. She didn't seem to have suffered. Then he got in, and towed the tin under the seat aft. Elizabeth followed. The boy watched them. Robin began to take the tyer ff the mainsail. He wished the boy would go—after ll, it was rather cheek to have come on board like that. But the boy didn't go.

Presently he spoke again.

" Nice boat, she is," he said. He spoke defensively, but at the same time as if he wanted to be friendly. Robin was now busily engaged clearing the jib halyards. Elizabeth glanced at his back, then up at the beach-boy on the jetty. She wanted to laugh. Then with a sudden impulse she asked the beach-boy if he would like to come on board and look round.

" But, of course," she added, " you've seen her already, haven't you ? "

" I was only keepin' an eye on 'er," said the boy, uncertain of what Elizabeth's last remark implied. " I didn't do no 'arm."

" Of course not," said Elizabeth. Then she repeated her invitation. The boy looked quickly along the beach in the direction in which his companion had disappeared.

" Bert's 'opped it," he said, and slid down into *Tern's* well.

" Who's Bert ? " said Elizabeth.

" 'Im what was 'ere with me," said the boy. " 'E's opped it. Thought you mightn't like us being 'ere. There's some as don't," he added reminiscently.

Elizabeth went to the mainsail halyards and began undoing them from the cleats.

" 'Ere, let me do it," said the boy. He pushed past her, and in a couple of moments had the mainsail set. Robin came aft.

" Do you know about boats ? " said Elizabeth.

The boy nodded. " My dad's got a smack," he said. " She's a beauty. I go wiv 'im sometimes, after sprats.

That's where she lies"—he pointed towards the mouth of the creek—"and that's my dad aboard 'er now. *Maisie* 'er name is."

Robin looked inquiringly at Elizabeth—they were all ready to start. It was time the beach-boy went. Robin still wished he would hurry up and go—but not quite so much as before, now that he knew his father was the owner of a smack. He had noticed *Maisie* several times as they went to and fro in *Tern*: she was a small square-sterned boat, untidy but workmanlike, of about eight tons.

The beach-boy hopped on to the jetty and cast off *Tern's* rope. He stood holding it in his hand. Robin took the helm, and waited for him to let go. But instead of letting go he looked hard at Elizabeth, a little pucker between his eyebrows.

"I *was* going off to 'er now," he said. "To *Maisie* —to my dad."

Robin and Elizabeth exchanged glances. Robin nodded.

"We'll take you if you like," Elizabeth said. "In *Tern*." The pucker disappeared from between the boy's eyebrows, and his face became one large grin of pleasure.

"You will?" he said, and jumped nimbly back on to *Tern's* foredeck, rope in hand. Then he shoved her head off; the mainsail filled, and *Tern* began to gather way.

They threaded their way amongst the moored boats and clustered dinghies towards *Maisie*. The beach-boy was in high glee, handling the jib sheets while Robin steered. Evidently he approved of *Tern*.

"Where'd you get 'er?" he said. "She don't look like one of ours."

"We built her ourselves," said Robin.

The boy stared at him in astonishment. "You *did*?" he said. "Coo, that's a bit of all right, that is."

Robin's heart warmed to him.

Another tack brought them to *Maisie*. The boy lowered the jib, and Robin took *Tern* alongside. A fisherman in a blue jersey was chipping paint off the inside of her bulwarks with a scraper.

"Hallo, Dad," said the boy.

The fisherman suspended his work, and nodded them a greeting. The boy took *Tern's* rope and jumped on board.

"You coming too?" he said. "Dad won't mind, will you, Dad?"

The fisherman looked *Tern* over with a benevolent eye, and returned to his scraping.

"You're welcome," he said mildly.

Maisie was untidy, dirty, and smelt of fish. One side of her deck was cluttered with her trawl. Robin liked her. The boy showed them round proudly. He made them examine the fish-well and poke into the tiny fo'c'sle forrard. Especially he made them admire the auxiliary engine.

Elizabeth was glad they had made the acquaintance of the beach-boy, because she was extremely anxious to find out more about Arthur's battle; so when they had finished their inspection of *Maisie* and were ready to go off again in *Tern*, she suggested to the beach-boy that he should come too. It was obvious to her that Robin would no longer mind. The beach-boy was delighted: it was, in fact, exactly what he had hoped for himself.

Unless you actively dislike a person, it is difficult not to feel friendly when you are sailing together in a small boat. Neither Robin nor Elizabeth disliked the beach-boy: on the contrary, Elizabeth liked him very much, and Robin—helped by his admiration of *Tern* and his obvious skill in handling her—was quite ready to do the same. Indeed (thought Elizabeth), you could hardly help liking him—unless you were Arthur.

When they reached the main channel, the beach-boy pointed away up towards the Quay where, in the distance, they could see a group of white sails close together.

"There they come," he said. "They'll be finishing in half an hour."

It was the race—the boats were half-way round on the last lap. Elizabeth stared hard, and thought she could distinguish an orange hull; but the boats were a long way off and she couldn't be sure.

"*His* brother's racing," she said, indicating Robin.

"'E is?" said the beach-boy. "What boat?"

Elizabeth glanced sideways at Robin.

"*Whynot*," she said. Robin remained intent upon his steering. The beach-boy whistled.

"Coo," he said. "*'Er?*"

Elizabeth nodded. She had a strong desire to giggle, but restrained it. The beach-boy was obviously embarrassed. He looked at Elizabeth suspiciously.

"That bloke . . . is 'e a friend of yours?" he said.

Elizabeth shook her head.

"No—not really," she said. Robin compressed his lips and said nothing.

"Honest?" said the beach-boy.

"Honest," said Elizabeth.

The beach-boy seemed reassured. He came aft and sat down by Elizabeth. He turned his head and fixed her with a bright but indignant eye.

"D'you know what 'e did? 'E 'it me, 'e did." He paused to give his announcement time to take effect. Elizabeth nodded sympathetically, hoping he would go on. Robin waited expectantly—he definitely liked the beach-boy now.

Presently the beach-boy continued: "And I 'adn't done nuthen," he said. "Me and my mates weren't doing nuthen to 'urt—jest keepin' an eye on 'er, as you might say . . ."

" Like you were on *Tern*," murmured Elizabeth.

" Eh ? " said the beach-boy with a momentary return of suspicion. But seeing Elizabeth's face, he grinned.

" That's it," he said. " Like what we was on *Tern*. 'It me ! " he repeated. " That's what 'e did—'e 'it me ! "

Tern was rapidly approaching the race. They could now easily distinguish the orange hull. She was in a close group of other boats, reaching down the channel towards them.

" That's 'im," said the beach-boy with a jerk of his head. " Coo, don't 'e think 'imself a toff : not 'alf 'e don't."

" You saw him last night, didn't you," said Elizabeth, " on the beach ? "

The beach-boy chuckled. " Last night ? " he said. " Not 'alf we didn't . . ." He paused, and his eye gleamed with pleasurable memory. " You see," he went on, " when he turned nasty when we weren't doin' nuthen—when 'e 'it me—me and my mates wasn't goin' to stand for it, see ? So we give 'im what for, see ? Calls 'imself a toff, 'e does—'im and 'is 'at ! " He ferreted about in his pocket for a moment, and pulled out a small object which he tendered to Elizabeth. " See 'ere what I've got," he said. It was a badge made of braid with a crest on it.

" What is it ? " said Elizabeth.

" It's off 'is 'at," said the beach-boy. " Coo, 'e warn't 'alf wild." He put it carefully back into his pocket. Then he nodded his head with great solemnity. " And what's more," he said, " 'e'd better mind out, or there'll be more comin' to 'im."

" What do you mean ? " said Elizabeth.

" 'E'd better mind out," repeated the boy.

There was no time to explain further at the moment, for all their attention was needed to pass safely through the crowd of racing boats. Robin knew that it was a breach of etiquette to interfere with a boat which was racing : to take her wind, or press her to go about—even if you were on the starboard tack ; and *Tern* was on the port tack, which made it even more necessary to keep out of the way. The boats were very thick and close together, and Robin was too much occupied even to notice *Whynot*, more than with a sidelong glance, as she slipped past. Elizabeth, however, waved, and Antony waved back—himself too busy to observe their passenger. Arthur, who was steering, did not deign to turn his head. A minute later the fleet was astern. The beach-boy chuckled.

" Coo ! " he said ; " did you see 'im ? Thinks 'e's at the 'elm of the old *Britannia* ! " And he gave an imitation of the King's helmsman in a race, which made Elizabeth and Robin burst out laughing. " Some sailor, ain't 'e ? " went on the boy. " All spit and polish and fine weather, that's what 'e is."

" Why fine weather ? " said Elizabeth, still laughing.

" Do you think 'e'd take the *Whynot* out in a breeze ? " said the boy. " Not 'im— An' if 'e did, he'd turn 'er over as like as not."

" You couldn't capsize *Tern*," said Robin.

The boy grinned and cocked his head knowingly. " Na-a-ow," he said. " *Tern's* all right, she is."

Elizabeth was anxious to know more precisely what the beach-boy meant when he said that *more was coming* to Arthur if he continued to misbehave ; and as they sailed *Tern* back to the creek she made several efforts to get an explicit answer. But she was not successful.

" 'E'd better mind out," said the boy again ; and with that Elizabeth had to be content.

They had a small iron ration each just before they got back to *Maisie* ; here they left the beach-boy with his father, and then set off again for home.

CHAPTER XXII

ANTONY had enjoyed his race in *Whynot.* He and Arthur had come in third out of fifteen starters. He was telling Robin about it (again) as they lay in their bunks that night in the cabin they shared on *Ianthe.*

"Honestly, Robin," he said, "*Whynot's* a jolly good boat. Arthur knows how to handle her too."

"He'd never take her out in a breeze," said Robin. "He wouldn't dare."

"How do *you* know?" said Antony.

"And he wouldn't go out of the harbour, either."

"Don't be a fool," said Antony. "You know nothing about Arthur. Just because you don't like him, you think he can't do anything. He jolly well knows how to sail a race."

Robin felt miserable. He knew much more about Arthur than Antony did, but it was almost impossible to make Antony understand. He had told him about how he and Elizabeth had taken the beach-boy out in *Tern*—he had told him as soon as Antony had got back from his race ; but Antony had not really been very interested. His thoughts were too full of what he had just been doing himself. Robin had done his best to make him see how beastly Arthur had been to the beach-boy, especially to *their* beach-boy ; but Antony had only half-listened and refused to take what Robin said seriously. Indeed, he was even inclined to think that beach-boys in general *were* a nuisance, and that they had no business to mess about with other people's boats. It was no good Robin explaining that they hadn't done, or intended to do, any harm—any more than their own beach-boy had done any harm to *Tern*.

"They jolly well ought to keep off," Antony said. "Besides, just because one of them's all right, it doesn't mean they all are. I bet there are others who wouldn't mind smashing *Whynot* up—or *Tern* either."

But Robin was not convinced. "I'm not talking about the others," he said, "at least, not really—I don't think they *would* do any harm. But I mean *our* beach-boy. It was him Arthur hit ; it was him he was a beast to."

"What if he did ?" said Antony, and there was something in his tone which made Robin for the moment unable to say any more. He lay stiff in his bunk, more miserable than ever. He thought of the lovely time they had had building *Tern*—especially those last weeks when Arthur had had mumps—the excitement of launching her, the feeling of triumph when they found that she was good, and of the way he had looked forward to the best summer holidays they had ever had, sailing in her : sailing in her all together, all knowing that she was the best boat in the world. But now the holidays were going to be spoilt. Antony didn't really like *Tern* at all. He liked *Whynot* instead. *Tern* was too slow—too slow to windward. At least, he expected she was, though they hadn't had their race yet. He hoped they would never have it, because if *Whynot* won (and she probably *would* win) it would be worse still. It was all Arthur's fault—and Arthur was a beast.

Ianthe was silent. They lay in their bunks, one on each side of the little dark cabin. Everybody else was in bed too. The only sounds were the lapping of the tide past *Ianthe's* sides, and the occasional lazy tap of ropes against the mast. Antony knew that Robin was miserable. He thought he was being silly, but at the same time he was sorry. Presently he broke the silence.

"Robin," he said. "Let's have a long sail to-morrow. Let's go round Brownsea, and properly explore."

"H'm," said Robin.

Antony waited a moment; then, "We might take the beach-boy too," he said. "Would you like to?"

"N-not specially."

"Why not?"

"Antony . . ."

"What?"

"D-do you *l-like* Arthur?"

Robin's voice was so small and woebegone that Antony could not help laughing.

"You know I think he's an ass," he said. "I've told you so hundreds of times."

"I know," said Robin, "b-but . . ." Here he stuck, and before he could go on, Antony spoke again. Anyway, he knew what Robin was going to say.

"You are an idiot, Robin," he said—and Robin was comforted; for it's nice to be called an idiot in the right tone of voice. "Anyway," Antony went on, "Arthur's not nearly so bad as you think. He swanks frightfully, and he's an awful ass. But he's not bad really. I like going on his motor-bike and it was fun racing in *Whynot*. After all, we've got heaps of time for *Tern*."

"I know," said Robin. "But all the same, Arthur *is* a beast."

Antony laughed again. Then he stretched out his arm and just touched Robin's shoulder.

"Good night," he said.

Elizabeth, of course, had also told her family about the sail with the beach-boy. Mr. and Mrs. Rutherford were not at all surprised (Mr. and Mrs. Chale, on the other hand, *had* been slightly surprised—but there was no knowing what the Rutherford children would do) ; but Mr. and Mrs. Rutherford were well used to Elizabeth's partiality for odd small boys, and to Anne's too, though advancing years had in her case made it less evident than it used to be. Mrs. Rutherford, indeed, had a similar partiality herself ; had she not had it, the apples in the garden at the Cottage would never have been allowed to disappear as quickly as they always did. Moreover, she heartily shared Elizabeth's indignation at Arthur's behaviour. Mr. Rutherford, though he had no definite antipathy to odd small boys, nevertheless began to fear for the privacy and comfort of *Tessa's* saloon, if this particular small boy's companions turned out to be as delightful in Elizabeth's opinion as he was himself. The Bosun approved of what Elizabeth had done, for practical reasons. It was just as well, he said, in the present circumstances, to have the beach-boys on their side. He was inclined to be suspicious of beach-boys in general ; but they could undoubtedly be excellent allies in dealing with a person like Arthur. They had, indeed, already proved their value in a signal victory.

Next morning it was Antony who turned up on *Tessa's* deck by way of the bobstay and the bowsprit shrouds. This excellent method of bathing was becoming a habit : who called on whom had to depend, of course, on the tide ; just now the tide was flowing in the mornings, so it was Antony or Robin who called on *Tessa* before breakfast, and Anne who called on *Ianthe* (if she wanted to) later in the day. Elizabeth had not yet made the passage, though Anne was sure she could do it quite easily; but she would probably make the attempt before long, properly convoyed by Daddy in the dinghy.

It was early when Antony called; about eight o'clock. *Tessa's* deck was still wet with dew. It was a windless morning, and wreaths of mist, not yet drunk up by the sun, lay about the reaches of the harbour. The water was pearl-coloured and as smooth as ice. Later it would be hot—and the Bosun thought there would be a breeze.

Antony announced that he and Robin had decided on a long exploratory sail in *Tern*.

"I asked him," he added with a touch of embarrassment, "if he'd like to take that boy—you know, the one you took out yesterday. But he said he wouldn't."

Elizabeth was pleased with Antony for saying this; she had been half afraid, for Robin's sake, that he would be going out again in *Whynot*; or even if he didn't, that he might have been annoyed with Robin for so obviously taking sides with Arthur's enemies. She thought the proposal of a long sail in *Tern* was a good one, and Anne thought so too.

"We'll take lunch and tea," said Antony.

"Yes," said Elizabeth. "It will be almost a cruise."

"It's not a cruise," said Anne, "unless you sleep on board."

"Or in tents," said Elizabeth. "Like last year, with *Puffin* and *Sheldrake*."

"And I expect," said Mrs. Rutherford, "that you'll soon be wanting to do that in *Tern*."

"We jolly well will," said Antony.

Obviously, a cruise was necessary. They had all decided on it long ago, before *Tern* was even finished. But it had seemed best to spend a few days practising in her first, and getting used to her ways. All boats are different, and because you can sail a dinghy (or even because you can steer *Tessa* or *Ianthe*) you cannot therefore handle a boat like *Tern* really confidently and properly without a certain amount of practice. Moreover, *Tessa* and *Ianthe* were themselves going away in a few days' time, to take part in the annual meet of the club, to which both Mr. Rutherford and Mr. Chale happened to belong, in the Beaulieu river. They might both be away for a week, and the most sensible thing was for *Tern* to have her cruise at the same time.

"Let's decide now," said Elizabeth, "exactly when we can start—on our proper cruise, I mean."

"The meet's next Sunday," said Mr. Rutherford, "but I expect we shall be off a day or two before then."

"Daddy wants to go on Thursday," said Antony. "He says he's getting sick of doing nothing."

"If we went on Thursday," said Mrs. Rutherford, "it would give us nice time for the New Forest."

"New Forest?" said Elizabeth. "What do you mean?"

Mrs. Rutherford laughed. "You've forgotten?" she said.

"Why the New Forest?" said Antony.

"Mummy means the riding," said Anne.

As a matter of fact Elizabeth *had* forgotten. Neither she nor Anne had mentioned it since the evening when Mrs. Rutherford had made the suggestion that they should go, and neither of them had thought of saying anything about it to Antony or Robin. Antony, however, was interested.

"Riding?" he said. Mrs. Rutherford then explained what they had planned. Antony listened eagerly.

"Gosh," he said, "that would be marvellous."

"We might go on Tuesday," said Mrs. Rutherford. "If that's all right for Daddy—and the Bosun."

"Me?" said the Bosun. "It doesn't matter to me. I don't ride. The horse was never built that could carry me."

Antony shivered, and hugged his wet ribs with his arms.

"Robin can't ride," he said, "but I don't expect he'll mind." Elizabeth didn't think he would mind either—but then an uncomfortable thought occurred to her. She glanced at Antony.

"Does *Arthur* ride?" she said.

"I don't expect so," said Antony

"I bet he doesn't," said Anne, "except a motor-bike."

Antony grinned. Certainly, it would be difficult to imagine Arthur on a horse.

"Antony's getting cold," said Mrs. Rutherford.

"Come on," said Anne, "I'll take you back." She pulled up the dinghy and she and Antony got in. Elizabeth and Mrs. Rutherford went below to see if the kettle was boiling for breakfast.

After breakfast the mists had melted, and a small summer breeze was beginning to ruffle the surface of the water. It was blowing from the sun, a sure sign of a fine day to come. Anne, Elizabeth and Mrs. Rutherford spent a busy half-hour packing food; and on *Ianthe* Alf (directed by Mrs. Chale) did the same. Then Antony and Robin came off with Alf in *Ianthe's* dinghy. Mr. Rutherford took Anne and Elizabeth, and all four boarded *Tern*. An extra journey had to be taken by Mr. Rutherford because they had forgotten the chart; at the same time he brought a small methylated spirit-stove which they had bought in Newport before leaving in *Tessa*. They hadn't used it yet ; but to-day he thought it might be useful. The food and the coats (it was a hot day, but in sailing one never knows, and it is best to be prepared for emergencies) were stowed in the fo'c'sle, on the port side, clear of the anchor and warp, and the spirit-stove and matches under the seat aft, next to the tin of iron rations.

When everything was tidy Robin hoisted the burgee. (I forgot to mention the burgee before. Anne, in accordance with Antony's suggestion before *Tern* was even begun, had made it. It was of blue bunting and had a flying tern embroidered on it in white cotton.) Then, as *Tern* was lying head to wind and tide, Anne set the mainsail, while Robin got the jib hooked to the stay, and the halyard and sheets bent on ready for hoisting. When the jib was ready, Robin went aft to the tiller, and Antony hauled up the anchor. *Tern's* head canted to port, Antony hoisted the jib, the mainsail filled, and they were off. They waved good-bye to *Tessa* and *Ianthe* (Mr. and Mrs. Chale were on deck watching them start), Alf wished them a prosperous voyage, Mr. Rutherford who, like Alf, remained resting on his oars nearby, shouted to them to be back before midnight (or the Bosun would be anxious), and *Tern* with a fair wind and tide slipped quietly and swiftly up the narrowing channel of the South Deep towards Green Island.

What is more delightful than sailing on a fine day with a fair wind and a fair tide? If you hear some sailing man arrogantly assert that he prefers beating to windward against half a gale, don't believe him. The great thing in sailing is to be ready to take what comes—but when what comes is fair weather and a fair wind, then the real sailor is thankful.

It was Elizabeth's weather, so Elizabeth steered. Robin and Antony were squatting on the floorboards, their heads close together and the chart spread out. Every now and then one or the other would look ahead, verify a mark or perch, and tell Elizabeth on which side she must pass it. Brownsea Island, high and woody, lay on their right ; Green Island and Furze Island were ahead—the harbour indeed was full of islands ; and little twisting channels ran between. Inland, too, on their left, narrow creeks wound up between marshes or heath, all calling for exploration, all unknown water, silent, lonely and inviting. They would enter all of them soon, when their real cruise began ; they would circumnavigate every island, sail up every creek to its end, until the whole harbour was home. They would find nooks to pitch their tents in, and secret anchorages for *Tern* in places which even the buccaneers of old Poole, never knew.

Robin was happy again. What had happened yesterday had faded away in the pleasure of the present and in the anticipation of what was to come. He looked out of the corner of his eye at Antony as they bent over the chart together. Was Antony wishing he were in *Whynot*? No ; Antony was enjoying himself too.

At the western end of Brownsea the navigation became more intricate. Antony went to the tiller, and Robin kept the chart. Once or twice *Tern* touched the bottom, but they were able, by pulling up the centreboard and pushing with an oar, to get her off again. About the middle of the morning they anchored under the bank for their first meal ; there was no need to anchor, but it was pleasant to do so. It made it feel more like cruising—and there was plenty of time. It wasn't meant to be lunch, because it was early—only about twelve ; but having begun, they somehow went on, and lunch it became. They were quite hungry enough. There was pressed beef and lettuce and tomatoes and cheese and biscuits and cake—and some fresh figs. They hadn't expected the figs, but Mrs. Chale had slipped them in. They had come from the garden at the Manor, originally a large basketful, and still there were a few left. The peaches—also from the garden at the Manor—were finished ; but it is natural that peaches should be finished first, both because they go squashy sooner, and also because they are even more delicious. There were five figs, and Elizabeth had the extra one. Then, as the meal had turned into lunch, and as lying at anchor under a remote and sheltered shore is only less delightful than actually sailing, Anne suggested that they should try the spirit-stove and boil a kettle for cocoa. They put the stove in the fo'c'sle (the proper place for cooking), and, as *Tern* lay with her head to what little wind still reached them under the sheltering shore, they found that the flame burned steadily. It was a long and satisfactory meal and, except for the cocoa-mugs, which they sluiced over the side, there was no washing up.

When they got under way again the tide had begun to ebb ; so once more they found that they had arranged to have a fair tide both ways.

The breeze had gone round with the sun and got stronger, as it often does in fine summer weather. It was now almost southerly. *Tern* was reaching along the north shore of Brownsea. Robin was steering. The seclusion of the narrow creeks was gone ; there was a broad expanse of water on their left, lined and dotted with innumerable beacons, perches and buoys, right over to the shore by Poole Quay. A lot of other boats were about, and suddenly they recognized one that they knew.

Anne saw her first. "Look," she said. "Antony, look—there's the Yellow Peril."

There was no mistaking the orange hull. She was

about a quarter of a mile ahead of them, bound in the same direction.

"Gosh, so it is," said Antony.

Elizabeth looked at Robin, who said nothing.

"Let's chase her," said Antony. "Not that we'd ever catch her, though." He looked critically at the trim of the sails, and gave her another inch of jib sheet. "Come on, Robin," he said.

A few minutes later they saw *Whynot* come up into the wind and go about; she was coming to meet them.

"He's recognized us," said Antony.

The gap between the two boats was quickly closed. When Arthur was just in front of *Tern* he put *Whynot* about again, and when his sails filled on the other tack, the two boats were sailing side by side with not more than a dozen yards between them. Arthur shouted greetings and Antony replied. Robin remained as intent as he could on his steering.

"Are you going back to your moorings?" shouted Antony.

"Yes."

"We'll race you."

Arthur raised his hand in assent and gave a small extra pull on his main sheet.

There was a fine breeze now, and both boats were sailing fast. *Whynot* was heeled well over, and Arthur was sitting right up on the weather gunwale. Robin looked sideways at her as often as his steering would permit. He noticed with satisfaction that when the stronger puffs came, *Whynot* had to ease up a little into the wind: she would be better, Robin thought, with a reef. *Tern*, on the other hand, made easy weather even of the strongest puffs; she was only slightly heeled—indeed, it wasn't necessary for more than two of them to shift their seats to windward. No reefs for *Tern*, thought Robin. Why, she could do with much more sail than she had. How stiff she was—yes, stiff as a church. If only it would really blow. . . . She charged along with a curling wave under her forefoot and a hissing of bubbles at her stern.

They were gaining on *Whynot*. Each time the heavy puffs came, *Whynot* eased her sheet, or luffed, and each time she lost a little ground. Robin saw that Antony was pleased. . . . It was *Tern's* weather. . . . If only it would blow harder! A real blow—that was what *Tern* wanted. If only it would come, *Whynot* would be nowhere.

The boats were no longer side by side. *Whynot* was now definitely behind, following in *Tern's* wake. They could see Arthur perched precariously on the weather gunwale—" sitting her up ". Antony waved a gay, derisive hand. Arthur did not reply.

" Hoorah," said Elizabeth, " we're beating him."

" Good old *Tern*," said Anne.

" He'll be jolly annoyed," said Antony.

Robin did not speak. He clutched the tiller with fierce determination. He had for days past dreaded the race with *Whynot*; now it had unexpectedly happened. But *Tern* was doing well—marvellously well: much better than he had dared to hope . . . and Antony was pleased. Dark on the water a puff came down. *Tern* bowed to it and increased her speed. Antony laughed, his eyes on *Whynot*—" Look at her! " he said.

Whynot's sails were shaking—Arthur had been forced to bring her to the wind. Antony picked up the loose end of the main sheet and held it high above his head for Arthur to see.

" Want a tow? " he shouted. But Arthur was too far behind now even to hear that hoary jest.

Antony looked up at the burgee, which was flickering like a snake's tongue.

" She's jolly fast," he said.

Robin inwardly rejoiced ; but he said nothing, and minded his steering. If only it would blow harder . . . if only, all the way home, the wind would be free . . . But Robin knew that very soon, at the eastern end of Brownsea, they would have to turn, and beat to windward home. Antony knew it too ; but Antony didn't mind—not as Robin minded. Robin knew perfectly well that *Tern* was slow to windward, but it was not that fact which worried him. Had there been no Antony, it would have meant nothing to Robin to be beaten by *Whynot* every day. But there *was* an Antony—and an Arthur too. And Antony didn't know yet what Robin knew—that *Tern* was the best boat in the world, however slow to windward she might be. A twelve-metre racing yacht was faster to windward than a Bristol pilot cutter, or even than a Brixham trawler ; but only people like Arthur would despise the pilot cutter on that account. And Antony too? That was just the trouble. . . .

Round the end of the island the Haven was in sight, and the shipping in Brownsea roads. The breeze held true from the south, raising a chop against the ebb tide. *Tern* could no longer hold her course for home. The sheets were trimmed, and Robin, still at the tiller, settled grimly down for the beat to windward.

He glanced back at *Whynot*—she was well behind. She was heeled steeply over and little slaps of spray flew over her weather gunwale as she hit the waves.

" I wish it would blow, I wish it would blow," muttered Robin to himself.

Antony was watching *Whynot*.

" Let me take her for a bit," he said to Robin. Half thankfully, half regretfully, Robin abandoned the tiller to him. Antony was a good helmsman—perhaps it would be better to let him steer. Robin went forward, to be ready to handle the jib sheets.

Anne was watching *Whynot* too. " She's gaining," she said.

Elizabeth, with a look at Robin, denied it.

" She is," said Anne. " Isn't she, Antony ? "

Antony nodded. " Obviously," he said.

Indeed, it was true. Tack for tack the two boats beat down the channel, and at every tack *Whynot* crossed *Tern's* path a little nearer. They could see Arthur's face now : he was grinning.

With an impatient jerk Antony pulled the mainsheet tighter.

" The beastly boat's gone dead," he grumbled.

" You're p-pinching her," muttered Robin. " The sheet's too tight."

Antony slacked it off again irritably. " If we had a mainsail double the size," he said, " she might sail."

On the next tack *Whynot* passed only just astern. They could see half her bottom as she heeled. The spray flew.

" Gosh, she's moving," said Antony.

On the next tack she would pass them. Robin knew now that it was no good even wishing that it would blow. He looked at *Whynot* away to leeward under the island : he could not but admit to himself that she looked lovely—and that Arthur was handling her well. Yes, there was no doubt about it, Arthur knew how to sail a race. And there was no doubt that next time he would be ahead.

" Come on, Robin," said Antony. " You take her again. It's like trying to sail a tar-barrel."

Robin went back to the tiller. Antony began to whistle. Robin and Elizabeth exchanged a rapid glance.

" She's sailing j-jolly well," muttered Robin.

" Who? *Whynot?* "

" No, *Tern.*"

Antony laughed. " She's not bad with a fair wind," he said.

Whynot had gone about. Rapidly their tracks converged. Robin saw that it was hopeless : *Whynot* would pass easily ahead.

And of course she did.

The race was lost—as Robin knew it would be lost ; but knowing did not make it any the less hard to bear. Arthur had been right—in the Building Shed, ages ago, with his first horrible supercilious look. The heavy stern . . . slow to windward . . . he had seen it, and he had been right. *Tern's* transom *was* awkwardly designed ; she *was* slow to windward ; and Arthur no doubt was already rejoicing in his perspicacity, and despising *Tern.* And Antony—was Antony despising her too? That would be hardest to bear of all.

Antony had gone forward to tend the jib sheets ; Robin looked at his broad straight back and crisp brown hair, and wondered. Antony knew about boats, really ; he wasn't a fool, like Arthur. . . . But all the same, Robin was afraid.

Meanwhile *Tern* plodded doggedly on down the channel through Brownsea Roads, and *Whynot* with every tack drew farther and farther ahead. Presently they saw her come up into the wind and lower her mainsail.

" Hullo," said Antony, " he's hanging on to a mooring. He's waiting for us." He came aft and took the tiller from Robin. " Stand by the halyards, Robin," he said. " I'm going to run up alongside him."

Robin unwillingly obeyed ; but it was no good objecting : Antony had decided. Arthur, with *Whynot* made fast to the mooring-buoy, was sitting at ease in the stern and watching their approach. In a few minutes Antony had *Tern* alongside. Arthur tossed them a rope. He grinned—Robin thought he looked worse than ever when he grinned.

"You didn't do badly—considering," he said.

Robin inwardly fumed.

"Considering what?" said Elizabeth, not in her politest voice. Arthur ignored her.

"We'll take you on again," said Antony.

"There won't be time," said Anne. "We're going cruising." Arthur raised his eyebrows.

"Cruising?" he said. "Good for you. That's more your line, isn't it? If you want to race, Antony, you'd better come with me again. Still," he added condescendingly. "*Tern's* not a bad old tub. She'd blow along quite fast—with half a gale behind her."

Robin longed to say that with half a gale behind her—or in front, or anywhere else—*Whynot* would sink. Nevertheless, he kept silent. He wished Antony would let them go—there was no point in staying here. He began to fiddle with the main halyards.

"We jolly well left you on the reach," Antony said, "before we had to beat."

Robin was grateful for that.

"You wouldn't have, if I'd had a reef down," said Arthur.

"B-b-but you hadn't," said Robin.

Antony laughed. Poor old Robin, he thought, why should he be so solemn and earnest about it all?

"We might have another go to-morrow," he suggested.

"No good," said Arthur, "we're going out in *Zephyr*. But Tuesday would do."

"Not for us," said Anne. "We're riding."

Arthur looked surprised. "Riding?" he said. "Good Lord, where?"

"New Forest."

"*Billing*—something," said Elizabeth.

"Not Billingham?" Anne nodded.

"Why?" said Antony. "Do you ride too?"

"Lord no," said Arthur scornfully. "But I know Billingham. A pal of mine lives there. I say," he went on, "how are you going?"

"Bus," said Anne.

Arthur thought for a moment. Then he looked at Antony.

"I tell you what," he said. "I'll take you on the old bike." He grinned at the others. "There's only room for one, I'm afraid. What about it, Antony?"

Antony nodded. "Fine," he said.

"I could look in on Charles," said Arthur. "And it would be amusing to see you mount the gee-gee—what?"

"Don't be an ass," said Antony.

"You'll come, though?"

"All right."

The two boats got under way again. *Whynot* heading for her mooring in the creek.

"Hi! Arthur!" called Antony, before he was out of earshot. "Don't let the kids down you. Would you like an escort?" Arthur did not answer, but busied himself with tiller and sheet, as if he hadn't heard. Antony chuckled. "Poor old Arthur," he said.

It was still quite early in the afternoon—not nearly midnight, in fact—and there was no reason why *Tern* should go straight home. Moreover, there was some food left. They spent some time, therefore, in cruising about in Brownsea Roads watching the other boats coming in or going out, and critically examining (always an agreeable occupation) the various yachts at anchor. It was good practice too to sail past them excessively near, so that one could reach out a hand and touch their sides. Presently Elizabeth noticed *Maisie*, and drew Robin's attention to her.

"Look," she said, "they're both on board."

"Who do you mean?" asked Antony.

"The beach-boy—our beach-boy—and his father."

"Let's go close to them," said Robin.

Antony was curious to see Robin's beach-boy, so he willingly consented. The beach-boy had seen *Tern* long before she reached *Maisie*, and was on the look-out to greet her. His father, the fisherman, was not chipping paint because it was Sunday; he was putting a new lacing on to the head of the mainsail instead. He went on doing it even when Antony brought *Tern* to the wind alongside.

"'Ullo," said the beach-boy. "She looked proper nice, she did, beatin' to windward out there."

"We were racing," said Elizabeth. Then she caught Robin's eye and wished she hadn't said it.

"Coming aboard?" said the beach-boy.

Antony shook his head at Elizabeth. "Not time—not now," he said to her.

"We can't now," called Elizabeth.

The beach-boy looked disappointed. The fisherman continued his task. Antony let the mainsail draw, and *Tern* began to gather way.

"Hi!" shouted the beach-boy. "My dad says he'll take you out trawlin'."

"Gosh," said Robin, "I'd love to go—shall I shout to him?" Antony nodded. "When?" shouted Robin. "When can we come?"

The beach-boy appeared to have a hurried consultation with his father.

"Any when," he shouted back. Robin waved to show that he had understood—for *Tern* was now moving fast away. Robin kept his eyes on *Maisie* until it was time to go about. Then he waved again, and the beach-boy answered.

" When *shall* we go ? " he said.

" There's not much time," said Antony. " We're starting our cruise on Thursday."

" Robin," said Elizabeth, " why don't *you* go on Tuesday—when we're riding ? "

Robin pondered the suggestion, and found it satisfactory. He nodded his head quickly.

" All right," he said. " I will."

Tern sailed back up the South Deep towards home. Robin and Antony went aboard *Ianthe*, and Anne and Elizabeth took *Tern* to her anchorage. The Bosun fetched them. Tea was finished—but only just. It was quite possible to put a little more hot water in the pot.

" The Yellow Peril beat us," said Anne as she drank her tea.

" Poor old Robin ! " said the Bosun.

" But he's going out on a trawler on Tuesday," said Elizabeth. " When we're riding."

Yes—that would be some comfort, at any rate, for Robin. When he lay in bed that night he didn't talk much to Antony. But he thought a lot. Why could they never get away from Arthur ? Arthur was a beast . . . " you didn't do badly, *considering* . . ." Yes, he *was* a beast. If only he could prove—prove to horrible, condescending Arthur—and to Antony too—that *Tern* was a far better boat than *Whynot*. Antony ought to know. And he would know—if it wasn't for Arthur. It was all Arthur's fault. . . .

But he was going trawling on Tuesday : trawling in *Maisie*. . . . What had the beach-boy said—about *Tern* beating to windward ? " *She looked proper nice.*" O course she did : of course she looked marvellous. But it was good to know the beach-boy thought so too. It was comforting : and it was comforting too to think that he was going trawling on Tuesday. . . .

CHAPTER XXIII

WHEN Tuesday came, Robin was the first of the four children to begin the day. *Maisie* was going out early, after sprats in the bay. Robin therefore was called by Alf at half-past six, and given a cup of tea and some bread and butter. The rest of his day's food had been packed up the evening before, by Mrs. Chale's direction, in a basket. After breakfast Antony rowed over to *Tessa*, and the Bosun took the whole party—Anne, Elizabeth, Mrs. Rutherford and Antony—ashore in the dinghy. It was rather a heavy load, and it was a long pull, but the Bosun said resignedly that he was used to it and mustn't complain. In any case (as Anne remarked) he would have plenty of time during the rest of the day to sleep it off if he wanted to.

Arthur was on the look out for them, and met them at the jetty. He had his motor-bike ready, so he and Antony started first. Mrs. Rutherford, Anne and Elizabeth made their way to the bus.

The bus-ride took an hour and a half. The bu

eemed strange after *Tessa* and *Tern*. They had been iving afloat not much more than a week, but it was nough to make the land seem unfamiliar : it was not nly that they had land to look at instead of water ; but eople were different too, and clothes, and noises, and mells. And it was hot—with a different kind of heat.

When they arrived at Billingham they found Antony nd Arthur waiting for them at the bus-stop. Then they nade their way (Mrs. Rutherford knew it) all together o the stables. Mrs. Rutherford was doubtful at first if he would ride herself, because she had not got her iding clothes, but Anne and Elizabeth said it would be ickening if she didn't, and that she obviously must.

"You'll be perfectly all right in your trousers, Mummy," said Elizabeth.

Mrs. Rutherford didn't really want much persuading ecause she liked riding as much as Elizabeth and Anne lid (it was she who had taught them), and she had been lubious about her trousers merely from the point of view f propriety, and not at all of her own comfort. As it appened, none of the children were properly dressed, ither. They all had shorts on. But they got over the nconvenience of this by saying to the man at the stables hat they would ride bareback. The man accepted this— nd Mrs. Rutherford's trousers—with as good a grace as e could. It was not quite what he was used to—but it s difficult to combine the life of a mariner and a horseman vithout a small breach of etiquette.

Arthur stood by while they mounted. For a moment e rather wished he hadn't come ; all the others, he felt, ad with the mounting of their horses suddenly receded nto a world in which he had no share. It was vexing o know nothing about horses and nothing about riding. t would have been better (he thought), even though he idn't ride himself, if he could have made a knowledgeable comment or two. But he couldn't, and that made him sulky.

Elizabeth was the last to mount. She had a New Forest pony: a grey, with a patient but wary eye. Anne and Antony were walking their horses round the stable-yard, to try them. Mrs. Rutherford held hers in by Elizabeth, as the stable-man helped her on.

"All right?" she said.

"Lovely," said Elizabeth, leaning forward and patting the pony's neck.

"She'll be all right, M'm," said the stable-man. "He's used to children and as quiet as they make 'em."

Mrs. Rutherford caught Elizabeth's eye: she was not at all afraid of Elizabeth's ability to manage her pony.

"Come on, Mummy," called Anne.

Mrs. Rutherford and Elizabeth moved forward to join the others. Mrs. Rutherford thought how nice Antony looked on a horse; it was the first time she had seen him ride. Gay and gallant—that was what she called him in her mind. Arthur was watching Antony too, but sullenly and a little enviously. As they were preparing to move away, he got astride his bike and started the engine. At the sudden burst of noise, Elizabeth's pony tossed his head and edged a little sideways. Arthur raced his engine, still watching Antony. Antony's horse stopped and backed. Arthur raced his engine again. Anne's horse too showed signs of uneasiness and alarm.

"Do stop that beastly row," Antony called. Once more, just for a second, Arthur opened his throttle.

"Sorry, old chap," he said. "Doesn't the horse like it?"

Antony disdained to answer. Mrs. Rutherford looked at Arthur with disfavour. Anne and Elizabeth were too busy with their mounts to say anything.

Then Arthur let in the clutch, and sputtered away

owards the road. Just at the gate he stopped and looked
back.

"How long will you be, Antony?" he shouted.

"A couple of hours or so," Antony called.

Arthur raised his hand, and was gone. The four riders
noved off into the road, from which after a few minutes
hey turned and found themselves in a green lane winding
hrough woods. Antony was annoyed with Arthur; he
ıad obviously raced his engine deliberately to frighten
he horses. He ought to have known better; but then
Antony thought) Arthur knew nothing whatever about
ıorses, and he was an ass anyhow. But Antony soon
orgot him in the pleasure of the ride.

Arthur, for his part, did not forget Antony—or any of
he others—as he went racketing along the road on the
vay to see his friend Charles. He too was annoyed;
ıe was annoyed with Antony for the way in which he
ıad told him to stop revving up his engine, and for the
vay in which he and the others, but especially Antony,
ıad ridden off—or started to ride off—without taking
ıny notice of him. There was no reason why Antony
hould be so infernally conceited just because he was on
ı horse. Horses weren't much, anyhow: not nearly as
good as motor-bikes. And just because a chap was on
ı horse he thought he had the right to tell you to shut up.
The thing was absurd.

Then it occurred to Arthur that it might be amusing
o beat them all up a bit (that was how he put it to
ıimself) on their way back. Not, of course, that he'd
lo anything to hurt; he'd just make the horses skip a
ittle, by way of a joke. They all thought themselves
uch jolly superior riders, anyway, that they could hardly
bject. That horse of Antony's was a wicked-looking
levil—not that he knew one horse from another, really—
out that beast certainly had some kick in him. Antony

would look a fool if he came off—or anything like that. As for Mrs. Rutherford, she was quite a sport on the whole, and wouldn't cut up rough—in any case there would be nothing to cut up rough about. He was only going to make them jump. . . .

Arthur knew the general direction in which they intended to ride, and he knew that they would have to come back along the same stretch of road as that by which they had set out. Accordingly, after an interval of about two hours, he saw to it that he was on that bit of road, at a point about a quarter of a mile from the stables. He stopped his machine and shoved it off the road amongst the trees which bordered it. Then he sat down to wait, in such a position as enabled him to see the road and to remain hidden from anyone who might be travelling along it.

He waited for a quarter of an hour (he kept looking at his watch), but nobody came along the road but a couple of cars and one old woman pushing a perambulator filled with faggots. First he felt impatient, then he began to feel a trifle foolish : it was a kid's game, he thought, hiding behind trees. However, he might as well wait a bit longer—they'd be here any minute now.

Then he heard them coming : clop clop along the road. He peered out from behind his tree. There they were—Mrs. Rutherford and Elizabeth in front, Anne and Antony close behind. He thought Antony looked more cocksure and pleased with himself than ever—and there was the kid Elizabeth, humming to herself as usual, he supposed.

He waited until they were well past him, and then pushed his machine out on to the road. He started his engine and followed them. As he got near he hooted on his horn—sharply, twice, just to wake them up. Antony's horse and Elizabeth's pony each turned an pprehensive ear, and fidgeted. Arthur slowed down, nd hooted again—several times. Elizabeth's pony gave sudden start, but she pulled him in. Antony looked ack.

"Confounded idiot," he muttered. Then he signed vith his hand for Arthur to slow right down. Arthur till came on. Elizabeth's pony was getting more restive nd alarmed. With an angry gesture Antony shouted o Arthur to stop. He didn't stop. He still came on, ıst at the heels of Antony's horse ; and once more he lew his horn.

"Mind out," he called. "You might give me a bit f room."

Antony was just going to yell to him again, when lizabeth's pony reared in a panic and swung out on to he wrong side of the road, directly in front of Arthur's ıachine. Elizabeth set her teeth and clung on. Arthur, o save himself from running into the ditch, accelerated, nd shot past all four horses with his engine roaring. Ie missed Elizabeth's pony by an inch. The pony lunged in terror, flung Elizabeth from his back and alloped off riderless amongst the trees.

Mrs. Rutherford was off her horse in a second, and at lizabeth's side. A moment later Antony, white faced, as there too. Elizabeth was on the grass at the side of ıe road, lying face upwards with her pigtails spread out. Irs. Rutherford on her knees, slipped an arm under her ıoulders.

"Elizabeth, Elizabeth," she muttered with a sort of gonized urgency. There was nothing else to say. ntony and Anne watched, in dumb misery.

Then quite suddenly Elizabeth sat up, tossed back her igtails, and looked all round her with startled eyes.

"My pony," she said, "where's he gone? We must atch him."

Something turned over inside Mrs. Rutherford. Sh
felt weak and wobbly ; sudden and violent relief is almos
as hard to bear as pain.

" But are you *hurt* ? " said Antony. He had tossed hi
reins to Anne, and he too was on his knees beside Elizabeth. Then he put his arm round her. " Let's hel
her up," he said.

" Gently," said Mrs. Rutherford.

" It's all *right*," said Elizabeth. " It's perfectly al
right. . . ." She got to her feet.

" Are you sure there's nothing . . ." said Mrs
Rutherford.

" Oh, Mummy," said Elizabeth, " of course there isn't
Don't *fuss* ! "

Never before had Mrs. Rutherford been so happy t
hear an irritable word.

" My pony," said Elizabeth again. " Do go and ge
him, Antony."

Antony was only less relieved than Mrs. Rutherford
He took his reins from Anne, vaulted on his horse an
cantered off like a cowboy in pursuit of Elizabeth's pony

All this time Anne had been silent. When Antony ha
mounted, she drew in a breath through dilated nostril
lips tightly compressed.

" I could *kill* him," she said.

Antony quickly caught Elizabeth's pony and brough
him back. A minute after his return, they saw Arthu
walking back along the road towards them. His hanc
were in his pockets and he was walking slowly, with
hangdog look. When he came up with them he sh
a furtive glance from one to another of the group. Seein
Elizabeth apparently safe, he tried to speak with as littl
concern as possible, to hide his confusion.

" I say," he said, " no damage, I hope ? "

There was a silence. Arthur fidgeted uneasily.

"Arthur," said Mrs. Rutherford, "I simply don't know how you *could* . . ."

The three others kept their eyes resolutely on the ground. Arthur grew more uncomfortable.

"Well, dash it," he said, "the beastly horse coming right across me like that . . . it jolly nearly had me in the ditch." His voice was half plaintive, half blustering.

Antony looked straight at him, in astonishment and anger. "Good God . . ." he began; but for the moment he could say no more.

Arthur began to whine: "I only meant to stir you up a bit," he said. "It was only a joke. I didn't think it would do any harm. . . ."

Then Antony could contain himself no longer. "You fool," he burst out. "You unutterable fool. Bittle . . . Elizabeth . . . might have been *killed*. . . ." His face was white with anger. Arthur's lower lip trembled.

"But dash it all," he stammered, "you needn't . . . after all, she isn't hurt. . . ." But Antony wouldn't let him go on.

"Get out," he said with contempt; and then again, savagely: "*Get out!*"

Arthur turned and slunk back down the road to his motor-bike.

Elizabeth was standing by her pony, holding the bridle. Mrs. Rutherford was watching her. Antony, who was still on his horse, moved over beside her.

"Shall I lead him back for you?" he said.

"No," said Elizabeth. "I'll ride."

"Just a moment," said Antony. He dismounted, tossed his reins to Anne, and helped Elizabeth on. "All right?"

"Yes, quite."

"Sure?" said Mrs. Rutherford.

"Of course, Mummy."

Then the four rode back to the stables. On the return journey there was (of course) one extra in the bus.

During the bus-ride Anne said to Elizabeth: "Bittle, did you hear what he said—about your pony nearly having him in the ditch?"

"Yes."

"That's exactly what he said ages ago, at the cottage, when he nearly killed Sally. Do you remember?"

Elizabeth nodded.

"Yes," she said. "He *is* a beast, isn't he, Anne?"

"I should jolly well think he is," said Anne.

"Gosh, so should I," said Antony, who was sitting on Elizabeth's other side. "An unutterable beast."

. . . .

Meanwhile Robin had had a great day on *Maisie*. To enjoy trawling you must be interested either in fish, or in boats—or in both. Robin was not interested in fish, but he was excessively interested in boats. Therefore he was happy. *Maisie* he loved: she was not at all like *Ianthe*; nobody minded if you walked on her deck in boots; she was rough, and thick, and strong. She was even less like *Whynot*. She was (Robin thought) a little bit like *Tern*. Not, of course, in detail or design—or size, for *Maisie* was a sea-going vessel of eight or nine tons; but Robin did feel very strongly that if only *Tern* smelt of fish she would definitely belong to the same family as *Maisie*. Both *Maisie* and *Tern* looked as if they were built for work.

He had great pleasure too in watching the casual but extremely efficient way in which the fisherman handled her; everything he did seemed to be easy, even though it wasn't. Nothing hurried him, nothing bothered him.

They were out all day, and though Robin helped to haul and shoot the trawl at regular intervals, for most of the time he had nothing to do. But he wasn't bored for a moment. The fisherman talked little and asked no questions, but Robin liked him ; for Robin himself never talked much either, and when people are doing important work together (like trawling) there is no need to invent conversation. The beach-boy, too, was more silent than he had been on *Tern* ; he kept his eye on his dad, and jumped to obey orders when any were given. He was proud of *Maisie*, and obviously glad to find that Robin approved of her.

It was sunset when *Maisie* got back to her moorings, and the light was already beginning to fail. While the fisherman was stowing gear and seeing to his catch, Robin noticed that the beach-boy (whose name, by the way, had turned out to be Sammy) was scanning the foreshore by the jetty in an interested manner.

" What are you looking at ? " he asked him.

Sammy, however, seemed embarrassed by the question. He turned away, and pretended that it was nothing important. Robin looked where Sammy had looked—and Robin too became interested.

It was low water, and *Whynot* was lying on the sand in her usual place. It was always easy to recognize the orange hull. But the interesting thing was not *Whynot* herself, but the fact that two boys—evidently beach-boys—were busily occupied with her. She was too far away for Robin to see what it was that they were doing ; one of them, however, was squatting on his haunches close to her side, while the other was standing near him, apparently—so it seemed to Robin from the way he kept looking this way and that along the foreshore—keeping watch.

Robin turned to Sammy. " I s-say," he stammered, " wh-what are they doing ? " The sight of them, and the fact of Sammy's embarrassment a moment before, when Robin had asked what he was staring at, had brought to Robin's mind the veiled and mysterious threat which Sammy had uttered during their sail in *Tern*.

"*He'd better mind out*": that was what Sammy had said; and he had refused to say any more.

Robin was disturbed. The behaviour of the two boys was undeniably suspicious. Nobody could pretend that they were merely engaged in the general (but irritating) task of "keeping an eye" on *Whynot*. What they were doing was something more definite than that; and the fact that they were doing it in the gathering dusk, boded no good either to *Whynot* or to Arthur. Robin, though he would have welcomed most things which might contribute to Arthur's discomfiture, could not but rebel at the idea of actual damage to his boat. And it was for that reason that he was disturbed.

He passed his tongue along his top lip, and, rather huskily, spoke again to Sammy.

"But wh-what *are* they doing?" he said.

Sammy was evasive. "What are '*oo* doin'?" he said. "Them boys? That's Bert Simmons an' Eddie Crouch. Aow do I know what they're doin'? Just messin' around, I reckon."

He looked out of the tail of his eye at his father as he spoke. But his father—fortunately—seemed not to have heard. At any rate he took no notice.

But Robin was not satisfied.

"Sammy," he said, speaking low so that Sammy's father should not hear; "they wouldn't . . . they wouldn't . . . bust her up, would they?"

Sammy sniffed, and spat over the side into the water.

"Bust 'er up?" he said. "Naow! They won't do nuthen. . . ." Then he edged a little nearer to Robin, and when he spoke again it was ingratiatingly, and almost in a whisper. "See 'ere," he said, "what Bert an' Eddie does ain't my business, see? An' 'taint yours neither, see?"

"I know . . ." began Robin, but Sammy interrupted him.

"That bloke," he went on, "'im what 'as the *Whynot*, 'e ain't no friend o' yourn."

He paused, and stared fixedly at the water where he had spat. Robin was uncomfortable. He liked Sammy, and he couldn't bear Arthur; still, the turn that things seemed to be taking was, to say the least of it, awkward. He wished Antony were with him.

"B-but," he stammered—but once again Sammy would not let him speak.

"G'arn!" he whispered. "Don't you worry. They won't do no 'arm."

Robin, however, was not so sure.

At that moment, to his great pleasure and surprise, he saw Antony rowing towards *Maisie* in *Ianthe*'s dinghy. When the dinghy got near, Antony turned his head and shouted a greeting.

"Hullo," called Robin. "I didn't know you were coming."

Antony pulled alongside and shipped his oars.

"I saw you pick up your moorings," he said. "We've been home ages. I thought I'd row over and fetch you."

This was eminently satisfactory. Robin had just been wishing that Antony were with him; now here he was. Moreover, Antony's coming would save Sammy's father the long row to the South Deep. Robin said good-bye, and added his thanks for the day's outing—"You're welcome" was all that Sammy's father said in reply—and then got into the dinghy with Antony.

"I'll row," he said. He took the oars, and pulled a few strokes. "I've had a lovely time—*Maisie*'s marvellous. I say, Antony . . ."

" What ? "

" I was just wishing you were here. I wanted to tell you. Those boys . . . those beach-boys . . . not *our* beach-boy . . . not Sammy . . . but the others . . . they're doing something to *Whynot.* I'm sure they are. I was watching them from *Maisie.* We ought to stop them, oughtn't we ? Of course, I couldn't see very well, but . . ."

Antony did not let him continue. " *Doing* something ? " he said. " Doing what ? "

" I don't know. I couldn't see," said Robin.

" Something *bad* ? " said Antony.

Then to Robin's astonishment he went suddenly very red, and said—quietly, but with a sort of intense urgency and conviction : " Gosh, I hope they *smash* the beastly boat."

Robin stared round-eyed. Antony looked straight at him and said : " Robin, you were right. He's a beast. Arthur's a beast. An absolute beast." He then told Robin the story of what had happened that afternoon during the riding. Robin slackened his strokes as he listened. When Antony had finished there was a moment's silence.

Then Robin said, " But do you mean, he d-did it on *purpose* ? "

Antony shrugged his shoulders in a gesture of contempt. " If he did," he said, " he was an utter cad ; if he didn't, he was an utter fool. He was a beast, anyhow. Gosh—he might have killed her—he might have killed Elizabeth ! "

Robin rested on his oars : it was impossible to go on rowing just at that moment. First Elizabeth had been nearly killed—by Arthur ; then he had never seen Antony so angry—and his anger was against Arthur. Robin had always known that Arthur was a beast ; but he hadn't known he was *that* sort of beast: he never thought he would deliberately—if it *was* deliberately—charge on his motor-bike through a crowd of people riding, just to frighten them. He was even worse than he had thought. And Elizabeth—she might have been killed . . . He felt a little cold black emptiness inside him—horrible. But it passed, and he felt instead a secret joy: *Antony* knew that Arthur was a beast. He had never known it before; but now he did; he was boiling with rage against him.

But what about *Whynot*? Suppose the beach-boys really had done something serious, oughtn't he and Antony to find out and warn him? It might be dangerous—besides, it was a dreadful thing to tamper with a boat: with anybody's boat, even Arthur's.

"Antony," he said huskily.

"What?"

"Oughtn't we to go and *see* what they were doing?"

Antony waited a moment before answering: then, "All right," he said. "And I jolly well hope we find they've bashed her bottom in."

Robin couldn't help chuckling at the violence of Antony's words.

"Let's go now," he said. "They've gone by now, and we shall be able to see before it's quite dark."

Antony agreed; so Robin turned the dinghy round and rowed back into the creek. All the wind had gone with the setting of the sun, and the water was glassy smooth. The yachts in the roads had their riding lights up: yellow stars in the dusk. The clank of the dinghy's rowlocks deepened the quietness.

The foreshore by the jetty was deserted. Silently they beached the dinghy opposite where *Whynot* lay, took off their shoes and got out. They hauled the boat up a yard or two, for the tide was rising, and laid out the anchor.

"There's nobody c-coming," whispered Robin.

Antony, too, looked left and right through the dusk, along the pebbly sand.

"Come on," he whispered.

They padded stealthily on their bare feet up the stretch of sand.

Robin peered over *Whynot's* gunwale. "She l-looks all right," he said. At any rate her bottom wasn't bashed in. Meanwhile Antony was going carefully over her, stopping every now and then to take a precautionary look along the sand, in case anybody was coming; for, though they were doing no wrong, they nevertheless both felt that it would be unpleasant if anyone were to see them.

"What did he *seem* to be doing, when you saw him?" Antony whispered. "I can't find anything—can you?"

"It was difficult to tell," answered Robin, "they were so far off. But one of them was sort of crouching down. . . ."

"Inside her, or outside?"

"Outside. And I think the other was keeping watch."

"Which side was he on?" said Antony. "This side, I suppose—or you wouldn't have seen him."

Robin nodded. Antony once again examined *Whynot's* side—the starboard side, nearest the water. He peered close in the dark.

Suddenly he straightened up. "Robin," he said, "I've got it. Look. It's the shroud plate."

Robin peered. "It's loose," he said.

The shroud plates are flat narrow pieces of iron, with a loop on top; they are screwed to the sides of a boat, with the loop projecting above the gunwale, so that the shrouds (or backstays) can be made fast to them. If they break, the stays of course collapse too, and almost certainly the mast goes over the side—and that is a major disaster.

" They've unscrewed it," said Antony. " And they've bored out the screw holes, and pushed the screws in again."

" So that it wouldn't show," said Robin.

" It's quite loose. Feel it. It wouldn't last a second. But he easily might not notice—until it was too late. Gosh, it's pretty cunning."

" It wasn't Sammy," said Robin.

" Of course not. I know. He was with you."

Robin fingered the plate. He was thinking. Arthur was a beast—there was no doubt about that. Antony too knew it now. He was a beast, and it would serve him right if he went out sailing in *Whynot* and his mast broke. He'd be furious—and he would look a fool . . . It wasn't as if they had done it. He and Antony had done nothing. It was the beach-boys—and they too had plenty of reason for thinking Arthur a beast. It was a fair revenge. . . .

But at the same time, nobody *ought* to damage a boat. It was much worse, really, than damaging anything else—a motor-bike, for instance.

" B-but, Antony," he began.

" What ? " said Antony.

" We ought to t-tell him, oughtn't we ? "

" *Tell* him ? Why ? "

Robin knew why, but it was difficult to explain. Antony was much too angry to listen to reasons.

" *Tell* him ? " he repeated. " Good Lord—but don't you realize what he's done ? Why on earth *should* we tell him ? "

It was queer for Robin to have to argue on behalf of Arthur against Antony—against this new and angry Antony. It was queer, and difficult as well. But Robin couldn't give it up.

"But suppose," he said, "suppose the mast broke and he was drowned, or . . ."

Antony stopped him with a laugh. "Don't talk rot, Robin," he said. "Of course he won't be drowned—though I jolly well wouldn't care if he was. Anyway, he never dares take *Whynot* out if there's any wind. Not even *that* idiot could drown himself in the harbour on a calm day. Come on; let's get back to *Ianthe*."

Robin had to consent, though unwillingly. He was sure that they ought to warn Arthur. It was one thing to loathe a person, but it was quite another to allow his boat to be tampered with, and so bring him into danger. But perhaps Antony was right: perhaps there wasn't really any danger. It was true, as Sammy had said, that Arthur never went out in *Whynot* in rough weather—and it was unlikely that he would venture outside the harbour, even if the weather was calm. Robin, however, could not help wishing that they didn't *know* about the shroud plate.

Nevertheless, in spite of his doubts, Robin was inwardly happy; he was happier than he had been for a long time.

CHAPTER XXIV

It was a tired Robin who tumbled into his bunk that night at half-past ten. He had had supper when he got back to *Ianthe*, and had told his father and mother about his day's trawling ; he had not, of course, said anything to them about *Whynot*. Nor had Antony : that sort of thing is much better undisclosed.

Antony had seen the Bosun after their return from the New Forest. The story of Arthur's behaviour in the New Forest was still being amplified and commented on in *Tessa's* cabin when he arrived on board. Antony joined in, and added to the general chorus of indignation. Mr. Rutherford thought that they should never have anything to do with Arthur again. The Bosun was furious.

"That fellow," he said, "will never be drowned, if that's any comfort to him. He was born to be hanged."

Then he had told Antony how he and Mr. Rutherford had spent the day in laying in stores for the coming cruises : for *Tessa's* cruise to Beaulieu, and for *Tern's* cruise to—well, where *Tern* was going was not yet decided. All was therefore ready for the start on Thursday. It would have been quite possible to do the provisioning on Wednesday, but the Bosun pointed out that he was always fond of work, and that he and Mr. Rutherford had to have some sort of occupation during their lonely day: moreover, something was pretty sure to be forgotten, and it would be convenient to have a spare day in which to make up the deficiency.

"Your father always forgets things," he said to Elizabeth. "He's a poor caterer."

"He doesn't," said Elizabeth. "Anyway, Mummy doesn't."

"I said your father," replied the Bosun. "He does it on purpose."

"Why?"

"Because he thinks it's more economical."

"But it isn't," said Elizabeth. "He has to go again afterwards."

"Exactly," said the Bosun. "That's what I tell him."

But whether or not Mr. Rutherford and the Bosun had forgotten anything, they had certainly remembered a great deal. The parcels were mountainous.

"They're all over my bed," said Anne. "And Bittle's."

"Ungrateful child," said the Bosun.

Elizabeth had herself inspected the stores. Her inspection was not thorough; it was hasty, but purposeful. She didn't mind particularly about the bacon and the rice, and that sort of thing; but it was important to be sure about the bananas and the chocolate and the raisins.

Next morning, which was Wednesday, Antony and Robin both appeared on *Tessa* by way of the bobstay and the morning bathe. Anne was cooking breakfast.

She left the frying to Mr. Rutherford and went on deck. Elizabeth was already there.

"Hullo," said Antony. "I could smell your bacon as we were swimming over."

"Haven't you bathed?" said Robin.

Elizabeth and Anne hadn't; they were not as regular in early morning bathes as the boys were. Besides, this morning was not quite so fine as it had been.

"The glass has dropped a bit," said Antony.

"Half a tenth," said Robin.

"I know," said Anne. "The Bosun tapped ours."

"I hope it'll keep fine for to-morrow," said Antony. "Alf thinks it will."

"The Bosun says there might be thunder," said Elizabeth. "But I hope not. If there is, Daddy says we mustn't go outside the harbour."

Antony exchanged a glance with Robin. He wondered if he ought to tell Anne and Elizabeth about *Whynot*, but decided that he wouldn't. It was better, he thought, not to have more people arguing about it. He himself was feeling less sure than he had felt last night about the rightness of saying nothing to Arthur, and the fact of feeling less sure made him the more unwilling to discuss it with Elizabeth and Anne. Not that he was any less angry with Arthur, or any less contemptuous of the way he had behaved; his anger and contempt were as strong as ever; indeed, he was ashamed of having pretended to himself so long—just for the sake of rides on the motor-bike and races in *Whynot*—that Arthur was really not nearly so bad as the others (especially Robin) seemed to think; but he was beginning to feel, with Robin, that it might be mean to let him go out without a warning in an unseaworthy boat, even though there was no real danger.

It was therefore a relief to him when, as they were all

four sailing in *Tern* after breakfast, they saw that *Zephyr*, on her moorings in Brownsea Roads, was preparing to get under way, with Arthur on board. They passed close to her out of curiosity, but not too close—out of delicacy. Arthur was wearing a new pair of white ducks and his yachting cap ; Elizabeth wanted very much to see if it had a new badge on it, but she couldn't. He looked so repulsive, Antony thought, that his scruples about *Whynot* began to weaken again, but only momentarily. It *was* an awkward situation ; but it was a good thing that it was not yet critical, for there was no need to decide absolutely to-day whether or not to tell him : he would be safe to-day at any rate, because he was going out in *Zephyr*.

Robin was still secretly and solemnly happy, even more so than last night. They were all four, so to speak, together again ; the miserable feeling that Antony no longer belonged to them, as he had belonged last year, was gone ; there was no fear now that he was turning in his thoughts away from *Tern*, and towards other things—Arthur's things. And not only was Antony with him again, properly with him, but they were also on the eve of a cruise, the first real cruise that *Tern* had ever had. And though the trial trip from Yarmouth had been splendid, and though sailing about in the harbour for the past days had been good too, neither had been equal to what a proper cruise would be. Poole Harbour was a wonderful place for cruising in ; it would take years really to grow familiar with its creeks and islands and lonely places ; it was better even than the Roach at Burnham where they had cruised last year in *Puffin* and *Sheldrake*. *Tern* herself, too, was far better than a dinghy ; she was a real *boat* ; they could go outside the harbour if they wanted to—to Old Harry, or even Swanage. For *Tern* had proved her qualities in the open sea. . . .

"Antony," said Robin suddenly.

"What?"

Robin had meant to ask Antony if he didn't really think now that *Tern* was a much finer boat than *Whynot*—in spite of the fact that she was not so fast to windward. But his courage failed him. He was pretty sure that Antony did think so; and it would have been comforting actually to hear him say it; nevertheless, it wasn't, after all, easy to ask him. In fact, the words refused to come.

"Oh . . . n-nothing," he stammered.

Antony laughed, and asked Robin to come and take the tiller. Robin did so.

They sailed about till lunch-time, not going anywhere in particular, but just sailing. The afternoon was occupied mainly in loading *Tern* with stores for the cruise. There was a lot to put on board—more than they had had to put in *Puffin* and *Sheldrake* the previous year, because all the most interesting anchorages in Poole Harbour are a very long way from shops, and it would not be possible to get fresh provisions every day without spoiling the cruise. In addition to food they also had to stow the tent (this belonged to Antony and Robin), the blankets, the air-mattresses, and a considerable amount of extra clothing in case of wet, cold, or other emergencies. Then there were the cooking utensils, and the primus. By the time everything was on board, *Tern's* fo'c'sle was packed tight, the locker under the seat aft was full, and there was a good deal just lying about on the floorboards—the kind of things one can't possibly find a place for, like mackintoshes and an unexpected extra basket of apples and a tin can of paraffin.

In the evening *Tessa's* whole company went to supper again on *Ianthe*. One might have expected that it was *Tessa's* turn to entertain *Ianthe* this time, and so it really was; but *Tessa* was smaller than *Ianthe*, and nine people at supper in her saloon would have made an almost intolerable squash. Mrs. Chale realized this, and told Mrs. Rutherford that it would be much more sensible if they came again to *Ianthe* ; besides, Mrs. Chale also knew that it would be rather flustering for Mrs. Rutherford to have to cook supper for so many people, whereas Alf was used to it. Mrs. Rutherford—though she wouldn't have admitted it—secretly agreed.

Supper was a good deal less demure than it had been on the previous occasion. This was partly because they knew each other better, and partly because there was so much to talk about with all three vessels on the eve of a cruise. Elizabeth sat next to Mr. Chale. She didn't actually have an accident with her chop, but, as even round *Ianthe's* table nine people were a tight fit, she did have a certain difficulty : there was no room to raise her elbows properly in order to exert the necessary strength to carve it. So she abandoned the attempt.

" Will *you* do it ? " she said to Mr. Chale. Mr. Chale (to show there was no ill feeling) complied.

In addition to discussing details of the coming cruises, they also talked a good deal about the weather. People on shore talk about the weather when they've got nothing else to say ; but people at sea talk about it because it is extremely interesting and important. Both on *Tessa* and on *Ianthe* few people during the course of the day had passed the barometer without giving it an interrogatory tap ; and the disturbing thing was that it had fallen a little bit more. Only a little. But it *had* fallen. Alf had become less confident in the continuance of fine weather, and more inclined to agree with the Bosun that there was probably thunder about.

Mr. Chale and Mr. Rutherford both impressed upon Antony (for Antony would, of course, be in charge of *Tern*) that unless the weather obviously improved to-morrow they must on no account go outside the harbour.

"And it will be no hardship, either," said Mr. Rutherford. "The harbour is a splendid cruising ground. You've sixty miles of waterways to explore—and you hardly know any of them yet."

Antony promised to obey. He knew it was important; and he knew he was responsible for the safety of the other three. Nevertheless, it was a pity that the glass was falling. It would have been pleasanter to feel that they could go outside into the bay if they wanted. Of course, they might *not* want to do so; but one never knew. . . . However necessary it might be to bind himself by a promise, it was nevertheless irksome.

"And remember," said Mr. Chale, "taking unnecessary risks at sea is neither courageous nor commendable. It's simply silly. No sailor ever does it. He is ready to face what he must face, but he makes everything as safe and easy as he possibly can. Sometimes he can't—so much the worse for him. But if he can, he does."

"Like a good billiards player," said the Bosun, "who always leaves himself an easy shot."

While the conversation about the weather was going on, Antony could not help feeling more and more uncomfortable about *Whynot*. On several occasions he felt Robin looking at him, and he knew that Robin's thoughts were running in the same direction as his own. He knew that he was (so to speak) captain of *Tern*, and, as captain, responsible for the rest; and the serious way in which his father and Mr. Rutherford—and the Bosun too—had been talking about the folly of taking unnecessary risks, impressed the feeling of responsibility on him more deeply; and it was difficult to be responsible for the safety of one boat's crew and at the same time deliberately to ignore the safety of another. For he was coming in spite of himself to feel that it *would* be dangerous to let Arthur go out in *Whynot* without a warning. At first. the idea of danger had not occurred to him. Perhaps he had been too angry to think at all. His one wish, the result of his rage, had been that Arthur should suffer in return for what he had done. But now it all seemed a bit different. He was still just as angry ; but he had had time to think. He knew that Arthur was a timid sailor ; but even a timid sailor may be caught out in a thunder squall. Perhaps, after all, they would have to tell him what the beach-boys had done. . . . It would be pretty beastly, telling him. He never wanted to speak to him again. Nevertheless, it might be necessary.

The supper party broke up early, because it is a good thing to get as much sleep as possible on the night before a cruise begins. For on the night after it has begun one seldom gets any sleep at all. But though the four children all went to bed early, it was a long time before Antony was asleep. He was worried. He talked to Robin as long as possible ; but Robin went to sleep.

After that there was nothing to do but think. So he lay on his back in his narrow bunk and thought. He listened to Robin's regular breathing, and wished he could go to sleep too ; but he couldn't. He reached out a hand in the dark, and it touched Robin's cheek. Robin from his sleep made a small noise as if he had recognized the touch, and burrowed deeper into his blankets. Good old Robin . . . he had made him pretty miserable once or twice lately . . . but Robin always took things hard. It was a pity he didn't like racing, and motor-bikes, and things like that . . . they were jolly good fun really, and he had enjoyed going out with Arthur. But he'd die rather than go again. Robin had been right about Arthur from the beginning—Robin had always loathed him, even before he had actually *done* anything. It was difficult to see why. Perhaps he *did* see, though it wasn't easy to explain, even to himself.

Then he thought of Elizabeth again—Bittle—falling from her pony, and lying for that horrible moment motionless in the grass by the side of the road, and a new surge of anger came up in him. Because of Elizabeth—yes, and because of Robin too—he felt once more that Arthur deserved anything he might suffer in the way of punishment. Why should he warn him of what those boys had done? It wasn't *his* business . . . Arthur had been beastly to them too. . . .

But the glass was going down. There was thunder about. Any time now there might be a squall. Arthur would stay ashore if he knew it was going to blow; but perhaps he wouldn't know. Perhaps he would be caught . . . and it might be dangerous. What he did to Bittle was dangerous too . . . but he didn't *mean* it to be. To let him sail in *Whynot* without a warning would be different: it would be bringing him into danger on purpose. Even in calm weather—even in harbour—an accident to a boat can be dangerous. He remembered how his father at Creeksea years ago had capsized *Ladybird*, when he was on board. Uncle Lance was on board too. It had not seemed dangerous; but Uncle Lance had told him afterwards how his father, just as *Ladybird* went over, had noticed that the end of the main sheet was round his body, and had jerked it free. It might have pulled him under.

"Robin," Antony muttered. "Robin—we must tell him." But Robin was asleep. He didn't even grunt. But he was right—Robin was right: it was their plain duty to tell Arthur what the beach-boys had done.

Antony lay staring in the dark at the deck-beams close above him. The slow night went on. He heard *Ianthe* stir at the turn of the tide, and her chain clank faintly. A few drops of rain pattered sullenly on the deck. It was a long time before he was asleep.

. . . .

When Antony awoke in the morning Robin was already up. Mr. and Mrs. Chale were dressing in their cabin, and Alf was laying breakfast. Antony hurriedly put on his clothes and went on deck.

"Hullo," said Robin. "I've been up for ages."

"Is it going to be fine?" said Antony. "I say, Robin, we must tell him. I've been thinking it over. We must tell Arthur."

"When?"

"Before we start. He may be on *Zephyr*. We can sail over and see. Or he may be ashore."

Robin did not say anything; but he was glad. He knew Antony was right.

It was a bright morning with not much wind. There was no mist, and the distances were sharp and clear.

"The glass hasn't gone down any more," said Robin.

"Good. What does Alf think?"

As a matter of fact Alf had been less cheerful than the morning was when Robin first saw him. He had shaken his head and looked doubtful.

"Maybe it'll keep fine," he said. That was not very satisfactory, but Robin couldn't get him to say any more.

Mr. Chale, when he came on deck, was doubtful too. After breakfast, when Antony and Robin had said good-bye to Mrs. Chale, Mr. Chale came over with them to *Tessa*, and had a consultation with Mr. Rutherford and the Bosun. All three were agreed that *Tern* must not venture outside the harbour while *Tessa* and *Ianthe* were away. In a spell of settled fine weather, such as they had had during their first few days, it would have been all right ; but not now.

"No unnecessary risks," repeated Mr. Chale.

Mr. Rutherford looked at Antony. "All right ?" he said.

Antony nodded. "All right," he answered.

Ianthe and *Tessa* were both preparing to get under way. *Tern* was all ready, and could start at any minute. Antony, however, was anxious not to start before *Ianthe* and *Tessa*, because everybody would wonder why *Tern* was going to the jetty in the creek, and at the end of the cruise they might ask questions. Antony knew that there was nothing to hide now that he had decided to tell Arthur ; but at the same time he preferred not to discuss the affair of *Whynot* with his father or Mr. and Mrs. Rutherford. It was convenient, therefore, that he suddenly remembered about the tent-pegs.

"Oh, by the way," he said, "we must go ashore before we really start. We've got to get some more tent-pegs. There aren't enough."

The tent-pegs were meat skewers ; they had bought the last lot in the butcher's shop in the High Street at Burnham, last year.

"Bother," said Elizabeth. "It's a waste of time."

Antony and Robin exchanged glances.

Then the four children got into *Ianthe's* dinghy, and Mr. Chale rowed them across to *Tern*. Mrs. Rutherford came too, just to see them safely aboard—though she could have seen just as well from *Tessa's* deck. Mr. Rutherford and the Bosun were busy preparing *Tessa* for sea.

"Take care of yourselves," said Mrs. Rutherford. "Good luck to you."

"Good luck to *Tessa*," said Antony.

"And to *Ianthe*," said Anne.

Mr. Chale began to pull away. " And don't forget," he said. " No unnecessary risks."

" Of course not," said Antony.

Then they all said good-bye, and Mr. Chale took Mrs. Rutherford back to *Tessa*, and himself returned to *Ianthe*—where Alf and his mate were as busy as Mr. Rutherford and the Bosun were.

In a few minutes *Tern's* mainsail was set, her jib clipped on the stay, and her anchor up. Antony went to the tiller, and they were off. Once more they waved and shouted good-bye to everybody on board the two yachts. As *Tern* slipped past *Ianthe*, Alf raised his hand in salute and grinned.

" Jib up, Robin," said Antony. The clip hooks rattled on the stay. *Tern*, with the wind behind her, headed between the buoys at the entrance to the South Deep.

" Where are we going first ? " said Elizabeth. " Oh—the tent-pegs, I suppose."

Antony caught Robin's eye, and waited a moment before answering.

" As a matter of fact," he said, " we've got to see Arthur."

" *Arthur ?* " said Anne. " Why on earth ? "

" They've been m-messing about with *Whynot*," said Robin. " We've got to tell him."

" Who have ? "

" The beach-boys."

" Not Sammy ? " said Elizabeth.

" No—the others."

" What did they do ? " asked Anne.

Antony explained.

" Gosh," said Anne. " It would jolly well serve him right if we *didn't* tell him."

" I know," said Antony. " But we must all the same."

" Why ? " said Elizabeth.

" Because we must," said Antony.

Zephyr lay up stream a little, on their left. Antony altered his course to pass near her. He could see one of her hands polishing brasswork on deck.

" He d-doesn't seem to be there," said Robin, his eyes on *Zephyr*.

" Perhaps he's down below," said Antony.

The deck-hand looked up from his work as *Tern* passed.

" Anyone on board ? " called Antony. The deck-hand shook his head.

" The boss may be coming later," he said.

Antony bore away and headed for the entrance to the creek.

" Perhaps he's with *Whynot*," he said. " Or if not, we'll find him at his house."

" I hope we *d-do* find him," said Robin.

" Of course we shall," said Antony shortly.

Tern entered the creek. All four children looked towards the place where *Whynot* usually lay. She was not there.

" Where's she gone ? " said Elizabeth.

" *I* don't know," said Antony irritably.

Robin lowered the jib. He knew Antony was feeling anxious and worried.

" I expect she's at the yard," he said.

" Why should she be ? "

" For repairs—he may have found out."

Antony told Anne to pull up the centreboard. Anne fumbled at the cleat.

" Oh, buck *up*," Antony said. " We'll be aground."

Tern ran alongside the jetty. Robin jumped out and took her rope and made it fast. Antony lowered the mainsail. They all got out.

At the top end of the jetty, Antony hesitated. He

looked again over to where *Whynot* usually lay. No : she was not there.

Elizabeth plucked Robin's sleeve. " Look," she said, " there's our beach-boy."

Robin looked. " S-sammy," he said.

" Where ? " said Antony.

Robin indicated with a nod. " There," he said, " by the sheds."

Sammy had seen them, and was coming down the foreshore towards them. He too looked worried and anxious.

" Hullo," said Robin when he got near.

Sammy did not answer his greeting.

" Are yer lookin' for '*im* ? " he said, with a jerk of his head towards the place where *Whynot* should have been.

Robin nodded.

" Where is he ? " said Antony.

" Gorn," said Sammy.

" Gone ? Gone where ? "

" Swanage way—round Old 'Arry."

" Good Lord . . . Are you sure ? "

Sammy was sure.

" How do you know ? "

" I 'eard 'em saying so at the yard."

There was a deep pucker between Sammy's eyebrows. He looked from Antony to Robin, and back from Robin to Antony.

" It wasn't me wot did it," he said defensively. " 'Ow did I know 'e'd go off like that ? "

But Antony wasn't listening. He had only one thought in his mind. Arthur was in danger ; in real danger. They had been too late. He had gone. And—what was far worse—he had gone to sea. Even in the harbour it would have been bad enough. But he wasn't in the harbour ; he had gone outside, round Old Harry Rock, on the way to Swanage.

He saw one of the men from the yard at the entrance to the sheds, and hurried towards him. Perhaps after all Sammy had made a mistake.

" I say," he began breathlessly, " do you know where *Whynot* is—where she went, I mean ? "

" *Whynot ?* " said the man casually. " She was off a couple of hours ago. Going Swanage way, I believe. Quite a change for the young gentleman ! He doesn't often go outside the harbour."

Antony's heart sank. Sammy had *not* made a mistake. The man from the yard looked up at the sky.

" He'll have a breeze, maybe. I told him it wasn't *Whynot's* weather. See there ? " He pointed with his thumb to windward.

Antony looked. Over the trees on Brownsea the sky was no longer clear. Clouds were coming up. But there was still very little wind.

" Thunder," said the man.

For a moment Antony thought it might be possible to get back to *Ianthe* or *Tessa* before they started. Now that Arthur was really in danger, he would tell them everything ; he would ask them to go after him, to tell him, to take him on board, or—if they were too late for that—to save him somehow. He ran down to the end of the jetty, ignoring the others who looked at him in anxious enquiry. From the end of the jetty he could see across into the South Deep. He stared hard, straining his eyes—and again his heart sank. *Ianthe* was gone ; and that brown mainsail—just coming into the main channel past the buoys—yes, that was *Tessa.* They were too late again. By the time *Tern* had beaten out of the creek against the wind, *Tessa,* too, would be out at sea, far beyond recall.

For an instant a horrible feeling of helplessness almost overwhelmed him. Then he made up his mind. He turned on his heel and walked firmly back to the others.

"What are we going to do?" said Anne.

"We're going after him," said Antony. "There's not a moment to lose."

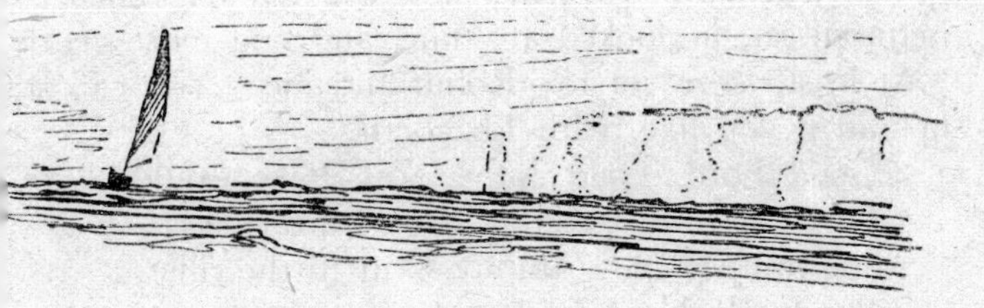

CHAPTER XXV

"COME on, Robin. Quick!"

Antony ran down the jetty and jumped on board. ɩobin and Elizabeth followed close behind him. Anne ung back. Antony went straight to the main halyards nd began hauling up the mainsail. Robin cast off the ɔpe and held it in his hand ready to shove off the ıoment Antony gave the word.

Anne hesitated, looking down into *Tern* from the jetty.

"Get in, quick," said Elizabeth. Anne took no notice. he was looking at Antony. The halyard had jammed, nd he was tugging at it.

"Antony . . ."

Antony jerked the halyard free, and continued to aul.

"What?" he said.

"Our promise . . ." said Anne. Her forehead was rinkled with anxiety. "Our promise . . . we promised ot to go outside . . . not to take risks . . ."

"Not to take unnecessary risks," said Antony without

turning his head. He made the halyard fast, and bega
to set up the peak. "This is a necessary one."

"But . . ." said Anne.

"There's no but about it. We've got to go." Anton
spoke with a new urgency and conviction. Then, th
mainsail set, he looked at Anne, and said more gently
"At least, *we've* got to—Robin and me. You can sta
behind if you like, with Elizabeth."

"Good Lord," said Anne, "as if we would!"

"Of course we wouldn't," said Elizabeth.

Anne jumped in. Antony went to the tiller.

"Ready, Robin?" he said.

"All ready."

"Let go, and shove her off."

But just before Robin let go the rope, there was
shout from the top end of the jetty.

"It's Sammy," said Elizabeth. Robin hung on.

None of them had given Sammy a thought since thei
first seeing him. Now he was running down the jett
as fast as his legs would carry him.

"Oy!" he shouted. "Oy! Take me wiv you
Guv'nor."

And without waiting for permission he jumped on t
the foredeck.

"Chuck me the rope, mate," he said. Robin chucke
it, gave *Tern's* head a shove, and jumped on board too
The others were too much surprised to make any objection
Sammy seized the jib halyard and ran the sail up hanc
over hand. "I'm in on this, I am," he said half tru
culently. "Think I'd let you go off on your own? No
me! If that bloke's coming to any 'arm, we'll get 'in
out of it together, see?"

Obviously it was no time for arguing. There wa
much too much to do, and much too little time to do
it in. Along the creek it was a beat to windward—anc

here was very little wind. The tide was coming in gainst them. Robin got the oar out, and pulled; he ulled till the sweat ran down his forehead, and slowly *Tern* crept over the tide. When he was tired, Antony owed; then Sammy; and at last they got her to the nouth of the creek, and could hold their course for the ntrance of the harbour and the open sea.

With the rowing finished and the wind on their beam, here was now nothing to be done but steer, and wish hat *Tern* would go faster—and, of course, keep a look-out.

Sammy stowed the oar under the thwarts, rubbed his nose with the back of his hand, and grinned at Antony.

"You ain't goin' to cut up rough, are you, Guv'nor?" ie said.

"What do you mean—cut up rough?"

"With me—jumping aboard like that."

Antony looked at Sammy, then up at the burgee.

"You oughtn't to have let them do it," he said. "The hroud plate . . ." Then, recollecting himself, he added, vith a little twist of his mouth: "But then . . . *I* let hem too—really."

"That's where it is, Guv'nor; we didn't oughter."

Sammy kept his eyes on Antony, hoping that he would inderstand how he felt—hoping that he would see that ie was sorry, and that if there was to be danger for any of them, he wanted to share it. And Antony did see; for after thinking a moment, his eyes still on the burgee, he glanced at the beach-boy and smiled.

"It's all right, Sammy," he said gently.

Robin was glad that he said that. Sammy was obviously relieved; he hopped up from where he was sitting on the floorboards and cocked his head to windward.

"Coo!" he said. "Look at that—'e's goin' to cop it presently—and us too, I reckon."

Antony and Robin had both for some time been awar
of the sky to windward ; but neither of them had wantec
to mention it. There was still very little wind, and t
the eastward the sky was bright. The sun was shining
but over the hills to the westward the clouds which the
had seen from the jetty were gathering and rising, creep-
ing upward, dirty and dark and cold, slowly eating u
the blue.

Yes. Sammy was right : they were going to cop it

Elizabeth had her back to Antony. She was kneelin
at the entrance to the fo'c'sle, by the side of Robin, an
they were both eagerly scanning the sea ahead in th
hope of seeing *Whynot*. A ribbon had come off one o
her pigtails. Antony wished that he had not let he
come. Neither Elizabeth nor Anne ought to have come
He and Robin—and Sammy—should have done this jo
by themselves. It was going to blow.

Antony bit his lip and looked sideways again at th
advancing murk. As for Arthur, he wouldn't stand
chance. He was miles away—they couldn't even se
him yet—and at the first puff of wind his mast would go
Then probably they'd never see him at all. But the
would do all they could ; they would scour the sea fo
him . . . but he wished the girls hadn't come.

But how (he thought) could he have left them behind
They had nowhere to go. *Tern* was their home. The
would have had nowhere to sleep, no food . . . even i
they had consented to stay. And they would not hav
consented. Yet he wished they were not there.

For a moment Antony's courage failed him. It wa
a hard thing to be in command. He wished desperatel
that his father were with him. Or the Bosun.

Then suddenly Elizabeth gave a shout : a high, shrill
excited shout.

"I can see him. Look ! It's *Whynot*. Over there."

All strained their eyes to where she pointed. Far away n the lee bow a little white triangle of sail gleamed for second in the sun, and then turned grey again. Sammy umped on to the foredeck.

" Is it him ? " said Anne. " Can you see ? "

Sammy shaded his eyes with his hand, and shook his ead. Then he climbed for a couple of hoops up the nast, and looked again.

" That's 'im ! " he called.

" Sure ? "

" That's 'im all right."

Antony gave the tiller to Anne.

" Let me come up," he said to Sammy. " Let me ook." Sammy slid down on to the foredeck. Antony limbed.

" *Is* it ? " said Robin. Antony came down again. He nodded.

" Yes," he said. " It's *Whynot*."

" Thank goodness," said Robin.

" I can see her hull—orange," said Elizabeth excitedly.

The boat had turned slightly, and the sun had caught er side. The colour gleamed. It was *Whynot*, without doubt.

Antony, for the moment at any rate, forgot his fears. ike the rest of them, his whole thought was filled with he task they had to do : somehow or other to warn rthur of his danger before it was too late.

Whynot was a long way ahead—at least a mile, and erhaps more—she was well beyond the Bar. It was ucky that there was so little wind. Had there been breeze, she would have been already so far that there vould have been no chance of even seeing her—provided, f course, that her mast had held. But now she was in ight. True, *Tern* would never catch her ; but, when he squall came—if it did come—they might—if anything

happened, be able to reach her in time. Meanwhil
there was nothing to do but wait.

Tern was sailing intolerably slowly. One by one th
black buoys on their left crept by. A little oily swe
slopped in from seaward ; it shook what wind there wa
out of the sails, and made *Tern* lazy and stupid. An
all the time the murk was climbing up the sky to th
westward.

Then suddenly the sun went out. The sea was grey
glistening, and cold. Anne shivered ; she dug for he
sweater amongst the gear in the fo'c'sle. She foun
Elizabeth's first and threw it to her.

"Put it on, Bittle."

"I'm not a bit cold," said Elizabeth.

"You'd better put it on."

Elizabeth put it on. A few drops of rain fell : larg
thick scattered drops, which pitted the surface of the se
The rest of the sky had been swallowed at a gul
There was no blue left.

Antony and Robin exchanged glances. Then Anton
looked away to the left, where the coast towards Hengis
bury should be. It wasn't there. It was as if it ha
been smudged out with a dirty finger. *Whynot* was sti
in sight—but only just. The air between her and *Te*
seemed to have thickened.

Now there was no wind at all. The tiller was slac
in Antony's hands. *Tern* lolloped uneasily and absurdl
in the swell.

For several minutes nobody spoke. They kept the
eyes on *Whynot*, fearful that they might lose her. The
suddenly Anne said : "Listen ! What's that ?" Sh
spoke sharply, and her voice made them jump. The
they heard what she had heard : a whispering on th
sea—coming swiftly nearer. Antony looked towards th
sound ; the water looked whitish, and roughened.

"Quick," he said, "oilskins."

Anne, being nearest, dived into the fo'c'sle again. She scrabbled for the oilskins and chucked them out one by one.

Before they could get the oilskins on, the rain reached them. It came, solid and soaking. It hissed down, making a million tall but tiny splashes in the smooth sea. They struggled into their oilskins, but they were already wet. There was no oilskin for Sammy.

When they looked again towards *Whynot*, she was gone. She was blotted out. There was nothing to be seen but the murk and the rain and the pitted sea. Still there was no wind.

Anne and Elizabeth crouched at the entrance to the fo'c'sle. There was no room to get right in, because of the gear. The motion of the boat, lolloping in the swell, made it impossible to sit comfortably. Rain was trickling down inside their clothes. It was beastly. Robin was still staring at the place where *Whynot* should be. Sammy, coatless, was sitting on the middle thwart, soaked to the skin but chirpy as a sparrow. He was grinning. Antony jerked irritably at the slack tiller.

"Blast the boat," he muttered. "I wish there was some wind." The rain was streaming off his hair and getting into his eyes.

All round the air was thick with rain. Even the near shore by Studland was scarcely visible. There was a flash, and Robin involuntarily ducked his head. Two seconds later came the thunder: it was like someone beating an enormous drum—quickly first, with light strokes; then slower and heavier; then three great whangs.

"Blimey," chirped Sammy, "ain't we 'avin' a lovely sail?" He spat the rain water out of his mouth over the side.

Antony felt grateful to him. He was anxious—

horribly anxious. He was afraid not only for *Whynot*, but for *Tern*. It was he who was responsible. Sammy's cheerfulness was comforting.

Still they couldn't see *Whynot*.

Then the wind came. Its coming was a relief. Suddenly the sails steadied, the jerking boom went to sleep ; *Tern* heeled, and gathered way. She was alive again, and in the pleasure of it Antony at the helm almost forgot the rain. The wind came westerly off the land, not very strong, but strong enough to drive *Tern* hissing through the water with her sheets eased.

" Can you see her yet ? " called Antony.

" No."

Anne was about to crawl from her shelter, to help the look-out again, but Antony checked her.

" Better keep under cover—all you can," he said.

Tern was sailing finely. Now that she was moving she hardly felt the lollopy swell. The bar-buoy was well astern. Everybody's spirits rose. They were sure to see *Whynot* soon ; unless——? Antony felt a little wave of sick fear in the pit of his stomach. It might be that that first puff had dismasted her. He prayed that the weather might clear—even if it blew.

The wind eased again as suddenly as it had begun. Then another puff came, nearly ahead. The sails shook, and Antony hauled in the sheet, and was forced to alter his course a little—away from the land. The wind was backing southerly. There was more lightning, and another whang on the drums—this time only one second later. It was so loud that it made them jump and feel queer inside. But Sammy only grinned.

" She's goin' fine," he said, glancing at Antony.

Antony smiled back at him, and minded his steering. The rain drove at them aslant now, so that it was difficult to keep their eyes open.

"Are you looking?" called Antony. "Can you see
ıer?"

Sammy shook his head.

"Can't see a th-thing," shouted Robin.

The wind backed more southerly still and blew a bit
ıarder. You could hear the puffs now as well as feel
hem. They came with a *whoosh.* *Tern* was heading
ıbout south-east, towards the open sea. The cliffs round
Studland were farther away than they were, and scarcely
visible through the rain and haze.

Antony wondered if he ought to put *Tern* about and
nake a tack in-shore. But what was *Whynot* doing?
He didn't know. If he tacked in-shore, he might miss
ıer when it cleared; if he kept on, still he might miss her.

It was blowing quite hard now. Antony had his hands
ull looking after *Tern.* He called Robin aft to hold the
nain sheet. Elizabeth and Anne joined Sammy in his
ook-out.

"I'm wet, anyhow," said Elizabeth. "I wish we
could see her."

Tern was sailing grandly; but she was pressed. The
sea was still fairly smooth, for the land sheltered them.
The waves were long but not steep, and *Tern* rode them
easily, like a seagull. There was another thunderclap,
out not so loud.

"She's a fine ship," said Antony.

"If only we could see *Whynot,*" said Robin.

They were getting farther and farther off-shore. Old
Harry and the cliffs were gone in the haze. *Tern* was
ılone in her own little circle of sea.

It was blowing harder now. Robin had to ease the
sheet when the puffs came. *Tern* was labouring a little.

"We'll have to reef," muttered Antony. "I wish it
vould clear. He may be anywhere. It's hopeless like
his."

A vicious puff came. *Tern* dipped her lee-deck under and Elizabeth was thrown off her balance and staggered against Anne. Robin let the sheet fly. There was a violent rattle and slatting of canvas and blocks. Anne looked scared.

"That was a good one," said Antony. He tried to speak lightly, but there was a catch in his voice. Robin got the sheet in again, but another puff hit them, as strong as the first. The sea was getting rougher. "Come on," said Antony. "We must reef."

Sammy jumped to the halyards. Antony eased *Tern* into the wind.

"Lower away," he shouted.

Robin clawed the sail in as Sammy lowered. *Tern's* head was blown round as the mainsail came down. Half of it came on top of Elizabeth. She struggled free, and clutched at the gunwale. *Tern* rolled horribly in the trough of the waves. Everything was in a mess. Robin and Sammy got the mainsail in-board somehow, though it was difficult to stand, *Tern* rolled so: she flicked them first this way, then that. Antony stayed at the helm and kept her before the wind.

"Buck up, for goodness' sake," Antony said.

Robin and Sammy pulled two reefs down. Anne helped them tie the points. All their fingers were clumsy but they got it done somehow.

Then Robin and Sammy went to the halyards and the mainsail was set again.

The rain had stopped. While they were reefing they hadn't noticed if it was raining or not. But it still blew if anything, it blew harder. Still they couldn't see the cliffs. They couldn't see anything.

Robin was holding the sheet again, sitting close to Antony. Antony had brought *Tern* back on the wind. She was much easier with the reefs. But Antony felt ost ; the boat having run off the wind while they were ying down the reefs, and the weather being thick and nothing in sight, he didn't know where he was or where *Tern* was heading. Perhaps the wind had backed again : here was no sign by which to tell.

The sea was much rougher. They were getting off he land. The waves were steeper, and had little white crests on them. *Tern* was close hauled ; she plunged and struggled, her speed checked by the waves. She had gone dead again—but with the reefed sail she was safe.

" We must make a tack in-shore," thought Antony. ' We're getting much too far out—I'm sure we are. If only we could see something."

Robin's hands were stiff with holding the sheet, and he rope cut into his fingers. Anne and Elizabeth had gone back by the fo'c'sle, crouching to get what shelter hey could. The spray flew.

" Antony," said Robin.

" What ? "

" She can't possibly live in this—*Whynot*—her mast must have gone. We'll never see her."

A big wave rushed at *Tern*. Her bows lifted, then plunged. A solid sheet of spray swept across her, almost blinding the three boys.

" All aboard for Rio," sang Sammy, dripping from head to foot. Antony glanced at Elizabeth—she looked a bit white.

" Come on, Robin," he said, " we'll put her round."

Sammy heard him and reached for the jib-sheet. Antony was just about to put the helm down, when Sammy stopped him.

" 'Old on, Guv'nor. There she is ! " His voice was sharp with excitement.

" Where ? "

" Over to loo'ard. Look. Over there."

Antony and Robin looked where he pointed. Anne and Elizabeth scrambled unsteadily to their feet and looked too.

" I can see her," shouted Elizabeth.

" She's sailing."

" Her mast's not gone."

" Oh, Antony, quick—we'll get to her. We'll reach her in time."

It was indeed *Whynot*. The haze had suddenly thinned and there she was, not half a mile away to leeward. And she was still sailing : by some miracle her mast was not gone, and she was still sailing.

Antony put the helm up and steered straight for her. It was incredible that her mast had held—incredible that she was still alive. With the wind free *Tern* once more sailed gallantly and fast, sucking down into the troughs and surging forward on the crests. No spray flew. The sky was clearing. And *Whynot* was still safe. Antony felt that he could shout aloud with relief.

Sammy climbed on to the foredeck. He waved one arm and clung to the swaying mast with the other, yelling *Whynot, ahoy !* with all the force of his lungs. But *Whynot* was much too far away to hear. There was nothing to do but settle down to the chase.

The spirits of all of them were high. There was no need now to crouch for shelter. There was no rain, the wind was free, and *Tern* with her reefed mainsail was making easy weather of it. They had all been scared—except Sammy. Even Antony had been scared. But you can't go on being scared for ever, so long as things don't get worse ; and things had not got worse—they had got better.

" We'll c-catch her," said Robin.

" It's *Tern's* wind," said Antony.

" He must have seen us," said Anne.

But whether Arthur had seen them or not, he made no sign. *Whynot* held on her course.

The seas were getting bigger as the two boats drew away from the land. They could see *Whynot* only when they were on the crest of a wave, in the troughs she was hidden, except sometimes the tip of her sail. *Tern* was going splendidly. Antony had hard work to hold her in the puffs, and when she yawed on the crests.

" Gosh, isn't it blowing," he said to Robin. Sammy started to sing : a long song about roses and somebody's mother. He was enjoying himself. The thunder was all gone, and the whole sky had cleared. The coast-line was clear too, but the cliffs by Old Harry were a long way off. Far ahead the Isle of Wight lay on the sea, light as a cloud.

But the wind was increasing. It had shifted more westerly with the passing of the thunder, and *Tern* and *Whynot* were running before it. Antony watched the seas rolling up on the quarter with an anxious eye. *Tern* had never been out in anything like this before. But it was all right—provided it got no worse. He wondered what it would be like when they came to beat back—against the wind.

A harder puff struck *Tern*. She seemed to bury herself and drive into the sea, then yawed violently as the next wave passed under her. Sammy stopped singing.

" Come up, my beauty," he said. Then suddenly his eyes grew round. He jumped from the middle thwart where he had been sitting and scrambled up on to the foredeck.

" Look *out*," shouted Antony. " Come back inside."

" Can you see 'er ? " shouted Sammy. He clung to the mast on the swaying deck and stared at the sea ahead. All thought that on the crest of the next wave they would see *Whynot* as before. But the wave came—and they did not see her. Then another, and still the sea was empty.

Horror seized them.

Sammy climbed three hoops up the mast.

" Don't, Sammy, don't," cried Elizabeth, her voice shrill with fright and not far from tears.

Sammy hung on, and scanned the sea. Then he shouted again.

" There she is ! Cripes, she's turned top."

" Where ? " yelled Antony. Sammy pointed, clinging to the mast with his other arm.

" Dead to loo'ard."

" How far ? "

" Not far."

Then Anne saw her : an upturned orange hull. In a moment she was gone again. Another wave hove her up, and Robin saw her too, and Elizabeth. *Tern* was racing towards her. A few seconds more, and she was plain in sight, lifting and dropping, a dead thing in the sea.

" Is he there—can you see him ? " called Antony.

They couldn't. Then Sammy, still up the mast, let out a joyful yell.

" There 'e is, Guv'nor ! "

Robin scrambled on to the foredeck. " He's the other side," he shouted. " I can see his arm—hanging on."

" Oh, Antony, be quick," Elizabeth wailed.

Antony said nothing. His mouth was set, and he was thinking. It's no joke picking up a person from a sea like that. Then he made up his mind.

" Sammy," he shouted. " Get the mainsail down. Quick ! " In two seconds Sammy was back in the well. " Help him, Robin."

The halyards were started. The sail flogged. Robin clutched and clawed at it to drag it in-board as it came down. Anne helped. *Tern* rolled horribly. They were flung across the boom, and back again. Elizabeth crouched on the floorboards, trying to keep out of the way of their trampling feet, half sick with fright. But they got the sail down.

" Get forrard again," shouted Antony. " I can't see her. Keep pointing." Robin obeyed.

" More to the left—not too much—that's it. Keep her so," yelled Robin.

Tern was travelling fast, even under her jib alone—too fast. They must check her way still more. Sammy was already at the jib halyard, waiting a sign from Antony. Antony nodded at him.

" In a minute," he said. Then he turned to Anne. " Get a rope—quick. The anchor warp."

Anne got it.

" Pass it up to Robin."

Robin hove it up on to the foredeck. *Whynot* was very near. They could all see Arthur now. He had one arm round *Whynot's* upturned keel. The wave crests passed over him as they swept by. But he was hanging on. Robin tied a bowline in the end of the warp.

" Down jib," shouted Antony. The jib rattled down. *Tern* surged slowly on. Antony's heart was in his mouth. The boat wallowed and rolled horribly. It was almost impossible to steer, but she bore down, lurching and tumbling, on *Whynot*. If he went too near, Antony knew he might kill Arthur ; if he didn't go near enough, Robin wouldn't be able to throw him the rope.

Robin had the coil on his arm now, ready to throw. His other arm clutched the mast. He had a hard job to keep his feet. They could see Arthur's face ; it looked green, as if he were half-dead ; but he hung on. A big wave swept *Tern* closer—they were almost on him. The tiller was useless—it was luck now, if they got him or not. *Tern* drove broadside on, in the trough of the seas, almost rolling her gunwales under. One more wave—one more —and they would get him—or crush him. Antony held his breath, in an agony of helplessness. Robin watched his chance. Nobody spoke.

The wave came and *Tern* surged sideways sickeningly on its crest. Robin staggered, regained his balance, and with all his might flung the heavy rope at Arthur's upturned face. For an instant Antony shut his eyes. If Robin had missed . . .

" Got 'im, by gum," yelled Sammy.

" Hang on, Robin," shouted Antony.

Robin passed his end of the warp round the mast, and hung on.

" Catch a hold, mister," yelled Sammy. " Get yer 'ead through it. Don't drop it, for Gawd's sake. We've gotcher. Hang on, bully, an' all aboard for England."

Arthur had grabbed the rope as *Tern* was swept past on the wave. With an effort he succeeded in getting the bowline over his head. Only a yard or two separated the two boats—it was dangerously near in that sea. Antony came forward and sent Robin to the tiller.

" Let go," he shouted to Arthur. " Let go of your boat, and we'll haul you in."

Arthur let go. A wave went over him. He reappeared face uppermost, struggling. Antony and Sammy hove with all their strength. The next wave swept him to *Tern's* side. He clutched it, gasping. Antony and Sammy got their hands under his arm-pits.

" Wait till she rolls," Antony panted. " *Now!* "

They hove. Arthur was half across the gunwale. With the next roll they tumbled him in.

There was no time even to get Arthur comfortable; still less to ask the questions which were seething in their minds. The immediate need was to make sail again. The two boats were weltering close together in the big

Robin watched his chance.

waves—sucking together in the troughs. A collision would be fatal. They left Arthur in a heap on the floorboards. Sammy set the jib ; Robin at the tiller got *Tern* moving again before the wind. She still rolled abominably. Then they got the mainsail up—trying not to trample on Arthur, or on Elizabeth who was crouching by his side. Arthur took no interest in what was happening ; he lay huddled ; inert and exhausted.

It was better with the mainsail set. *Tern* was sailing properly again. But it was still blowing, even harder than before. Anne dragged a blanket from the fo'c'sle and put it over Arthur. Elizabeth stayed by his side, watching him. He was absolutely done, and shivering with cold. Sammy dragged at his legs to straighten him out a bit, so that he lay less bunched, then shoved another blanket under his head, squashed up, for a pillow.

"It's all right, mister," he said. "We got yer. You'll be as right as rain in a minute."

Robin had all he could do to steer. Antony was by him, holding the mainsheet.

"Is he all right ?" Antony called.

"Fine," said Sammy.

Something like a smile flickered on Arthur's blue lips. His teeth chattered.

"I'm only c-c-cold," he said. His voice sounded faint and strange. Anne got more blankets from the fo'c'sle and piled them on him.

Antony was too busy with sailing the ship to pay much attention to Arthur yet. It was enough to know they had got him and that he was safe. Moreover, he must decide what to do. Beating back to Poole in that wind and sea would be pretty frightful anyhow, and quite impossible with Arthur lying all over the bottom of the boat. He would have to carry on as they were for a bit longer. He was getting anxious again about the seas :

they were alarmingly big, and it was really blowing like smoke. Even before the wind *Tern* was pressed more than he thought was safe. He decided once more to reduce sail. There were no more reefs to take down, so he told Sammy to trice up the tack of the mainsail a bit, and lower the peak. That made a lot of difference, and *Tern* was much easier.

Then Arthur suddenly sat up.

" That's better, mister," said Sammy.

Arthur grinned—rather wanly—but still, he grinned.

" Gosh," he said. " I thought I was done for."

" Didn't you see us coming ? " said Antony. " We came after you, to warn you."

Arthur looked blank and didn't answer.

" About the mast," said Elizabeth.

" The shroud plate," said Robin.

Sammy was whistling between his teeth and not looking at Arthur.

" *Shroud* plate ? " said Arthur. Then he understood. " Oh, *that* . . . Good Lord, you thought . . . you mean, what those blasted ki . . ." He looked at Sammy and checked himself. Sammy went on whistling. " I got that repaired before I started," Arthur said. " It was pretty obvious."

The full significance of that remark was apparent only to Robin. As he kept *Tern* before the rolling seas, there was on his lips a small inward smile of immense satisfaction. When she started, *Whynot's* gear was sound ; now she was a wreck. But *Tern* was sailing on. It was what he had always known. Now, at last, the others must know it too. Even Arthur—especially Arthur.

Arthur was still weak, and badly shaken. He didn't want to talk much. But he was recovering quickly. Anne opened the iron ration tin (it was easier to get at than the food in the fo'c'sle) and made him eat some chocolate. That helped a lot. Then, little by little, as *Tern* surged and swung before the wind to the eastward, Arthur's story came out.

"I knew you all thought I was a funk," he ended, "that I'd never take *Whynot* outside. So I jolly well did. . . . Especially after . . . well, you know what I mean . . . after what I did that day . . . when Elizabeth fell off her horse. I say, you know . . . I didn't *mean* to do any harm. But I knew you loathed me for it . . . and thought I wouldn't dare . . ." His voice trailed off.

"But they said you were going to Swanage," said Antony.

"I was. I meant to. But when that squall came, I had too much sail. *Whynot* nearly turned over then. And it got rough. She wouldn't go to windward, somehow. I got sort of blown off-shore. It was beastly."

"But when you *did* capsize . . ."

"She broached to. Gosh, it was awful. I hadn't a chance. I say," he added shyly; "it was jolly decent of you. . . ."

After that they had chocolate all round. There hadn't been time to realize before that they were hungry. Now they did. They emptied the iron ration tin.

Antony knew that he must put *Tern* about; yet he shrank from doing it. It was more than an hour and a half since the first thunder-squall had hit them, and *Tern* was at least six miles out at sea. Long ago they had left the shelter of the land. The seas were really big now, and there was no sign of the wind growing less. But for every moment they continued to run on, there was the smaller chance of being able to get back.

"Come on," Antony said. "We're going about. Get the peak up, Sammy."

Sammy obeyed. Antony hauled in the sheet as Robin

cautiously eased the helm down. *Tern's* head swung up towards the wind. A wave leapt on her broadside ; the crest burst against her bows and a sheet of spray swept across them, blindingly. *Tern* reared, plunged, and wallowed. There was a violent slatting of canvas. It was a moment of horrible confusion.

Antony seized the tiller from Robin, and pushed it hard up. Another wave leapt as *Tern* was in the trough. She was rolled over until the water poured in over her side. Then her head came round, and once more she was running before the wind.

Antony felt his knees were trembling. He bit his lip to steady himself. Sammy grinned.

" That one wet me, Guv'nor," he said.

Antony laughed rather uncertainly. " She won't do it," he said.

Sammy triced up the tack again and eased the peak. *Tern* was safe—but she was not going home.

Evidently there was nothing to be done but to continue running until the wind eased off ; or until—but what the alternative was neither Antony nor anybody else knew, or even liked to think of.

For another hour they ran on, taking turns at the helm. Arthur had quite recovered, and took his trick with the others. His clothes (which had indeed never been wetter than Sammy's) had partly dried in the sun and wind, and Antony and Anne (being the biggest) had each lent him a sweater. *Tern* was now in the middle of the bay, the cliffs of Studland as remote and visionary as the cliffs of the Isle of Wight. The coast on their left was a far brown line. The wind did not ease. As far as the eye could reach the sea was flecked with white, and one after another in endless procession the great seas rolled up, menacing and powerful. But each time *Tern* lifted, and they passed beneath her. But steering was hard and anxious work. All the boys knew that it would be dangerous if the seas took her anywhere but dead astern : they had not forgotten the horrible moment when Antony had tried to bring her to the wind. And Antony knew that even as it was *Tern* was overpressed ; if the wind increased any more, they would have to lower the mainsail altogether, and drive along under the jib alone. Nevertheless, as time passed and *Tern* survived each succeeding wave, their confidence in her grew greater. There had been terrifying moments ; but they were getting used to it now—and so was *Tern.*

Arthur was at the tiller. He was a good helmsman.

" Gosh," he said. " She's a good boat. I'd never have thought she'd do this. And if she hadn't," he added, " there wouldn't have been much left of me."

" She's not so bad," said Antony ; and Robin knew from the way he said it that he was proud of her.

" Antony."

" What ? "

Arthur had some difficulty in saying what he wanted to say ; but he got it out.

" If you knew about the shroud plate, and wanted to warn me, why did you wait so long ? "

" Because . . ." said Antony, and stopped. It was an awkward thing to explain.

" He was in a rage," said Elizabeth. Antony looked at her and smiled a bit shamefacedly. " About me," she added.

" I was—as a matter of fact," said Antony.

" So were we all," said Anne. " But Bittle and me didn't know about *Whynot.*"

Arthur swallowed hard, and became very intent on his steering. When he spoke he avoided looking at any of them.

" I guess I jolly well deserved it," he muttered.

" Ow ! " said Elizabeth. " What an enormous wave." She clutched Anne for support as *Tern* rolled. " But we aren't now," she said. " We're not in a rage, I mean."

" Of course not," said Antony.

" How c-could we be ? " said Robin.

" What about Sammy ? " said Anne.

Sammy whistled a short stave between his teeth and looked at Arthur out of the corner of his eye.

" Na—ow," he said. " We're all together like, ain't we, 'avin' a lovely trip and Gawd knows where we'll fetch up, 'cos I don't."

" S-sammy wanted to come," said Robin.

" He wouldn't *not*," said Antony. " He jumped aboard as we were starting."

" You did—you really did ? " said Arthur. " In spite of what I . . ." But Sammy interrupted him.

" Mebbe I did," he said casually. " And what my dad'll do when I get 'ome summat about next week . . . coo ! "

" What *will* he do ? " said Anne.

" Wop me."

" Poor Sammy," said Elizabeth.

" 'Oo says I'm pore ? " said Sammy indignantly. " If yer own dad can't wop yer, I'd like to know 'oo can, and it won't be the fust time neither."

Antony for a minute or two past had been looking out to windward. " I say," he said suddenly, " it's not blowing so hard, is it ? "

It wasn't. The wind was definitely easing off. If it continued to do so, Antony thought they would soon be able to put *Tern* round and start for the long beat home. Then a new thought struck him. It was already late in the afternoon, and they were miles and miles from Poole ; and beating to windward in a small boat in a rough sea—

for the sea would be rough for a long time even if the wind eased—was terribly slow. It was slow even in *Ianthe.* In *Tern* they would make hardly any headway at all. In another three or four hours it would be dark.

"Robin," he said.

"What?"

"The wind's much lighter. We'll put her round."

"Will it be like last time?" said Elizabeth. "Oh, Antony, please don't."

"Of course it won't. There's not nearly so much wind."

They put *Tern* about. No water this time came aboard; there was no horrible rattling and banging—but it was pretty horrible all the same. It was horrible because *Tern* seemed suddenly to have died. She was no longer a boat, but a log. Laboriously she climbed the waves, then fell with a sickening crunch into the hollows behind. And she didn't seem to move at all. She was helpless. And all the time the wind was getting lighter.

Before, there had been moments of terror, moments of excitement, moments even of delight. Now it was just vile.

Anne was the first to be sick. Then Elizabeth was sick too—but more cheerfully. She managed it neatly over the lee side, and when it was over she said she felt lovely. Arthur wasn't quite sick, but he went pale green and felt awful. Antony and Robin and Sammy survived.

A couple of miserable hours went by. Daylight was going, and they seemed no nearer to the distant cliffs. It was quite obvious they could not get home before dark.

The wind was almost gone. Fortunately the sea was going down too, and *Tern's* motion became less unbearable. But still she was barely making headway. The three sufferers got over their sickness. They all had food

—their first meal since breakfast, except for the iron rations—and felt better. But they were no nearer home.

Darkness grew upon the sea. The wind died altogether, and *Tern* lay becalmed. The water was much smoother now, and though *Tern* still pitched and rolled the motion was gentle and kindly.

"I wish there was some wind," muttered Antony.

"I'm glad there isn't—not in the dark," said Elizabeth.

"We shan't get home."

"I know."

Indeed, it was all too obvious. But the fact when it was mentioned was somehow less disturbing than when it had been only a private thought in each of their minds. They would be out all night. In *Tern*. In an open boat, on the wide sea.

Nothing could be done about it; so the best thing was to accept it.

Elizabeth chuckled. "Who's going to bed in the fo'c'sle?" she said.

They cleared the anchor and warp out of the starboard side of the fo'c'sle (the other side was packed with stores) and made it secure on the foredeck. That made a cabin for one. Elizabeth went to bed first. It was rather fun being in bed, though she didn't sleep much. She was allowed three hours, and then Anne had a turn. Of the boys, two at a time remained on watch, and two huddled down as best they could in the bottom of the boat and wrapped themselves in blankets and sweaters, and dozed. It was excessively uncomfortable and squashed, and rather cold. But it was fun all the same. As for getting home that night, once they had given up the hope they had given up the desire too. Once you know a thing must be, it is seldom so bad as when you still think it needn't be.

Besides, a night at sea is marvellous, once you've stopped being frightened of it. And it was calm: there was no more danger. And there was (thank goodness) a great deal to eat on board. Everybody nibbled almost continuously, when he wasn't sleeping, or trying to sleep.

Robin was very happy : probably happier than any of the others. That was because he was the proudest of *Tern*. And during one of his watches with Antony, when the others were huddled heaps under their blankets, and the Needles Light was blinking at them miles away to the eastward, and the sea was hushed, he had a lovely private conversation with Antony, in which he made him admit that *Tern* was the finest sea-boat in the world, and that it didn't matter that she was a bit slow to windward.

"It did blow, didn't it?" he whispered. The night and the solemn loneliness of the sea made them unwilling to speak aloud.

"Rather!"

"Almost a gale."

"Jolly nearly."

"Not really a gale. I saw a gale last winter—at Rocken End when I found the timber for the stem. It wasn't like that. Thank goodness it wasn't like that."

"It blew though."

"And *Tern* didn't mind."

"Not a bit."

"Antony, she's a marvellous boat."

"Rather!"

"Better than *Whynot*."

"I should jolly well think so," said Antony.

There was mist in the night. No shore-lights were visible. But all the time whoever was on watch could see the bright eye of the Needles Light, and the bright eye of the light on Anvil Point. Not a breath of wind stirred. *Tern* hung motionless, not answering her helm.

They couldn't keep her head in any one direction ; but it didn't seem to matter.

When Antony and Robin went off watch, one light was ahead, the other astern. When they came back on watch two hours later, one was on their left, the other on their right.

" Which is the Needles ? " said Robin.

Antony wasn't sure. It depended which way *Tern's* head was pointing ; and that nobody seemed to know. The coast was invisible ; mist hid the stars. But it still didn't seem to matter.

Antony wished a breeze would come. The night was very long. What worried them now was the thought of Arthur's parents. Probably *Whynot* would be found—and Arthur not there. They would be certain he was drowned. And heaven knew how long it would be before they could let them know he was safe. Thank goodness *Tessa* and *Ianthe* were at Beaulieu. Mr. and Mrs. Rutherford and Mr. and Mrs. Chale little knew what *Tern* had been doing . . . Long before they were home, *Tern* would be home too ; and though it would be bad to have to confess, it wouldn't be *very* bad. And they had, after all, saved Arthur's life. . . . They all wished a breeze would come.

It came an hour before dawn : a lovely light rustling breeze. It took *Tern* straight ahead, so that her sails shook. Antony let her pay off on the port tack. When the sails were full, he found that with the wind abeam *Tern* headed well to the right of the light on Anvil—just about (he thought) where the entrance to the harbour should be.

Tern glided easily and sweetly over the smooth sea. The new motion brought all the ship's company out of their blankets. It was lovely to be sailing again—and getting swiftly nearer home. It was still dark, but

Robin thought he could detect a faint lightening low down in the sky. He pointed it out to Antony. But Antony laughed.

"Not yet," he said. "That's not the dawn. It's the wrong way."

"But it *is* lighter," said Anne.

"It can't be," said Antony.

Elizabeth was looking at the sky over the mast. The mist had thinned.

"Antony," she said.

"What?"

"Is that the Great Bear?"

"Yes——"

There was silence as they all stared up at those familiar stars.

"Gosh," said Robin, "we're g-going the wrong way."

It was true. There was the Great Bear; and there too was the Pole Star—and the Pole Star was on their left hand. They were sailing east.

"That *is* the d-dawn," said Robin.

"And that light's not Anvil; it's the Needles," said Arthur. They were not going home at all; they were getting farther and farther away.

"Go about. Quick!" said Anne. Antony took no notice.

"Antony . . ."

Antony interrupted her. "I've got an idea," he said. "Look here: yesterday, before it was dark, we were just as near the Needles as we were to Poole. Nearer if anything. We still are. The tide may have taken us nearer still. . . ."

"Well?" said Anne dubiously.

"Why not go on?"

"Where to?"

"I know," said Elizabeth, in sudden excitement. "To the Solent. To Beaulieu. To Mummy and Daddy."

"That's what I meant," said Antony.

"We'd be there just as soon," said Robin.

"We could telegraph from Yarmouth to Arthur's father."

"And to Sammy's."

It was a good idea ; and when the daylight came, it was evidently a better idea still ; for the rising tide during the latter part of the night had taken them several miles nearer the Needles than they had been before. It would be much quicker to finish the crossing of the bay than to put back whence they had come.

And it would be much more fun.

CHAPTER XXVI

After a long, hard and comfortless night at sea, nothing is so refreshing as the dawn. Though nobody had really slept, yet when the dawn came nobody felt tired at all. Moreover, they were no longer faced with the weary beat back over the way which they had come; they were going on—and the wind was free. It was a lovely light northerly breeze, blowing off-shore, with a smooth sea. No wonder that nobody felt tired.

They had breakfast: corned beef and bread, and marmalade, and butter. Anne had a passionate desire for a hot drink—cocoa if possible; and her desire was swiftly communicated to the others. Antony thought it might be possible to light the stove. Anne tried—and it *was* possible. She cleared everything from the starboard side of the fo'c'sle, and put the stove right in the forepeak, as far as it would go. Then around it she erected an impenetrable zareba of tins and blankets, cunningly piled, to exclude the draught. She lit it—and it didn't go out.

The cocoa was the most delicious thing in the world.

Luxuriously they sipped it, from tin mugs, while the bow wave whispered and daylight broadened over the calm sea.

Two hours of sailing brought them to within sight of the buoys which mark the entrance to the Needles Channel. There was the lighthouse, whose blinking eye they had watched through the night, and the jagged rocks, and the pearl-grey cliffs. None of them were quite sure what the buoys in the channel meant, so it was lucky that they met an old tramp steamer coming out. Antony and Robin noticed carefully which side of the buoys she went.

The last of the flood tide carried them in, past the shingly beach of Hurst (remembered from the trial trip last holidays) and into the Solent. Yarmouth was under the lee. They ran into the familiar harbour, and tied *Tern* to the steps of the old stone quay. The clock on the church tower pointed to ten minutes to nine. They sent their telegrams. Sammy's telegram was the more difficult; Sammy, being unfamiliar with telegrams, wanted to write a long explanation of his inexplicable conduct, in order to soothe his dad; but it would have cost at least five shillings, so Antony was firm. He merely wrote: *Quite safe, home to-morrow, Sammy.* And Sammy had to be content.

Then they had another breakfast, with coffee instead of cocoa, in the shop at the corner of the square. After that they embarked again, and set sail for Beaulieu.

There is no need to describe this final voyage. It took a long time, because the tide had begun to ebb and was therefore against them. But every moment of it was delightful. They felt that they had been at sea for ages and ages; *Tern* was their trusted ship and their home; and they had the lovely feeling of being once more in sheltered waters after discomforts endured and perils past on the wide sea.

Anne knew the entrance to the Beaulieu river, and i
was she who piloted them in. Many yachts were
anchored inside, for the Meet had not yet all dispersed
They saw *Ianthe* first, then *Tessa* a little way beyond.

"Let's hail," said Elizabeth. But she said it doubtfully

"You do it," said Anne.

But none of them wanted to hail. When you have
done something excessively surprising, you can't, somehow, behave just as if you had merely been to fetch the
potatoes. It didn't feel right merely to give an ordinary
cheerful hail. They sailed on in silence.

When they drew near *Ianthe*, they saw Alf on deck
polishing the stanchions. He looked up and saw them
His blue eyes popped.

"Sakes alive, it's Master Antony and all," he said.

"Are they aboard?" said Antony.

"No. They've gone over to *Tessa* yonder."

Antony grinned at Alf and waved a hand. Alf continued to stare, his leather suspended.

Tessa was quite near. The Bosun was on deck. They
saw him stare too, take his pipe out of his mouth, stare
again, then spin round and push his head down the
companion-hatch. A moment later Mrs. Rutherford was
on deck; then Mr. and Mrs. Chale; and Mr. Rutherford
emerged simultaneously from the fo'c'sle hatch.

Robin dropped the mainsail with a run. *Tern* came
alongside with a bump—but nobody cared. The Bosun
jumped into her.

"I'll look after *Tern*," he said. "Get aboard all of
you."

That was nice of the Bosun—but he was always good
at understanding things.

They scrambled out: the girls first, then Antony and
Robin. Anne hurled herself into Mrs. Rutherford's arms,
Elizabeth into Mr. Rutherford's; then they changed

parents and did it again. The Chale family was similarly occupied.

It was a very surprising meeting indeed. It all took a long time to explain, and presently they went below in order to do it better.

"You see," said Anne, "we thought he'd be drowned."

"He would have been," said Antony.

"I nearly was," said Arthur.

Mr. and Mrs. Rutherford and Mr. and Mrs. Chale were thinking that it was not only Arthur who might have been drowned; but they didn't say so—at any rate yet. The whole story was very sudden and very bewildering. One thing at least was obvious: all the children were safe.

"There was a gale," said Elizabeth.

"N-no," said Robin, "it wasn't a g-gale; but . . ."

"It blew jolly hard," said Arthur.

"We were quite safe," said Antony.

"Sammy was marvellous," said Elizabeth.

They suddenly realized that Sammy was not there.

"Where *is* Sammy?" said Mrs. Rutherford.

"He must have stopped in *Tern*."

"With the Bosun."

"Fetch him—at *once*," said Mrs. Rutherford.

"I'll go," said Elizabeth.

Sammy came into the cabin with Elizabeth. Mrs. Rutherford embraced him too. Sammy looked pleased, but rather embarrassed. He sat down on the extreme edge of a vacant bit of settee, and kept quiet while more of the story came out (as complicated stories do) in mixed pieces.

Later on they all had tea. Some had to have it on deck, because they were too many for the cabin table. One thing was still bothering Antony. "Daddy," he said, when tea was nearly finished, " I know I promised . . ."

Mr. Chale waited for him to go on. His face was serious, but there was a kind of a smile hidden somewhere in the corners of his mouth.

" . . . not to go outside the harbour—not to take unnecessary risks. But this *wasn't* unnecessary."

The smile at the corners of Mr. Chale's mouth became more conspicuous. " Unfortunately," he said, I'm afraid it wasn't."

" I think," said the Bosun, " that you're a lot of lunatics. Your parents and I are very angry with you (here he looked at Mrs. Rutherford who did her best to smile too ; but it wasn't altogether easy). But (here he lifted his tea-cup and looked at Robin over the rim) . . . you did right. What about it, John ? "

Mr. Rutherford had to agree. " It's a lucky thing," he said, " that we made *Tern* such a powerful boat."

" She's the b-best boat in the world," said Robin.

. . . .

The end of an adventure usually coincides with the end of the holidays. But this time it didn't. On the next day the three boats returned to Poole. Anne and Elizabeth went in *Tessa.* So did Sammy ; for the sooner he got home, the sooner he would get the first interview over with his dad. Mrs. Chale wanted Antony and Robin to go in *Ianthe*, but they were both so anxious to make the return journey in *Tern* that she was forced to submit. The Bosun went with them. Arthur was invited to take his choice between the three vessels. He chose *Tern.*

There is nothing more to tell. After a few days' interval *Tern* finished her interrupted cruise ; or perhaps I should say started on a second. It was very delightful, but not so exciting as the first. This time they explored the harbour.

Sammy was wopped by his dad ; but he didn't mind. Sammy was extremely fond of his dad, and didn't in the least see why he shouldn't wop him if he wanted to.

Whynot was salvaged. Her mast was smashed and her sails ruined ; but her hull was sound. She was soon refitted and sailing again. During the last few days of their time in Poole Robin had several trips in her. He quite enjoyed it. It was impossible to be bosom friends with Arthur ; but still—he was no longer a beast. And whenever he spoke of *Tern*, he did so with the utmost respect. He had learnt to agree with Robin—and with Antony—that *Tern* was at any rate *one* of the best boats in the world.